T0278108

# The
# SCARLET
# ALCHEMIST

**Books by Kylie Lee Baker
available from Inkyard Press**

*The Keeper of Night*
*The Empress of Time*

\*

*The Scarlet Alchemist*

# The
# SCARLET
# ALCHEMIST

## KYLIE LEE BAKER

ISBN-13: 978-1-335-45801-8

The Scarlet Alchemist

Inkyard Press
22 Adelaide St. West, 41st Floor
Toronto, Ontario M5H 4E3, Canada
www.InkyardPress.com

**Printed in U.S.A.**

To Ruby

This one's for you

# CONTENT NOTE

During the Tang dynasty, Chinese alchemists tried to create an elixir of immortality. This story is what might have happened if they'd succeeded. Because this is an alternate history that reimagines China as it might have developed a century after this discovery, many historical details have been consciously changed. As such, please do not use this book as an authoritative source on Chinese history or culture.

In particular, please note that while the alchemy in this book is based loosely on the principles and goals of eighth-century Chinese Taoist alchemy, the depiction is entirely fictional and is not reflective of historical or modern Taoist practices. This book also includes contemporary Mandarin and Cantonese words, which differ greatly from the Middle Chinese that was spoken during the Tang dynasty. The author made this decision for the sake of relatability and ease of reading for modern Chinese speakers (as well as a reluctance to learn a dead language for the sake of a fantasy novel).

# PROLOGUE

I remember the day of darkness, even if no one else does.

When I close my eyes, I'm standing in a city my aunt says I've never visited, with my parents, who no longer exist.

The city of Chang'an is like a lifetime in a single moment, brimming with words in a thousand languages, the ghosts of footsteps softening the rammed dirt roads, silk clothes that shimmer like fish scales as people glint down the wide streets. At the faraway end of the road is a great stone gate with five doors opening into darkness.

I don't know what's behind the gate, but I move closer, away from my parents, past the merchants and their goatskin bags spilling wine, the pilgrims in robes the color of dust, the dancers in jewels that sharpen the sun's rays and cast them back at me like daggers.

There is something beyond the gate. I'm sure of it. The five archways are screaming mouths, calling out for me.

A gong echoes, then the world flips and disappears, a door slammed shut in my face. I reach out for my mother, and my fingers snap in all different directions with a thousand tiny pops, like fireworks. I'm falling through a world that's turned to sand, tumbling into the night sky. The universe unfolds my skin and stretches me across its endless dark, a pale tent over all the stars. I am the night that birthed the world. I am the bones of all the planets. I am silence. I am the end.

I hear my father's voice speaking to me in a language that I've long forgotten. The words rise and fall like slow gusts of wind spilling across a valley, shivering through the grass. Somehow I know that they're of great importance, but I am made of silk and the words flow through me. The only word I understand is my name. *Zilan. Zilan. Zilan.*

I wake in a bed in Guangzhou in my mother's arms. My parents tell me it was a dream, but I know better.

I know because the way they look at me has changed. They watch me when they think I'm not paying attention, their gazes crawling up the knobs of my spine. They're waiting for something.

*What did I do?* I think one thousand times over. But no one will tell me.

Then my mother dies and my father vanishes, and there is no one left to ask.

I am the only one who remembers.

# CHAPTER ONE

*Year 775*
*Guangzhou, China*

At high noon on the first day of the summer solstice, old man Gou barged into the shop carrying a rancid hemp bag over his shoulder. Even if I ignored the suspiciously human-shaped bulge inside, or the brown ooze sloughing onto my floor, or the purple fingertips dangling out the untied end, I would know that scent anywhere.

I closed my book and set down my tea that now tasted sour, the smell of hot corpse knifing up my nose and making saliva pool at the base of my throat, like I was going to be sick. I liked to think I was good at breathing through my mouth and swallowing back the nausea like a professional, but I typically only came across corpses when I was expecting to.

"You can't bring that in here," I said, taking a quick sip of tea to force down anything besides words that wanted to come up.

Old man Gou kept walking forward like he hadn't heard me, hitching the bag higher on his shoulder. "I need you to—"

"I know what you need," I said. "That's not how this works. You make an appointment and you go around back after dark."

He bristled at being interrupted, but I didn't care. People with leverage didn't come to me asking for help. His gaze twitched around the shelves packed with ceramic horses and tiny servants on their knees, thousands of glazed clay eyes witnessing his sins.

My family owned a míngqì store at the far west end of Guangzhou. Uncle Fan and Auntie So molded clay into ghost vessels to bury with the dead, and my cousins and I sold them to grieving families. No one could take real people with them to the afterlife, but they could take our painted ceramic steeds and beautiful glazed clay women and faithful servants the size of your palm. They crammed as many as they could into their tombs, hoping that cold clay would turn to warm flesh once their souls crossed over, that they wouldn't be alone in death.

When I was younger, I asked Uncle Fan if any of that was true. He scoffed and said *It doesn't matter if it's true, the dead can't ask for refunds*, and slammed the kiln door shut. But the dead could do a lot more than he thought.

That was only our business during the daylight hours. Uncle Fan and Auntie So were blissfully unaware of where the other half of our money came from.

"Take me to the back, then," old man Gou said, as if it were that simple.

I shook my head, praying that no one had seen him dragging a rotting corpse to our shop in broad daylight. Getting hanged for forbidden life alchemy would certainly interfere with my upcoming travel plans. "I'm watching the shop now. That's why you need an appointment."

He narrowed his eyes, his irises glinting gold—a side effect of eating too many gold nuggets. These days, the diet of the rich was no longer steamed bear and phoenix pears but handcrafted gold pieces with pearls as garnish, still steaming from their alchemical transformation. Some said they ate it with spoons instead of chopsticks because they didn't have the patience to eat the pieces one at a time.

A century ago, the royal alchemists learned the secret recipe for gold that stopped you from aging and made your blood run the color of sunlight. As long as you kept eating it forever, your smiles would never carve scars into your cheeks, your bones would never grow brittle and creak during rainstorms, your skin would never sag or speckle or crease.

But even ageless bodies were still made of soft human flesh, and neither gold nor gems would protect the rich from disease, or accidents, or whatever the hell had happened to the rancid corpse that old man Gou had dragged in. Those who could afford the gold of immortality often stayed locked away in their mansions to protect their investment, but clearly Gou's family hadn't felt the need. No one truly believed in death until it happened to them.

"There was only a small window of time that I could remove his body unnoticed," old man Gou said, lowering his voice, as if anyone unfortunate enough to pass by would actually process his words before falling unconscious from the stench.

"Which I might have been able to accommodate, if you had come here yesterday and *made an appointment*."

Old man Gou huffed. "Is this trinket shop more important than my brother?" he said, his grip tightening on the bag.

*Important to me, or to you?* I wanted to ask but knew better than to say that to a man, even one who was breaking the law and probably wouldn't risk making a scene. There was a dagger under the counter that I had no qualms about drawing if he grew too upset, but bloodstains were annoying to clean and hard to explain to Auntie So.

One of the problems with the death industry was that everyone came to you with pain so great that they were convinced no one else could have felt it before. They didn't like that I had rules, that I charged for my time, that their tears didn't move me.

*It doesn't matter that death is sad. This is a business*, Uncle Fan always said when customers cried. *If you make a poor man's business a charity, within a week he'll have twice as many beggars and nothing left to give.*

Besides, old man Gou didn't need my charity, and if he wanted someone to cry for his brother, he could buy a couple mourners down the street. His satchel bulged with coins and his purple silk robes twinkled with golden embroidery. His hands had no callouses, no dirt caught under his nails like the farmers or artisans. He hadn't fallen on hard times, clearly.

He must have read the sternness on my face and decided to change tactics, because he finally set the bag on the floor with a heavy sigh. I prayed whatever swampy liquid sloshing around inside wouldn't stain the floor.

"Surely you don't have many customers these days," he said, strolling over to a shelf and lifting a ceramic ox. I opened my mouth to demand he put it down, but he let out a breath and a cloud of dust flew up into the air, the soft powder swirling around the horribly smug look on his face.

"We have enough," I said, gripping the edge of the counter. People who couldn't afford life gold were still planning funerals, of course, but there were no more aristocrats emptying our shelves when their fathers passed. Most customers bought one or two míngqì and cried over the counter while begging for a lower price. We gave it to them, not because we were good people but because a few coins were better than none at all.

Old man Gou raised an eyebrow. "You'd be better off making chamber pots."

I didn't reply, because I'd actually said the same thing to Auntie So. *People can shit in a hole in the ground, not in my art,* she'd responded.

I shook my head. "Closing at random times is bad for business."

"Zilan síuzé," he said, offering me a stiff smile, "please, my brother has two young daughters."

It took an immense effort not to roll my eyes at how sweetly he said my name. When I was younger, he'd laughed when his son called me gwáimūi—*ghost girl*—and didn't scold him when he ripped up all the purple orchids that grew at the edge of the city, chewed them up, and spit them at my feet. I couldn't even be that mad at him, because I also wanted to chew up my name and spit it out in a purple slurry.

Zǐlán—written with the characters for *purple orchid*—wasn't the kind of name that you gave a girl who would be someone important someday. It was what you got stuck with when your father was a foreigner and your mother had—for some bizarre reason—let him name you even though he barely spoke Chinese. Maybe it was fine for Scotian girls to be named after flowers, but in Guangzhou, names were our parents' hopes and dreams for us, not just pretty things they saw in the dirt.

My cousin Wénshū's name had the character for *book* in it, because even before he'd proven his annoying aptitude for reading, he was destined to be a scholar. My cousin Yǔfēi's name was a misty shroud of snow and rain, the hidden face of a beautiful goddess. But zǐlán was a flower so common that it couldn't even be sold, so fragile that a few days of rain would tear it apart. It was pretty for a moment, and then it was dead.

The shop was truly starting to smell now, and if I'd hoped for any customers today, they certainly wouldn't come if old man Gou stood there any longer with his brother's leaky corpse. It was best to just deal with him quickly.

I sighed. "Lock the door."

Old man Gou turned and drew the wooden bar across the door behind him. He cleared his throat, stepping farther into the room. "I want—"

"Payment first," I said, tapping the counter.

He froze as if slapped. "You haven't even looked at him yet."

"A consultation costs fifty gold."

His expression curdled, but he obeyed, emptying his satchel onto the counter. Gold coins spun across the polished wood. These were the diluted kind used for currency, not the nuggets eaten for immortality. I could tell that from the tarnish alone.

I picked up one of the coins and held it up to the window, examining its shine, then dropped it in my cup of tea. Real gold always sank to the bottom, but fool's gold—the cheaply transformed kind that would turn back to coal in the next hour—would float.

"My brother had heart pains," old man Gou said as the coin sank to the bottom of my teacup.

I picked up another piece and put it in my mouth, biting down gently. Real gold was soft and malleable. This one came out with the impression of my back molars. Satisfied that they were real, I began to count.

"Cinnabar and mushrooms didn't help," old man Gou went on.

"I am not a healer," I said, because his voice was distracting me from my counting. "His diagnosis doesn't matter to me as long as he's in one piece."

Old man Gou's upper lip twitched as I lined up his gold in neat rows. He was probably unaccustomed to being spoken to so casually. Bags of gold could buy him many things, but my respect was not one of them.

"This is forty-seven," I said at last, holding out my hand for more.

Old man Gou waved his hand at me as if it didn't matter. "Surely that's enough for a consultation."

I raised an eyebrow. "You want a consultation worth forty-seven gold pieces?"

*"Please,"* he said, teeth clenched.

"As you wish," I said, leaning over the counter. I squinted at the sack's hemp fabric, stained with gray liquid. I took a deep breath, the scent of death making my eyes water.

"No," I said, swiping his gold off the counter into my clay bowl. "Thank you for your business."

*"No?"* old man Gou said, red rushing to his face. "How can you call that a consultation?"

"The smell," I said, taking a long sip of my tea that now had a metallic tang, like blood. "You waited too long to come to me. I'm not going to reanimate a corpse with maggots for eyes and send him on his way."

"He has eyes!" old man Gou said, his voice rattling the row of ceramic singers beside him. "You didn't even look at him!"

I took another sip of tea. "Looking costs ten more gold than what you paid me."

*"Three* more! You said fifty!"

"That was before you tried to shortchange me," I said. "Now it's ten more."

Old man Gou huffed and reached into another satchel,

shaking his head as he counted out ten coins and slammed them onto the counter. I added them to my bowl, then ducked under the counter and into the shop room.

I pulled back the hemp cloth, revealing a stiff and bloated body the color of cold porridge, his nails and lips blue. His nose dripped with a tar-black liquid that ran down his cheeks and pooled at the corners of his mouth. I touched his arm and felt the skin shift back and forth as I moved my fingers, like a piece of loose clothing. Old man Gou gagged at the smell.

"He's already started purging," I said. "His skin could slip off at any moment. I can't fix that."

"But you can bring him back?"

I looked up, frowning. "Did you hear me? You want a brother with no skin?"

"We'll sew it back on," he said, waving his hand like it was a minor inconvenience. "Anything's better than death, isn't it?"

I narrowed my eyes. "To *you*. He won't be able to go outside. His appearance will alarm people."

"Our house is large enough that he won't be bored," he said. "Can you do it or not?"

If I could afford to have a conscience, I would have said no.

But soon, my cousins and I would take our civil service exams, and if all went well, we'd be moving to the capital for the second and third testing rounds, leaving half our savings behind for Uncle Fan and Auntie So. I pictured them sitting in the dark, stretching out the last bags of rice into thin soup.

"Six hundred," I said.

Old man Gou scoffed. "I heard you were charging five hundred last week."

"Last week, gold was worth more."

"How dare you—"

"If you don't like it, find someone else."

There was no one else, and he knew it. Alchemists who could repair broken toys or heal skinned knees were easy to find, but experimenting with life alchemy—or soliciting it—was punishable by death.

Old man Gou glared back at me, probably unsure if I would truly walk away from five hundred gold. But I had seen death and decay, things far more fearsome than an angry old man, things that Gou could never imagine in his endless, gilded life.

At last, he nodded.

"You can leave the body in the pigpen," I said. "Come back after dark with the money."

His eyes narrowed, the gold flecks knife-sharp. "I'm not leaving my brother in a pigpen."

"Oh, then let's prop him up to greet customers," I said, rolling my eyes and standing up to move behind the counter again. "I'm not the one who dragged a corpse here at midday with nowhere to put it."

"Can you not help me *now*?"

"My cousins are busy, and I need their help," I said. "Besides, you haven't paid me yet."

"What is it with you Fans and money?" he said. "Have you no compassion?"

"None," I said, taking another sip of tea. I was used to people berating me for my prices.

"That's why your family is so unlucky, you know," he said, hefting the sack onto his shoulder once more. "You all have bad karma."

I made sure not to change my expression, not to show him that his words affected me. He was probably talking about my parents. Guangzhou had been smaller back then, and every—one had heard about the girl foolish enough to marry a foreigner who left her on her deathbed. Or maybe he meant

Auntie and Uncle, whose poor health was no secret. But our bad fortune had nothing to do with our prices, and everything to do with gold guzzlers like old man Gou.

"Buddhist morals don't apply to an alchemist," I said, draining my teacup and setting it heavily on the counter, "and the devas will abandon you for this. If you want your brother back, then I'm your new god."

Old man Gou scoffed. "Imagine," he said, shaking his head, "someone like me on my knees praying to someone like you."

That could have meant a thousand different things, but in the end, it didn't matter. China had long split into a great chasm, with Gou's family on one side and mine on the other.

"I don't want your prayers," I said. "I just want your money."

# CHAPTER TWO

I found Wenshu sitting on the floor of our bedroom among dozens of unfurled scrolls. His eyes tracked up and down the text, not bothering to look when I appeared in the doorway. I could have set the roof on fire and he probably would have kept reading until his skin started to bubble.

He went outside far less than me or Yufei, so his complexion nearly matched the white of his hemp robes. Yufei and I joked that he would make a better bride than either of us because he was wispy as a stalk of silver grass, had soft hands, hair that never tangled, and bathed so often that he perpetually smelled like soap beans.

"Gēgē," I said. "We have—"

"Wait a minute," he said. "I'm concentrating."

His gaze stayed locked on the parchment, reading faster than I could ever dream of. He had an irritatingly good memory, and it was probably the fifth or sixth time he'd read the same scroll, so I didn't feel too bad about grabbing one of Yufei's stray socks from the floor, balling it up, and throwing it at his face.

The sock bounced off his forehead. He finally looked up, his expression flat. "I'm studying."

"It's tax day," I said. "Come with me to the tax office and buy more tattoo ink on the way. We have a job tonight."

"Ah." He looked down at the scroll before him like a lover he couldn't bear to part with, slowly rolling it up. He'd gone to school for a few years, but ever since business declined, he'd had to split his time between the shop and studying on his own. Though he wasn't the most patient teacher, he'd managed to teach Yufei and me some basic characters, and the rest we'd learned for ourselves.

At some point that I couldn't remember, we'd all joked about passing the civil service exams together and moving to the capital, Chang'an, as government workers, where we could send Auntie So and Uncle Fan enough money to buy ten new houses. Then one day, as we studied with only the light of the thinnest slice of crescent moon coming through the paper windows, we realized it was no longer a joke. We'd spoken it aloud and slowly it had taken shape, gone from the soft haze of a dream to something with hard edges and sharp corners that we could hold tight in our hands. Now, in two weeks' time, we'd take our exams and see if our studying had amounted to anything, or if the dream would pour through our fingers like sand.

So, whenever we weren't working, Wenshu and Yufei studied Confucian classics for the bureaucratic exam, while I studied for the alchemy exam to become one of the royal court alchemists.

I'd read every alchemy book in Guangzhou that I could find or borrow or steal. I'd learned how alchemists were masters of the five elements, using all kinds of rocks and minerals as catalysts to reshape the world. At first, the earliest alchemists' only goal had been to create an elixir of immortality.

They had managed to kill five emperors with their toxic concoctions before they finally succeeded for Empress Wu—over one hundred years old and still fresh as a pond lily.

Now, with their greatest dream accomplished, there was little that modern alchemists wouldn't attempt. They could rend mountains in two, change the course of rivers, boil the oceans, raze cities to ashes—nothing was impossible if you had the right stones and were willing to pay the price.

My first text had been my father's notes on alchemy—the only thing he'd left for me, besides my ridiculous flowery name. My aunt said he'd heard that alchemy was more advanced in China than in the West, so he'd traveled along the Silk Road with the hopes of learning our secrets. He came from the other side of the world, from a small country called Scotia that spoke a strange language called Gaelic, where they still thought of alchemy as pseudoscience and myth just because they'd never mastered it. Auntie So said my father was tall, pale, and pinkish like uncooked jellyfish, with coppery hair and watery blue eyes. I still remembered the soft line of his smile, but after ten years, my memories had grown tattered at the edges.

Because of him, I would be a great alchemist one day. Not to make him proud, but to spite him. Because when my mother got sick, he'd simply left and never come back. I could still feel her stiff, withered hands in mine while she said, *Your father has gone to get help. He'll be back any moment now.* But there was no help beyond our local healers, and as the moon grew thin and dark in the sky, I knew he would never return. My mother, who had never hurt anyone, who braided my hair with orchids and picked the peppers out of my soup for me and sang to me every night until she died, had believed in him until her last breath.

So I had taken his notes as my own, because it was the

least he could give me after dumping me on Auntie So. His research was the only advantage I could hope to have over the schooled alchemists. He wrote half in Chinese and half in Gaelic, which Wenshu had helped me decipher, saying it had roots in the Slavic languages that were used along Western trade routes.

It was obvious that the Scotians really had no idea what they were doing with alchemy. My father's notes described unstable and overly ambitious transformations mixed with rants about a magical elixir hidden in a mythical Penglai Island. Sometimes, that ambition had led him to questions that would have gotten him jailed if he'd said them in Chinese.

*Why must the dead remain dead?* he'd written in his last notebook. *Alchemists wield life energy for their transformations, so why is death untouchable? Surely, with the right stone, it's possible.*

He'd focused his efforts on chicken-blood stone—a mix of clay and bloodred quartz—as the key material in a transmutation that could revive the dead. He hadn't stayed long enough to find out that he was right.

Putting his notes into practice had taken some trial and error, plus a lot of screaming and praying from Auntie So when the pig she slaughtered for dinner was suddenly alive again in the afternoon. But the first time I'd tried it on humans, I'd realized that this was as close as I would ever get to being a god. For a single moment after every transformation, I was no longer a poor merchant's daughter but an artist of the universe, repainting the constellations, smoothing mountains into valleys and parting seas.

My cousins tried alchemy when we were younger, but neither of them had been able to do much more than create bubbling pools of sludge that smelled so sharp that we nearly fainted from the fumes.

"There's probably a genetic component," Wenshu had said. "Your father did it, that's why you can."

But I suspected that Wenshu just preferred reading scrolls to getting his hands dirty.

"You smell like old fish," Wenshu said, rolling up his last scroll and setting it with reverence on his desk.

"No, I smell like purge fluid."

"Oh, that's much better," he said, putting his brushes in their drawer. I waved my hands near his face and he flinched away. "Wash your hands, you demon."

I jokingly reached for his pillow and he grabbed a handful of soap beans from the jar on his desk, hurling them at my head.

"If the smell bothers you now, good luck tonight when you actually see the body," I said. "It's leaking from every orifice."

"The body isn't standing in my bedroom touching my pillow," he said, turning and pulling out the inkstone from his desk drawer, holding it to the light, and scraping the crusted bits from the near-empty pan. He would have to make more before nightfall.

Yufei appeared in the doorway, holding a bundle of fabric. Our room truly was too small for three people, and Yufei and I were definitely too old to be sharing a room with a boy, but unless one of us slept in the hallway, there was nowhere else to go. Her long skirt had red dirt stains at the hem, and her hair had fallen down from the intricate bun that Auntie So did for her every morning.

"Why is there a body in the pigpen?" Yufei asked.

"That's for later," I said, gathering up the soap beans from the floor.

Yufei blinked but didn't inquire further. She had such a small range of facial expressions that neighbors whispered about how she wore a porcelain mask instead of a real face. Wordlessly, she unfolded the fabric in her arms, dumping whitish-brown mush all over the floor.

Wenshu made a strangled sound and backed up. After seeing the body that afternoon, my first thought was that I was looking at several pounds of human fat. But death had a distinct smell, and this one was sharp and sweet.

"Sweet potatoes?" I said.

Yufei nodded. "Can you fix them?"

I nodded, moving over to my bedside drawer. "Yes, but why did you smash them?"

"And why did you dump them all over the clean floor?" Wenshu said, gripping his hair.

Yufei shrugged. "Needed something heavy, and they were already ruined," she said, sitting down cross-legged.

"You needed something heavy while buying vegetables two blocks away?" Wenshu said, glaring accusingly at the mashed potatoes.

"Men are annoying," Yufei said, as if that explained it all. At our blank looks, she rolled her eyes and elaborated, "They wouldn't leave me alone and I had eggs in my other hand."

"Oh," I said. "You bludgeoned someone with potatoes?"

She nodded.

Quite a few men were desperate for Yufei's hand in marriage, but she was just as determined to convince them they would be better off with a wild boar than have her for a wife. One unfortunate suitor had slipped her a love note last month, which she'd torn to pieces and eaten in front of him. Another man had come to the shop to give her wildflowers, which she'd tossed into the kiln. Auntie So kept telling people Yufei was fifteen, even though she'd been fifteen for over four years now, because she was getting embarrassingly old to be unwed. But no matter how hard she tried, the well of suitors never seemed to dry up.

Wenshu let out a massive sigh, hunched over his desk. "Did you kill anyone?"

Yufei shook her head. "Too many witnesses. But even if I did, Zilan could just fix him."

Wenshu groaned and flopped facedown onto his bed. "I have demons for sisters."

"All the more reason to stay on our good side," I said, digging through my drawer for the right stone and hiding a small smile. Something in me always warmed when Wenshu or Yufei called me their sister. Sure, we'd grown up together, but I was really only their cousin. It was painfully obvious just by looking at the three of us together—I was taller than both of them because that was what happened when you had a towering Scotian father. My hair had a strange coppery tint in the sunlight, my arms and legs were so long that Auntie So called me grasshopper, and the shoemaker told me only men had feet so big.

When we played by the river as kids and I saw our mismatched reflections rippling in the muddy water, the word *sister* felt like a lie. I had not always been their sister, which meant one day they could decide I wasn't their sister anymore. It was fine now, when we were all living under Auntie and Uncle's roof. But maybe one day, Yufei would finally meet a man that didn't disgust her, and Wenshu would marry because it was the logical choice, and I would be alone. Unlike Yufei, I wasn't pretty enough to persuade a man to pay a dowry for me. The fact that I was a hùnxiě—half Hàn Chinese and half foreigner—certainly didn't help my case. Part of me wished all of us could be like Yufei and just pretend to never age, so we could stay together forever.

I pulled three small moonstones from the drawer, warming them between my palms. Moonstone was a waterstone, useful for healing and repairs. All the stones in the world had different properties based on their elements—most metalstones could reshape other objects, earthstones were good for transforming the mind, woodstones worked well for manipulating plant and animal life, and firestones were agents of destruction or great change. There were still thousands of stones with untapped uses, and even more hybrid stones that alchemists tried to forge for more powerful reactions, like the chicken-blood stone my father had studied.

I'd bought an old alchemy-stone manual a few years ago for half price because it was so outdated, then taken notes in the margins as I tried out each stone to verify what the book said. I knew by heart how to use any stone I could find in Guangzhou, and carried a satchel of the most common ones with me at all times: moonstone for healing, iron for reshaping, amethyst for breaking.

For small repairs like this, a few moonstones would do the trick. I held three of them in my hand, sunk my fingers into the mashed potatoes, and closed my eyes.

The real reason I could do alchemy and my cousins couldn't was that they couldn't hear the river flowing inside them. I'd asked them about it once and Wenshu had checked my forehead for a fever.

Qi—breath, energy, life—circulated through all our bodies, an endless river inside us keeping our hearts beating, making our lungs expand, warming the food in our stomachs. Alchemy was about drawing the power of the natural world into your qi. When I closed my eyes and let my breath grow shallow, I could hear it rushing over smooth stones and golden sands, pouring into the vast ocean of my heart.

My palm grew cool as it soaked up the healing properties of the moonstone, the river inside me running cold, thin layers of glassy ice forming across it and shattering in the current. I breathed out a cloud of water vapor, my skin prickling with goosebumps. Then, like an unstopped dam, the moonstone's energy bled out my palms and into the potatoes.

The starchy sludge grew firm beneath my hands, the skin sealing back up, soft spots of overripeness growing firm. Five whole sweet potatoes sat on the floor beneath my hands.

My fingers stung as if frostbitten, one of my nails cracking as I rubbed my hands together to melt away the coldness.

Whenever I called on alchemy, it bit back. That was one of alchemy's central principles—*you cannot create good without also creating evil.* For small things like reconstructing potatoes, the cost was negligible. For bigger transformations...it was always a question of whether it was worth it.

"Thanks," Yufei said, gathering up the potatoes. She paused, raising an eyebrow as if contemplating something of great importance. "We should do this with the food the merchants throw out at the end of the day. Save some money."

"That's not a bad idea," I said.

"It is absolutely a bad idea," Wenshu said. "You want to eat rotten fruit and spoiled meat?"

"Zilan can unspoil it," Yufei said.

"You would lick soup off the floor. Your standards for food safety don't reassure me."

"*I* wouldn't lick soup off the floor," I said.

"No, you would just resurrect potatoes with hands covered in corpse juice," Wenshu said.

"The moonstone purifies—"

"Eat what you want," Wenshu said. "There's a very short list of things I would die for, and potatoes are not on it."

KYLIE LEE BAKER

I turned to Yufei. "You and I are on that list, but second to his soap beans."

Another handful of soap beans flew across the room, raining over me and Yufei.

"Did you want me to go with you or not?" Wenshu said.

I nodded, biting back another jab. Taxes for our ward were due at the end of every week, and it wasn't a good idea for a girl to walk alone to the other end of the city on a day that everyone knew she'd be carrying money. I had cinnabar crystals in my pocket that I could use to explode a thief's brains if I wanted to, but it was better for our business for me to simply walk with Wenshu and avoid conflicts altogether. He always offered to go by himself, but I knew he didn't have enough of a spine to stand up to the market commandant.

"I'll come too," Yufei said.

"You already went out today," Wenshu said. "Mama will be mad if you get too tan."

"I want rice cakes," Yufei said, as if that would ward off Auntie So's anger.

Wenshu rolled his eyes and handed me a straw hat from the hook by the door, taking one for himself as well. I didn't particularly care if I got tan, but I knew it would give Auntie So one less thing to worry about. Both she and Uncle Fan had been too sick to work lately, so if me having the complexion of raw whitefish made them smile, I wouldn't question it.

I grabbed the bag of gold from behind the counter while Wenshu took out our sales ledger. We left through the side door, locking it tight behind us and stepping out into the sharp sunlight.

# CHAPTER THREE

Our shop sat at the end of what locals called the "Road to Hell" because it was where the market commandant had forced the death shops to relocate, saying we brought bad luck to the rest of the market. A funeral parlor sat across the street from us, an exorcist to our left.

The road had a slight downhill slope, so when the butcher poured buckets of lamb and pig blood outside, the whole street bled like a fresh wound. Most of us were too poor to buy anything but white, undyed hemp robes, so the hems of our clothing always soaked up the blood, making it clear to everyone in Guangzhou where we were from. We were far from the shade of orange trees at the inner part of town, so summer sunlight stripped the color from our lattice windows and painted signs, as if the whole street was an echo growing quieter by the day.

I tilted my hat so it blocked the glare of the sun and followed Wenshu to the end of the road, Yufei trailing behind. Wenshu walked in front of us only because we knew it would embarrass him to be seen dragged around by two younger girls.

To the east, just beyond the clay walls that marked the border to our wards, merchant ships bobbed nauseously in the black waters. Many seamen could no longer afford both their ships and their homes, so the harbor of Guangzhou had filled up with families living on leaky wooden boats with torn sails, vomiting into the shallow water from the restless wrenching of the tide. At the start of each week, at least a few of their corpses would float to the shore, and whoever got to them first would steal their clothes and scrap their boats for parts to sell.

We turned to the main road, where Yufei immediately draped herself across a pastry cart and batted her eyelashes at a flustered young man until he handed her a slice of niángāo. She shoved it at my face and wouldn't move until I took a big, sticky bite, then gobbled down rest of it.

Much of the street was packing up for the day, merchants herding pigs and goats back to their stables, wrapping up and boxing yards of hemp. It was the unlucky month—the fifth lunar cycle of the year—so few people wanted to stay out at night until after the Dragon Boat Festival at the end of the week. The air smelled of pomegranate and ixora flowers that hung in garlands over storefronts to ward off evil spirits, though I suspected that any demons would still smell our fear even through a whole meadow of flowers.

Around us, people spoke in Guangzhou dialect that my cousins and I used less and less each day. We tried to speak the language of the Northern capital as much as possible, partially because the civil service exams had an oral section that wouldn't test the southern dialects, and partially because Auntie So and Uncle Fan didn't understand it. We could discuss our resurrection plans over dinner and they'd think we were practicing for our exams. Wenshu used to be called Man-syu, but when he was eight, he'd learned that Wénshū was how his name would be pronounced in the capital of Chang'an, and had refused to answer to Man-syu unless it was Auntie or Uncle calling him. Yufei's name was the same in either dialect, but with a different tone. For me, the Northern dialect transformed my name from Zee-lahn to Zih-lahn, the same cheap flower no matter the inflection.

The main block still stood in shambles from the fires that had ripped across all the thatched roofs last week. I heard rumors that in the capital, roofs were made of shiny tiles that deflected fire, but that felt like a lie. Surely roofs made of tile would be too heavy and crush everyone inside.

The merchants who'd lost their shops were forced to improvise, moving the last of their unscorched wares onto carts and blankets under thin gauze canopies of whatever frames remained standing. The weaver at the end of the street had lost half her pongee—poor man's silk so thin that a harsh ray of sunlight could tear through it. It wasn't good for much else than the appearance of wealth. The burnt bits were in a bin on the ground for people to buy as scraps, the rest hung up on thin lines, a dozen colors blowing in the wind like a strange celebration before the singed ruins of her shop. She smiled as my cousins and I walked by, but they averted their eyes and didn't see the way her smile thinned. It was the same smile my mother had worn, toward the end. The kind that never reached her eyes.

I pulled out a small piece of moonstone from my pocket, then cracked it into three pieces, sinking my hands into the scrap bin.

"We have plenty of scraps," Wenshu said, but I ignored him as my fingers grew cool and damp. The moonstone drank up the burns on the fabric, blackened sections replaced by lavender and deep red and pale blue, the fabric no longer stiff and crunchy beneath my fingers but soft and new. My hands suddenly ached like I'd been molding míngqì all day.

I stood up quickly, ignoring Wenshu's glare. It was unwise to practice alchemy in this part of town. While the rich coveted alchemists, some commoners despised us for widening the income gap and would spit in our food or overcharge us if they saw my stones. They didn't care that most alchemists in the south never even came close to the royal palace, much less learned how to make life gold.

I turned at the sound of fabric tearing.

A low-ranking state official—I could tell from the blue hue of his robes—had torn a sheet of bright yellow pongee in half and cast it up to the sky, where the wind carried it away.

"Ten gold pieces is too much for this shit," he said.

Yufei made a low sound of anger, but Wenshu grabbed her sleeve before she could intervene. She stayed back not because he was actually strong enough to restrain her, but because she knew we couldn't afford the trouble.

"Any less than ten and I'm losing money," the woman said, taking a step back. "I can give you a half sheet for five?"

The man responded by tearing another sheet in half and casting it behind him, two lavender ghosts floating up to the sky. The woman took another step back as the man crossed his arms. It was always the wealthy who haggled down to the bone. The rest of us knew that while prices were flexible to a point, there was a limit.

I jammed my hand into my pocket, feeling for the right stones. Yufei stood in front of me on the off chance anyone was looking, while Wenshu sighed but didn't protest.

I eyed the rickety frame of the withered storefront. The wood was already weak from the fire. Were it to suddenly topple over, no one would suspect a thing.

I fished out three small pieces of amethyst—a firestone—from my bag, clenched it in one fist, and pressed my other hand to the wooden banister.

Destroying was much easier than creating.

All you needed was a tiny ember of hate and the will to set yourself on fire, let the river inside you run dry until the parched earth shattered like a porcelain plate.

With a sound like thunder, the frame split down the middle and caved inward. The man scarcely had the chance to look up before the sharp end of the broken wood cleaved into the side of his head with a wet crunch. He screamed and stumbled back, half of his face painted with blood. The woman reached out to help him, but he shoved her away and stumbled down the street, dizzy trails of blood behind him.

"Zilan," Wenshu said, yanking my sleeve to pull me back toward the road, "do try your best not to murder people while we're doing errands."

"I didn't," I said, at the same time Yufei said, "He deserved it!"

I hadn't intended to kill the man and didn't think I truly had, since he'd been well enough to run away screaming, but it was hard to conjure much pity for a rich man berating a merchant over fake silk. Every day that the wealth gap yawned wider, I began to realize that evil was not found in the demons or spirits we could ward away with fragrant flowers, but in the men who thought that everything on earth could be bought.

I pulled the brim of my hat down farther to avoid eye contact with peddlers and Buddhists looking for converts until we finally reached the market commandant's office, a white clay building with a fenced-in courtyard and barrier of plum trees. We waited our turn in line behind the other merchants,

Wenshu shifting from foot to foot, wiping his sweaty palms on his robes.

"Could you at least clean your face?" he said to Yufei.

She blinked, sticky brown rice-cake crumbs lining her mouth. "Is he going to tax each grain of rice? What does it matter?"

"He'll say we have too much to eat," Wenshu said, trying to scrub Yufei's face with his sleeve, but she ducked under his arm and stepped back, nearly toppling the person behind us in line.

"All he can see is what I *didn't* eat."

"Just eat it now and be done with it!" Wenshu said, trying to grab Yufei again. She pulled his straw hat over his face and shoved him backward into me. I caught him under the arms, grunting as he dug his heels into the dirt to right himself. He managed to yank my sleeve so hard that the seam tore, sending him to the ground with the fabric in one hand.

The doors to the commandant's office slid open. "Next!" a man called, glaring down at the three of us.

I dumped out the entire bag of gold onto the market commandant's tray. This was meant to be our entire week's worth of earnings for them to count and remove taxes from, but no one was foolish enough to be honest.

We knelt on the floor while the commandant sat on a raised cushion before us, draped in enough blue silk that he looked like a bald head emerging from the sea. I wondered how old he really was—you could never tell with gold eaters. But I knew from the color of his robes that he was low-ranking, so he couldn't be gorging himself on too much gold—the price of it went up the farther south it had to be imported, as only the royal alchemists in Chang'an knew how to make it.

"Fan Wenshu," my cousin said, handing over our ledger while the assistant began counting our coins.

"What do you sell again?" the commandant said, barely looking up from his notes. The man spoke the dialect of the capital, like all government officials, even though few merchants in Guangzhou could. When I was young, Uncle Fan had pantomimed his way through these meetings, always getting shortchanged or berated.

"Míngqì, sir," Wenshu said.

The man nodded. "The new adjusted rate for míngqì next week is twenty-five gold."

Wenshu nodded but said nothing. Gold was getting devalued every day, so the increase wasn't surprising. The market commandant was responsible for regulating prices.

"And the new tax rate is twenty percent."

I looked up. "You're increasing our prices by five coins and our taxes by ten percent?"

"Orders from the Empress," the assistant said. "There's a shortage of ceramic."

"There isn't," I said, narrowing my eyes. "We make our own. We would know."

"Zilan," Wenshu said, elbowing me. We both knew it was just for show. It would reflect poorly on Wenshu if he let his sisters speak freely to a high-ranking officer. But it would look even worse if we said nothing at all—this was supposed to be our entire week's earnings, and quiet complacence while half of it was stolen would make them suspicious.

"It is not my job to question the will of the Empress," the commandant said, "and certainly not *yours*."

He said the last word like even mentioning us put a sour taste in his mouth. Was it our low rank, or the fact that I was a hùnxiě, or the food still on Yufei's face?

Our coins clattered into a porcelain bowl as the assistant swept a quarter of them off the tray.

"You can't charge us next week's tax rate on last week's profit," I said.

"I counted correctly," the assistant said without sparing us a glance.

"Count again," Yufei said, crossing her arms.

Wenshu sighed and pinched Yufei's ear in one hand and mine in the other, yanking us down into a bow. We were allowed to be defiant because the commandant would trust that Wenshu would punish us at home. Defiance from Wenshu himself wouldn't have been so easily tolerated.

"I apologize for my sisters," he said. "Please, would you humor them? I'll never hear the end of it otherwise."

The assistant huffed and stiffly removed the coins, recounting as the three of us watched his every move. The amount he placed in the bowl was smaller this time.

"Inspections are next week," the commandant said. That meant they would come to our shop, break a few míngqì in their attempts to "inspect the quality," and turn over every drawer looking for the money they knew we hadn't given them. But I had sealed our savings into the walls, and they had yet to find it.

It wasn't even as if the taxes we paid were of any use to us. Most of the money went to Chang'an to repave the roads in gold. No one cared about the dirty south.

The commandant dismissed us with a wave of his hand, and it took everything in me not to hurl my bag of gemstones at his face. I had the power to raise the dead and fix any broken thing or creature, but alchemy wouldn't stop the commandant from taking our money. No matter how much I hated him, I couldn't just bring the roof down and crush him under straw and wood beams—another man would take his place the next day. There was nothing to be done but save what we could and, one day, if we were lucky, become one of the rich that we hated so deeply.

Wenshu and Yufei stood up, but when I moved to follow them, my legs prickled with numbness and I sank back to the floor.

"Zilan?" Wenshu said, gaze darting back to the commandant, who no doubt wanted us gone. I opened my mouth to explain, but the words lodged in my throat, breath choked away, a strange and wordless sound falling from my lips like dead bark off a rotting tree. Yufei said something, but her voice blurred before it could reach my ears, and I couldn't tear my gaze from the long swathes of blue silk of the commandant's robes, rippling and stretching to the edges of the room like a nauseous sea pooling hot under my feet. The room grew dim around us, paneled walls falling away and a night sky unfolding overhead, and when I turned my head up to find the stars, I toppled forward, my forehead smacking against something hard.

The ground beneath my face pulsed like a heartbeat, so many footsteps all at once. I tasted parched dirt, scorched earth, bright with spices. A stranger called my name, and when they lifted me off the ground, I fell to pieces, shattered ceramic twinkling back down to earth in a thousand sharp chunks.

I woke with my face against Yufei's sweaty robes, blood pooling in my head. I was upside down, tossed over Yufei's shoulder. The hot sun burned my neck, my face jostling against her back as she walked.

"Put me down," I said.

She stopped walking, squatting down until my feet touched the road. I stood up straight, my body tingling as blood rushed back down to my feet. I pressed a hand to my forehead, rubbing where I was sure a bruise would form.

"You okay?" Yufei said, standing too close, shielding me from the busy road.

"Where's Wenshu Ge?" I said.

Yufei looked over her shoulder as Wenshu stomped toward us, arms full of fruit. He didn't look relieved to see me upright, eyes narrowing as he approached.

"Did you eat *anything* cold today?" he said, shoving a cucumber at me.

I took a bite rather than answer. The thought of eating fruit before we left had crossed my mind, but Yufei had eaten the last pear yesterday and I'd wanted to avoid exactly this— Wenshu spending money we didn't have on fruit that wouldn't help me.

Every now and then, I blinked and woke up thrown over Yufei's shoulder while she carried me home, the last few minutes scraped from my memory. Other times, the world rippled like the surface of a pond before swallowing me whole. Auntie So said I fainted because my fire element was unbalanced, so I needed to eat lots of cucumbers and melons to quench it. Wenshu thought it was an illness, but I never actually felt ill. It was more like I'd stopped existing. Somehow, I didn't think all the cucumbers in the world could change that.

Wenshu pushed my hair aside, poking at the sore spot on my forehead and frowning. "You need to say something before that happens," he said.

I nodded, even though I knew I couldn't have said anything, and by this point Wenshu surely knew it too. Just like the rules of the commandant, it was out of my hands, up to some higher power who cared nothing for me at all.

# CHAPTER FOUR

In hindsight, attempting a resurrection half an hour before dinner was probably not the best idea we'd ever had. We'd come back from the market to find Auntie So insisting she felt well enough to cook all the potatoes Yufei had bought, meanwhile old man Gou was loitering by the pigpen with crossed arms and a sack of gold, unwilling to leave without his brother. We could have made him wait until the sun fully set, but having a rich man standing in our backyard with a bag of money would make the neighbors ask questions.

"Can you do it in less than an hour?" Wenshu whispered to me, glancing at old man Gou glowering over Yufei while she counted his coins.

I wasn't sure, but soon I would be taking the royal alchemy exam and would have to do transformations under far more pressure than my aunt yelling for me to come eat. I imagined my father traveling across the world, using alchemy to slay wild beasts with a flick of his wrist, climbing mountains and wading through rivers. Surely he had faced more peril than a cranky old man, so if I wanted to be better than him, I would have to get used to performing with an angry audience.

Yufei finished packing up the gold, giving me a nod from across the yard.

"Let's get ready," I said.

So, as the smell of sweet potato and ginger wafted out the windows, we locked the door to the pigpen and took out our tools, old man Gou waiting just beyond the gate.

Our pigpen was a wooden cage screened in with windows that had once been meant to keep the pigs cool in the summer, back when we could afford our own pigs. Now it was just a cool slab of dirt and old hay with snakes hissing in the thatched ceiling. It was better to do this sort of complex alchemy after the sun fell completely and no one walking by could see us, but days were stretching longer and longer in the summer months, and pale orange light still glowed through the windows.

"Let's make this quick," Yufei said, cracking her knuckles. "I'm hungry."

"You look at rotting human flesh and think of food?" Wenshu said, counting out his needles.

"I see unappetizing things all the time," Yufei said. "I eat dinner next to *you*, don't I?"

I couldn't quite bring myself to laugh, too focused on the corpse on the ground. I had to be in the right mental space for this level of alchemy.

I bent down and pulled the sheets off the body—old man Gou had said his name was Gou Jau Gam—and rolled him onto his back. I could hear his organs sloshing around inside of him like a mushy pie, his skin doughy under my fingers. Yufei handed me a knife, and I split his robes down the middle, exposing the grayed skin of his back and jutting knobs of his spine. The smell of human rot mixed with the scent of hot potatoes from inside the house, creating a nauseating sweetness that coated my throat.

I opened my bag of gemstones and fished out three chicken-blood stones, turning them over in my palm under the dim light of the pig pen. Bloodstone was a hybrid gem, made of clay, quartz, and cinnabar that together made an earthy stone with bright splashes of scarlet. I'd only ever been able to find it when merchants from Zhejiang passed through our city. I'd spent enough time studying gems that I could identify most of them by touch, but there was no room for error with this kind of alchemy, so I always triple-checked that I had the right ones.

Larger alchemical transformations like this were easier if three people were involved because everything in alchemy followed the rule of threes—Heaven, Man, and Earth, the cosmic trinity. You needed all three things in some form to produce alchemy. Three symbolic gemstones were often good enough stand-ins, but for intense creation magic, having three people made the transformation more stable. Or at least, less likely to take too much from me. Alchemy always had a price. Sometimes it didn't take what you offered, but what it wanted.

Wenshu heated a blade over a candle until it glowed a furious red, sterilizing it. He dipped it in a cup of water to cool it, the metal hissing and steaming in protest. When the steam began to abate, he passed the blade to Yufei and offered her his palm, turning away. He could never manage to do this part himself because the sight of his own blood made him woozy. Yufei gripped his wrist and carved a thin line against his palm. Wenshu winced but didn't make a sound, clenching his fist and letting the blood pool into a small bowl.

Yufei sliced a line across her own palm, then passed the

knife to me. The blade was a bit too dull, dragging unevenly across my skin, but it did the job. I added my own blood to the bowl, squeezing my fist to force more of it out.

Wenshu's face had gone pale as he swirled his calligraphy brush around the blood offering, but he scoffed at my offer to do it for him.

"Your handwriting is atrocious," he said, though his words had no bite. He kept his hand steady as he grabbed Yufei's arm, painting the character for *Heaven* over the blue rivers of veins just beneath her skin: 天

On my arm, he painted Earth: 地

And on his own wrist, Man: 人

We jolted at the sound of metal striking wood and turned toward the house.

"*Yufei!*" Auntie So called, probably banging a spoon against the window frame. "*Come help me cut onions!*"

"In a minute, Mama!" Yufei said. "I'm studying!"

"*You should be* studying *how to cook, or your husband will bring you back to us and ask for a refund!*"

Wenshu scoffed, not managing to hide his smile before Yufei glared.

"Gohgo says he'll come help you!" she shouted.

"Hey!" Wenshu said, shoving Yufei's shoulder.

"*I don't want him in my kitchen!*" Auntie So said. "*He'll faint trying to lift a pot of water.*"

Yufei barked out a laugh, while Wenshu grimaced.

"Mama, we'll all come help you in a minute!" I said.

Auntie So made a noise of acknowledgment and didn't press further. Old man Gou coughed from outside the pen, an unsubtle sound of impatience.

I took a deep breath, then knelt before the body.

"I'm ready."

Wenshu knelt on one side, ready with his needles, a dry palette of ink, and shallow bowl of water. Yufei knelt on the other side of the body, resting her hands on the back of his neck and the small of his back, the easiest way to hold him down on her own, because Wenshu and I would be too busy to help her once we got started.

I closed my eyes and placed my hands on his upper back, just above the heart meridian.

The sounds of pots and spoons clanging inside our house faded away and all I could hear was the slow bleeding river inside me, smoothing over rocks, carving canyons into the earth. The current soothed away the feeling of cracked dirt against my knees, the sweat on the back of my neck, the sweltering summer air that made breathing feel like drowning. The river inhaled my entire world until there was nothing but cold darkness and water whispering the secrets of the universe in my ear.

For simple alchemy, this was as close as I needed to go.

But this time, instead of just listening to the sounds of the river, I sank my feet into it.

Cold water bit into my ankles, the river suddenly made of teeth. The water was in me and all of me, and it knew my heart's intentions. It latched its jaws into me like a tiger trap locking around my ankles. *Stop*, it whispered. *You will go no farther.*

But I only took orders from people who paid me.

I yanked my ankles out of the water, my skin peeling back as the river tried to tether me there, painting my feet with hot blood. I stepped up onto the riverbank that felt like it was made of glass instead of soil, a jagged surface that quickly grew slick with my blood. Behind me, the running waters fell silent, holding their breath. I walked forward into the darkness, my wet steps echoing a thousand times into the sky.

I couldn't see anything at all, but it didn't matter. This was not a place that you could navigate with a map. It was a place of endings—the last dead end in a winding, lightless labyrinth of caves. It was getting lost in the forest after dark, when the trees breathed you in and wouldn't let you go. It was the heavy silence after a heart stops beating, when all you can hear is what *was*.

Footsteps wouldn't take you anywhere in a place like this. Desire was what pulled you deeper into the dark, bit into you like tiny hooks and lured you forward on a clear fishing line cast far across an ocean of night.

*Gou Jau Gam*, I thought, over and over again in my mind, tracing the characters across the empty sky.

At last, the ground sloped downward and I stood in the withered canyons where a river used to be. Not the river of my own qi, but someone else's, where now there was nothing but dry dirt. I followed the path across crooked roots and fish bones and loose rocks.

I knew I was getting close when I heard someone's jagged breaths. I hurried down the riverbed until I came across a man dressed in white, curled up on his side as snakes writhed around him.

"Come on, get up," I said, yanking him up by the arm. He was far lighter than he looked, easy to pull to his feet.

The man jerked away, his eyes dark and empty, his face bloodless. He was a shell of the real Gou Jau Gam, an empty vessel like our unpainted míngqì, nothing but powdery white clay.

"Who are you?" he said.

I didn't answer, waving for him to follow me down the

empty riverbed. I didn't like to be in a place like this any longer than I had to. There was always the chance that you wouldn't be able to find your way back. I took off walking, and after a moment, his uneven footsteps stumbled after me.

Sure enough, just around another bend, we reached a stone wall that formed a dam in the riverbank, just barely restraining the water as tiny leaks dribbled down the stones. I let out a tense breath. At least some water was still getting through.

I sank my fingers into the cracks between the stones and pulled hard, jostling a few stones but not managing to pull any out, the surface too slick. I looked over my shoulder at Gou Jau Gam, who watched me with hollow eyes.

"Are you going to help me or not?" I said. "This is *your* qi, not mine."

He shook his head. "The dam won't break. I've tried."

"Of course it won't break for just *you*," I said. People couldn't go around resurrecting themselves, after all. "I've used bloodstone to get here. It will break."

When he still didn't move, I sighed. "The longer we wait, the stronger the wall will become."

His eyes widened and he stepped forward, hands ghosting across the wall, feeling for weak points but not quite daring to use any force. I returned to my own section, and after a few minutes of loosening stones, I finally managed to yank one out. Water sprayed through a hole the size of a coin, the pent-up force of it like a solid punch to my ribs. While the qi of the living always ran clear, this river was scarlet, tainted from the bloodstones. Red water pooled around our feet, the parched riverbed drinking it up instantly.

Gou Jau Gam froze, staring at his wet feet, toes tapping in the ground that was now soft instead of sharp beneath him.

"This is mine," he whispered in wonder, as the last of the water disappeared into the earth. "This is my life, isn't it?"

I sighed, my hands slipping off another stone. "What's left of it," I said. "There's more where that came from if you hurry."

At once, he turned to the wall and started grabbing at the stones with fervor, splitting his nails and cutting his palms. When that didn't work, he slammed his fists against it, stones clanking against each other, the whole wall trembling.

With a heavy crack, the wall folded in toward the center.

The water spilled through slowly at first, lapping over the sinking lip of the wall, then all at once, it gushed over and roared toward us.

The stones flew at us first. I'd barely thrown an arm over my face before the river pummeled us with rocks, forcing my breath out in a choked gasp as they slammed into my ribs. I couldn't draw another breath before the waters surged on top of us, crushing us to the riverbed.

I threw out a hand and grabbed Gou Jau Gam's robes as the river scraped us along the bottom of its parched maze. He thrashed in my grip until I managed to grab his wrist. I had to make sure to take him back with me, or all of this would be for nothing. I sank my fingernails into him until I drew blood, just to be sure he was tethered to me. Then, just as my lungs started screaming for air, I opened my eyes.

Gou Jau Gam was thrashing on the floor of our pigpen, Yufei sweating as she forced him into the ground. I knelt before him, bone-dry, hands crushed into his spine, the blood-stones in my left hand gone, choking down deep gasps of air that tasted like corpse and ginger.

His body rattled like a cage full of snakes, fingernails raking up handfuls of dirt, teeth gnashing into the ground. I'd dragged the heavy anchor of his soul back with me and dumped it onto the mortal plane. Just like creatures of the deep sea, dead souls didn't take kindly to being forced up into the sunlight. His soul would flee again if it wasn't bound.

I kept my hands clenched just above his heart meridian. I was the one holding the anchor, and if I let go, he would plummet back down.

"Jiějiě, hold him harder," I said to Yufei, struggling to even form words when my mouth tasted like bloody water and silt. It was hard to keep my grip on the body with how slippery his skin was. Some of it was tearing near his nape, so I readjusted my grip, hoping I wouldn't accidentally peel him like a grape.

Wordlessly, Yufei pressed her knees into the small of his back, her hand driving his face into the ground. Despite being half my size, her strength was immense. It wouldn't shock me if she could one day break bricks in half with her bare hands.

"Gēgē, *now*," I said, gritting my teeth.

Wenshu knelt beside me, pulling a patch of skin taut. He wielded a tool that looked like a calligraphy brush, but with sharp needles instead of hairs. He'd gotten it from one of the Bǎiyuè people from the southern coast when they'd traveled to Guangzhou for trade. The needles were coated in black ink that Wenshu would tediously slip under the skin, spelling out the name of the dead man in writing that wouldn't wash away. His hands moved fast over the grayed flesh, the characters appearing line by line.

As he finished the first character, the man jolted and Wenshu hissed, reeling back so as not to stab any stray marks into the skin.

"Harder, Yufei," he said.

Yufei leaned more of her weight into his neck and Wenshu carried on, sweat dripping down his brow. My hands were starting to grow numb, and it was getting harder to hear the river the longer the man grunted and thrashed beneath me. This man's soul was farther away than usual, a thin kite string I was trying to snatch out of a clear sky.

Finally, Wenshu leaned back. Three characters, red and inflamed, marked the man's spine.

高
有
金

Gou Jau Gam.

# CHAPTER FIVE

Gou Jau Gam fell still in the dirt, his lungs expanding with rattling breaths. I finally dared to lift my hands, which trembled even though I could no longer feel them. My arms had a pale purple tinge, hair standing up and bones shuddering with cold. I had to remind myself how to breathe, my heartbeat punching against my chest like it wanted to break me open from the inside.

Old man Gou burst into the pen, apparently taking the sudden silence as confirmation that we'd finished.

"Is he back?" he said, bending down and grabbing the dead man's shoulder.

I tensed. "Don't—"

But Gou Jau Gam's skin tore like wet paper, splitting at the base of his neck, syrupy black blood oozing out. Old man Gou froze, but his brother only winced and sat up. His eyes were still pale and blue, his complexion still like old porridge. He coughed and brown purge fluid spilled past his lips, down his bare chest.

But old man Gou hugged him anyway, squeezing out more of the black blood, like his brother was nothing but a rotten soup dumpling. Over his shoulder, Gou Jau Gam's eyes met mine. They widened, as if remembering, but he would only know me as a hazy character in a bad dream.

*"Dinner!"* Auntie So yelled from beyond the window.

Me and my cousins flinched from the sound. It was hard to think about things like food after dragging a man back from death.

Wenshu raised the sheet over Gou Jau Gam's shoulders. "You need to leave now," he said.

Old man Gou nodded, helping his brother to his feet. Gou Jau Gam listed to the side, but his brother held him steady. His limbs would still be stiff for a while, his qi just beginning to circulate once more.

"He'll be all right now?" old man Gou asked.

"Eventually," I said. "Besides the skin, which I warned you about."

Old man Gou nodded. "If he… I mean, can he die again?"

*"Yes,"* I said, frowning. "Of course. He's alive again. Anything alive can die. He shouldn't be out looking like that anyway, so it shouldn't be hard to keep him from dying in your house."

Old man Gou nodded. "And are there any long-term side effects?"

I glanced at his brother, his milky eyes staring past me as if seeing into another world.

*You cannot create good without also creating evil.*

That was alchemy's key truth. Surely new life came at a great cost. Surely a soul couldn't simply be dropped to the bottom of the dark sea and then resurface as if nothing had happened, especially if their body had decayed.

But my hands didn't even hurt after the transformation. I felt a bit tired as my heartbeat slowed down and warmth crept back into my bones after my journey through the river, but that seemed too cheap a price for raising the dead.

It had been years since my first resurrection, and I still hadn't figured out the true cost. There was no one for me to ask. My father had been the one to do the research, and he was gone.

"No," I said, because that answer was better for business. I didn't feel too bad about lying, because I knew that no possible side effect would have changed his mind. If I turned out to be wrong, it wasn't as if he could report me to the market commandant to get his money back.

"He should cough up the rest of the purge fluid in a few days," I said. "Just stitch him back up if his skin slips."

*"Dinner!"* Auntie So called again.

Yufei held the door open for the men as they shuffled outside, the sheet pulled higher to hide Gou Jau Gam's face. Wenshu sighed at his bloody palms, fingers twitching.

"Go wash up and distract Mama," I said. "I'll clean up here."

Wenshu whispered his thanks and hurried into the house. We needed to wash down the floor, or else the smell of purge fluid would waft inside. Uncle Fan and Auntie So didn't have a very strong sense of smell anymore, but we didn't want them to have a reason to investigate the pen and find our supplies.

"I'll get water," I said, hitching a bucket over my shoulder.

Yufei nodded and watched me go. She knew I always wanted time to myself after big alchemical transformations. Jumping back and forth between planes felt a bit like splitting myself in half. There was the Zilan who lived in the dark, and the Zilan who lived aboveground, jolted from a vivid dream.

Time passed differently by the river—I felt like I'd been there for hours, but the sun was only just sinking into the dusty horizon as I headed down the street to the public well.

Wenshu liked to keep his own water that he would reuse for washing throughout the day, but we had to trek to the well if we wanted water for any other purpose. The shops had already closed for the day because no one traveled on the Road to Hell after dark, so for once, I walked the street alone.

My hands moved on their own, hooking the bucket and drawing water up from the well as my thoughts wandered. When I turned around, clutching the bucket in both hands, a man stood before me.

I wondered for a moment if I was still caught between planes, because this man didn't look like he belonged on our street.

He wore the purple robes of the highest class and shoes so clean that surely he'd never walked a step in his life. His eyes were dark and round, like the water deer that ate flowers at the edge of the city, ready to lope off if startled. He looked about my age, but his skin sparkled with gold flecks, so he might have been my age for a very long time.

He took a small step closer and I nearly dropped the bucket. Handsome men only ever looked at Yufei, not at me.

"You're a hùnxiě, right?" he said.

I nearly bit down on my tongue, the breathless feeling of his attention withering inside me. *I'm just a spectacle*, I thought. *He's just never seen anyone like me before.*

But the young man spoke in a crisp Chang'an dialect, and we didn't get many Northerners in these parts. What was someone like him doing on the Road to Hell, gawking at me?

"Do you understand me?" he said, misreading my hesitation. "Oh no, I'm not good at dialects. Umm…*nei si bat si wan hyut*—"

"Stop," I said in his dialect, grimacing. I'd been told that southern dialects were harder for Northerners to learn than vice versa, and his upside-down pronunciation only confirmed it. I should have just pretended not to understand, but he was too painful to listen to. "I need to go," I said, turning away. I wouldn't stand here and be a spectacle for him when dinner was waiting.

"Wait, wait!" he said. I stopped, only because the water was so heavy and my palm hurt from being cut open. "What's your name?"

"Hùnxiě," I said, "since that's apparently all you care about."

He winced. "I'm sorry, I just…" He jammed a hand into his pocket and pulled out a thin brown stem and crumpled purple petals. It unfolded in his palm, five delicate petals spreading out. My breath caught in my throat.

A purple orchid. *Zǐlán.*

"In Chang'an, they speak of a hùnxiě in Guangzhou who is a great alchemist," he said. "They say that you can find her name in the fields at the border of the city. I went to the border and this is what I found." He held up the flower. "I asked around for Zǐlán, and everyone told me to find the street covered in blood."

I looked between the crumpled flower and his wide brown eyes. *People speak of me in Chang'an?* Many of the revived dead tended to leave Guangzhou rather than explain how they'd come back to life, but I hadn't thought they'd ever mention me again.

"It's you, isn't it?" the man said, lowering the flower.

For some reason, I couldn't bring myself to lie. Unlike everyone in Guangzhou with sharp teeth and jagged edges, this man felt like the world after a rainstorm, a morning when the earth was fresh and untilled.

"Chang'an is full of royal alchemists," I said, rather than answer his question. "If you wanted an alchemist, why come all the way to Guangzhou?"

The man dropped his gaze to the red road. "I have a reputation in Chang'an," he said, "and the alchemists there can't do what I need."

"Which is?"

He looked around, then took a step closer. "They say you can raise the dead."

The winds died down around us, as if the whole world was listening. I glanced back at the house, where Yufei had left a light burning for me.

When people in Guangzhou came to me for help, I knew who they were, who their families were, where they lived. I never feared them turning me in because no one would cross a skilled alchemist who knew where their children slept.

But I knew nothing of this man. Not even his name.

"You've got the wrong person," I said, turning toward the house. "Good night."

"I'll pay you one hundred thousand gold."

I froze. Slowly, I looked over my shoulder. For a hundred thousand gold, we wouldn't have to worry about the míngqì shop for the next year, maybe two, if we were careful. Our taro soup would have pork again. We could find a better healer for Uncle and Auntie.

I carefully smoothed out my facial expression. I didn't want this man to see just how much that money would mean to me. I felt like one of the painted míngqì in the shop, waiting to be bought.

"This dead person must be very important to you," I said at last.

He scratched the back of his neck. "Well, you could say that. Will that be enough for you?"

I pretended to deliberate for a moment before nodding and setting down the bucket.

"Where is the body?" I said at last. Then an awful thought crossed my mind. "Please tell me you didn't bring it all the way from Chang'an." I imagined the smell of dead flesh after a hot carriage ride and my stomach clenched.

The man looked away, blinking quickly again, like something was in his eye.

"What is it?" I said. "Is it in bad condition?"

His silence only made my stomach clench even harder.

"Is it in pieces?" I said. "Did someone fall off a tall building? Get mauled by a leopard? I can't help you if—"

"No, no." The man shook his head. "Nothing like that."

"Then take me to it," I said. "I need to see what I'm working with."

The man sighed, then spread his palms out as if offering me something. "It's…it's me."

I blinked. Perhaps I wasn't as good at Northern dialects as I'd thought.

"Do you even understand what resurrection means?" I said.

He glanced around the street, taking a step closer to me. He smelled like cloves and frankincense and travel. "I don't think I'm going to be alive for much longer," he whispered.

I took a quick step back, one hand on the knife in my belt. "Are you a criminal?"

He shook his head. "No, I just… I just *know*."

"Okay…" I said, frowning. "How?"

"I can't explain right now," he said. "I'll give you one thousand more if you don't ask questions."

I closed my mouth, hating the fact that this man thought he could buy anything he wanted, and that I needed the money so badly I was proving him right.

"I need you in one piece," I said, crossing my arms. "Minor damage is fine, but it won't work if your head isn't attached to your neck, got it? The sooner I get your body, the better. If it's been more than a week, you don't want me to wake you up again. Trust me." I grimaced, thinking about the half-melted corpse I'd just revived, but old man Gou hadn't cared about the risks.

He nodded quickly, shoulders relaxing. "Yes, yes, that's fine. Thank you."

I waved a hand to dismiss his words. "How will I know when you're dead, and where do I find your body?"

"You'll come with me to Chang'an, of course," he said, gesturing for me to follow him.

My feet stayed rooted in the dirt. "Now?"

"Yes." He turned around. "I need to return immediately."

"I can't just leave," I said, frowning. "I'm taking the imperial alchemy exam in two weeks. I have to be in my home province for that. And my family is here."

One hundred thousand gold was a lot, but it wasn't enough for a family of five to live off of for the rest of our lives. Especially with the value of gold dropping by the day. It certainly wasn't enough for me to give up my plans of working in Chang'an and slide into early retirement. Besides, if I wasn't an alchemist, I would have to become a bride. And a bride like me would not have her choice of men. I grimaced at the prospect of marriage, and how someone like the man in front of me probably thought I had more in common with pond scum than a potential bride.

His eyes went wide. "You don't want to be a royal alchemist," he said. "Trust me."

"It's not about wanting," I said, rubbing my bruised forehead. Of course someone like him would never understand. Alchemy was the only thing I was good at, the only thing I could get paid for. As much as I loathed the idea of helping the rich spin more gold for their breakfast, there was no such thing as an impoverished royal alchemist, and I wouldn't let my family starve just so my morals could thrive.

"I know the royal alchemists," the man said. "They would tell you the same thing."

"They don't know me," I said. "And neither do you."

"Do you want more money?" he said. "Two hundred thousand?"

"I am not a cow that you can purchase!" I said, raising my voice more than I probably should have on a quiet street at night, but the neighbors wouldn't understand this dialect anyway. "Unless you intend to support my family for the rest of our lives, you cannot pay me to miss my alchemy exam!"

"Zilan, please—"

*"Zilan?"* I echoed, my eyes narrowing.

"Xiǎojiě," he said quickly, "please—"

"When I pass my exams in two weeks' time," I said, my jaw clenched, "then, and only then, will I go to Chang'an. I will go there to be a royal alchemist, not as your purchase."

His shoulders drooped. "I worry I may not have that long—"

"Then die in Guangzhou," I said, "or find someone else."

I grabbed the bucket, ignoring the twinge in my palm, and brushed past him down the street. He called out for me, but I did not turn back, locking the gate behind me.

# CHAPTER SIX

I stuck my face in a bag of soap beans and scrubbed my palms to chase away the scent of corpse before dinner, but it was the kind of smell that you could never really wash out. Just the memory made my throat close up. By the time I came downstairs, the soup was no longer steaming, and I could tell from the water lines on the inside of the clay bowls that Auntie So had already given half her portion to me.

I sat down beside Yufei and put a mouthful of lukewarm ginger-and-sweet-potato broth in my mouth before Auntie or Uncle could ask why I was so late. Their faces looked brighter than last night, so luckily Auntie So hadn't been lying again about feeling well enough to cook. Just yesterday, their skin had gone gray, fevered gazes darting about the room like trapped dragonflies, never settling on any one thing for too long. Their coughs scraped up their throats and shook the shelves, rattling the míngqì.

Last month, the local healer had shrugged and said the red rope demons killed the elderly in the summer, that there was nothing to be done. But my mother had died of a similar sickness, and she hadn't been that old, so maybe the healer just didn't know what to do.

Across the table, Wenshu stirred his soup like he would rather eat dirt, and I remembered that these were the potatoes I'd resurrected with "corpse hands." Last year, the soup would have had pork, scallions, vinegar, soy paste, and rice. Now it was just hot ginger water and mushy potatoes. Still, it was more than some of our neighbors had, so none of us would complain.

The extra money we made from resurrections had helped us to at least buy vegetables now and then, but most of it went to the increasing rent, clay, firewood, our savings for Chang'an, and money for Auntie and Uncle to use after we left, since they couldn't manage it on their own anymore. There was no telling how long the process of imperial exams would take, how many months the five of us would have to live without pay before we could send money home.

Yufei had already finished her soup but had left a few bits of potato at the bottom, pushing them around with a spoon so that Auntie So wouldn't refill her bowl. Uncle Fan let out a hacking cough, sending ripples through the soup pot in the center of the table. He settled back in his spot in the corner, half asleep, pieces of potato on his face.

"You smell like old lamb," Auntie So said to me. "Why are you late and stinky?"

Wenshu choked on a piece of potato, hacking it back into his bowl.

I didn't know what kind of lamb meat Auntie So had been sniffing, but at least she didn't recognize the smell of corpse.

"We went to the market to pay taxes today," Yufei said, not even hesitating or looking up from her bowl. "The heat is baking the butcher's cuts."

"Did you look at it or bathe in it?" Auntie So said, narrowing her eyes. She finally noticed Yufei's bowl and snatched up the ladle like a weapon, sloshing some of her own soup into Yufei's bowl before she could protest.

"I'm full," Yufei said.

"Liar," Uncle Fan said, opening one eye, then closing it again.

"You would eat this table if it was well-salted enough," Wenshu said.

"And *you* will be shorter than your sisters for your whole life if you don't eat your food," Auntie So said.

"Yufei and I are the same height!" Wenshu said, his face red.

Auntie So scowled. "She's a fifteen-year-old girl!"

"Liar," Uncle Fan said.

Auntie So sighed, turning to me, her new target.

She scooped out another spoonful and dumped it into my bowl. "I don't like sweet potato," she said before I could protest. "Eat it so it doesn't go to waste."

I eyed her bowl that had hardly been touched. "But you haven't—"

"You want to waste food?" she said, raising the ladle as if to bludgeon me with it.

"Just eat it," Wenshu said in the Northern dialect. "She's not going to anyway."

"You first."

He wrinkled his nose. "Your undead potatoes taste like shoes."

"Stop keeping secrets!" Auntie So said, banging the ladle on the table, rattling all the cups and bowls.

"We're practicing for our test," Yufei said. "It's coming up in two weeks." It was impressive how smoothly she lied.

"Those tests are for rich people," Auntie So said. "People who go to school."

Wenshu's shoulders slumped. Of course we all knew that it would be hard to compete against people with teachers and tutors. But sitting here waiting to be married off was hard too. Being berated for charging more and more gold that would buy us less food each week was hard. Having to obey sleazy old men like Gou was hard. The chasm between the rich and poor was yawning wider and wider each day, and soon the distance to the other side would be too far to jump.

Uncle Fan sighed, patting Wenshu on the back. "She means that people train their whole lives for this exam, so don't be disappointed," Uncle Fan said.

"Why would we be disappointed?" Yufei said, glaring. "We're going to pass."

Auntie So grimaced but didn't argue—there was little point in arguing with Yufei because not even her parents could make her do something she didn't want. They'd learned that the hard way after trying to arrange a marriage without her consent. The man was young and objectively quite handsome and polite and probably didn't deserve to be pelted with pig manure, but he'd understandably withdrawn his proposal after his first meeting with Yufei. Still, I didn't know how she could speak so candidly to Auntie and Uncle without feeling ashamed.

Around Uncle and Auntie, I always wanted to be smaller, wishing I could fold up into a neat little cloth square, tuck myself away somewhere unobtrusive. I never wanted to give them a reason to resent me. I always said *yes, Mama* and *okay, Baba* and never complained in front of them. It wasn't a question of *if* they loved me, but of how much. Because at the end of the day, they had never asked for me.

They'd already had a brilliant son and a beautiful daughter, then my mom had married a jellyfish man and had a gwáimūi girl and then had the audacity to die, leaving Auntie So no choice but to take me in or be seen as heartless. A lot of poor families drowned their daughters in the ocean, so I should have been grateful that I was even alive. They fed me and gave me clothes and called me a Fan, but just saying something didn't make it true. Part of me always thought I was one outburst or broken plate or uneaten vegetable away from being an orphan again.

I'd never worried about that with my own parents. *You are my whole world*, my mother had said to me. I could remember those words, even though I couldn't see her face anymore. Back then, I'd thought that love was something endless and unbreakable, as constant as the beat of the tide on the shore. It wasn't until my parents were gone that I realized nothing in life is a promise, that everything good can simply stop existing one day, that the sun might not rise and the tides might lay still and the sky will go cold and dark. The world owed me nothing, and everything that I thought was mine could always be taken back.

I finished my soup that somehow tasted like nothing at all, and my thoughts drifted back to the strange man by the well. Had he given up and returned to Chang'an to meet his death? It wasn't my problem, but I couldn't help but wonder.

The three of us cleaned up after the meal, sending Auntie and Uncle to bed. Technically, this was women's work, but Wenshu always complained that we wouldn't know what *clean* really meant if it ran us over in the street. I brewed tea, and we went back to our room and studied our scrolls with only the dim light of a candle and the moon. Wenshu and Yufei fell asleep over their papers around dawn, but I stayed awake until the light through the window turned orange and the candle went out, thinking of our impending exams that would change absolutely everything, of a new life somewhere far away, and of the man who would die in Chang'an.

The last two weeks before our first exam spun by in a haze of midsummer heat and burning rain. Two people came by looking for resurrections, but I turned them away, knowing we needed every spare moment to study. We took turns yanking each other's hair to keep awake when one of us fell asleep reading.

I studied my alchemy texts in the shop, pinching myself awake whenever my eyes began to close. I wasn't like Wenshu, who could read with ease thanks to his years at school, or Yufei, who could recite texts back fluently after only a quick glance. For me, studying felt like painstakingly carving a tattoo into my brain the way Wenshu did to the spines of corpses. But I would do it if it meant being a better alchemist than my father.

Still, I heard his voice at times when I studied. Not the words, but the rhythm and warm cadence of a language I'd long forgotten. Whenever I heard that low rumble, it was easier to remember his notes, easier to recall the stones and all their properties. My fingertips warmed as if alchemy was sparking inside them, waiting to break free.

At least Wenshu and Yufei had an idea what their first exam would entail. They had to memorize all the Confucian classics, then write long essays explaining his ideas and how they applied to government. They'd be locked in cells, stripped of their clothing, handed a chamber pot and a wooden slab, and wouldn't be allowed to leave until they finished or time ran out. If anyone died during the test, they would be rolled up in a reed mat and tossed over the compound wall, rather than let family into the sacred testing zone to claim the body. If they scored high enough, they could go to Chang'an for the next round. Wenshu had tried practicing by going without food or water from sunrise to sunset, but Yufei always managed to sneak snacks when he wasn't watching.

Fewer people spoke of the alchemy exam, for it was an ever-changing practical test. Some said that alchemists were thrown in deep pits with live tigers and had to fight their way out with alchemy. Others said you were tied to anchors and dropped down a well with a handful of alchemy stones and had to climb your way to the top or drown. The worst rumor of all was that the judges didn't bother actually holding an exam in the southern provinces and simply promoted anyone who could pay.

All I could do was focus on studying my texts until dawn and napping facedown on the counter in between customers. I practiced identifying my stones by touch alone, hiked down to Dongguan and sifted minerals from the sand to replenish my stock, and even dipped into my savings to buy some of the rarer stones at the market—jades for woodstones, ammonite for waterstones, ruby for firestones.

When the day of our exams finally arrived, our eyes burned from dryness and our faces had purple shadows from weeks of shallow sleep. My stomach wanted to gnaw itself open from nerves, but I shoveled down some porridge to quiet it and forced Yufei and Wenshu to take at least a few bites, since none of us would eat or drink again until nightfall. Yufei combed my hair and pinned it back and told me I couldn't look like a farm girl with my usual sweaty ponytail. I thought it was pointless, because the type of women who didn't sweat in a kiln all day used gold pins and ornaments in their hair, but Yufei only had copper scroll clips.

We walked to the city center just before sunrise, and

Wenshu and Yufei hopped onto the back of a farmer's wagon that was heading west to Foshan. I'd be going east to Huizhou, about three hours in the opposite direction, and needed to wait for my own passage.

The sight of the two of them on the carriage together—without me—only worsened the twisting in my stomach. They looked so perfectly like brother and sister—the same height, the same narrow faces and round black eyes. They looked like a family.

"We'll meet back here tonight," Yufei said, taking my hand, "after we've all passed."

I nodded, not trusting myself with words.

"Remember," Wenshu said, "if any men bother you—"

"—I jam the heel of my palm into their nose," I said. Yufei had become all too interested in self-defense techniques as of late, which she insisted on teaching Wenshu and me as well.

The horse neighed and the cart jolted forward, my cousins moving farther and farther away from me into the morning mist, waving as the landscape of tall grass swallowed them whole. I stood alone in the cool dawn on the empty street, waiting for my own dream to begin.

Eventually, the next wagon to Huizhou let me hop on. I sat among the hay bales hugging my knees as we rolled over rocks and the sun rose above the countryside.

We finally reached the walls of Huizhou along the path of the Pearl River. The air smelled of green tea leaves, the scent blowing down the valley from the rolling fields in the distance. The ride had only taken me a few hours from Guangzhou, but the dialect was different enough that I could only catch fractured pieces. Auntie So said the language here was mixed with the words of the Hakka people who came south from central China.

I stepped off the wagon and handed the driver a few coins, then pushed through the wall of words I didn't understand toward the city center. Merchants and horses and carts crammed together in the dirt roads, fighting for passage. More trade moved through here than Guangzhou, which was why the royal court had chosen it for the exam location.

It wasn't hard to find the city center, because scholars in their blue robes were all moving in the same direction through the streets. Down by the muddy silt of the river, two court officials in fútóu hats stood with scrolls in hand, the path of scholars narrowing into a single line that awaited their approval before moving into the gated market. I gripped the straps of my bag and got into the line, ignoring the strange looks of the men around me. At the front, each competing alchemist passed the guards a handful of gold and received a strip of cloth with their name on it, which the guards tied tightly to their wrists.

When I reached the front, the two guards stared at me for a long moment, the disapproval in their gazes making my palms sweat. I was used to being looked at like vermin—no one liked merchants, after all—but it was easier to glare back when safe in my own shop with a knife under the counter than here, alone in a new city. The taller guard narrowed his eyes and shouted something in Huizhou dialect at me.

"I'm here for the alchemy exam," I said in Chang'an dialect. "My name is Fan Zilan." I offered them fifty gold coins in my hand, the entrance fee.

They stared at my palm like I'd offered them a dead frog. The man's eyes skimmed over me, lips curling. Long ago, he might have turned me away just for being a woman, but Empress Wu's perpetual reign had changed everything. If a woman could be the sole Empress, then women could serve her as scholars. But just because it was allowed didn't mean it was common. Most women didn't go to school, so few had the means or motivation to take the exams.

"*You're* an alchemist?" the taller one said.

"Yes," I said, moving my hand closer and shaking the gold as if to tempt him. The guard relented, scooping the coins from my palm.

"Are you a hùnxiě?" the other one said.

I bit down on my tongue, afraid I might say something that would instantly disqualify me. Instead, I nodded stiffly. He made a note of something on his scroll and I nearly snatched the brush from his hands. What did that have to do with an alchemy exam? All that should matter was my skill as an alchemist.

The other one grabbed my arm and tied a cloth around my wrist tight enough that my hand nearly popped off. He hadn't even asked what characters to use for my name, so how did he—

I froze at the two characters scrawled messily onto the fabric, ink bleeding down my wrist.

混
血

"This says *hùnxiě*," I said.

"Ah, so you *can* read," the first guard said, trying to wave me past.

I clenched my jaw. "That's not my name."

The guard shrugged. "There is only one hùnxiě here, so it won't be a problem," he said. "Now go inside or get out."

A firm hand shoved me past, and then I was in the testing grounds, the line rushing up behind me. I considered tearing the cloth strip off, but that would probably disqualify me. I crossed my arms to hide the wristband and stomped deeper into the yard.

In the town square, people peered through their windows and sat fanning themselves in the shade of the buildings, snacking on pears and berries. A crowd of young men hovered in the center, talking among themselves—some of them wore the blue robes of scholars, so they were probably the other alchemists. On the red dirt pathway, cleared of merchant carts, were what looked like a hundred metal cages, hardly large enough for pigs. Were we meant to trap some sort of animal? Perhaps they'd set loose wild boars and we'd have to capture them or be gored on their tusks.

I moved closer to the cages, but a guard stepped in my path.

"Place your bag here and empty your pockets," he said, holding out a wooden tray piled with other small bags and loose gemstones.

"But I need my stones," I said, clutching my satchel to my chest.

"Transformation materials will be provided," he said. "Everyone gets the same things."

I supposed that was fair. It felt like handing over my firstborn child, but I sighed and dropped my satchel on the tray, and the guard whisked it away. That was at least one hundred gold pieces worth of stones that I prayed I got back.

"What are you doing here, little girl?" one of the alchemists said, his voice loud enough that another group nearby turned to stare at me. He had a pale face and a wiry mustache, wet and tangled with scraps of tea leaves. For once, I was glad that I wasn't small like Yufei—none of the men could look down on me.

The alchemist grabbed my sleeve, inspecting the hemp fabric stained brown at the ends from clay. "Is your dress made from used diapers?" he said.

I snatched my sleeve back as the other men laughed. "Is your mustache made from cockroach legs?" I said.

A few of the other men laughed softly, but were quickly silenced by the first man's glare. He stepped closer, his warm breath reeking like baked fish.

"Why don't you just go home to your husband?" he said. "Or are you here because no one wants to marry you? Can't say I blame them."

He grinned darkly, one of his front teeth unnaturally white and smooth. Those who could afford it sometimes had their teeth replaced by pearls or gold if they fell out. Or sometimes they'd pull them out just to replace them with a more expensive gem.

But if he thought I could be scared off by a couple of rich men, he was wrong. I was Fan Yufei's ugly sister, the gwáimūi girl of Guangzhou, and there was nothing he could say to me that I hadn't already heard.

"Find some entertainment that doesn't involve me," I said. "There are easier targets, believe me."

The men seemed stunned at my words, so I took the chance to push past them.

A hand closed around my wrist, yanking me back into their circle. I looked over my shoulder at the man with the mustache.

"You're not pretty enough to get away with being so mouthy," he said.

I clenched my fists, and instead of pulling away, I closed the distance between us, looming over the man, arm tense in his grip.

"Do you really want to find out why I'm here?" I said.

I didn't want to get disqualified before the exam had even started, but I wouldn't let this man tug me around like a rag doll. I was here because I was an alchemist, not a plaything.

He was incredibly lucky that the state official in a yellow robe banged a drum at the other end of the street. He released me and stormed off, the rest of the men shoving past me as they followed him.

The official cleared his throat, standing on an elevated podium at the far end of the yard. The crowd fell quiet as everyone drew closer to listen.

"Aspiring alchemists," he said, his voice wispy with age, but perfectly clear in the nervous silence of the courtyard, "welcome to the preliminary round examination for imperial alchemists, held in this year 775, in service to the Perpetual Empress of the House of Li. We gather here in service to her, and the family that Heaven has chosen for us. It is my hope that the best among you will earn a place among her ranks, and bring pride back to the southern provinces."

He held out a shaking hand, gesturing to the rows of metal enclosures in the courtyard before him.

"Now, alchemists," he said, "please enter your cages."

# CHAPTER SEVEN

*Enter your cages?* I thought. *Those are actually for us?*

If this surprised the other alchemists, they didn't show it. All of them bent down and crawled inside, so I hurried into one as well, hugging my knees to make myself smaller, metal bars digging into my back. The guards came around and locked the doors, one by one. When they finished, the official in yellow once again stepped forward, and all eyes turned to him. He stood beside a long table of five men in red and green robes, a massive wooden board beside him covered in blank scroll paper.

"Aspiring alchemists," he said, "your task is to break free within the hour, but you will soon find that these are not normal cages. Our judges—" he turned, gesturing to the table of scholars "—will be watching you carefully. The first ten to escape will move to the second round in Chang'an. Best of luck to you all."

Then he moved back, and more officials came up and down the rows, laying trays of alchemical stones on the ground in front of our cages. I supposed this was meant to make the exam fair, so that the wealthy scholars couldn't bring wagons full of every stone in the world.

I peered through the bars while I waited for them to reach my cage, trying to discern the stone types from color alone, but I needed to feel them to be sure. My fingers twitched as the other alchemists started sifting through their supply. I couldn't sit here and wait patiently for my turn. I needed a strategy.

I ran my fingers up and down the bars. *You will soon find that these are not normal cages*, the official had said. What did that mean?

The metal was silver-colored, at least on the surface. I closed my eyes and tried to identify the metal type by feel, but I was used to holding stones in my hand, testing their weight against each other. I scraped my thumbnail against the bars but couldn't scratch the surface.

At last, the guards reached my cage. I leaned forward, gripping the bars as the man shifted to set a tray in front of me.

He hesitated, his gaze dropping to my wristband. Then he stood up swiftly, withdrawing the tray and instead setting it down at the next alchemist's cage.

"Wait!" I said, swiping a hand out as if I could snatch the stones back, but the guard ignored me, hurrying to distribute the rest of the trays.

My hands shook against the bars, heartbeat throbbing in my ears as I realized what was happening. It didn't matter how good of an alchemist I was. They weren't even going to let me try. They'd decided it the moment they'd learned what I was.

I smashed my fists against the floor, the echo ringing out across the courtyard, making the other alchemists flinch.

"Hey!" I shouted. "You forgot about me!"

The judges glanced at me and whispered to each other, but made no move to intervene.

"Shut up!" a man said somewhere behind me. "Some of us are trying to concentrate here."

I whirled around, shooting him a look that could melt iron. "This isn't fair!" I said, slamming my fist against the top of the cage, even though it rattled through my bones and would probably break my hand if I kept going. "I paid fifty gold like the rest of you!"

"You should have stayed home, little girl!" someone shouted from across the row, and I recognized his voice as that of the annoying mustache man. A few others made sounds of agreement.

I slumped against the cold metal floor of the cage, my skin burning, out of breath and ready to tear my hair out or scream until the world ended. The urge to cry crashed over me in a hot wave and I swallowed it down, fingernails pinching into my thighs. I thought of Wenshu and Yufei, who were probably locked in their testing rooms by now, worrying about trying to recall Confucius's words instead of yelling like a feral animal. At least they had a chance.

I turned to the alchemist in the cage closest to me, who was busy sorting through the stones that should have been mine.

"Give me some of yours," I said.

His eye twitched, but he ignored me.

"I'll pay you," I said. That was all rich people cared about, wasn't it?

He scoffed, shaking his head. "You wear rags. I doubt you could pay me enough for a bowl of rice."

"Give them to me or the second I get out of here I'll rip your ears off with my teeth."

The man hesitated for one glorious moment before shaking

his head. "You don't scare me, hùnxiě," he said, even though that was definitely a lie.

He grabbed three pieces of silver and pressed them to a pile of copper-colored stones. With a flash, the silver disappeared and the copper re-formed into a short blade. The man began sawing at the bars.

"*This* was supposed to be my competition?" I said, hanging my head. The bars were obviously hard metal. Copper wouldn't do anything to it.

"Shut up," the man said, sawing harder.

I sighed and turned to the cage on my other side, where an alchemist had heated a pile of rubies into a small fire and was trying to melt the bars. That might have worked if he'd had a few hours to spare, but the flame was small and ate through the rubies quickly. The metal glowed a weak blue before quickly cooling back down.

The color made me pause, a memory coming to me as if floating to the surface of a dark pond.

The metal fire pokers that we used in the kilns to bake míngqì always changed color when heated. Iron pokers, which we used most often, turned red. Steel pokers turned blue.

These bars were the right color and hardness for steel. The most common metals—gold, silver, brass, bronze, nickel—were all too soft to damage it.

Had they given the other alchemists anything harder than steel to use? I pressed my face between the bars, searching for iron or diamond or tungsten among my neighbor's stash, but the alchemist frowned and turned his back to me, shuffling his stones out of my sight.

I leaned heavily against the door and crossed my arms, rattling the lock.

*The lock.*

I sat up straight. If they'd given the alchemists a soft metal to melt down, they could carefully pour it into the lock and then quickly cool it with a waterstone, attach a handle, and then it would no longer matter if you could break the bars. You would have a key.

"If I tell you how to get out, will you give me the rest of your stones?" I said to the alchemist on my right.

"I know how to get out," he said, molding another blade.

"Clearly not. If you would just—"

"You're wasting your breath," he said. "Stop distracting me."

No matter how much I rattled the bars, insulted him, and criticized his attempts, he kept ignoring me. For an excruciating amount of time, I watched him heat and reheat all the firestones he could find and hold them to the bars, even when his palms burned and blistered, the air reeking of cooked flesh. With a feral grunt, he wrenched the glowing bars apart a fraction. He was wiry like Wenshu and managed to force himself out of the gap, singeing his robes. He fell onto the ground outside his cage, panting.

"The first alchemist has escaped!" the official announced. Then he turned to the wooden board, dipped a brush into a pool of ink, and drew a single tally mark across the paper.

My hands tightened around the steel. Only nine more people could pass.

I slipped my arm through the bars, reaching out for the alchemist's discarded stones. Auntie So always said I was long-limbed like a wind sock, so I prayed that would finally be good for something. But the stones were too far away, no matter how much I stretched.

On the other side of the yard, metal clinked and clanged,

and the audience cheered as the official drew another tally mark on the board. Soon after, a third.

As the tally marks kept coming, panic ignited in my stomach and I started hammering my fist on the cage again, even though it wouldn't help. I knew the answer. All I needed was a few stones, and I could be out in moments. How could I come so close and go home with nothing?

The man with the cockroach mustache strolled over to my cage, shoving a quartz key into his pocket. Apparently not all the men were fools, but I loathed that *this* was the one who had found the same answer as me.

"Poor thing," he said, kneeling in front of my enclosure, eyes glinting with gold. "Nothing but a little caged bird now, aren't you?"

"You're actually proud of yourself?" I said. "You can't even win a fair fight."

"I don't need to prove myself to *you* to be worth something," he said.

In a burst of rage, I reached out and grabbed his beard through the bars, yanking him face-first into the dirt. He bit down on his tongue, red spilling past his teeth.

The satisfaction lasted only a moment before he spit a mouthful of blood at my face, then grabbed the dirtied hem of my skirt spilling through the cage.

I didn't see what stone he'd grabbed for his transformation, but my dress burst into scraps of fabric, fluttering to the ground around me. I had nothing but a long, thin undershirt made of pongee to cover me. The man reached for me again, but I raked my nails against his outstretched hand, shifting against the other end of the cage so he couldn't take what little clothing I had left.

I shivered and hugged myself to hide what I could, the steel cage burning against my skin from the afternoon sun.

The man sat back and laughed as the scraps of my dress settled around him, the horrible sound echoed by at least a dozen other men. Hands pawed at me through the bars, no matter which side I leaned to. Someone grabbed my head, and my hairpins clattered to the floor of the cage, hair falling over my face. Someone else sloshed hot tea over my bare back, another hand tugging at the edge of my undershirt. There was nowhere safe but to curl deeper into myself, wishing for the thousandth time that I was smaller, that I could fold myself up and tuck myself away like a used rag. Tears burned at my eyes. Was it not enough to take away my dream? They had to humiliate me for daring to try?

The man with the terrible mustache reached through the bars again and swiped a thumb across my face, catching the traitorous tears. I wanted to push him away, but no matter where I went, more hands would seize me.

"If you ask me nicely, maybe I'll let you out," he said. "Just admit that you can't do it yourself.'"

*I can* do it myself, I thought, unable to stop more tears as another hand ripped at the seams of my shirt.

Far away, I saw the official drawing the eighth tally mark on the board.

The bars around me started to blur into a lake of silver. I placed my bare palms against the burning metal just to keep myself grounded. *Please, not now,* I thought. Starbursts flashed behind my eyes, the white sky dripping into the horizon like sheep's milk. This really wasn't a good time for one of my fainting spells. Who knew what these men would do if I stopped fighting. I fell onto my forearms and pressed my head to the cool metal, sucking in deep breaths as the world spun around me.

The man's words fell over me in sharp waves, and in the distance, the official called out another number, another mark painted on the board, another chance gone.

*This isn't fair,* I thought. But what part of my life had ever been fair? I was foolish to expect them to let me compete. I wanted to cry in Yufei's arms and let her break all these men's faces. I wanted Wenshu to take me home and feed me and scrub the tears from my face until my skin was raw. Everyone who would help me was far away.

And then, strangely, I thought of the handsome stranger by the well, and the purple orchid crushed in his palm.

*I will go to Chang'an to be a royal alchemist,* I'd said to him. I'd been so certain at the time. So naive. I'd thought that skill and dreaming were enough.

That man had come all the way from Chang'an for *me,* not for any of these men. I was a great alchemist that they whispered about in the North. I was worth traveling across half of China to meet. I could do things that no other alchemist could dare to dream of. I was Fan Zilan.

I closed my hand around the man's wrist, the cold touch anchoring me, the dizziness ebbing away. Maybe he thought it was desperation, because he didn't pull away, even as my nails dug into his pale skin.

"Ready to give in?" he said.

I smiled, the sharp expression startling him back, but it was too late. I already had him in my grasp. Maybe they hadn't wanted to give me any stones or metal to work with. But alchemy was everywhere—in the earth, the sky, the seas, our breath, and our blood.

I grabbed one of my hairpins from the floor and stabbed it into his wrist.

A tortured wail ripped from his mouth and he reared back, but I held his wrist tight as blood gushed across his white skin, splashing over the floor of my cage. If I couldn't get a key, then I needed something harder than steel to saw my way out, and blood was full of iron.

The copper in my hairpin acted as the catalyst metal, drawing the blood up from his wrist, splitting the wound wider as an iron blade ripped from his veins, clattering to the floor of the cage. The reaction was unstable because I'd neglected the rule of threes, singeing my palms and bare knees and casting dizzy shapes across my vision, but it didn't matter. Let the alchemy take what it wanted from me, crack me open and tear me to pieces, as long as it gave me its power.

The man fell back, scrambling away and screaming as I hacked at the bars with my iron blade. Everyone had backed away from my cage in terror, watching the bleeding man stumble drunkenly as red painted the dirt. The bars of my cage fell away, and at last I rose to my feet, standing in only my blood-soaked underclothes.

I raised the blade at the crowd of gawking alchemists, who flinched back, retreating. I turned to the judges and the stunned official in yellow, still holding the brush in his shaking hand. Ten tally marks had been painted across the board. I was too late.

*"Damn all of you!"* I said to them, tearing away my wristband, hurling it to the ground, then grinding it under my heel.

"Who the hell is she?" I heard one of the judges whisper, cowering away.

I hurled my blade at their feet. One of the judges screamed

and threw up his hands to shield his face as the knife staked itself in the dirt.

"Fan Zilan," I said.

"Zilan xiǎojiě," one of the judges said, raising his trembling hands, "please—"

"Go to hell," I said, stomping toward them. They shrieked and cowered, but I only snatched my bag of stones from their table and turned away. I grabbed a jacket from a spectator, who bowed and apologized as I tore it from her shoulders, then stormed off to wait for the next merchant cart back to Guangzhou, where I could say goodbye to my dream of ever becoming a royal alchemist.

"Stop!" I said as Yufei sloshed another bucket of freezing water over me. I stood in our backyard at sunset in only my underwear. "That's enough!"

Yufei tossed me a rag and I caught it with trembling hands, then scrubbed the blood from my face. Wenshu had nearly passed out when he saw me waiting for him and Yufei in the city center in nothing but a blood-drenched undershirt, and hadn't let me into the house until I cleaned up.

"You missed a spot," Yufei said, snatching the rag and scouring the back of my neck. My teeth chattered, but I let her finish.

Even though my bloodstained, half-naked appearance had certainly soaked up all the attention upon our reunion, I hadn't missed how gray Wenshu and Yufei had looked after their test, lips cracked and eyes shadowed. They both said it had been "fine" but the word felt too careful, too rehearsed.

"Are you not allowed to discuss it?" I'd said, after ten minutes of them avoiding eye contact.

Wenshu shook his head. "Zilan, I don't know how I did,"

he said. "It's like I spent a year in a cave and only just saw sunlight. Maybe it was fine, or maybe I don't know what words are anymore."

It was the most humble Wenshu had ever sounded about his own abilities, so I stopped asking questions, and neither him nor Yufei had offered any more information.

Yufei wrapped me in a blanket and led me back inside, where Wenshu peeled himself from bed and stood in the hallway long enough for me to get dressed in our room, then the three of us lay unmoving on our backs like garbage washed up on the shore.

"I'm going to kill all of them," Yufei said, once I finally told her and Wenshu the details of my test. Wenshu crossed his arms and glared accusingly at the wall.

"I'll cut all their greasy fingers off and make them swallow them," Yufei said. "I'll—"

"It doesn't matter," I said. "It's done. I failed."

"You got out of the cage," Wenshu said, frowning. "Was that not the test?"

"I wasn't fast enough," I said.

"Maybe they'll make an exception?"

I huffed and gripped my blanket. "Don't you get it?" I said. "They didn't want me there! They wouldn't even take my name! What are they going to do, write *hùnxiě* on the results list?"

"Only one of us needs to pass," Yufei said. "The rest can follow and get other jobs in Chang'an."

Wenshu made a face but didn't argue. He knew as well as I did that wasn't exactly true. Life in Chang'an was expensive, far more than in the south. We would need high salaries if we hoped to both live somewhere decent and send money home to Auntie and Uncle. It was pointless to move to the capital just to be merchants again.

They were both looking at me like I was just another question on their test to figure out, and I knew what they were thinking: *Do we go to Chang'an without her?*

Maybe they would pretend to ponder it for a few days out of courtesy, but eventually I would tell them to go. What kind of monster would I be to make them stay?

I would have to remain at home and work in the shop. Wenshu and Yufei together would probably have enough money to afford a real doctor for Uncle and Auntie, and maybe even some food. If that didn't work, I could sell myself as a bride. Maybe if Auntie So advertised me as "Fan Yufei's little sister" and I wore enough makeup, I could trick someone my age into marrying me before they realized what I really was.

A wave of bitterness rushed through me like sickness and I rolled over onto my side in bed, unable to look at my cousins any longer. We'd all worked equally as hard for our future in Chang'an. But in the end, they'd had their chance, and I hadn't even been allowed to try.

Eventually, they blew out the candles. Yufei pulled the blanket over both of us and threw her arms over me, but I lay stiff beneath her touch, unfairly furious with her. Why did she deserve parents and beauty and a chance at her dreams, while I got nothing at all?

By morning, my anger had drained away and I felt like a ravaged sea vessel, its treasures spilled out into the ocean, just rotting wood bobbing in dark waters. A good sister would have gone with Wenshu and Yufei to the town center, where the list of second-round candidates would be posted. But instead I just lay in bed and told them I didn't feel well, even though all of us knew it was a lie.

They shut the door and left me in the dark, and I remembered the hands of the men scraping across my bare back, ripping away everything I'd ever wanted. Tears wet my pillow, so I pulled my blanket over my head and ignored Auntie So asking if I was going to open the shop. The idea of selling míngqì the rest of my life in that tiny store made me want to disappear.

I hugged my bag of stones to my chest and wondered what my father would think of me now. He'd been a great alchemist in the West, but his only child would be no one at all.

I lay there even after the sun grew too bright for sleeping and began to scorch my cheek, then hid my face under the blankets, because if I was to be a bride, I couldn't get too tan.

The door slammed open.

I winced, but didn't lift my face, even when someone tore my blanket away.

"Zilan," Wenshu said, breathless. "Get up."

"No thanks," I said, determined to crush my face into my pillow.

"Zilan, we're going to Chang'an," Yufei said.

"I knew you would," I said, too tired to even feign enthusiasm. A cruel part of me had hoped at least one of them had failed, just so I wouldn't be alone.

Wenshu sighed, yanking my pillow out from under me, my forehead smacking the floor.

"Hey!" I said, sitting up. "What are you—"

"Not just me and Yufei," he said. "All three of us."

# CHAPTER EIGHT

We filled our bags with lychee and oranges, the only cheap foods we didn't need to cook. Then we split our gold between all three of our bags, with smaller satchels sewed into our undershirts and hats, loose coins tied into my braids and stuffed into our socks so that even if someone robbed us, they wouldn't leave us with nothing. Yufei had suggested swallowing some of the coins whole for safekeeping, but Wenshu had shot her such a horrified look that I'd laughed and insisted she was joking before he could start yelling.

Wenshu had, unsurprisingly, ranked eleventh out of all the scholars in Lingnan, the southernmost district. Yufei had just made the cut at rank number forty-six, even though her raw score probably would have disqualified her if she'd tested in the North, but there weren't many southern candidates who knew the Northern dialect well enough for the speaking exams they would face in Chang'an. When they'd checked the list of alchemists, they'd found my name second on the list. Not *hùnxiě*, but Fan Zilan.

I'd run back to see it for myself, and sure enough, my flowery servant name had been written next to the number two.

Part of me had been convinced it was someone else, but for once I was grateful for my name destined for nothingness, because at least it was unique. I thought of all the men who hadn't passed, their burning shame when they told their parents they'd failed, their lifetime of expensive classes worth nothing at all. They'd thought I was just a joke when they'd seen me, but none of them were laughing now. For a brief, brilliant moment, I allowed myself to imagine life in Chang'an as a royal alchemist, able to practice alchemy without fear.

But that dream was still half a world away. After telling Auntie and Uncle, we started planning for our move in earnest.

The first chunk of our savings bought us two horses named Kumquat and Turmoil, who both seemed suspiciously old, but the merchant swore up and down that they could make it to Chang'an. We could have walked there in a month and a half, but our second-round exams were in four weeks, and horses could take us there in three if we were lucky. We had a hasty riding lesson that resulted in all three of us falling into water troughs and hay bales, but once we all could cling to the saddle long enough to make it up and down the street, the merchant took our money and waved us off.

I transformed my hairpins into three copper rings and slipped them onto my index, middle, and ring fingers. That way, I could transform most materials just by touch, without fishing a stone from my bag. I knew our journey would be long and potentially dangerous, and I didn't want to be helpless if someone cut the strings to my satchel and my stones scattered across the road.

Two days after the exam, we said goodbye to Uncle and Auntie, who crammed our bags full of even more fruit and a few strips of smoked sea snake.

"You bought that?" I said, backing away as Auntie So tried to shove it into my bag. I couldn't remember the last time I'd eaten meat. We'd given Auntie and Uncle enough money to last them a few months, but hadn't intended for them to use it on us.

"You can't ride to Chang'an eating only oranges," Auntie So said, grabbing my bag and yanking me toward her, then shoving bananas out of the way to cram the paper-wrapped snake into the top. "You'll fall off your horses before you make it out of Guangdong."

Uncle Fan slipped me a dagger when Auntie So wasn't looking. "A girl needs one of these," he said.

"Don't worry, Baba. Wenshu will be with us," I said.

Uncle Fan raised an eyebrow, glancing at Wenshu pulling Yufei's hair to stop her from taking his bananas, loose soap beans spilling from his bag out into the road.

"Yufei will be with us," I amended.

Uncle Fan stifled a cough, closing my hand around the dagger.

Yufei and I managed to settle ourselves on Kumquat's saddle, while Wenshu sat on Turmoil. I wrapped my arms around Yufei as she grabbed the reins, then looked over my shoulder at Auntie and Uncle standing before the store. I'd never really noticed how small they were until I saw them huddled in the shade of the awning, leaning into each other. I had a sinking feeling that I would never see them again—they were old and sick, after all. What if they died while we were gone? I wouldn't be around to resurrect them. I knew that the five of us couldn't keep living on broth, that my resurrections alone weren't enough to keep up with how fast gold was losing its value, that they wouldn't survive the journey to the North with us, and a thousand other reasons we had to go. It was a logical choice, an investment in all our futures, the smart thing to do.

But Uncle Fan's eyes misted over and he held Auntie So's hand as he waved goodbye, and some cruel part of my brain whispered, *Remember this, Zilan. This is the last memory you'll ever have of them.*

I wanted to go back, but the horse lurched forward and I clung to Yufei to avoid falling off, and after that I couldn't bring myself to turn around until we passed the city walls.

We'd ventured east toward Huizhou as children to trade along the river, but we'd never gone north into Qingyuan. Beyond the city walls, there was little more than farmland and open sky. We passed through deep valleys of young sugarcane, its leaves waxy and green and lush, the air tinged with sweetness. Cicadas chirped in the grass, flies swarming around our horses. I'd never before seen so much open land, like the whole world was a scroll unfurling into forever.

"I'm going to throw up if you keep squeezing my stomach like that," Yufei said.

I loosened my grip probably less than she would have liked, but I didn't want to slide face-first into the prickly sugarcane. Kumquat started trotting faster downhill and I grabbed Yufei's shoulders for support.

"How much farther for today?" I called to Wenshu, who looked only marginally more dignified than me and Yufei because he had more space in the saddle, though he still clutched the reins with stiff hands.

"We should at least ride until sunset," he said. "Do you hate Kumquat that much?"

"Shut up," I said. I knew he'd seen me flinch away from the horse's gigantic black eyes before the merchant helped me into the saddle. I remembered my mother riding horses along the shore when I was a child, her hair loose, smiling while my father and I swam in the sea. I wanted to be as graceful as her, but something about horses unnerved me. Their big eyes were such a cavernous, glossy black. Their hoofbeats made the whole earth tremble, rattling my bones.

"I can't believe you're fine with dead bodies but don't like horses," Wenshu said.

"They're just so large," I said. "Like trees, but they can run toward you."

"Now you know how people feel when they stand next to you."

I would have thrown something at Wenshu if I hadn't been hanging on for dear life.

Once we'd traveled for several hours without falling off, we picked up the pace a bit, because according to Wenshu, *If we were going to go this slowly, we might as well have paid for donkeys.*

We reached a town in northern Qingyuan just as the sun was setting. It wasn't nearly as far as we needed to go, but our legs were sore from riding and we all practically fell off our horses.

People called Qingyuan the gate to the wilds of Yuebei. The south of Qingyuan, where we'd come from, was mostly trading villages. But to the north of Qingyuan, we'd pass through towering bamboo forests, sloping mountains, rice plantations, and wild bananas trees.

We walked our horses to the closest inn and tied them up. When we ventured farther into the farmlands, we would likely have to sleep outside, but it wasn't safe to do that so close to a city. Our throats would be cut in our sleep, our gold stolen. If we could just make it north to the Cháng River, we could follow the postal route straight to Chang'an.

I couldn't help but wince as Wenshu handed over our gold

coins to the innkeeper. After hoarding gold for years, spending so much of it at once felt wrong.

A night at the inn apparently came with a bowl of porridge. We weren't quick to turn down hot food, so we stumbled into a pub so loud that it made my head throb, men's voices far too boisterous and cheerful for so late in the day. Wenshu pointed me and Yufei to a bench in the corner and handed us each a bowl.

At the bar, a pair of scholar alchemists were practicing party tricks, turning beer into blocks of ice. The innkeeper laughed uneasily and gave them new drinks on the house. Wealthy men like them could use their alchemy to charm free food and gifts from merchants, partially out of reverence and partially out of fear. It was a dangerous game to show off alchemy with so many desperate for life gold, but few would bother the sons of aristocrats and risk imprisonment.

As a merchant alchemist, I had no such protections. I'd heard of other lower-class alchemists who woke up shackled in dark rooms, tortured or starved until they made life gold, even if they didn't know how. The punishment for kidnapping a commoner was only forty lashes with a light stick, a low price for an aristocrat to pay in exchange for eternal life.

A group of men in cyan robes drank rice wine across from us—probably the local magistrate and his right-hand men, based on the color of their clothes and the way their skin sparkled with gold flecks. I shoveled soup that tasted like dust into my mouth and willed myself not to fall asleep sitting up.

I was stirring the slurry in my soup together when feet stopped in front of our bench. Wooden shoes that curled up at the tip, gold designs carved into the sides.

"What lovely wives," a man said.

Wenshu choked on his soup. For a moment, his expression was so pained that I thought he actually might vomit it back into his bowl, but he swallowed it down and shook his head. "Sisters, sir," he said. Then elbowed us and we ducked our heads in a bow.

"Oh, unmarried, then?" the magistrate said, sliding onto the bench next to me. I wanted to recoil, but Wenshu left me no room to move. The man smelled like wine and sweat. He must have been close to Uncle Fan's age. Yufei clutched her spoon like she fully intended to scoop the man's eyes out, but I was too tired to conjure any anger right now and dropped my gaze back to my soup.

"How much for the pretty one?" the man said.

I didn't need to look up to know that he meant Yufei. She moved to stand and most likely pour her soup over his head, but Wenshu grabbed her wrist.

"They're not for sale," Wenshu said, somehow managing to sound polite. He could have been a court actor in another life.

The man sighed. "The hùnxiě, at least?"

I stifled a sigh. I would have preferred "the ugly one" or "the tall one." Yufei moved again, but Wenshu tightened his grip around her wrist.

"We have business up north," Wenshu said evenly. "They need to work for me for a few more years before they can marry."

It was a vague enough response that it might stand a chance at appeasing the man, if he was decent and honorable.

The smile dropped off his face. His gaze slid across the three of us, gold flecks glittering in his irises, his lip curled.

"I see," he said, turning without another word. He said something to his companions, and soon their conversations died down and they left the pub. We returned our bowls in stony silence and headed up to our room. Wenshu didn't even complain about not having water to bathe, which truly spoke to how exhausted he was. We were all shivering, so I fished out some firestones and made a small flame in the hearth, jabbing it with a fire poker. The bright flames reminded me of Uncle Fan's kilns, but I swallowed down my tears before Wenshu or Yufei could see them.

The room had only one bed, so Yufei tugged me onto it beside her and wrapped her arms around me like an octopus. Wenshu curled up on the floor beside us.

The two of them dropped off to sleep quickly, but even though my whole body felt like it was covered in heavy clay, I couldn't fall asleep. Moonlight spilled across my face from a tear in the paper window and scorched away any hope of slumber, yet I couldn't bring myself to move away from it. It took me a while to realize that it was too quiet. The only sounds in the room were the passing footsteps of night guards and the distant hum of cicadas in the fields.

I sat up, rubbing my eyes, wiping away the haze of half sleep.

My cousins were motionless beside me, completely silent.

They weren't breathing.

They lay still as corpses, dust settling on their white, waxy skin, blankets unmoving.

I seized Yufei by the shoulders and shook her. She was still so limp and warm. Dead bodies quickly grew stiff, unable to bend at the joints.

She sucked in a sharp breath and slapped my hands away, driving a foot into my ribs.

"What are you doing?" she said, shoving me back when I reached for her pulse. Beside her, Wenshu stirred, rolling over and cracking open one eye.

"Why are you making noise when it's still dark?" he said.

"I just thought..." I hesitated, unnerved by their glares.

I knew they were only exhausted and irritated to be awoken in the middle of the night, but their anger was so rarely pointed at me.

"Bad dream?" Yufei said, her gaze softening.

I nodded because that seemed the easiest answer.

Yufei leaned over me and yanked Wenshu up unceremoniously. He folded over the bed, grumbling in protest as she manhandled him under the blanket, sandwiching me between them. He swore under his breath but flopped over onto his stomach obediently. Yufei curled up around me, and then both of them were warm beside me, chests rising and falling, like when we were children, all small enough to share the same bed. They fell asleep again quickly, and this time I was the one lying stiff as a corpse.

This happened every now and then, ever since I'd woke them up three years ago.

When I was sure they were sleeping, I sat up against the wall. The moonlight fell through the paper windows, lighting up the pale white scars on the back of their necks that spelled out their names:

範　範
文　雨
書　霏

When I was thirteen, my cousins had started bleeding from their eyes. Yufei fell down while carrying eggs and twitched like her bones were trying to break free from her skin, foaming at the mouth, thrashing on top of the eggshells. Wenshu coughed up black blood and screamed and cried that his organs were melting. The healer said it was because they'd played in the tall grass, where the grass demons hid.

*Then why not Zilan?* Auntie So had said. *She goes everywhere with them.* But the healer had no answer. I always wondered if Auntie So truly wanted to understand what had caused their illness, or if she wished it had been me instead.

Uncle Fan had busied himself making lots of míngqì to bury them with—soft baby lambs and tiny ponies and wise teachers. *They will be well taken care of, where they're going,* he'd said. My cousins grew smaller and smaller, skin tight across their bones, somehow looking younger even though their faces were wrinkled from thirst.

My aunt prayed, but I didn't bother. If praying could save lives, then my mother wouldn't be dead. Hadn't my aunt prayed for her sister before she'd died? Didn't she know by now that prayers were useless?

My cousins stopped breathing as the sun fell. I sat on the floor between them and didn't tell my Auntie or Uncle because they were too busy praying and carving and doing things that didn't help, didn't matter, didn't change anything at all.

My cousins went cold and stiff as clay, like they were turning into the míngqì on the shelves, and I was alone again. When I was eleven and my mother had died, I'd cried because I'd thought that was the worst pain I would ever feel. But this was like baking in one of Auntie's dragon kilns, my lungs filled with fire, organs cooked and skin scorched off.

I bit the side of my hand to stop from crying, because if Auntie and Uncle heard me, they'd send their bodies off to the coroner and I'd never see them again. I tasted blood but only bit down harder, scarlet painting my chin and neck.

The floorboards creaked in the hallway. I froze, my pulse hammering through the wound in my palm, but after a moment, the footsteps moved past and a door closed at the other end of the house.

I had to do it now, or I'd never have a chance again.

I threw open the chest at the foot of the bed, blood splattering over all my notes, all my stones. I'd already resurrected mice and pigs and pangolins. If that worked, then why not this?

I put three bloodstones in each hand and took Yufei's cold palm in my left and Wenshu's in my right, my blood running down their wrists.

A hot breeze rolled by and my father's notes spun across the room, fluttering down in front of me.

*You cannot create good without also creating evil*, they said.

I didn't care.

Let all the evil in the world sink its teeth into me. Turn every clear river to sour blood, scorch every forest, hammer every mountain peak into the ground, take every piece of goodness left in this crooked world and give it to my cousins, and we'd figure out what to do about the rest. All I needed was them, even if there was no world left for us.

I clawed apart the darkness to bring them back from the river and carved their names into their spines with an old knife, and when the sun rose, there were three of us once more.

It didn't matter then what the cost was, or when I would pay it. In the years since, sometimes I'd forget that there was any cost at all. But then I would wake up and my cousins' eyes would be white and frosted, their bodies still, like their souls had once again crossed the river and had to be called back. They told me they didn't feel dead, that they didn't even feel sick anymore, that I'd saved them and didn't need to worry. *Whatever the cost is, it can't be worse than death*, Wenshu had said, and never wanted to bring it up again. But while

Wenshu knew more about literature than me, he didn't understand alchemy or its intractable laws. Nothing this important could be free.

At last, I couldn't fight my exhaustion anymore, and I fell asleep to the sound of my cousins' breaths.

I woke to my teeth slamming into the floor.

I jolted awake, my hands scrambling for purchase, my mouth filled with blood. Hot fingers latched onto my hair and dragged me back.

Wenshu was facedown on the floor, a man in a cyan robe jamming a knee into his back. Yufei was spilled halfway over a table, another man yanking her across it by her hair.

The man from the pub loomed in the doorway, his arms crossed, gold flecks in his skin sparkling in the pale sheet of moonlight bleeding through the window.

*Of course he came for us*, I thought. What rich men couldn't buy, they took.

I clamped my hand around the wrist above me, releasing the tension on my hair, and drove my elbow backward. A man huffed out a surprised sound of pain—surely he thought a woman would scream and cry and fall limp like a wet flower. I didn't give him a chance to recover, grabbing him by the beard and yanking his face down to my level. I clapped my hands over his eyes, my copper rings heating up, and transformed the gold flecks in his eyes into needles, skewering his irises. He screamed and stumbled away, hands clapped over his eyes, bloody tears pouring past his fingers.

Yufei had already rolled to her feet and jammed the heel of her palm into the other man's nose with a crunching sound and a burst of blood down his face. The man collapsed against the wall and probably would have given up at that point, but Yufei stomped on his hand and then his groin.

I whirled toward Wenshu, who was still struggling to get up while another man crushed his face to the floor. My copper rings had burned up in my last transformation, so I snatched my satchel and tightened the rope, slamming it into the side of the man's head.

He fell off Wenshu, tripping over the table and onto Yufei, who kicked him under the chin. I heard Wenshu groaning but getting up behind me, probably panicking at all the blood on the floor.

The magistrate stood in the doorway, his face white and eyes wide.

"What kind of demons are you?" he said, his voice trembling as he took a step back.

"I thought you wanted us as brides?" I said, cuffing the blood from my face.

Before the magistrate could answer, his gaze settled on something behind me. I didn't have time to turn before Wenshu shoved past me and gouged the magistrate with the fire poker, spearing him into the wall. He gasped and clutched at the wound, blood gurgling past his lips.

"I said they're not for sale, asshole," Wenshu said, spitting at his feet.

As the man slumped to the floor and fell silent, we looked around at the ruined room—table overturned, walls splashed with blood.

Wenshu inhaled a shaky breath, pulling his hair from his eyes. "We need to go," he said.

We crammed our possessions back into our bags, abandoning a few bloodstained bananas, and hurried out into the night.

*Is this what the rest of our journey will be like?* I thought. It seemed that fate frowned on those who ventured too far from home.

We managed to climb back on our horses and headed out into the quiet night unnoticed. Once my heart stopped thundering in my chest, I felt shaky and sick. I pressed my cheek to Yufei's shoulder, hugging her from behind, and this time she didn't complain. We rode out into the wilds of Yuebei as the sun rose bright red over the fields of sugarcane, toward a world that would do anything to keep us away.

# CHAPTER NINE

We arrived in Chang'an in three weeks and three days. For what felt like an eternity, we'd ridden through farmlands, fields of rice and soybeans, mosquitoes and locusts buzzing in our ears. Our bags quickly grew lighter as we had to eat all our fruit before the summer heat spoiled it, our stomachs sloshing with citrus as we rode over jagged, unpaved ground.

Any time we stopped in a city, Yufei and I kept our hats on and our heads low, walked behind Wenshu, and pretended not to speak Chinese. If anyone asked, he told them we were tribute girls from southern Asia who Wenshu was delivering to the Emperor. Few would dare try to steal the Emperor's slaves, after all.

For long stretches of time, there was no water. We grew dizzy from the heat, our skin parched and pink. I fainted only once and managed to dismount Kumquat first, whereas Wenshu toppled off Turmoil twice. We all but fell into the Cháng River when we finally reached it, and from there onward, the roads were always paved and lit with lanterns, a tavern never too far away, for this was the path that postal couriers took to Chang'an. We'd had to sell Kumquat and

Turmoil about a day's walk from the capital because only nobles could ride horses through the city streets.

I knew when we'd arrived because the golden walls of the city glistened from far in the distance, brighter than any star. Though Guangzhou had walls too, they were barely my height, made of rammed dirt, and were mostly meant to mark the city limits and stop the sheep from wandering out into the fields to eat all the crops. But the walls in Chang'an were made of golden desert sand packed into bricks, three times my height, as if to keep something out. A moat was carved into the earth surrounding the walls, like the whole city was a lonely island floating in black waters.

We filed into the line to pass through the gate, where imperial guards interrogated weary travelers before letting them into the city. People at the front of the line gave the guards handfuls of gold coins, though I couldn't make out how much. As we drew closer to the gate, the guards started yelling at a couple in white robes, shoving the woman to the ground.

"We don't need more beggars in Chang'an," the guard said. "If you can't pay, get out!"

The couple hurried away, the line shuffling ahead. Wenshu's fingers twitched as he counted the remaining coins in his satchel. We had a few more sewn into our clothes, but this wasn't the best place to undress, and we needed that money if we didn't want to sleep on the streets for the next few months. We'd already far overspent what we'd estimated just to get here in one piece. We couldn't arrive in Chang'an with nothing at all.

The family in front of us passed through the gates, and soon the guards loomed over us, palms outstretched.

"How much?" Wenshu said, his voice even as he unhitched his satchel, like the price was inconsequential.

"Fifty for men, thirty for women, twenty for children,"

the man said, jerking his open palm toward Wenshu with impatience.

Wenshu pressed his lips together and pretended to count, but I knew from his face that we didn't have enough. How could we have come all this way just to be sent away at the city gates?

I slipped a hand up my sleeve and yanked the thread binding two pieces of gold to my clothes. I'd never attempted alchemy on money before—it was said that the capital gold was made from unstable materials, and the punishment for counterfeiting coins was death.

But as Wenshu grew pale, eyes darting around while cataloging his options, I decided there was a first time for everything.

I clenched the coin in my hands, crushing it against my new trio of copper rings. I used the copper catalyst to thin the gold, splitting the coin in half and reshaping the pieces into smaller coins that I hoped looked passable.

I didn't even have a chance to check before the coins multiplied again, bursting from my fist and spilling down my sleeve, rolling in the red dirt. Everyone turned to stare at me, then the coins at my feet. Wenshu's gaze fell to my right hand, where my copper rings had mysteriously disappeared, his face sinking into a tight grimace. I could almost hear his searing thoughts: *Did you really do illegal alchemy standing right in front of the city guards?*

He sighed, then grabbed my arm and threw me to the ground.

"You stole from me again?" he said. "I knew I was missing some."

"Forgive me," I said, bowing deeper into the dirt. Hopefully, the guards would think I was just a disobedient wife and not trying to counterfeit coins.

But the guards didn't seem inclined to investigate further. From my spot on the ground, I heard Wenshu drop my coins in their hands and tie up his satchel. I watched his feet moving, Yufei shifting from foot to foot, horses and pigs passing by.

"Come on," he said at last, yanking me up by the back of my dress. I stumbled after him until we passed the guards, then I took his wrist in one hand and Yufei's in the other.

"Run," I said in Guangzhou dialect.

"What?" Wenshu said. "Why?"

"Hey!" the guard called out. I looked over my shoulder and caught a glimpse of the guard holding a handful of ash spilling through his fingers. That answered one question at least: fake gold only lasted a few minutes.

"Run!" I said again, and this time they listened, darting around horses and carriages and carts, shoving our way through married couples and families, stumbling across spilled fruit and splashing through murky puddles.

People shrieked behind us as the guard thundered his way through the crowd. I jammed a hand into my bag of stones, fishing around for something useful while trying not to crash into anyone. Yufei grabbed my arm just in time to yank me away from a child chasing after a ball. Ahead of us, a man was pulling a cart of cabbages out into the street. I grabbed three chunks of amethyst in one hand and slammed my other palm into the cart.

It burst into wood splinters, cabbage leaves flying up into the air and raining over the crowd, cabbage heads rolling into the street. The guard tripped over a spinning cabbage and landed face-first into a puddle. I hardly had time to laugh before Yufei pulled both me and Wenshu into a side street, tucking us behind an abandoned cart. Only moments later, heavy footsteps rushed past us.

We panted for breath, cuffing sweat from our foreheads.

"Sorry about pushing you down," Wenshu said. "It seemed preferable to beheading."

I waived a hand in acknowledgment, wishing I had some water.

"I think we've made a good first impression," Yufei said, sagging against the wall and feeling through her bag for oranges that she knew weren't there.

"I'll check if the coast is clear," I said, rising to my feet even though my legs felt like paper, then hobbling to the mouth of the alley.

I flinched at the sound of a gong, sure that it meant the guards had somehow found us. But no one paid any attention to me. Everyone rushed to clear the streets, pressing themselves against buildings, ducking behind merchant carts, scooping up their children onto their shoulders. Wenshu and Yufei rose and stood behind me, trying to get a closer look.

Purple-robed officials on white horses trotted down the street, not even sparing a glance at the people below them. Their faces had a sharp brightness to them, like the ocean sparkling under midday sun. I'd heard that the more gold you ate, the more luminous you became, but I had never seen anyone with such a glow around them, as if the sun wasn't shining on them but from within them. How much gold did they have to eat to look like that?

Behind the officials, four servants carried a gold-embossed palanquin at their waists. Everyone bowed as it passed, but when the wind blew the silk curtains back and I caught a glimpse of the person within, I couldn't bring myself to move.

The warm, golden pools of her irises blazed as they captured the sunlight, matching the huādiàn on her forehead made of delicate gold foil and insect wings. Gold ornaments and flowers decorated her elaborate hairstyle, shimmering constellations in the glossy night black of her hair. She looked more like the perfect clay míngqì women in our shop than anything real, as if she had been shaped with exquisite care, hand-painted, polished with a ceramic glaze, baked at a perfect temperature until the colors grew deep and rich. She turned slightly and, for a single moment, met my gaze.

I suddenly felt bloodless, my feet rooted to the ground, breath trapped in my chest. Something about her stare felt almost physically sharp, like a hand clamped around my throat.

Someone tugged my sleeve—a merchant scowling at me from where he knelt on the ground.

"Are you a fool?" he whispered. "Bow or the guards will come for you."

I dropped to the street as the palanquin rode past. "Who is that?" I asked.

The man's frown deepened. "Do you live under a rock?" he said. "That's the Empress."

My gaze snapped back to the retreating palanquin. Empress Wu—who the people called the Eternal Empress—was celebrating her hundredth year as regent, one hundred years since the Emperor grew too ill to rule on his own and handed her the reigns to his kingdom, and still she looked barely older than me and Yufei.

In Guangzhou, the scholars said that under the Empress's command, alchemists had discovered ways to measure time, ways to heal the sick, and of course, ways to stop aging. The Empress had thousands of questions about how the world worked, and using an obscene amount of the Emperor's money, she'd set out to answer them all.

Following behind the Empress, with noticeably fewer guards, two young girls on horseback laughed and tried to race each other, forcing the disgruntled guards to grab the horses' reins. They didn't look older than ten, but if they ate gold like the rest of the royal family, their appearance said little about their true age. I'd heard of some aristocrats who liked to keep their daughters small and cute for decades.

The crowd began to murmur, some shouting curses as the girls rode past. Someone threw a persimmon at them, startling the horses, who took off faster down the road. The merchant beside me spat in their direction as they passed.

Wenshu nudged me to the side so he could get a better look. "What have they done?" he asked the merchant. "They're only children."

"They're the traitor's daughters," he replied. "The Empress only lets them live out of kindness."

"What traitor?" I said.

The man turned to me, expression pinched as if physically pained by my ignorance. "Consort Xiao. She killed the Empress's daughter in her cradle," he said slowly, "yet the Empress is merciful and lets the traitor's daughters live as princesses."

I mumbled my thanks and watched the princesses hurry after the Empress in a flurry of rotting fruit and insults. The last horse in the procession thundered past us, far too close. I jumped back and a sudden pain lanced through my head like a fire stoker.

I fell to my knees and kept falling, the ground nothing but silk under my palms. I tumbled forward into an empty sky and crashed onto my stomach, slamming the air out of my lungs. My fingers twitched across soft dirt, powdery red under my nails, ghosts of footprints beneath my fingertips. Voices spun above me in watery clouds, but even though they seemed miles away, I knew that some of the shapeless sounds were screams; I could feel the terror and agony in the pitch even without understanding the words.

I sat up and faced a wide, empty street of red dirt. In the distance, a gate with five great arches yawned open into nothingness. Their hungry darkness sapped the light from the street, swirling deeper, beckoning.

"Zilan?"

I blinked, the ground coming into focus beneath my hands. I was on my knees, Wenshu gripping my shoulder. When I raised my gaze to the path that the horses had followed, I saw the same five arches at the end of the street.

"I've been here," I said, grabbing Wenshu's sleeve. "I've been here before."

Wenshu looked past me, probably at Yufei. "That's not possible," he said. "You need food and water."

"No, *listen to me*," I said, but he and Yufei—mostly Yufei—were already hauling me to my feet, dragging me away from the crowd. I heard Wenshu asking about shade, then they were pulling me down the street in the opposite direction from the gate. I tried to turn back, but my head still felt like it had been split open, so it was easy for Yufei to force me around a corner, where I couldn't see the gates anymore.

I stumbled alongside the drainage ditches, glimpsing my watery reflection in the murky pools of rainwater. I smelled the sharp scent of citrus, then Yufei pushed me down by the shoulders, forcing me to the ground under the shade of an orange tree. She plucked the straw hat from my head and fanned me with it. I hadn't seen where Wenshu went, but he reappeared moments later with three pieces of húbǐng—a flat bread covered in sesame seeds.

"Eat," he said, sitting in front of us. "Both of you."

I took a bite and then couldn't stop eating until the bread

was gone and my stomach felt tight. I'd finished before both Wenshu and Yufei, who looked at me like I was a caged animal. Yufei tore off a piece of her bread and offered it to me, but I pushed her arm back.

"No, I'm full," I said. "And my head hurts, but I'm not losing my mind. I've definitely been here before."

Wenshu sighed. "Zilan, you lived down the street from us for as long as I can remember, which is longer than *you* can remember, because I'm older. Your parents never took you this far north, and our parents certainly didn't. Why would any of us come here?"

I pressed my lips together. It certainly would have been a long and difficult journey, especially for a child.

"Maybe you can see the future," Yufei said, between bites. "Wouldn't be the weirdest thing you've done."

I supposed not. But I hoped that wasn't the future, because whatever I'd seen was not just the streets of Chang'an, but pain and darkness.

Wenshu wouldn't let me stand until I'd eaten an entire orange and my stomach felt ready to explode from food. Once he was satisfied, we headed back down the main street with the intention of finding a place to stay, though that plan was quickly derailed by Yufei trying to sample food from every single cart we passed.

There were more people here than I'd seen in my entire life in Guangzhou. I'd never really felt small before, but the scale of everything in Chang'an was immense—the rammed-dirt walls twice my height, the bamboo buildings with clean thatched roofs bound together with gold twine, the red-and-black pagodas in the distance stabbing into the pale sky. At every intersection, we passed a police post with stone-faced guards and bridges sloped over drainage ditches carved deep into the ground like the city's wet veins. I'd expected a big city to stink, but Chang'an smelled mostly of elms and junipers and other fruit trees that lined the streets, probably to keep people from toppling into the ditches.

We wandered toward the eastern wards, where Yufei charmed a guard into buying her tánghúlu. He didn't even flinch when she ate the hawthorn berries whole—seeds and all—and handed him the skewer to throw away as she told him how far we'd come to take our second-round exams.

"I should escort you to the dinner, then," the guard said, inching closer to Yufei. "It's almost time."

"Dinner?" Yufei said, grip tightening around his arm. "What dinner?"

"For the arriving scholars," the guard said. "The royal family is welcoming all the candidates tonight at sundown. You didn't know?"

I shared an uneasy glance with Wenshu. We'd received almost no instructions from the Guangzhou magistrate other than the date and location of our next exam. It might have been a miscommunication, since we'd left for Chang'an quite soon after the first exam and mail from the North to the South was slow. But I also knew that the local school hadn't been thrilled that one of their dropouts and his unschooled sisters had passed while some of their paying students hadn't.

"What will they serve us?" Yufei said, pressing closer to the guard. "It's real food, not gold, right?"

He tipped his head back and laughed, slipping an arm around Yufei's waist. "No, the royal family won't share gold that easily. But if they like you enough, they'll keep you around to serve them forever."

*Forever*, I thought. So much for retirement.

The guard led us to another eastern ward, this one lit with

white paper lanterns painted with gold cranes, casting the paved courtyard in warm light as the sun sank behind it. We crossed a bridge over a silvery pond where golden carp shimmered beneath the water—was everything the rich owned made of gold, all the way down to their fish?

The guard left us at the gates and tried to kiss Yufei on the cheek, but she laughed coyly and ducked away. The smile dropped off her face as soon as the guard turned to leave.

"I'm surprised you tolerated that," Wenshu said.

Yufei lifted a small red satchel from her pocket. "I took his money."

Wenshu's eyes widened. He spun around, making sure the guard was gone. "He'll come back for you!" he whispered in Guangzhou dialect, eyeing the other guards in the courtyard.

"He'll assume he dropped it," Yufei said, stuffing it into her pocket.

Wenshu turned to me, as if I was the one pickpocketing. "We can't do that here! Who knows what their jails are like!"

I nodded. "Yeah, Jiějiě, that's probably not the best idea."

"Thank you," Wenshu said.

"You should let me do the stealing next time," I said. "I can put holes in their pockets so it's easier to believe they dropped it."

Wenshu sighed but didn't bother arguing as we walked closer to the building. Muffled voices and laughter echoed across the yard, the smell of salt and garlic and pork carrying across the lake on the gentle breeze. If being a royal alchemist meant attending feasts, maybe I could get used to it.

Another guard waited at the door, a scroll in one hand and a sword tucked into his belt. He frowned as we approached, unmoved by Yufei's soft smile.

"This meal is for scholars," the guard said before Wenshu could even open his mouth.

"We *are* scholars," Wenshu said. "We've come from Guangzhou."

The man's gaze shifted across the three of us. "Guangzhou?"

"It's in Lingnan," Wenshu said, his words tight. "The south," he continued, when the guard's expression didn't change.

"The south?" the man said. "I heard that southerners stuff baby mice with honey and let them scurry across the table for guests to catch and eat raw."

I grimaced. I'd heard rumors of older people doing that, but I'd never met anyone who'd actually tried it. There were easier ways to get food.

"No," Wenshu said, expression flat. "Check your list."

The guard's grip on his scroll tightened. "There's a dress code," he said. "You can't sit among royalty looking like that."

My gaze fell to my dirtied skirts. It was difficult to wash blood entirely from white cloth, so our clothes had taken on a brownish tinge, made worse from sleeping outside on our journey. Was this man really going to deny us a meal over our clothes after we'd spent weeks traveling?

I sighed, jamming my hand into my bag of stones.

"I don't want your bribes," the guard said. But I had already found three pieces of slate. I grabbed Yufei's sleeve in one hand, the stones in the other. The slate drank up the blood and filth from her clothes, leaving her in a wrinkled but bright white gown. The excess poured down my wrist, pooling on the ground.

"Is that clean enough for you?" I said, my palms burning as I shook the blood and dirt off my hands.

The guard drew his sword, leveling it with my nose. The

three of us froze, eyes fixed on the blade. I'd never had such a sharp weapon pointed at me before and was sure a wrong breath would slice my nose clean off.

"Only royal alchemists can practice outside the training compound," the guard said.

"What?" I said softly, afraid to move my lips too much. "In the south, we're allowed to do lower-level alchemy in public."

"And in the North, we have rules. Our alchemists actually have skills beyond skinning hogs and squishing beetles. If you leave now, I won't have you thrown in jail."

"Don't worry, we're going," Wenshu said, bowing and grabbing both me and Yufei before either of us could argue.

We moved wordlessly down the streets, Yufei casting sad glances back at the building as the smell of food faded. It was her expression more than my own pride that made me look over my shoulder at the guard growing smaller behind us, wishing I could rip his veins open. I would remember his face, and when I was a royal alchemist, I could make him crawl around and catch honey stuffed mice to eat raw.

Wenshu finally ground to a stop when we were a safe distance from the guard, his face red and jaw clenched. Had the encounter really upset him that much? Had risking jail more than twice in one day been the last straw?

"Gēgē," I said quietly, "I—"

"Zilan," he said, his voice low. "How long have you known how to do that?"

I blinked. "Do what?"

He grabbed Yufei's clean sleeve and yanked it up in the air.

"Oh. That's pretty easy," I said, not sure why *that*, of all things, was the focus of his wrath. "A few years, maybe?"

He dropped her arm, fists clenched. "In that case," he said, "then *why the hell have I been doing all of our laundry this whole time?*"

"*That's* what you're mad about?" Yufei said.

"I'm not using up my slate on laundry!" I said. "You would have made me clean all your clothes every time someone breathed on them! A little dirt isn't a big deal!"

"What else can you clean?" Wenshu said, throwing his hands up into the air. "Can you wash vegetables? Scrub the floor?"

I looked at the ground.

"You *can*!" he said. "I can't believe you! You think I *enjoy* cleaning up after you two?"

"*Yes,*" Yufei and I said at the same time.

"Can we talk about dinner now?" Yufei said.

"Yes," I said, taking her arm and hurrying us away from Wenshu's wrath.

Wenshu let out a withering sound of anger but stomped obediently behind us. "You could at least clean my clothes now."

Though we'd hoped to stay somewhere close to the training grounds, we quickly realized that everything in the eastern wards was far too expensive. What their inns demanded for one night could have bought us food for a month back in Guangzhou. By the time we made it to the western side of the city, it was just after sundown and all the wards had closed their gates for the night, leaving us stranded in an abandoned labyrinth of dirt walls and worn paths.

We sat by a drainage ditch under a pear tree. It wouldn't be the first time we slept outside in recent weeks, but something about it felt distinctly and conspicuously poor in a city as magnificent as Chang'an. We were invited here as scholars, the best in Lingnan, and yet we were sleeping on top of rotten fruit.

Maybe it was something about the vastness of the streets

when empty, but I couldn't relax enough to grow tired, despite how far we'd traveled. I rolled onto my side, wincing when a stone jammed into my hip. When I reached down to move it, I knew at once from the touch that it wasn't a stone.

I scooted to the side, making Yufei grumble, and picked up a single pearl covered in muddy red. Even through the dirt, I knew the scent of blood. I brushed aside some smashed pears and found several more scattered pearls jammed into the ground.

I glanced at Wenshu and Yufei's sleeping forms, then stuffed the pearls into my pocket to clean later. Maybe I could trade them for gold to buy us breakfast. I leaned back against the tree until my eyelids grew heavy, and when I finally sank into a dream, it was solid and unchanging as a painting, nothing but five tall archways leading into darkness.

# CHAPTER TEN

We woke to the sound of gates creaking open. The sun was already hot enough to turn the smashed pears around us to a sticky jelly, but somehow its light hadn't disturbed us—a testament to how exhausted we'd been. We sat up and brushed off our clothes, then Yufei and I tied back each other's hair while Wenshu stared half-awake at the horses pulling carts down the street. I pulled Yufei's hair just a bit too tight when I remembered I'd have to leave her and Wenshu again as we went to our respective practice grounds. The guard she'd pickpocketed had been kind enough to mention that all the candidates were supposed to meet today for a welcoming ceremony.

We stumbled sleepily through the streets, munching on pears, until we had to part ways at the eastern courtyard, where the alchemists were supposedly meeting. It didn't ease my nerves that a stern guard before the only door was eyeing me with his arms crossed. I knew I'd earned my place beside the other alchemists, but if my experience in the south was any indication, I didn't think they'd be thrilled to see someone like me among them.

Yufei punched me in the spine.

"Ow! What are you—"

"You're slouching. At least pretend you're confident or they'll walk all over you."

I sighed but straightened my spine a few degrees.

"Good," Yufei said. "Now go destroy them."

"It's an informational meeting. I'm not destroying—"

*"Destroy them,"* Yufei said, shaking her head. "No making friends until you pass."

"And keep your clothes on this time," Wenshu said. "We don't have any extra fabric."

"How boring," I said, trying to smile. I could feel the conversation ending, which meant my cousins would be leaving me again soon.

"Meet back here for dinner?" Yufei said.

I nodded. "Oh, I almost forgot." I reached into my satchel, digging around for a moment before pulling out the pearls I'd found, offering Wenshu a handful. "I found these where we slept. I want to keep some for my transformations, but we can trade the rest for gold. This should get you lunch, at least."

Wenshu frowned and picked one up, holding it to the sky. "Is that...blood?"

I shrugged. "Probably."

He clenched his jaw, carefully setting the pearl back in my palm, holding the hand that had touched it away from his body like he wanted to cut it off. "Do I even want to know where that came from?"

"The ground."

"I mean, who did it belong to?" Wenshu said. "It looks like a robbery gone wrong. We shouldn't get caught up in things like that." Bloody jewels were a telltale sign that they hadn't been earned by honest means. People often paid for míngqì with bloodstained gold nuggets.

116

"Of course you would find a way to scold Zilan for finding money," Yufei said.

"I'm not scolding her," he said, crossing his arms. "I'm just—"

"Asking too many questions about free money?" I said.

Wenshu shook his head. "We have enough for lunch. You hang onto them for now, and tomorrow we'll just trade them all for gold and wash our hands of whatever crime-scene evidence you've somehow stumbled upon."

"Yes, we know how much you like washing your hands," Yufei said.

I shrugged and added the pearls to my satchel. "Go now, or you'll be late," I said, waving them off so that they'd walk away rather than miss their own meeting because of me. As they turned away, I found it hard to breathe, my throat closing up and my eyes burning. *You're being childish*, I thought. I wasn't some little girl being dropped off at school for the first time. But this strange city felt so large without them, the dialect so sharp, the sunlight so bright. For the first time in my life, I felt small.

Luckily, the guard let me past the gates after I told him my name, and then the world opened up into a garden of dove trees and lily ponds full of sunlight. The courtyard had paths paved in gold so polished they cast my reflection back up at me. My shoes tracked red dirt onto them, which servants quickly swept behind me, brushing at my heels. I stumbled away from them, crashing into a stranger in red robes who looked at me like I was a dead rat before hurrying toward the grassy areas where the other alchemists were gathered.

China had fifteen divisions, and each sent ten alchemists, all of them now gathered in this shimmering courtyard. Some of them spoke in dialects I'd never heard and wore robes with plunging collars or widened sleeves, silk braided with

117

tiny jewels. Most of them were men, though several women stood at the periphery. I considered going up to them just so I wouldn't have to wander around like a leaf floating downstream, but their circle was tightly closed, and I couldn't imagine how to wedge myself into it.

To my dismay, I spotted the man from Guangzhou with the disgusting mustache, his right wrist still heavily bandaged. *It must have hurt holding a horse's reigns when traveling here*, I thought, which made me feel a bit better.

A gong rang at the back of the courtyard, and a man with a twisted mustache and purple robes cleared his throat and began to call attendance by region. Half the alchemists from Hedong and Hebei were missing, and the men around me whispered that they'd killed each other when their paths crossed on the way to Chang'an. I'd heard rumors of scholars poisoning each other or slitting the throats of their competition in their sleep, but that seemed to only be a problem among the Northern divisions. No one really thought of the south as a threat. We hadn't had a royal alchemist from Lingnan in the last decade.

"Fan...Zilan?" the man called.

I raised a hand, looking away as the other scholars snickered.

"Her name is Zilan?" one of them said. "Is she a servant?"

I dropped my hand as the man called out the rest of the names from Lingnan, hoping everyone would forget about me quickly. It was a bit too early to start making enemies.

"Zheng Sili?" the man called out. Across the yard, the man from Guangzhou with the terrible mustache raised his hand. The name sounded familiar, and I grimaced when I remembered it was the only one above mine on the lists of finalists from Lingnan. Of course, it had to be him. But he was in for a rude surprise when he realized that his high rank as a southern alchemist meant nothing to the alchemists of the North. Considering that we weren't even allowed to do basic alchemy in public without royal status, it seemed that in Chang'an, either you were a royal alchemist or you were no one at all.

The man at the front began his opening speech about the esteemed duty of royal alchemists, which I could hardly hear over everyone's excited chattering about the upcoming exams.

"It is our greatest honor to pledge service to the House of Li," he said. "You are the keepers of gold, which has made our kingdom great, which has cemented its place in eternity, which runs through the veins of the family that Heaven has chosen for us…"

I tried to subtly eavesdrop on some Northern alchemists near me, who seemed wholly convinced that the next round would involve fighting bears. It seemed ridiculous at first, but I supposed the palace was big enough to secretly store over a hundred massive animals. Besides, the government clearly spared no expense when it came to Chang'an.

At the sound of a door opening, the man at the front turned to his left with a look of relief on his face, mercifully wrapping up his speech. I followed his gaze to the far end of the courtyard, where a flock of servants rushed after a man in purple, hurrying across a bridge. He held up a hand to block the sunlight from his face, but as he crossed into the shade and dropped his hand, a wave of dizzying déjà vu washed over me, like when I'd seen the five gates.

This was the man who'd asked me to resurrect him in Guangzhou.

*Is he a court official?* It was unusual for an official to have so many servants, so he truly must have been rich beyond imagination. Whatever the case, it seemed he'd outlived his own predictions. What had made him so certain of his own death?

"Now," the man onstage said, "the Crown Prince wishes to welcome you all formally."

And, to my horror, the man who'd come to Guangzhou stepped onto the stage.

I'd known that Empress Wu had only one living son—Li Hong, Prince of Dai, the heir to the throne. Apparently, the man I'd spoken so casually to in Guangzhou would one day inherit the empire. This whole gilded city belonged to him, as did all the roads I'd crossed to come here, every stalk of grass, even the footprints in the dirt. When I'd refused to help him, he would have been well within his rights to tie me up, throw me over his horse, and take me back to Chang'an as a slave. So why had he asked me to help, rather than ordering me?

I tried to slide behind another alchemist so he wouldn't see me, hating the idea that someone so powerful even knew I existed. What if he remembered the thousand impolite things I'd said to him and had me thrown in jail? In truth, he hadn't seemed that cruel, but I knew better than to stake my life on the kindness of the rich.

The prince ascended the platform, his guards hovering nearby. In Guangzhou, he'd seemed so out of place, but here—gazing down at the crowd, the sun catching the gold flecks in his eyes and glimmering in the embroidery on his violet robes—he truly looked like someone who Heaven had handpicked as the future Emperor. Wenshu had always railed against the mandate of Heaven, saying that Heaven wouldn't choose emperors who neglected half the country and enslaved girls from across the sea, but I couldn't deny that something about the prince emanated power and certainty. It was as if he'd already read the story of his life and was merely acting out the part with the grace of someone assured of their destiny.

"Greetings, alchemists," he said, smiling as everyone bowed. "I will be brief, as I know you all have important duties, but I will say this much—do not underestimate your importance to our kingdom. Because of the noble art of alchemy, there are no limits to our dreams. Thanks to your talents, our empire is the strongest in the world. You will carve out a future that..."

He trailed off, squinting in the sunlight. It took me half a second too long to realize he was looking at *me*.

I tried to duck behind another alchemist again, but it was too late.

"Zilan xiǎojiě," the prince said, smiling. "I see you've made it, as expected."

All of the alchemists turned to me at once. I felt more exposed than when Zheng Sili had torn up my dress in public. Now everyone knew my name, and my face, and the fact that the prince—for some bizarre reason—was happy to see me. Most of the alchemists were slack-jawed and wide-eyed, probably confused that the girl with the servant name knew the Crown Prince. But some of their gazes burned, expressions sinking into sharp disapproval.

"Yes, *Your Highness*," I said, mustering as much bitterness as I could without being executed for my rudeness. His eyes dimmed and he cleared his throat, continuing his hollow speech. Slowly, the other alchemists turned away from me. They didn't dare to whisper while the prince was talking, but I knew what they were thinking. *She's only here because the prince likes her. She's probably one of his whores.*

Mercifully, his address ended quickly, and his servants swept him away. I let out a breath as soon as he was gone—it felt like a comet had ripped across the sky, dazzling everyone with its light, and now suddenly there was nothing but pitch darkness.

The first speaker returned to show us the training grounds through the next gate—a barren courtyard of pale dirt and stone walls. He gestured to the library just past the western gate, where we could study for our exam at the end of the week, but gave us no indication as to what it would entail. I could barely pay attention, feeling everyone's gaze on me as they whispered in dialects I didn't understand.

It seemed that despite my best efforts, I already had a reputation in Chang'an.

"There is absolutely no alchemy in the library," the librarian said. I would have thought a royal librarian would be the wiry, pale type like Wenshu, but this man looked like he could shove an ox aside and single-handedly drag cargo across town. As soon as I'd signed in as an alchemist, he'd put his hand out and demanded that I surrender my satchel of stones.

"I'm not going to do alchemy in here," I said. "I'm just going to read about it."

The librarian shook his head, his hair ornaments jingling. "The last alchemist we let in here with stones set fire to priceless, irreplaceable scrolls. You leave your stones with me."

Yufei crossed her arms, but Wenshu elbowed her before she could speak. "Do as he says, Zilan. It's the rules."

"What if someone steals them?" I said. "Do you even know how much I paid for those?"

"They'll be on my desk, where I can guard them," the librarian said.

I pursed my lips, clutching my satchel, but Wenshu sighed and nudged my shoulder. "Zilan," he said. "Just do it."

I shot Wenshu a murderous look, then turned and dropped

my satchel on the librarian's desk. Not because I agreed with Wenshu, but because openly disobeying my male "guardian" would make Wenshu lose face in front of all the other scholars who were just past the counter and undoubtedly listening.

We moved into the building, and luckily its vastness—unlike anything I'd seen in Guangzhou—was enough to make me forget about my stones. The royal library was a labyrinth of shelves packed with scrolls, maps, and paintings. Yufei helped me carry ten scrolls on Northern alchemy stones over to a table, while Wenshu gathered essays on Confucian analects, which he and Yufei promptly started fighting over, both wanting to read the same one. They agreed to take turns, but only when another librarian came by to scold them for making so much noise.

The scholars at the other tables moved away from us, mumbling that we smelled like rotten meat. It was definitely possible that the pig's blood on our clothes had seeped in and started to smell in a way we ceased to notice, but I thought it had more to do with us not having silk robes and speaking in Guangzhou dialect so they couldn't understand us. After a few hours, I convinced Wenshu and Yufei to move to a study room, saying the other scholars were too noisy, but really I just couldn't concentrate with everyone staring at us.

Soon, the sun set behind the windows and we read by candlelight. The sounds of the other scholars outside had gone quiet as the daylight waned, and I suspected most people had left. My eyes grew dry and the words I read began to lose meaning. The vastness of the library no longer seemed impressive but crushing when I started to realize how much I didn't know, how much information the formally trained alchemists had access to while I'd been poring over outdated texts. The children of scholars had probably read through this library ten times over, while I was about to have a breakdown after struggling through three scrolls.

"These scholars wrote about Penglai Island like my father," I said, slumped over a scroll. "They were looking for some sort of life elixir too."

"That's a myth," Wenshu said, not even looking up. "You should worry about things that will actually be on your exam."

"Well, sorry if I don't know the contents of every scroll before reading it," I said, rolling up the paper with more force than necessary.

Yufei groaned and flopped over her desk. "I'm starving," she said.

"We already had dinner, so deal with it," Wenshu said. "Besides, we already used all our gold for today."

Wenshu had counted our remaining money and calculated how much we could safely spend each day, assuming we all passed our next two exams and had to wait for the next lunar cycle for payment. With how alarmingly expensive food and board were in the capital, we could split one meal a day between the three of us, plus whatever street food Yufei could charm off of merchants. The question of what to do if we didn't pass our exams hung over us like a shadow, but none of us dared say it out loud.

"Fine, then I guess you don't want any," Yufei said, pulling an orange from her bag.

Wenshu's eyebrow twitched. "You can't eat in here."

"Are you going to tell on me?" Yufei said, already peeling it.

"I want some," I said, partially because I was hungry and partially just to spite the librarian for taking my stones.

"It will smell like oranges in here and they'll never let us back in," Wenshu said, trying to grab the fruit.

Yufei stood up, holding it out of his reach. "Get your own."

Wenshu huffed and got to his feet, trying to snatch the orange, but Yufei tossed it to me over his head. Before I could reach it, Wenshu smacked it out of the air. It hit the table, splashing juice onto the scrolls.

"You got ink on my orange!" Yufei said.

"As if that would stop you! You literally eat food off the ground!" Wenshu said.

We turned toward the door at the sound of shouting from the other side of the library. Yufei took the opportunity to snatch her orange back and shove half of it into her mouth, handing me the other soggy half. Something clattered outside, like a bag of marbles had spilled, then a chair screeched and wood splintered.

"Is that how Northerners study?" Wenshu said, scowling. "What are they doing out there?"

"I thought most of them left," I said. "Maybe the librarian is moving tables?"

"Or breaking them," Yufei mumbled, wiping her mouth with her sleeve.

Wenshu dug a rag from his pocket and hurled it at Yufei's wet face, his gaze still lingering on the door. "Maybe we should be worried," he said.

I crossed my arms. "About that jerk who took my stones?"

"No, that *someone else* has taken your stones," he said. "It sounded like a lot of stones fell on the floor."

My stomach sank. I stood up, shouldered past Wenshu, and threw open the door.

Shadows had swallowed the library, casting the tables in deep pools of black. The candles burned low, only weak white circles on the walls like ghostly moons. As I suspected, the Northern scholars were gone.

I crossed the room, turned the corner, and hurried toward

the main entrance, footsteps echoing behind me as Wenshu and Yufei followed.

But no one sat at the front desk. The door hung open, moonlight spilling inside, the candles by the doorway shivering from a high-pitched wind.

*That bastard promised to watch my stones*, I thought, charging toward his desk to rifle through his drawers.

Then the smell of blood crashed over me, my anger washed away like I'd been doused in cold water. I stepped around the desk.

The librarian lay on his back in front of the counter, jaw unlatched in an endless scream, teeth scattered around him, nose crushed into his face. Blood pooled underneath his head, almost black in the dim light, the stain spreading wider and wider like a portal of darkness opening beneath him.

Wenshu and Yufei appeared behind me, freezing at the sight of blood. I held my breath and gripped the edge of the counter, praying that the lightness in my chest wasn't a precursor to collapsing again. I really didn't want to be facedown in someone else's blood and teeth.

"Wow," Yufei said unsteadily.

Wenshu groaned. "I just wanted a quiet night at the library."

This sort of violence wasn't uncommon back home, where those who wore too many gold rings would have their fingers cut off late at night, but I'd expected the palace grounds to be safer. Perhaps the librarian had upset some of the Northern scholars who weren't used to being bossed around? Whoever had done this had come armed—the only bodies I'd seen with skulls crushed like grapes had either fallen from a great height or been bludgeoned with rocks.

"Should we alert the guards?" I said. I felt a bit bad about walking away from a dead body that I could have brought back, but since I wasn't even allowed to practice regular alchemy, getting caught using the most forbidden type of alchemy on a rude librarian wasn't high on my list of priorities.

Wenshu shook his head. "They'll find him eventually. We should leave."

"Why? It's not like we killed him," Yufei said.

"You think anyone else is going to see it that way?" Wenshu said, whirling around. "No one wants us here! They'll take any excuse to get rid of us."

I swallowed down the sharp taste of blood and peered around the desk. Just past the librarian's hand, gemstones sparkled across the floor, a blue satchel in shreds beside them. *My stones.*

I hopped over the body, making Wenshu grumble about bloody footprints, then bent down and started to gather up pieces of jade and iron.

"Zilan," Wenshu said, "we need to—"

"You go put away the scrolls," I said. "Jiějiě, help me gather these."

Wenshu ran off, clearly too stressed to argue, while Yufei passed me pieces of cobalt and diamond. I kept careful track of the stones I had on me, never wanting to be caught without what I needed. That was how I knew instantly what was missing.

"The pearls," I said. "Do you see them?"

Yufei frowned and looked around as Wenshu hurried back, face flushed, hands full of Yufei's discarded orange. "It's clean," he said. "We're leaving."

"The pearls are gone," I said.

Wenshu clenched his teeth. "Maybe it was a thief who took them," he said. "Does it matter?"

"Then why didn't they take her diamonds?" Yufei said, passing me a chunk of amethyst.

"Look, I'd rather not get caught standing over a dead body because of a handful of pearls," he said. "Can we go?"

"It was more than a handful."

*"Zilan!"* Wenshu said. "Please, let's go before we actually get in trouble."

I sighed and stuffed the rest of my gems into my pockets along with the scraps of my satchel. Wenshu was right. Pearls weren't worth getting thrown in jail. Perhaps they'd rolled under a desk somewhere. But something about this didn't sit right with me. I couldn't shake the sense that no matter how much I kept to myself, trouble was going to find me regardless.

Chang'an did not seem like a place where one could live quietly. It was a city with teeth, and it already knew my name.

# CHAPTER ELEVEN

In the morning, I tried to return to the library only to be swept up in a training exercise in the muddy courtyard. Though I wasn't keen on working with people who thought of me as a peasant or a whore, part of me wondered how formally trained alchemists practiced. Apparently, sparring was a regular part of their curriculum.

"It sharpens your mind," explained one of the female alchemists.

"For what?" I'd said. "Aren't we just making gold?"

She rolled her eyes. "Alchemists are expected to defend the royal family if the guards can't," she said. "Where did you study again?"

I'd watched the male alchemists pair off and take turns blasting each other's eyebrows off with firestones or transforming blunt weapons from the wet dirt, reluctantly laughing along with the crowd when one used earthstones to smash a six-foot hole in the ground, which his opponent promptly tumbled into.

Some of them had turned each stone into a ring to better arm themselves, although having several rings on each finger seemed to hamper their movements. Some, like me, had chosen only the most useful stones to transform into rings or bracelets or embroidered gloves, keeping the rest in satchels. One alchemist, who I'd mentally dubbed Fire Fingers, had apparently dunked his hands in a fire-retardant gel, embroidered silk gloves with traces of firestone, and used alchemy to activate them so that the flames devoured the fabric, leaving him with two blazing fistfuls of blue fire.

The longer I watched, the more I began to wonder exactly how much the rest of them had learned in school while I'd been working the shop. Beating the alchemists of Guangzhou was one thing, but the North practically bled gold, and its students clearly could afford the best alchemy tutors in the empire.

"Hey, hùnxiě," one of the men called. I knew the voice even before I looked up to find Zheng Sili, arms crossed. "Your turn."

I wanted to slink away and study, but everyone had turned toward me. "I have better things to do than bathe in mud like a pig," I said.

"Ah yes, you do that enough in your free time," Zheng Sili said, laughter rippling behind him. He crossed the circle, standing right in front of me. "You're too confident. You think you stand a chance against a trained alchemist? You only got out of Guangzhou because you flashed your skin at the judges."

I took a steadying breath. *You need to study*, I thought. *Fighting with Zheng Sili won't make you a royal alchemist.* "How's your wrist?" I said at last. "Did you tell everyone how I made you cry?"

Zheng Sili's eyebrow twitched. "There's no need to get defensive, Zilan. I know you're embarrassed that a whole town saw you without your dress, but it's not like there's much to see under your clothes anyway."

Without thinking, I shoved him hard. The crowd hurried away, murmuring as the circle opened up wider around us.

Fine. If there was anyone here I wouldn't mind fighting, it was Zheng Sili.

He smiled knowingly and took a step back, waving me into the circle with his palm facing up, like I was an animal. My face burned and I tightened my grip on my new satchel, which was nothing but some bundled-up scraps knotted to my sash.

Without warning, Zheng Sili reached a hand into his satchel. I didn't see what stones he grabbed, but with one smooth arc of his arm, he cast something to the ground and a circle of flames carved itself into the grass around us. Great walls of fire singed my heels, forcing me to step closer or ignite my dress.

What kind of firestone had he used? How did he have such precise control over the fire's shape? Was there already something flammable on the ground? I swallowed, even though the fire had sapped all the moisture from my mouth.

*Where did you study again?* the other alchemist had said.

*In an attic above a míngqì shop*, I thought bitterly. And I was beginning to feel that it wasn't enough to get me out of this.

I shoved my hand into my bag and pulled out three pieces of granite, sharpening them into a blade with the touch of the iron rings on my left hand. I probably should have thought of something more creative, something flashy to show all the other alchemists not to bother me anymore, but with so many eyes on me, it was the best I could think of.

I lunged forward and struck at Zheng Sili, but he wrapped his hand around my knife. His skin had turned the color of jade, a flexible but sturdy material encasing his hand as he snapped my blade off easily, casting it to the side. He'd moved so fast that I hadn't even seen what stones he'd grabbed before the transformation burned them up. With a flash of light against his jade hand, his index finger sharpened into a green blade.

He slashed at me, the strike so far from my center that I thought he was trying to tear my dress again, but instead he sliced my satchel apart, all my stones tumbling to the ground.

*Forget alchemy*, I thought, jamming my palm into his nose. The crunch and strangled scream that followed was satisfying for only an instant before he bit down hard on my fingers.

I tried to wrench my hand away in a panic, but his teeth only clamped harder. Human mouths were more than capable of severing fingers, and I wouldn't put it past Zheng Sili to try. If I were to lose a finger, I would be damned if it happened in such a ridiculous and embarrassing way as this.

I reached up to jam my thumb into his eye, but his jade hand grabbed my wrist and wrenched it back. His teeth had already broken skin, and bones would come next. I had no stones, and no free hands. The iron rings on my right hand were still intact, but what was I supposed to transform in Zheng Sili's mouth? His spit? His tongue? Transformations with metalstones like iron were meant for *things*, not bodies. Alchemical body augmentation was a science by itself, one that Zheng Sili had probably studied, but of course, I hadn't. I was half a breath away from surrendering just to save my fingers when his pearl tooth caught the light.

Now *that* was a stone I could work with.

I wrenched my hand back just enough until my iron ring clinked against the tooth.

With a flash of white light, the pearl popped out of his gums as it snapped into a spherical shape, releasing the tension on my fingers. Zheng Sili let out a startled breath and the pearl rolled across his tongue, shooting down his throat.

He shoved me aside and fell to his knees, choking. I took

my time gathering up my stones before casting a couple waterstones to the ground, turning the ring of fire into a thin sheet of smoke. Another alchemist rushed forward, striking Zheng Sili between the shoulder blades until the pearl popped out.

"Are you actually trying to kill me?" he said, panting. "We're sparring, not culling each other! There are rules!"

"You were going to bite my fingers off," I said, feeling oddly defensive as the other alchemists glared at me. No one had said there were rules. Everyone else seemed to fight dirty, so why couldn't I?

"No, I wasn't," he said, another alchemist helping him to his feet. "If you don't know what you're doing, you could have just said so."

As the wind washed away the smoke, the scowls of all the other alchemists fell into sharp clarity in the sunlight. Would it have been better if I'd lost? Or sacrificed my fingers for their approval? *Don't make friends*, Yufei had said. It seemed like that wouldn't be a problem.

I shoved past them, storming to the inner courtyard. Let them play their games. I had studying to do.

I finally found an unoccupied tree in the shade and threw my bag down, leaning against the trunk. My clothes still smelled of fire and my skin felt singed, but I unrolled my scrolls and started to read anyway, too angry to take in any of the words. I couldn't help but think about Zheng Sili and what other thousands of alchemy tricks he might know that I didn't.

I'd only been reading for a few minutes when a pair of silk shoes paused in front of me. I barely even glanced up from my scroll, catching a glimpse of jeweled bracelets probably worth my entire home back in Guangzhou. Was I really going to be a source of entertainment for all the other wealthy alchemists?

"I'm busy," I said, rereading the last line of my scroll. "I'll beat you up later, if you're that desperate."

"As tempting as that sounds, I was hoping we could continue our conversation from earlier."

I slid my gaze up the lines of purple fabric, squinting past the sunlight at the face of the Crown Prince.

I tensed, feeling like a lost child who'd just been spotted by a tiger. He knew damn well how much power he had over me, especially here, in his palace. I didn't want anything to do with someone like that.

He had a teacup in one hand and a scroll tucked under his arm, like he'd snuck away from a tutoring session. He looked more tired than when he'd addressed the other alchemists, and red scratches around his throat peeked out from under his collar. *Probably an overzealous concubine,* I thought, pursing my lips so I wouldn't say something rude out loud.

"You spoke so freely in Guangzhou," he said, when I spent a moment too long staring at him. "Why not now?"

I glanced around but didn't see any guards or servants attending him. "I don't think you want me to speak freely right now, *Your Highness,*" I said sourly.

He grimaced. "I've slipped away from my servants, so we're alone right now," he said. "You can say what you wish."

I raised an eyebrow. Surely he was joking. "You won't behead me for speaking out of turn?"

He laughed, shaking his head. "Even if I liked beheading people, the Empress wouldn't allow it. She's too fond of collecting alchemists."

*Collecting alchemists?* I thought. But there were more pressing questions, and I didn't know how many I could ask before a servant inevitably found us.

"You were wrong," I said at last. "You seemed certain you'd be dead by now."

He nodded, glancing around again. "When you wouldn't come with me, I took a long path back to Chang'an to buy myself some time. I've only just returned, hoping I would find you here."

"*Me?*"

He nodded. "You told me you would go to Chang'an to become a royal alchemist. I believed you."

I blushed, dropping my gaze to the dirt. I hadn't even fully believed it myself, but for some reason, he had.

"The people you've helped with your alchemy, they raved about you," he said, sitting cross-legged on the ground in front of me. "They showed me their babies, children they thought were gone forever, who are just now learning to walk."

I shook my head, drawing back against the tree. "That's not…" I trailed off. He made me sound like a hero, when I knew full well it had only been a job and nothing more.

He smiled. "You're so…"

I held my breath, praying his next words wouldn't be *kind* or *generous* or something else that I wasn't.

"…skilled," he said at last.

My shoulders relaxed. No one had ever said that to me before. No one had ever really shown that much appreciation for anything I did. I knew it was because I'd always asked for money instead of thanks, but the prince's words made me feel strangely warm.

"I've studied my entire life, but I've never *done* anything with it," he continued. "Not like you. No one has ever cried tears of joy because of me. I spend all day reading about things that don't matter."

To anyone else, his soft smile might have been endearing,

but something about his earnestness only reminded me how sharp I felt in comparison. He saw the good in me because he could afford to underestimate people. I was a novelty, but nothing stayed new and shiny forever. The prince would grow bored once he learned I was just a shrewd merchant covered in clay dust, not a hero.

He raised his cup to take a sip, the paint by the handle flaking away at his touch. I grabbed his sleeve, careful not to touch his skin. Commoners weren't allowed to lay a hand on royalty.

"Zilan xiǎojiě?"

I took the cup from him, held it up to the sun, and scraped away a flake of paint.

"This is lead glazed," I said. "You can tell because it cracks like alligator scales. You use this glaze for míngqì, not anything meant for drinking."

"I...will pass your comments on to whoever purchases my cups," he said, raising an eyebrow and reaching to take it back.

I poured his tea out into the dirt.

He let out a surprised sound. "Zilan—"

"Lead is poison," I said.

The prince went pale, grabbing his throat. "But my taste tester is fine!"

"Lead takes months to kill someone," I said, rolling my eyes. "If you're not sick already, you'll be fine. Just don't drink any more."

I handed him the empty cup, which he took with stiff hands.

"Thank you," he said quietly. "This is actually what I wanted to talk to you about. My return to the palace has been...precarious. Will you come inside with me?" He stood up, his gaze falling on the bite marks on the back of my hand.

"Is that from an animal?" he asked, eyes wide.

I thought back to the rabid look on Zheng Sili's face. "You could say that."

"Were you in the rhinoceros garden?"

I blinked. "You have a rhinoceros garden?"

"It was a gift from the prince of Champa, along with some elephants," he said, shrugging. "I'll take that as a no. Do you need medicine?"

I closed my eyes, my mind reeling. I remembered Wenshu crying when we ate our last pig a few years ago, meanwhile the royal family kept exotic pets just for entertainment. I looked between the prince's silk shoes and my own dirty feet.

"Why are you even talking to me?" I said. "I thought I made myself clear last time. I won't work for you."

"You were clear that you didn't want to travel with me to Chang'an," the prince said, "but now, you're already here."

"To study, not to serve you," I said. "I don't have time to help you. I haven't passed the second test yet, and I don't need you hanging around me, making the others think you bought my place here."

The prince frowned. "Are the other alchemists giving you trouble? I can talk to them—"

"*No,*" I said. "Defending me will only look worse."

"Then what can I say that will convince you?"

"Nothing."

"Surely there's something you want?" he said, clutching his cup. "I can give you anything."

I shook my head, bowing and turning to leave. My dreams couldn't be bought.

"Please," he said, taking my sleeve. I jolted back, for his hand had come dangerously close to my bare wrist.

"There is still danger," he whispered. "The reason I needed your help hasn't gone away."

"You seem to be surviving just fine on your own."

"As I said, I've been traveling," he said, tugging my sleeve again, pulling me a step closer. "But I have duties here. I can't avoid Chang'an forever."

"Well, perhaps you should confide in the Emperor about your certain death, and maybe he would protect you," I said. "What do you think is going to happen to you inside these gilded walls? Will you be crushed under your piles of gold?"

He grimaced. "My father is too ill to do much of anything," he said, "and I am the heir to the throne. That is a very good reason for many to dislike me."

I rolled my eyes. "It must be hard to be the wealthiest boy in the kingdom."

His expression slid into a frown. He released my sleeve, hand falling limp at his side.

"You told me to speak freely," I said. "Have you changed your mind?"

"I don't understand," he said. "Why does my wealth matter to you so much? Would you help me if I were poor?"

I let out a sharp laugh. "*I* am poor," I said, "and you never helped *me*. Or any of my people."

"What do you—"

"You cower away from death, like it's the worst thing that could happen to you, but in Guangzhou, people far younger than you die every day. We live with that fear. We don't go around begging for help, because we know no one will answer. No one will save us. Least of all the Emperor and his spoiled son."

I turned and stormed away, and this time, no one tried to stop me.

# CHAPTER TWELVE

I woke to a high, piercing whistle and shot to my feet before I was even fully awake—Uncle Fan always said that if I heard any unnatural sounds, the first thing I had to do was run to the kiln to make sure nothing was about to explode.

I tripped straight over Wenshu, kicking him in the stomach, and fell onto my hands. Yufei was already sitting up, looking out the window like she wanted to murder the first person she saw outside, and I realized we weren't in Guangzhou anymore, but in our tiny rented room in a cheap western ward of Chang'an.

Yufei groaned and shoved the window open, sticking her head out. *"It's too early for music!"* she shouted, and the sounds cut off with a sharp squeak.

Now that I was waking up, I heard the low rhythm of drums and blurry melodies in the distance.

I didn't like being woken up any more than Yufei, but it didn't seem that early—the sun was high in the sky, and most of the street seemed to be awake. We'd been up late studying again for our second-round exams.

"We should probably get up anyway," I said. "We can mail our letters to Baba and Mama."

Yufei huffed, slamming the window. "Not like we're going to get any more sleep with all this noise."

"I can't get up. Zilan kicked me to death," Wenshu said, lying flat on his black.

Yufei lifted a foot to stomp on him and he somehow rolled away even with his eyes closed, turning onto his hands and knees.

"How agile you are for a corpse," Yufei said.

The joke made my stomach clench, but Yufei and Wenshu didn't seem perturbed. I'd once asked Yufei how it felt to be revived from death, and she'd said it made her hungrier, which was a very Yufei answer, but I doubted it was that simple. When I asked Wenshu, he'd grown very quiet while he thought over his response.

"I think I remember death," he'd said at last, "but it feels more like death remembers *me*. Everywhere I go, it feels a bit like everything I do could be the very last time. Like I'm just a breath away from nothingness. Everything looks beautiful yet terrifying, because I'm so aware of how in just a moment, all of it could disappear."

Still, Wenshu's anxiety didn't sound like a heavy enough price to pay for the kind of alchemy I'd done to bring him back. Whatever debt he and Yufei had, I was sure it was still unpaid.

We dressed quickly and headed out into town to mail our letters and find food. My note was brief, stating that we'd arrived in Chang'an with all our limbs intact and that we'd send money home as soon as we passed our final exams. I hoped Auntie and Uncle would write back soon, because I hated not knowing how they were doing. Guangzhou could have burned down in our absence and we'd have no idea.

As we turned onto the main road, I clenched the letter tight to my chest, breath catching in my throat.

It seemed that Chang'an had exploded into a thousand colors overnight.

A procession of acrobats and musicians paraded down the street, tossing strips of bright red paper and gold foil into the white sky. Wagons rolled by, piled high with enough silk that it looked like a mountain was drawing nearer, a flutist seated at the top playing sweet melodies that disappeared into the clouds. Other women balanced tall poles vertically on their heads, somehow walking forward as other girls balanced nimbly at the top.

"Is that alchemy?" I wondered out loud as they strode past.

A woman beside us scoffed. "Not everything beautiful is created by alchemy," she said, then showered us in a handful of red paper. "Long live the Emperor."

"Is this...*carnival* his doing?" Wenshu said, brushing paper from his hair.

The woman shook her head. "It is the will of the Empress. We used to only have carnivals for the gods, but now she holds them in honor of the Emperor and his continued strength in the face of his illness."

The Emperor's inability to conquer an illness in over a century hardly seemed worth celebrating to me, but I held my tongue. Still, it was interesting that in the capital, such festivities were now for humans and not solely gods.

Auntie So still prayed and lit incense when she could come by it, but as the years went on, people seemed to put their faith less and less in the gods they couldn't see and more in the alchemy that they could. The Buddhists in particular had grown quieter over the years as their popularity waned. I suspected it was because people no longer needed the comfort of reincarnation after death when they could buy enough al-chemical gold to live forever.

As we crossed the street in search of food, something hard wedged itself up between the reeds of my sandals. I hobbled after Yufei for a few moments before pausing to shake out what I'd thought was a rock, but instead, a pearl fell into my palm.

My heartbeat hammered louder in my ears, remembering the dead librarian and my missing pearls. *This city practically bleeds jewels*, I told myself. *A pearl in and of itself doesn't mean anything.* I stuffed it into my pocket, though it felt oddly heavy.

When I looked up, Wenshu and Yufei had already disap-peared in the crowd. I spun around, searching for white hemp robes, but they'd vanished in the sea of colors.

A man shouldered past me, and when his arm brushed mine, his skin felt like a sharp breath of winter. A breeze blew back his long yellow sleeve, and beneath his robes, his skin looked like polished metal, glimmering white.

My feet ground to a stop, breath trapped in my throat as he continued away from me in the crowd. I finally turned when the cold sensation vanished, just as the man disappeared around a corner.

My fingers traced over the pearl in my pocket. The man's skin had been unnaturally polished, clean and rippling and white...like a pearl.

Once again, the image of the dead librarian burned across my vision. My knees shook and I started to feel untethered, like my soul was a kite rising over Chang'an, past the moun-tains of silk and flute melodies, up toward the faraway clouds. I held onto a cart for balance, then found myself moving for-ward as if the earth had sloped downward. Had the man with pearl skin even been real, or was my mind just hazy from the heat again? I stumbled after him, just to get a closer look, to be certain of what I'd seen.

There was a flash of yellow robes as he turned another corner. I hurried after him, slipping through the crowd, bumping into people who yelled and swore at me, but I only moved faster, as if magnetized. I tracked him deeper into a residential ward, twisting around clotheslines, farther and farther from the carnival on the broad main roads, the sounds of music growing softer.

In the stillness of the street, a high-pitched squeal tore through the air before cutting off abruptly. My footsteps slowed and I pressed a hand to the side of a building for balance.

Then came the smell of blood, so sudden and thick, a wave of bitter salt that stung the roof of my mouth.

A pig's severed head splashed into the road in front of me, its dull brown eyes wide, severed tendons splayed out like jagged ribbons.

I pressed a hand over my mouth to stop from gagging and leaned slowly around the corner, where the man in yellow hunched over the remains of a pig. He knelt in a pool of blood, making an odd watery noise, like the sound of Yufei raising her bowl to her lips and slurping down the last of her soup.

The man froze, the wet noises silencing. He started to turn, but I was already running the other way.

I fled back toward the main street, not quite sure where I was going, just following the music until I burst back onto the main road, panting. I glanced behind me, but the street was empty.

A hand gripped my sleeve.

"There you— Ow!"

Wenshu winced as I twisted his arm.

"Sorry," I said, releasing him.

"This is the thanks I get for finding you?" he said as Yufei approached with three pieces of húbǐng, handing one to me.

"You startled me," I said, gripping the bread so hard that it snapped in half.

"You're breathing fast and sweating," Yufei said, raising an eyebrow.

"I was running," I said, my hands trembling. "I saw a pig's head."

Yufei and Wenshu exchanged a glance. "And it...chased you?" Wenshu said.

I shook my head. "I think a man tore it off."

"You've cut pigs' heads off before," Wenshu said.

"No, this was a *pearl* man."

Wenshu grimaced, then tore off a piece of his bread and jammed it into my mouth. "It's too hot outside," he said. "Let's find some shade."

"I'm not making this up!" I said through the mouthful of bread.

"I didn't say you were," Wenshu said coolly, already walking away. "I just said I wanted to sit in the shade."

I shot Yufei a desperate look, but her face was blank, and she was already hurrying after Wenshu. She whispered something into his ear as they walked ahead of me, then cast a glance back in my direction, not even trying to hide the fact that they were talking about me. I wanted to yell, *I'm not some child you have to wrangle!* but as I stumbled behind them covered in sweat, juggling pieces of bread and shouting about a pig's head, I didn't think I was making a good case for myself.

We sat down underneath a fig tree. Wenshu announced he suddenly wanted water, which Yufei ran off to get, and both of them drank only half of theirs before declaring they were too full and refilling my cup.

I drank just to placate them, my heart finally starting to slow down.

"I think it has something to do with the librarian—"

"Shh!" Wenshu said, looking around before switching to Guangzhou dialect. "Don't talk about that here."

"Will you two *listen to me?*" I said, my voice rising. "I saw a man with pearl skin eating a pig. Don't you think that has something to do with that dead body and my missing pearls?"

"What is pearl skin?" Yufei said, frowning. "Is that an alchemy thing?"

"No. I mean, I don't know. Maybe?"

"Why don't you look it up the next time we're at the library?" Wenshu said. But his voice sounded too distant, too calm. He was frowning at me, like he saw something in my eyes that he didn't like.

"Why don't you believe me?" I said, dropping my gaze so I wouldn't have to look at them.

Wenshu sighed. "Zilan, it's not that we don't believe you," he said. I hated when he spoke for both himself and Yufei. "But whatever is going on, we need to stay as far away from it as possible. We're here for our tests, not to join the royal police."

I glanced at Yufei, because if she disagreed, she'd definitely say so, but she only stared at the dirt like it was the most fascinating thing in the world. It wasn't that I wanted to get all of us in trouble, but if danger was going to find us regardless, I would rather be one step ahead of it—whatever it was.

"Fine," I said, drinking the rest of Wenshu's water to make him happy. I would try to do what he said—mind my own business and pray that disaster conveniently avoided me, as if I hadn't been dreaming about it for as long as I could remember.

# CHAPTER THIRTEEN

On the day of my second-round exam, a royal officer announced the tragic, unexpected deaths of six alchemists from Longyou and three from Huainan. He assured us that all nine had definitely been accidental, and there was no need for us to worry.

But I'd seen the bodies being carried away that morning as I'd crossed over to the eastern wards, and I wasn't sure how you could accidentally get stabbed several times in the back. I wondered if the royal police were actually investigating and just didn't want us to panic, or if this sort of culling was standard in Chang'an. The one benefit of being a merchant from the south was that no one actually expected me to pass, so I didn't have to sleep with a knife under my pillow. At least, not yet.

The officer confiscated our stones and led us deeper into the palace grounds, opening the double doors to a dirt courtyard. Rows and rows of identical barrels sat across the yard in a grid, perfectly spaced like a strange wooden cemetery, trays of alchemy stones beside them. At the far end of the courtyard, the scholar who had given us the tour stood on a wooden podium, once again calling out our names, directing us to stand in front of barrels as they recorded who was still here.

By the time the names from Lingnan were called, only several barrels at the back remained. I ran my hands over the splintering wood, trying to gauge what was inside. Some strange poison for us to neutralize before it ate our flesh? A million little sand crabs that would scurry out and pinch us? After the last round, I truly had no idea what to expect.

"As is tradition, the second round will be proctored by two members of the royal court," the scholar said.

Servants opened a set of double doors near the front, and a woman in silver robes crossed the field, sat in a chair, and folded her arms without waiting for us to bow. She had tan skin and eyes like harvest moons the color of burning amber. A long black braid swung behind her, coming to a sharp point between her shoulder blades. She reminded me of the spiny orb-weaver spiders that sometimes crept into houses down south, carrying blazing red spikes on their backs to ward off predators. As she surveyed the crowd, I couldn't help but feel she wanted to be anywhere but here.

"The Moon Alchemist, head of the royal alchemists," the scholar said, bowing.

I held my breath as the other alchemists dropped into a bow. I'd heard some of the others whispering about her in the courtyard. They'd said that she'd once pulled the moon down from the sky for the Emperor to examine, thus earning her name. As the empire's prized alchemist, legend said she'd eaten gold even longer than the Empress so she'd never have to retire. She could reshape the moon and change the direction of the tides and bring about eclipses on command. Some even said she was the one who'd discovered life gold.

For one dangerous moment, I let myself imagine what it

would be like to train alongside someone like her, to learn the secrets of the universe, to hold the moon in *my* hands. I had tasted power during my resurrections, but surely the Moon Alchemist could teach me things infinitely greater than reviving moldy, rich old men. I folded into a bow and imagined that the dirt beneath my palms was the cool surface of the moon, then pinched myself to banish the thought. First, I had to pass this test.

"And of course," the scholar said, as we rose to our feet again, "the Crown Prince."

The prince rushed into the courtyard as if he'd run here, followed by his guards, and took a seat beside the Moon Alchemist. The other alchemists bowed again immediately, but I was so stunned that I stayed standing for a moment too long, and his eyes met mine across the courtyard. He smiled softly and I immediately dropped to the ground, hiding my face.

Alchemy required concentration, and the last thing I needed was the knowledge that the prince was watching me, comparing me against the tales he'd heard of me. Surely he imagined something much greater than I was. Whatever he saw would be a disappointment.

"As alchemists," the official went on, "one of your main duties is to preserve the eternal life of our kingdom."

*That means gold*, I thought. Of course they would make sure we knew all about gold. Nothing else mattered to the rich.

"The stones you work with are the keys that unlock all of alchemy's wonders," he said, "so you must know them better than your own souls, in darkness or light, at a moment's notice. And the most important stone that you will work with in your service to the Emperor is gold. Please open your barrels now."

I picked up a small hammer from the tray and started tapping the center ring, my hands slowing when I realized none of the alchemists were doing the same. Some had grabbed a few firestones to blast off the lid, but most were staring as if the barrels were exotic animals. Had they never opened one before? These men could conjure fire from air and uproot ancient trees with a single touch, but they didn't know how to open a plain wooden barrel?

I rolled my eyes and kept hammering the center ring. Auntie and Uncle received shipments of red clay and new dyes from the North in barrels like this. I wiggled off the top ring, then pried open the lid with the thin edge of the hammer.

A bright light shined up from inside, warming my face. *Gold.*

More than I had ever seen in my life, thousands of tiny flecks the size of my thumbnail, drinking in the afternoon sunlight and shimmering back at me so sharply that I had to squint. I couldn't help it—I sunk my hands into the barrel, the gold so smooth and cool that it parted for me like water, all the way up to my elbows.

But something was wrong. I picked up a piece and held it up to the sunlight. Its surface felt too firm, too unyielding in my hands. Gold was supposed to be weak and malleable.

"You must be the masters of gold," the scholar continued, once only a few alchemists were still struggling with their lids. "In each of your barrels, every piece is counterfeit except for one. Find it, and present it to me. You may use whatever means you wish, but you have only one chance to guess."

Immediately, the other alchemists took out their stones, sorting through them on the ground. I ducked down and did the same, even though my stomach felt like it was falling be- cause *I had no idea what they were doing.*

I'd looked for fake gold before, but I hadn't needed alchemy for that. Surely there was some sort of alchemical test far more accurate than my methods, or else the other alchemists wouldn't have been looking through their stones. Or was this just a test to make sure we'd handled gold before, that we actually worked with stones and didn't just read about them?

I took a deep breath and closed my eyes, trying desperately to think only about gold and not about the Moon Alchemist's cold stare or the Crown Prince's naive belief in me.

*Focus, Zilan*, I thought. *What is fake gold made of?*

Counterfeit gold was usually pyrite or cheaper metals plated in a thin layer of gold coloring. But I couldn't compare the weights because all the pieces were different sizes. I could try to scrape off the top layer and see if there was any discoloration underneath, but I risked scraping away real gold too.

Something whirred beside me. An alchemist was transforming a lodestone and some clear stones I couldn't quite see. He grabbed a handful of gold from the barrel and set it on the ground. When he held the lodestone to the pieces, they jumped toward it and stuck as if glued. He peeled the pieces away and set them aside, then repeated the process with another handful.

*He made a magnet*, I thought. I knew of magnets in compasses, but I didn't know how to make one and hadn't seen what he'd done with the lodestone. Was that something the other alchemists had studied in school?

The alchemist on my other side jumped back with a yelp, steam rising from the ground. The pile of gold pieces before him sizzled, the air suddenly smelling bitter. He must have poured an acid over the coins, hoping for some sort of reaction, but I didn't know what he was looking for. What was acid supposed to do to real gold that it wouldn't do to fake gold? Wouldn't all of it just melt into a gold soup?

At the front of the yard, one of the alchemists shot to his feet and rushed forward, holding out a gold nugget to the judges with both hands. The Moon Alchemist and the prince leaned forward with interest as the officer rose to inspect it.

*Already?* I thought, my heart sinking.

But the judge merely shook his head, tossing the gold over his shoulder.

"Leave," he said.

The alchemist fell to his knees. "Please, can't I have one more guess?" he said, clinging to the man's robes. But the scholar scoffed and yanked his robes away.

"*Leave,*" he said again. "There is no room for mistakes among the royal alchemists."

The man hung his head low and trudged away as if walking toward his death. That was really all it took to be sent home? One wrong guess and everything was over?

I chanced a glance across the courtyard. It seemed I was the only one who hadn't even taken any gold out of the barrel yet. My competitors were all hunched over their stones, pawing through their barrels. I swallowed down panic, clutching handfuls of cool stones to keep me grounded. Across the courtyard, the prince met my gaze. This time, he wasn't smiling.

I'd be damned if I looked like a fool in front of him.

I took a deep, steadying breath. *Let's do this my way,* I thought.

I grabbed some granite and iron and transformed them into a small cup. Then I picked out three water stones and used them to draw up water from the ground.

*I am in the shop, and old man Gou is trying to cheat me,* I thought. *It's just another day in Guangzhou. Same as always.*

I held a single gold nugget in my hand, rubbing my thumb across it. Already, I knew it felt too light, but I slipped it into my mouth anyway and bit down. When it didn't yield, I dropped it into my cup, watching it float on the top. I glanced up at the barrel, which probably had hundreds of thousands more pieces glinting back at me mockingly. I sighed, setting the first piece to the side.

As I worked, other alchemists started to bring their chosen pieces to the front. About half of them passed, earning the distracting applause of the Moon Alchemist and prince, while the other half were near tears after the court official turned them away. Most of them left with dignity, but several had to be carried out by the prince's guards when they groveled for too long in the dirt. The magnet man beside me passed, while the man with acid to my left didn't.

The sun rose higher in the sky, and in the uncovered court-yard, it beat down hard on the back of my neck. I'd forgotten to bring a hat, so it seared my skin and my hands grew slippery as I worked through the barrel. Little by little, the courtyard began to clear of all other alchemists. I stopped listening to who passed and failed, growing numb to the sounds beyond me, focusing with burning intensity on the gold in my hands.

Someone kicked over my cup, scattering my gold pieces. I glared up at Zheng Sili, his silhouette glowing in front of the sun.

"Oops," he said, smirking as he strolled to the back door, where he gathered his satchel and swung it over his shoulder. I hadn't been paying attention, but surely his smugness meant that he'd passed.

I clenched my jaw and refilled my cup. I couldn't afford to waste my energy on him right now. I was the only alchemist left, and all eyes were on me, burning far more than the sun on my skin.

As the sun rose higher, I found it harder to breathe. Images of the five gates flashed across my vision. I pressed my palms to my eyes as if I could crush the images away. *Not now,* I thought, bracing one hand on the ground so I wouldn't fall over. A sound like thunder roared all around me. I saw bright morning sky, blood spattering against a white road, searing light.

"Is she dead?" the court official asked.

I sucked in a breath. I had slumped deeper into the dirt, face-first.

"Perhaps you should go check on her?" the prince's voice said, a nervous edge to his words.

"If she's dead, she's disqualified and we can go home," the official said, his chair scooting back.

I rose onto my elbows, then snatched my water cup and poured the rest of it down my throat, even though it tasted like dirt and metal, shooting a dark look to the man who had just stood up.

"You are allowed to forfeit!" he shouted across the yard. "The rest of us would like to leave at some point."

I grit my teeth, grabbing three more water stones to refill the cup. "You said nothing about a time limit."

The official grimaced but sat back down without comment, crossing his arms.

I returned to my barrel, which was now almost halfway empty with no sign of real gold. The world fell away and one piece at a time, I sorted through the barrel as the day wore on.

I separated a few pieces into a "maybe" pile, but I knew from touch alone that all the others were fake. I refilled the cup three more times, either to drink it or after knocking it over in my haste. The sun began to descend in the sky, and my whole body felt like a withered flower. As I finally reached the bottom of the barrel, I took a deep breath and rose to my feet.

My legs ached from kneeling and I half expected to fall over before I reached the judges, but somehow I stayed steady as they watched me approach. Both the scholar and the Moon Alchemist seemed furious at having waited so long, but the prince only looked pale and sad.

"Well?" the official said. "What is your guess?"

I swallowed, my trembling hands clenching my skirt.

"All of these are fake," I said.

The official frowned. "I beg your pardon?"

"I said, *all of these are fake!*" I said, the words scraping up my throat. "There was not a single piece of real gold in my barrel!"

The scholar sighed. "Then you have failed," he said, rising to his feet. "What a waste of our time."

My face burned. "Show me the real gold," I said.

He kept walking toward the door, as if I hadn't spoken at all.

"If there's a real piece of gold in there, then show me!" I said. "Otherwise, you're just a liar and a cheat."

The official finally turned around, eyes narrowed.

"Listen here, you—"

"Do as she says," the Moon Alchemist said evenly.

She leaned her chin on one hand, drumming her fingers on her knee. The prince looked frantically between her and the court official, whose face flushed at the command.

"You are not an alchemist, so you could have made a mistake," the Moon Alchemist said, when the scholar didn't immediately move. "Go check and be done with it."

The scholar clenched his jaw, his cheeks so red that I thought he might burst, then stormed off down the path and knelt by my barrel, pawing through my gold.

"Thank you," I said, bowing to the Moon Alchemist.

She looked me up and down, then waved her hand as if my words were inconsequential. Now the scholar would realize his mistake. They would give me another chance. I wasn't a failure, hadn't humiliated myself in front of both the prince and the greatest alchemist to ever—

"Here," the scholar said, coming back up the path, a piece of gold in hand.

My heart sank. "Show me," I said, my voice shaking.

Before he could even agree, I'd snatched the piece from his hand. I pinched it between my fingers, but the shape didn't yield.

"This isn't real gold," I said.

The scholar shrugged. "Clearly, you don't know the difference."

"I know real gold when I see it!" I said. "I'm a merchant, I check for forged gold every day."

"Exactly," he said. "You are a merchant, not a royal alchemist. And that is why you've wasted all of our time pretending you had a chance here. Do you think we didn't notice that you had no clue what you were doing? That you can't make magnets or acid or do water-displacement tests? You may have fooled the backwater judges of Lingnan, but it takes more than luck and audacity to succeed in the royal court."

I stood rooted in place, too stunned to speak. He was wrong. He had to be. But I already felt half-dead from the heat, all my senses muddled, my head pounding from exhaustion. Maybe he was right. Maybe there were kinds of gold I'd never worked with before.

"Go home, hùnxiě," the official said, turning to leave.

My fist clenched around the piece of gold, so strong and firm in my hand, like steel or iron. I thought of my wristband at the first exam, *hùnxiě* scrawled across it like a brand.

They didn't want me to win.

"You're wrong," I said, my whole body trembling. "This gold is too hard. Real gold is malleable. Just feel it!"

"It's malleable enough," the scholar said, waving his hand to dismiss me as he turned away. The Moon Alchemist was already starting to leave, the prince looking morose as he slowly rose to his feet.

*Don't walk away from me*, I thought, my blood burning. *Don't you dare. I am not going home empty-handed.*

I jammed the gold into the back of my mouth and bit down hard.

A sharp *crack* ripped through my skull, a lightning bolt of noise and pain lancing through my jaw. It sounded like the world splitting in half inside my skull, and I didn't know if anyone else had heard it until all three of them spun around.

My mouth filled with a hot rush of blood. I spit out the shattered pieces of my tooth, holding up the bloody—and undamaged—piece of gold.

"You call that *malleable*?" I said.

"Zilan, your tooth!" the prince whispered.

"*I have plenty!*" I said, blood running down my chin.

The scholar had gone pale, taking a careful step away from me. It was the same look the judges in Huizhou had given me when I dared to escape my cage, when they realized that I was a merchant's daughter, and merchants wouldn't let you cheat them out of what they were owed.

"That's enough," said the Moon Alchemist.

She turned toward the scholar, arms crossed, her long shadow eclipsing his stunned face. "Do you think the Empress wants her alchemists losing their teeth because of your incompetence?" she said.

The man shook his head quickly. "There's no need to involve—"

"Do you think she would be pleased if I told her you wasted my afternoon?"

He dropped to the ground in a bow. "Forgive me," he said. "I can assure you—"

"I've had enough of your assurances," she said. Then she faced me, looking me over for a long, calculating moment. "The final exam is in one week," she said at last. "Don't be late." Then she turned away, heading for the door.

I let out a breath. A great lightness filled my chest, so strongly it almost overpowered the ache in my mouth. *I passed.* Only one more test stood between me and my dream. One day, I could be like the Moon Alchemist, with the highest-ranking court officials cowering on their knees before me. I looked up to the darkening sky and prayed that my mother— wherever her soul had gone—could see me now, so far from Guangzhou and so much more than anyone imagined I would become. And I hoped my father was ashamed that his purple weed of a daughter had done the kind of alchemy he thought impossible.

"Zilan xiǎojiě."

I winced at the sound of the prince's voice and bent to gather my stones as if I hadn't heard him. My mouth was really starting to hurt, and I wanted to get out of the prince's sight before I couldn't hide it anymore.

"Let me help you with your tooth," he said, stepping in front of me.

"I didn't ask for your assistance," I said, unable to hold back the bite from my words. I was tired, dried up like a raisin, sunburned, and with one fewer tooth than I'd had this morning. "Am I dismissed, *Your Highness*?"

"No."

My fist clenched around my satchel. *"No?"*

"No, you need to come with me to have your tooth examined first," the prince said, heading toward the door and waving for me to follow. "Please?"

"Is that an order?" I said, crossing my arms.

The prince sighed. "Yes, I'll have you beheaded if you don't let me help you," he deadpanned. "Just come with me, it will only take a moment."

"Tip your head to the side," the healer said, holding out a shallow bowl. I leaned over it as he irrigated my mouth with water, the bowl filling up with red.

He pried my jaw open with one hand while jabbing my gums with some sort of sharp instrument. I winced, my gaze drifting to the prince, who stood to the side looking queasy. He'd brought me to a small sitting area in what I suspected was the healer's private quarters.

The man released my jaw and drew back. "You had tooth fragments in your gums," he said, reappearing with a small cube of gold.

"What are you doing?" I said, flinching away as he tried to put the cube in my mouth.

"Rebuilding your tooth," he said, like it should have been obvious.

"But gold is—"

"It's mixed with copper to make it more durable," the healer said.

But that hadn't been my question. Having gold in my mouth felt like the mark of someone much more important than I was. Back in Guangzhou, some of the rich who ended up on the wrong side of town at night were beaten and had their gold teeth yanked out. More than once, people had paid for míngqì with bloody gold teeth.

"I can do it myself," I said, turning my face from the healer's hands.

He sighed. "You don't want a new tooth?"

"It seems like such a waste," I said. "I'd rather you just gave me the gold and remade my tooth with a rock."

Both the prince and the healer looked at me like I'd suggested amputating my own leg.

"It's just a tooth!" I said. "Plenty of people have no teeth at all."

"Will she be all right without it?" the prince said.

The healer grumbled but nodded, tucking his gold block away and not, unfortunately, handing it to me as I'd hoped. Maybe I should have just let him put it in my mouth, then extracted it later.

"Does it hurt?" the prince said.

"No," I said, bending to put on my shoes so he couldn't see my face.

"If it doesn't hurt, that means the nerve beneath your tooth has died, and we need to fully extract it," the healer said.

I bit back a curse. "It hurts a little," I said.

The prince frowned. "Do you want—"

"No," I said, before he could offer me anything else. I bowed in thanks to the healer, hurried to slip my shoes on, and left the room.

I heard the prince shut the door, his footsteps rushing to catch up with me. "The fastest way out is this way," he said, pointing to my left.

I pushed open the door, expecting another training compound, but froze at the sight of a garden. Two glassy ponds lay in the center of the pale dirt yard, perfect circles in mirror image of each other. Lily pads and yellow flowers speck-led the flat surface, the waters rippling as the largest ducks I'd seen in my life rushed to the edge at the sight of us.

"How many people do those feed?" I asked, incredulous.

The prince's face crumpled. "They're not *food*," he said.

"What, the prince of China is too good to eat duck?"

He glanced at the birds as if they might eavesdrop, then whispered, "I've eaten duck in the past, but not these ones."

"Then why are they so fat?" I said. "What have you done to them?"

He grinned. "Let me show you. Wait here." And with that, he hurried across the garden, disappearing into an ad-jacent building. I considered leaving, desperately wanting to go home and not deal with whatever nonsense the prince was up to, but I wasn't sure how to find the way out from here.

I sighed and squatted at the edge of the pond. All the bloated ducks stared as if judging me.

After a moment, a door slammed open, and the prince re-appeared with a basket in both hands, loaves of bread spill-ing over the top.

"This garden is right next to the kitchens," he said as he jogged toward me. "The cooks give me the stale bread." He knelt beside me and set the basket down, then tore off a piece and tossed it into the pond, where the ducks all converged.

"That one is Shu," he said, pointing to the closest bird. "That one is Cong, that one is Huluobo—"

"You named all of your ducks after vegetables?"

He shook his head. "After their favorite foods."

I pressed a hand for my forehead. Of all the reasons to not be passed out in my bed right now, this was the most ridicu-lous. The prince was certifiably a child.

"Bread is bad for ducks, you know," I said. "You're going to kill them."

The prince's eyes went wide, bread falling from his hands. *"What?"*

"There's no nutrients in it, and soggy bread can make them sick. In all your expensive classes, they didn't teach you that?"

The prince looked so horrified that I almost regretted speaking. "What am I supposed to feed them?" he said.

*What am I, your personal duck farmer?* I thought, but the prince seemed so genuinely devastated that I couldn't bring myself to say it out loud. "Auntie used to feed them seeds and lettuce," I managed.

Without another word, the prince stood up, abandoning the bread and heading for the door.

"At least show me the way out!" I shouted, but he was already gone. I sat heavily in the dirt, but thankfully the prince returned quickly this time. He had a head of lettuce in each hand that he all but hurled into the pond, startling the ducks away with a massive splash.

I stifled a laugh. Maybe the heat and dehydration had really fried my brain beyond repair if I actually found him amusing. "Here," I said, fishing one of the lettuce heads back toward me with a stick and peeling off some leaves. "They like it better this way."

The prince watched with rapt attention as I threw the leaves into the pond. I handed him the lettuce head and he quickly copied me.

"My cousins ask me about the secret life of the royal family," I said. "Now I know that it's just overfeeding ducks."

The prince smiled and shook his head, tearing off another leaf. "The ducks were a present from my father when I was younger. I cried for days when he told me I couldn't be a healer and had to be a prince instead. Father said my metal element was unbalanced and made me eat so much ginger that I cried even more."

"Most little boys actually want to be a prince, you know."

The prince shrugged. "That's what my father said, but apparently I was insufferable."

*"Was?"*

He scowled, but there was no anger behind it. "I'll have you know I am very reasonable."

"'Reasonable' would be eating these fat ducks," I said.

He shot me a flat look. "I could have you beheaded."

"I thought we already agreed that you wouldn't do that," I said, tossing a piece of lettuce at him.

"Circumstances have changed," he said, brushing the leaf from his hair. "My ducks are no laughing matter." He tore off another piece of lettuce, but I shook my head.

"If you overfeed them, they'll lay too many eggs. You'll have a hundred ducks here before you know it."

He pressed a hand over his heart. "If only I were so lucky." Then he stood up and stuffed the leftover lettuce into the bread basket. The ducks started swimming away, probably realizing their food source was leaving. The surface of the pond settled and went still, reflecting the darkening sky, the blurred images of cattails and silver grass, and a shadowed figure on top of the wall.

I looked up from the water to the masked man straddling the dirt wall, backlit in orange light, nocking an arrow and angling it down toward us.

I backed away instinctively, one hand in my satchel, and bumped into the prince. He fell backward with a surprised shout as an arrow lodged itself in his bread basket.

My fingers closed around three pieces of amethyst, which

I crushed against my copper rings and hurled at the base of the wall. The archer's next shot arced up into the sky as the wall shifted and crumbled beneath him. He fell backward off the other side with a crunch.

I grabbed three more stones and stepped forward, my heartbeat loud in my ears, but the flash of blue silk through the settling clay dust and panicked shouting on the other side of the wreckage told me that the guards were handling it.

"Not again," the prince said, sitting up. "Are you okay?"

*"Again?"* I said, hands shaking as I closed my satchel. "This happens often?"

"Often enough," he said, gathering up the lettuce that was starting to roll toward the pond. He didn't sound particularly upset, only tired. "Thank you for your help, but the head alchemist made me a boiled leather undershirt, so please don't take any arrows on my behalf. My organs are safe."

My face grew hot. "I wasn't! I just happened to be standing in front of you! As if I would sacrifice myself for you!"

"Still, thank you," the prince said, smiling. "I think I should send you home before anything more exciting happens. Nightfall is not the safest time to be at the palace."

He picked up the remaining loaves of bread and looked down at them in thought for a moment.

"Do you want this?" he said.

I frowned. "Why would I want your bread?"

"You said I never helped you," the prince said, shrugging, "so maybe this could be a start?"

"Help me?" I echoed, feeling numb. "With bread that you yourself won't eat? That you were going to *feed to the ducks?*" My voice rose the more I spoke, and the prince shrunk back. I had fought my way to Chang'an, even saved the prince's life a moment ago, and yet he didn't see me as anything more than a peasant.

"I thought…" he said quietly, speaking toward the dirt as if he knew my gaze would scorch him. "I just thought it would be better than nothing. I didn't mean to… I can get you fresh bread if you want."

I grabbed one of the loaves from him and ripped it in half, my hands trembling.

"Zilan xiǎojiě?" the prince asked hesitantly.

I hurled both halves into the lake. The ducks descended immediately, swarming around the food, their wings beating frantically, snapping at each other as they fought for scraps. Was that how the prince saw me? Just an animal who would eat whatever garbage he threw to it?

The prince wilted, somehow growing even smaller. "I didn't mean to insult you," he said. "Since we weren't giving it to the ducks, I just thought it was better than wasting it. I didn't—"

"*I am not one of your pets!*" I said. "I would rather starve than eat your scraps!"

"Zilan xiǎojiě—"

"I should have just let that archer skewer you," I said. "What a waste of my stones."

Then I turned and stormed away. I had passed two rounds of the royal alchemy exam—I could find my own damn way out of the palace.

# CHAPTER FOURTEEN

The aftermath of the carnival looked like a storm had blown through the city, red paper littering the ground, the dirt streets uneven from heavy foot traffic, the scent of firecrackers scorching the air. People in the western ward were busy fishing scraps of silk out of the mud to clean and resell.

I spotted a red piece of silk in decent shape jammed into a gutter above my head as my cousins and I walked back to our ward that evening. I plucked it free and quickly tucked it into my pocket, but an old man pawing through the mud had seen me.

"Please, xiǎojiě," he said, "could I have half?"

The three of us walked past him without a word. It was what Uncle Fan had always taught us—*Charity is for the rich. Show kindness once and by nightfall you'll have a hundred people at your door*—but after berating the prince for his lack of charity, I was too aware of the old man's gaze following me down the street.

I shook my head. This was different. The prince had enough wealth to feed a thousand mouths, while my cousins and I would run out of gold by the end of the week if we ate more than one meal a day. It was different because he kept his money for extravagant pets while we spent all ours to stop from starving.

We'd received a letter from Uncle and Auntie earlier that day, saying they were feeling healthier than ever, that they were doing well enough to manage the shop, so we didn't need to worry about sending money—lots of lies that only made us worry more.

Soon, I hoped we could give them enough for at least another month's rent. Wenshu and Yufei had both passed their second-round exams in the top twenty percent of their class, their success in the third round practically guaranteed.

Their final exam required recitation and debate in the Northern dialect. That seemed far easier to me than their written exams, but Wenshu would barely break from studying to eat. Northern words had started bleeding into his speech in Guangzhou dialect and he yelled at me when I pointed it out.

I was more worried for my own test, which I couldn't practice for the way my cousins could. Some of the Northern alchemists whispered that runners-up were sent to other provinces as teachers to make sure the pool of alchemists continued to grow. I couldn't imagine coming this far only to be ordered back to the south.

In the afternoon, Wenshu managed to talk down the price on some burnt rice, which we ate in our room so no one could covet our food. It tasted sharp going down my throat and kept catching in the space where my molar used to be. I told my cousins about the prince's irritating persistence while Yufei licked her bowl clean and Wenshu watched with his arms crossed.

"You shouldn't upset the prince," Wenshu said. "The last thing we need is a powerful enemy."

"He's not exactly the vengeful type," I said, frowning. "He probably just sat in bed and moped after I left."

"Who cares if he's upset?" Yufei said, scooping stray pieces of rice from Wenshu's bowl when she was finished with hers. "He thinks Zilan's a duck."

Wenshu sighed. "I know that death is inconsequential to us, but if someone's trying to kill the Crown Prince, we need to stay as far away as possible."

"It's not like I go looking for him!" I said.

I flinched at the sound of a knock on the door.

"You're too loud!" Wenshu said under his breath as he stomped off to answer it.

The bald man who rented us the room stood in the doorway.

"I'm sorry for my sisters," Wenshu said, bowing. "We'll be quieter."

The man shook his head. "They're burning the húlijīng soon, after the ward is locked," he said. "I'm letting you know as a courtesy—you're travelers, after all. If you don't attend, it looks bad for you."

Auntie So had talked about húlijīng—evil fox spirit shapeshifters—on occasion, but I'd never thought of them as more than folktales.

"There's a húlijīng here?" Wenshu asked.

"Likely more than one, which makes it all the more important that you go," the man said. "There's been trouble here for weeks."

"What sort of trouble?" Yufei said.

The man frowned at a woman speaking to him so casually, but Yufei was probably pretty enough to get away with it.

"Men with their throats slashed open, livestock cut to pieces."

"And you don't think it's wolves?" I said.

The man scowled. "Not unless wolves can scale our twelve-foot walls. Besides, the teeth marks are human."

I thought of the man tearing apart the pig the other day. Had they caught him?

"Let's go," I said, rushing to grab my shoes. This would show my cousins that I hadn't been exaggerating, that the capital really was full of monsters.

It wasn't hard to find the place the old man was talking about—half the ward was already crowded there, packed tightly together and murmuring.

"Why are you so excited?" Wenshu said, grimacing at the mud sticking to his sandals as he stumbled after me, Yufei close behind.

"I'm not excited," I said.

"Any kind of entertainment in this sad city is exciting," Yufei said.

We rounded the corner and found a crowd gathered around a pile of smoldering firewood, mostly the broken pieces of wagons that had rolled through town from the carnival.

But the person tied up in the mud wasn't the man I'd seen the other day. It wasn't a man at all.

A girl, probably no older than me or Yufei, was bound and gagged on the ground, flinching as men poured oil over her pink robes.

"That's not the right person," I said, quiet at first, then louder when no one acknowledged me. *"That's not the right person!"*

"Zilan," Wenshu said, grabbing my arm. "Don't make a scene."

"Why do they think it's her?" I said, yanking my arm away.

"She was seen feeding foxes after dark," a woman beside me said, casting a dirty glance at the girl in question.

"That's *it*?" It wasn't exactly a normal nighttime activity, but I'd done stranger things after dark. These people were just pinning their fears on an innocent person to make themselves feel better.

Two men yanked the girl up by her tied wrists and dragged her toward the wood. She screamed as her bare feet trailed over the smoldering embers.

I was already reaching for the stones in my bag when Wenshu seized my wrist. I shot him a warning look, but he didn't let go.

"If we make trouble here, they'll come for us next," he whispered. "We can't afford to stay in any other wards."

"So we'll sleep outside," I said, trying to tug away, but Wenshu held firm, his eyes like cold granite.

"Sleep outside?" he said. "You want to end up gutted like the librarian?"

I turned to Yufei for help, but she only stared wide-eyed at the girl. She wasn't arguing, which meant she agreed with Wenshu.

The girl screamed as the flames ate across her clothes. Racing comets of fire chased up the length of her hair, her skin dripping like one of the míngqì in Uncle's kiln when the fire burned too hot. A sharp smell cut through the dizzying heat, sweet and leathery, strong enough that I could almost taste it.

Smoke stung my eyes, blurring the street and casting the silent crowd in a ghostly haze. The gray clouds swirled into stormy shapes beyond the bonfire, like a herd of wild horses tearing from a billowing hurricane.

I didn't realize I was leaning into Yufei until she steadied me. She and Wenshu were staring at me, their eyes red from smoke, their backs to the fire.

"We won't end up like the librarian," I said, just to make them stop. "I wouldn't let that happen."

"It doesn't need to come to that," Wenshu said slowly. "Remember why we're here, Zilan."

I swallowed, thinking of the final exam, of Auntie and Uncle so far away, waiting for our money, probably afraid to buy more food until it arrived. I looked at Wenshu and Yufei, the flames reflected in their black eyes, flickering in tandem, their cold expressions exactly the same. I imagined them standing side by side when the Emperor gave them the purple robes of high-ranking scholars in only a few weeks, solidifying their home in Chang'an, with or without me.

*I can't lose them*, I thought, dropping my gaze as Yufei released my wrist. *I would rather die.*

We stood still as the screams fell quiet, the body a blackened pile of embers and bones. Some women and children finally began to leave, so we slipped away with them and headed back to our room.

Yufei and Wenshu both went to sleep not long after, but I stayed up staring at the ceiling, the taste of burnt flesh tacky in my mouth. And when they stopped breathing and the room fell silent, I could hear nothing but my own traitorous heartbeat, could see nothing but the moon casting its dim light across my open palms, like I was holding up handfuls of shimmering pearls.

# CHAPTER FIFTEEN

I woke to someone knocking at our door.

Yufei was already sitting up, holding one of her shoes like a weapon. Wenshu laid dead asleep until Yufei shoved him halfway onto the floor and he woke with a strangled shout.

Moonlight still poured through the open window. It was far too late for this to be anything good. I grabbed the satchel from beside my pillow and pulled out three pieces of iron, clenching them in my right hand.

"Zilan!" someone called from the other side of the door. "Zilan, please let me in!"

My cousins turned to me, Yufei lowering her shoe.

"Who the hell is trying to visit you this late?" Wenshu said, rubbing his eyes.

I groaned, raking my hair out of my face and rising to my feet. I recognized the voice, though I was still half-asleep and couldn't comprehend what on earth he wanted at this hour.

"You can drop the shoe," I said to Yufei, then slid the door open.

The prince stood in the hallway, his pale silk sleeping robes shimmering like moonlight cast over a pond. Yufei gasped, then clapped her hands over her mouth. Wenshu made a startled noise before throwing himself to the floor in a bow.

I rolled my eyes, tugging the prince in by the sleeve and slamming the door.

"Did you actually walk here in pajamas?" I said. "What if someone saw you? And how did you even find me?"

"Zilan!" Wenshu said, rising onto his palms and yanking Yufei down into a bow. "You can't talk to the Crown Prince like that!"

"It's fine," the prince said. "I'm sorry for waking you all, but I need Zilan urgently, so I checked the local register for your address."

"You need her?" Yufei said, raising an eyebrow and sitting up. "In what way?"

"Yufei!" Wenshu said, voice tight.

"In an alchemy way, I'm assuming," I said, stifling a yawn. "I already told you I'm not helping you."

The prince's eyes watered, then, to my horror, he knelt and pressed his face to the floor in a deep bow. Wenshu and Yufei gasped, backing up against the wall.

My skin burned, my bones locked in place. Royalty did not bow to merchants from Guangzhou. The royal family thought they were descendants of gods—they didn't humble themselves for anyone.

"I'm sorry about the bread," he said. "You're right, I never would have given something like that to someone of my status. I understand why you were insulted and I'm sorry."

"S-stand up," I said, still flustered at how the fucking *Crown Prince of Dai* currently had his face on my floor.

He looked up, still kneeling pitifully. "I thought about what I would have given to a princess, but I didn't think you'd want an elephant or a servant."

"*What?* No, no I definitely wouldn't," I said, gaze darting between Wenshu and Yufei, who were watching with thinly veiled shock. "Please tell me you didn't get me either of those things."

He shook his head. "You didn't want a gold tooth, so I assumed you didn't want gold jewelry."

I shook my head. "I don't want anything from you. I—"

"You can eat one of my ducks," he said.

Yufei snorted, clapping her hands over her mouth again.

"Is that a euphemism?" Wenshu whispered.

"No, no, it's not," I said quickly. I turned to the prince. "I was *joking*. I don't want to eat your ducks."

"But I was so rude to you," he said. "It only seems fair."

"Your ducks weren't rude to me! I don't want to eat them!"

"I do," Yufei whispered, before I shot her a murderous look.

"It's a sincere offer. You can have any one of them," he said, even though he looked like he was about to cry. Despite how horrifying the gesture was, I knew that the ducks were probably the only thing of true value to him, and the fact that he was willing to kill one for me was oddly sweet.

I pressed a hand to my forehead. "No, I don't need... You're forgiven, okay? I don't want your ducks, so please *get off the floor.*"

The prince sniffled, finally rising to his feet. "Thank you," he said quietly.

"Don't thank me," I said, still wanting to melt into the floor out of shame that this mess was unfolding in front of my cousins, "just tell me why the hell you came here in the middle of the night in your pajamas."

He grimaced. "It's my sisters."

*His sisters?* As far as I knew, the Empress had only had one daughter, and she'd died as an infant. So who was the prince talking about? Unless he meant his half sisters, who we'd seen on horseback when we first arrived in Chang'an.

"You mean the traitor's daughters?" I said, scrubbing my face, still far too tired for this conversation.

The prince sighed, rubbing his forehead. "Consort Xiao was not..." He shook his head. "It doesn't matter. Yes, that's who I mean. They've been taken to the dungeons."

"That's all?" Yufei said. "We took our first-round exams in dungeons, you know."

"You don't understand," the prince said. "No one leaves the royal dungeons unless they're in a coffin."

I thought back to the little girls racing on horseback, how they'd smiled even when the crowd booed and spit at them. I knew that coffins for girls that size could only hold five or six míngqì before the lids wouldn't shut. I'd seen so many children's funerals on our street, and they never got any easier. They always reminded me of Wenshu and Yufei, of how they could have been in those boxes instead of here with me.

"Isn't your palace full of royal alchemists?" Yufei asked, stepping closer. Her hair cascaded wildly around her face, like the mane of a wild horse.

"Yes, but they're too heavily guarded right now," he said.

"Are you not the Crown Prince of Dai?" Yufei said. "Can't you just order the guards to poke their own eyes out and free your sisters yourself?"

"It's not that simple," he said, grimacing. "The guards don't listen to me."

"Oh no," Wenshu said, switching to Guangzhou dialect and turning to me. "No, no, no. You know what he's saying, don't you?"

I blinked, still half-convinced I was dreaming.

"He's saying he doesn't have the authority to get his sisters out of jail," Wenshu said slowly. "Who has more authority than the Crown Prince?"

"The Emperor," I whispered, a cold pit opening up in my chest.

"Or the Empress," Yufei said.

Wenshu sighed. "I don't know what's going on between you two," he said, "but considering we haven't even passed our final exams yet, it's really not an ideal time to *get involved in a political conspiracy that could get all of us killed!*"

"Plus, what does Zilan stand to gain from this?" Yufei said, not even bothering to switch dialects for some semblance of privacy, instead glaring straight at the prince. "You're asking her to do something dangerous when she has more to lose than you."

The prince's eyes watered. "She's right," he said to me. "I know I'm asking too much of you. I know it's not fair, and if there was any other way, I would take it. But there is nothing I wouldn't do for my sisters. Please, Zilan. I'll give you anything."

*Anything?*

After the bread incident, I didn't think I could stomach any food that the prince bought us. I wanted to feel like my life in Chang'an was my own, not something that he'd handed me. But some things were worth sacrificing my pride for.

"When you first came to Guangzhou, you offered me one hundred thousand gold," I said. "I want you to send that to our parents."

"Of course," the prince said, all the tightness melting from his posture now that I'd agreed.

"Zilan," Wenshu said, "they wouldn't want you to do this for them."

"Then it's a good thing they'll never know," I said, grabbing my dress and pulling it straight over my nightclothes. It was lumpy and too tight, but I couldn't change in front of the prince.

My cousins still looked cross, but at least they'd stopped arguing. Even they knew it was too much money to walk away from. But more than that, I couldn't help imagining Wenshu and Yufei in danger, and the lengths I would go to, the people I would beg to help them if it came down to that.

"I'm going with you," Yufei said suddenly, reaching for her coat.

"No," I said, stepping between her and the coat hook. "It's already risky enough, you said so yourself. Sneaking around is harder with three people than two."

She scowled. "You think I can't take down a couple guards?"

"We can't *take them down*," the prince said, wincing. "The shift changes too often. We'd have guards swarming us at the sight of a dead body. What we need is a distraction."

"I can do it," I said to Yufei. "Just wait for me here."

Yufei crossed her arms and sat down on the floor. "If you're not back by sunrise, I'm coming after you."

I turned to Wenshu, who was worryingly silent. But he wasn't looking at me. He was glaring at the prince.

Wenshu stood up and approached him, and I couldn't help but remember how he'd skewered the magistrate with a fire poker when he'd tried to take me away. He stopped just short of the prince, a breath too close for a commoner to stand before royalty unless they were on their knees.

"You'll bring her back safely," Wenshu said.

The prince nodded quickly. "Of course I will."

Wenshu's gaze didn't waver. He probably would have burned holes in the prince's skin if I didn't interfere.

"Okay, we're leaving while it's still dark," I said, tossing the prince one of Wenshu's coats. Wenshu shot me a dark look, but I rolled my eyes. "Walking around in silver pajamas isn't exactly subtle," I said.

The prince held the hem of his sleeve to slide his arm into the coat, revealing three long scratches stretching down from his collarbone and disappearing under his shirt. He must have caught me staring because he quickly readjusted his collar.

"Problems with your exotic pets?" I said.

The prince grimaced. "Not exactly," he said, fastening the coat closed. "Let's go."

Our ward was mostly quiet at this time of night, and only a few men were still out smoking, the cool winds driving everyone else indoors. They glanced up as we passed, gazes lingering on the shimmering silk of the prince's sleeping clothes, but they made no comment.

I wondered how we'd make it out of the ward, but the prince pulled out a key from his sleeve and quickly unlocked the gate for me.

"It's a skeleton key," he said at my confused expression. "The city belongs to my family, after all."

I sighed. "Of course."

In the darkness, the main street looked vast, an ocean of shadows yawning wider as we drew closer. The gaping mouths of the five gates seemed even larger at night, as if breathing us in. I started to turn away, aiming for where I normally walked to the palace grounds, but the prince carried on straight toward the five tunnels.

"We're taking the shortcut," he said, jingling his keys.

He moved faster, waving for me to follow him up the stone stairs. Our footsteps echoed across the hollow street, but no matter how much I kept climbing, I never seemed to come closer to the top, like it was expanding forever upward. The black doorways loomed larger, eating the rest of the night sky until everything above me was a vast emptiness, the scent of dampness and moss. A sharp pain lanced through my head and I took another step but the ground dissolved beneath me. I leaned back for balance, my foot slipping off the stair—

A hand closed around mine.

I was kneeling on the steps, the prince clutching my hand.

*I could be killed just for touching him*, I thought as his grip tightened, strong and steady.

"What's wrong?" he asked. But my whole body felt numb and I couldn't figure out how to form words. Images came in flashes—the dark, gaping tunnels, hot bursts of bright sunlight, howling wind and hurried footsteps.

"Are you unwell?" the prince said, his warm hands cupping my face.

"No," I said at last, the word dry and cracked as it fell from my lips. "No, this just…this happens sometimes."

"This isn't the first time?" the prince said, frowning. "Zilan, have you seen a doctor?"

"Zilan *xiǎojiě*," I said reflexively, rising to my feet even though my joints felt loose. "We can't stay out in the open like this."

The prince's lips pressed into a tight line, but he took my arm and helped me up the rest of the stairs without further comment.

"I think I should take you back to your siblings," he said, once I stumbled up the last step.

"And then what would happen to *yours*?" I said, pushing him back when he reached for me again. "I'm fine."

As if to prove it, I turned and stormed forward into the tunnel. The prince sighed and hurried after me.

The darkness of the tunnel fell swiftly over us, like a cool curtain of night.

"This way," the prince whispered, his voice pulling me deeper into the heavy shadows. Eventually, the pale light from the city behind us grew so small that I could no longer see it, and my eyes adjusted to the stony darkness. The prince stopped at an iron gate that stretched all the way up to the rounded ceilings, then quickly unlocked it and shouldered it open with a rotting creak that made both of us wince.

The gate swung shut behind us, the lock latching, and a cold sense of finality washed over me. I felt like I was back in Huizhou, trapped inside the cage, hands reaching out for me from all sides. But there was no time to think too deeply on it because the prince was already moving into the next tunnel, one hand against the wall.

"I'm sorry about the darkness," he said. "I was in a bit of a hurry and forgot to bring a candle, but I know the way."

"How can you possibly know the way?" I said, scurrying closer to him when his footsteps drew farther away, irrationally afraid that I'd be left alone in here.

"I have to," he said. "These tunnels are a way to escape if the palace is ever attacked. Our enemies would be lost in the maze forever, but my family and I could escape in minutes."

He drew to a stop as the wall beneath his hands curved away and let out a disconcerting sound of contemplation.

"Don't tell me you made a wrong turn," I said.

"I did no such thing," he said, too quickly. "I am pausing to appreciate the beauty of these tunnels."

"While your sisters are locked in a dungeon?"

"Yes, I suppose that's unwise. We should go to them now, which means we should go...left."

He turned sharply down the left tunnel, walking faster.

"I can't believe I'm risking my life for you, of all people," I said.

We walked farther and farther into the darkness until eventually the air grew cooler and tasted less like dirt. We emerged in what appeared to be a vegetable cellar, behind a fortress of barrels crammed full of potatoes. The prince unlocked the gate and pushed it open, shoving barrels out of the way until we could cram ourselves through.

"I told you I knew where we were," he said, locking the gate behind us.

"The fact that the door was barricaded with potatoes means this wasn't the way you came," I said.

"Well, no, but I know where we are *now*."

He headed deeper into the cellar, waving for me to follow him. We passed barrels of carrots, shelves stuffed with bunches of green onions, bags of taro roots, sacks of rice. I hoped that most of it was to feed the servants and wasn't wasted on the royal family, who mostly ate gold.

We emerged into the garden, where the prince's ducks rushed toward us, expecting food. He shushed them and dashed through the closest door, keeping tight to the walls. I barely caught a glimpse of a guard disappearing around a corner before the prince hurried down a long, narrow path, deeper into the palace grounds than I'd ever been before.

The sounds of ducks splashing in the ponds and the stomping feet of guards grew quieter, the lanterns lighting the pathway spaced farther and farther apart, shadows stretching wider between them. The sloped roofs of the central palace loomed overhead, towering higher the closer we came.

The prince suddenly yanked me down another path, crushed me against a dirt wall, and clapped a hand over my mouth. Before I could protest, I heard footsteps crunching nearer. The prince's hand fell away and he pressed himself closer to me as a guard approached, both of us wrapped in deep shadows, as far as we could get from any lantern. His arms caged me against the wall, cool clay against my back and his warm chest and racing heartbeat flush against my front. I turned my head away so my face wasn't buried in the fabric of his coat, but I could still hear him swallowing nervously, could see the tense line of his throat, his hair blowing across my eyes with the whispered scent of soap and rice water.

The footsteps reached the mouth of the pathway and the prince held his breath, tucking my face against his throat. Maybe it was the sudden warmth in the cool night, but something about his closeness made me want to melt into him, to forget about the danger around us and trust that, for this one moment in this city with teeth, I was safe.

Once I could no longer hear anything but the prince's heartbeat, he pulled away and smoothed out his clothes. I brushed off my dress without even looking at it, feeling like I'd resurfaced from deep underwater, unsure what to do or say.

"Sorry," he said at last, looking down the mouth of the path rather than at me. "The guards were... And I was..."

"Scared like a baby deer?" I said.

"Um, I suppose that's fair," he said, waving for me to follow him back to the main path. "At least we're not dead."

"As if the guards would hurt you for walking around your own palace," I said.

The prince frowned. "Of course they wouldn't hurt *me*," he said.

"Then why—"

"Quiet, we're approaching another guard post."

We hurried down a smaller passageway to the left, which opened up to a clean-swept compound with small houses aligned in rows, surrounded by ginkgo trees trimmed into perfect spheres. To the right, there was a gray stone building with a towering green door and no windows, just an endless line of bricks with two guards stationed in front of it. I only got a quick glimpse before the prince pulled me back behind the wall.

"They've imprisoned my sisters in there," he whispered. "I saw them dragged off from my windows. Can you get us past the guards?"

I bit my cheek, thinking. The prince had already said it wasn't wise to simply attack the guards, and judging by how silent the inner palace was, I was inclined to agree. At the sound of fighting, every guard nearby would come running.

Which meant I needed to send the guards somewhere else.

As a child, I'd sometimes been able to keep Uncle and Auntie away from my resurrection practice by leaving snake boxes outside the pigpen to scare them off. But something told me that the palace guards wouldn't run away from danger but toward it. If I could create some sort of emergency, the guards would have to abandon their posts to attend to it.

"What's inside that house?" I said, pointing to the building closest to the dungeon, just across the yard. A gingko tree towered over it—if it happened to fall, the roof would cave straight in.

"I think that's where some guards sleep," the prince said.

I grimaced. I didn't want my fake catastrophe to actually kill anyone. "All of these buildings have people in them?" I asked.

The prince shook his head, pointing to the houses with thatched roofs farther to the left. "The inner ones are military storage."

"Like swords?"

He shrugged. "Swords, gunpowder, crossbows. Things they don't want the outer court to have access to."

"Gunpowder?" I said.

"Yes, it's an explosive that the military uses in—"

"I know what gunpowder is," I said, scowling.

I knew because royal military parades through Guangzhou were bright, expensive displays of burning lights that cast sparks on our dry roofs, tearing flames through our city before the procession headed back north to proclaim their message of glory delivered. I knew that thatched roofs were flammable, and gunpowder burned up fast once touched by fire. If a thatched roof caught fire, it would collapse quickly, and if a storehouse full of gunpowder went up in flames, the guards would need to put it out immediately, or they would have an empty storehouse to answer for.

I jammed my hands into my satchel and retrieved three firestones, then pulled off one of my socks and balled it up with the firestones inside. "Okay, I've got a plan. You might want to close your eyes."

"Are you sure—"

But he never finished his sentence, because I'd already ignited the sock and hurled it across the courtyard.

# CHAPTER SIXTEEN

The sock struck the top of the storehouse like a falling comet, and with a white flash, the whole roof burst into flames. I'd seen far worse fires start from far less in Guangzhou. The dim courtyard was suddenly alight with blazing orange, the fire roaring and churning smoke into the night.

The prince shielded his face, but I didn't look away until I saw the guards rushing through the smoke toward the burning storehouse.

"Come on!" I said, grabbing the prince's sleeve and yanking him across the courtyard before more guards could come running and spot us.

I coughed, stones slipping through my sweaty fingers as I wasted precious seconds fumbling with the lock. But with a few firestones, it unlatched and we rushed into the dungeons, slamming the door shut behind us.

The sounds of fire faded, the air suddenly cool and moist. We stood in a shadowed hall of slick stone walls covered in ominous black fungus, lit only by sputtering candles on the far ends that cast sickly circles of gray light across the doorways.

"No guards?" I said, rubbing the sting of smoke from my eyes.

"Only on the outside," the prince said. "They say the mold in here makes them sick."

"Wonderful," I said, already feeling like the air was coating my throat in slime. The prince hurried to the left, nearly skidding on the wet stone floor. He grabbed a candle from the wall and rushed down a spiral staircase, slipping on the last step as we emerged into a long, dark hall of cells with bamboo bars.

I hesitated in the doorway, even as the prince ran forward. I knew this scent.

This was the stench of corpses with teeth rotted from bloody vomit, skin spoiled with sores. As shops in Guangzhou shuttered with black X's painted across their doors, I had to charge half price for dead children because there were just so many of them. It was an illness that answered to no one, that stopped at nothing. Sick bodies started to rot even before they died, and they smelled like this.

"Yiyang!" the prince called out. "Gao'an!"

Formless whispers floated up from the cells, murmurs of pain or thirst, but nothing that told us where the princesses were.

The prince slipped his candle between the bars to peer inside. Most of the prisoners cowered, hair draped over their faces, shielding them from the light. What unspeakable horrors had these people done to end up here? Was I walking among Chang'an's most dangerous murderers with nothing but bamboo between us?

The prince's expression hardened as he moved down the hall, calling for his sisters. He was hurrying farther away with our only candle, so I plucked another from the wall and quickly lit it with some firestones.

A hand shot out from the closest cell, grabbing my sleeve, tearing the fabric. I gasped and pulled backward, breaking the weak grip easily, but my candle tumbled to the ground and extinguished itself in a puddle.

Through a cool sliver of moonlight pooling through the barred window, I caught a glimpse of a light brown eye with flecks of green.

Auntie So had always said my eyes were like honey, not warm and dark like my cousins'. *It's because of your father*, she'd said. I'd never seen anyone else with such light eyes, but of course, I'd never met anyone else with a Scotian father. Only foreigners had green eyes.

"You're an alchemist," the voice said. A man's voice, so distant that it was hardly there at all. He didn't sound like a foreigner.

I snatched my candle, edging away from him.

"It's all right," he said. "I am too. Or, I was."

*He's lying*, I thought. The prince had already said how much the Empress liked "collecting" alchemists, that she wouldn't hurt us because she needed us for her precious life gold.

"Touch me again and I'll break your hand," I said, fishing for more firestones.

The man shook his head, curled hair falling over his face. "I don't mean any harm," he said. "But I saw you walking with the prince."

"You saw *nothing*," I said through gritted teeth. I hadn't planned on killing anyone tonight, but if this man kept talking, I might have to.

He sighed, hunching over, sharp shoulder blades jutting from his back. "It's not as if anyone would listen to me, even if I told them," he said. "Once you get on the royal family's bad side, no one believes anything you say. You need to stay away from them."

"I don't take advice from people rotting in dungeons," I

said, lighting my candle. I only caught a quick glance of the man's gaunt face before he drew back at the sudden brightness.

"You want to be one of their lapdogs, don't you?" he said, his greasy hair shielding him so I could see only the gaunt silhouette of his profile. "They don't want your alchemy. They want your *soul*."

Cold rushed through me in a violent wave, my hand clenched against the wet stones. I rose to my feet, my skirts soaked through, and hurried after the prince. I didn't need warnings from a starving, disgraced alchemist probably hallucinating from all the mold and spores growing in the dungeon. Clearly, I could handle myself better than him. I was the one outside the cage.

"Zilan!" the prince called from the other end of the hallway.

When I caught up to him, he was kneeling on the ground before a cell, clutching two pairs of pale hands reaching through the bars.

Two round faces peered through the darkness, their bright skin smudged with dirt, streaked through with tears. I recognized them from the procession, but up close, I could see the way their faces glimmered with gold flecks, hinting that they were older than they appeared. They had papery pale complexions, sweet and smooth like newly bloomed azaleas, moon eyes, and full cheeks.

"Did they hurt you?" the prince said.

The girls shook their heads. "We're okay, but it's cold and wet in here," the older one said. The other one had angled herself toward me.

"Is this your girlfriend?" she said.

The prince let out a stiff laugh. "Umm—"

*"No,"* I said, frowning. "Don't say *umm* like you need to think about it!"

"I just didn't know what to call you!" the prince said. "You're my…" He turned to his sisters. "She's my… Well, we met—"

"I'm Fan Zilan," I said, before he could waste more time. "I'm getting you out of here."

I had so many questions about why the princesses were even here in the first place, but I knew we didn't have much time before the guards put out the fire.

"You're paying to replace all the stones I've used tonight," I said to the prince, digging out three more metalstones and warping them into a key. I didn't want to break the locks—hopefully, when guards realized the princesses had escaped, they would assume someone had taken their keys rather than used alchemy to blast free.

The doors swung open and the girls hurried out, crushing themselves against the prince. He wiped their faces with his sleeve and took one girl under each arm, ushering them to the door at the end of the hallway. By the time we emerged, the courtyard was completely shrouded in smoke.

The fire was mostly extinguished, but still smoldered warningly, embers flaring on what remained of the thatched roof. Guards and servants had spilled outside of the nearby houses to see what happened, so it wasn't difficult to slip past them unnoticed and make our way back down to the vegetable cellar.

"Where are we going?" the younger girl said to the prince as he locked the gate behind us.

"The nuns at the eastern convent can hide you," the prince said. "We can walk you halfway there, but then Zilan and I need to return before my absence becomes suspicious. It's a straight line from the midpoint, anyway."

"How long will we stay there?" the older girl said, clutching the prince's sleeve so hard that I worried she'd tear Wenshu's coat.

The prince didn't answer at first, our footsteps clattering across wet stones. "I'll send for you when it's safe," he said quietly. It wasn't a real answer, and I was sure the girls knew it, because they didn't ask again.

We hurried through the dark labyrinth for so long that I started to feel like I was sleepwalking, my numb legs shuffling forward on their own. When we reached a juncture of five tunnels, the prince pointed to the one farthest to the left.

"Continue straight until you see sunlight," he said, bending down to hug the girls. After peeling herself from the prince, the younger one crushed my legs in an embrace, making me stumble backward.

"Thank you for helping us," she whispered.

"I... Don't mention it," I mumbled, too aware of the prince's eyes on me.

Then the girls rushed off, and it was only me and the prince standing alone in the heavy darkness. As their footsteps retreated, the prince made no move to turn back, staring off into the tunnel that had swallowed them whole.

"The last time my mother sent a family member to the dungeons, they came out in pieces," he said, the words quiet. "Their body was chopped up and crammed into barrels of wine, which my mother served at a party. That's what I was expecting."

A weak wind shuffled leaves at our feet. I took a small step closer to the prince.

"You think your mother sent your sisters to the dungeon?" I asked.

"She's the only one who could," he said. He turned around, his expression tight, gaze focused sternly on the tunnel behind me. "My father is too ill."

"But why would she—"

"Zilan xiǎojiě," he said, his voice low, "if I tell you this, you cannot repeat it to anyone."

Something about the graveness of his voice unnerved me. The gold flecks in his eyes had never looked quite so sharp. But it was far too late to go home and pretend I had no part in this. "We have enough secrets to bury the both of us," I said. "What difference is one more?"

The prince nodded, letting out a tense breath. "There are things that I'm not supposed to remember," he said. "I was very young when it happened, and everyone thinks I've forgotten. But I could never forget how it sounded. And the silence that came after." He pressed his eyes closed, shaking his head. "They say that Yiyang and Gao'an are the traitor's daughters. But I was there when my sister died, and their mother did not kill her. *My* mother did."

The traitorous words echoed through the tunnel and fell quiet again before I could even begin to understand, much less believe them.

"The Empress?" I said slowly. "Why would she kill her own daughter?"

"Because she wasn't the Empress yet," the prince said. "It was easy to blame it on my father's other concubine. He had her jailed and married my mother, who became the Empress."

I closed my eyes, already wishing he hadn't told me. People had probably died to keep this a secret. I already had enough people wanting me dead—I didn't need to add another reason.

"I am the Crown Prince because of what she did," he said. "I thought that was what she wanted—a son to secure her position as Empress. I thought that meant I was safe." He shook his head. "But the servants say that she's begged my father to change the line of succession, to write me out of it so that if he dies, the empire belongs to her alone."

"And has he?"

"No, he's always refused. But..."

A breeze rushed through the tunnel and the prince looked up sharply, as if expecting someone to appear. I couldn't help looking over my shoulder, but saw nothing other than endless dark.

The prince sighed, gripping the ends of his sleeves. "Two months ago, something changed. I don't know why, but my mother seemed...uneasy. Death notices started coming in from my cousins, all over China. Everyone in the House of Li was turning up dead. Every day, my meals were poisoned. I lost twenty taste testers before I fled to Guangzhou to find you. Even now, I'm scared to eat. I hardly sleep. I've been attacked..." He trailed off, and in the dim light, I could make out the glossy scar tissue of the scratches near his throat. "I told Mother, but she wasn't concerned at all. I think... I think now that she's survived a century on life gold, she's realized that she doesn't need me to stay in power. She can be the Empress forever if there's no one left but her when my father dies."

I swallowed, though my throat felt full of rocks. When I'd lived in Guangzhou, the royal family had always seemed so untouchable. I had thought the rich had no problems, no worries, no fears.

"Have you told the Emperor?" I asked.

"No," he said. "I'm not even allowed to see him anymore. The healers say he's too ill, and since I'm the only legitimate heir, they can't risk me catching it. Do you understand what I'm saying, Zilan?"

His eyes blazed, begging me to say the treasonous words he had so long avoided. In the tunnels, where wet stones carried our voices into a secret darkness, the thought seemed almost too dangerous to speak. But I had to be certain. "You came to me because the Empress wants you dead," I whispered.

He nodded, his lips pressed into a tight line. "Yiyang and Gao'an are very far down in the line of succession. If she's trying to kill them now, that means that there's almost no one left but me."

Something splashed in the puddles behind us.

The prince moved in front of me, pressing me into the wet stone walls. I held my breath, but before I could speak, a rabbit hopped in front of us, darting down another tunnel. The prince let out a shaky breath.

"Please don't tell anyone what's happened here tonight," he said, huddling closer to me. "I suppose your siblings already know part of it, but no one else can. It puts all of you in danger."

"Don't worry, I'm not interested in angering the Empress," I said. He stood so close, the gold flecks in his eyes the only light in the darkness. The secret that had begun our relationship had somehow kept growing. Ever since the day I met him in Guangzhou, I'd felt my life starting to unspool, flying fast and far away from me. So much more was at stake now, and a wiser person would have fled.

But I thought about the prince walking through the labyrinth of the central palace in the dark, surrounded by guards who wouldn't listen to him and a mother who wished him dead. Did he even know how to fight?

"Are you really safe in the palace?" I said.

He shrugged. "I wander a lot at night, so I'm not easy to find. I have guards and taste testers and many locks on my doors. But I think that once I'm the last one on her list, the Empress will come for me, and I won't be able to stop her." He looked back at the tunnel where his sisters had disappeared into the shadows, then back at me, a gentle lie of a smile creasing his tired face.

"It's late," he said. "I should take you home so I can return before sunrise. I can't have anyone knowing I rescued my sisters. They'll likely suspect it anyway, but I don't want to give them any evidence."

With that, he turned and walked past me. I followed after him, beginning to feel the lack of sleep catching up to me. I hugged myself as a cold wind wafted through the tunnels, fingers catching at the torn sleeve where the prisoner had grabbed me.

"There was an alchemist in the dungeon," I said.

The prince didn't even slow down. "I'm not surprised."

"I thought you said the Empress didn't want to waste alchemists?"

"There are noblemen, and servants, and—as you saw—princesses down there too," the prince said. "If the Empress doesn't like you, it doesn't matter who you are. She'll make sure you never see sunlight again."

# CHAPTER SEVENTEEN

For days, I avoided the royal court, sure that if anyone saw me, they would drag me away in chains, gut me with a spike, and prop me outside the testing grounds as a warning to everyone else.

"If that happened, you would deserve it," Wenshu said, but he and Yufei humored me all the same, staying in our room to study. Yufei was clearly growing restless and went on long walks after every meal. She told us that more animals had turned up dead in the ward, but no more humans. Yet.

Wenshu still seemed put off by my midnight trip to the palace, hardly looking at me for days, leaving his coat that the prince had borrowed on the hook untouched as if soiled. Both he and Yufei had been so busy quizzing each other, talking over their texts, that at times it seemed they'd forgotten I was there at all. They barely acknowledged when I offered to get food, and Wenshu snapped at me if I interrupted for "pointless" reasons. I stormed out one night after he scolded me, shivering and staring up at the moon from the yard for an hour, and neither of them had looked for me, too busy practicing their recitations. Part of me wished I'd studied the classics like them, rather than trying to be an alchemist. What good were all my transformations if they put me a world away from my family?

It would be easy for them to live without me if I failed my exam. For me, being without them felt like clutching at driftwood in a nauseous sea, but they would always have each other, even if I was gone.

When three days passed without anyone breaking into our room and dragging me off to be executed, I started to think that maybe, just maybe, I was safe.

Then a man came from the royal palace.

Wenshu answered the door, jolting back at the sight of a royal guard. Yufei stood up with a scroll, ready to bludgeon him, but the man bowed and held out a wooden box.

"Delivery for Fan Zilan," he said.

Wenshu shot me a withering look, then accepted the box with both hands and dismissed the guard. He set it on the floor and crossed his arms while I untied the ribbon.

The box was full of red silk embroidered with gold cranes. Cranes were a symbol of eternity, a common image in the royal court full of gold eaters. I lifted the fabric and shook it out, the design flickering in the sunlight, as if the cranes were flapping their wings. Several gold coins fell out of the folds of the fabric, followed by a note that spiraled to the floor.

Zilan xiǎojiě,
Sorry about the guard, but I'm being watched very closely and can't come to you. Mother is suspicious but has no proof of my involvement.

You need to burn the dress you were wearing that night. A scrap of it was found on the dungeon floor and mother is searching the court for the owner.

I'm sending you this dress, partially because I'm not sure if you own more than one and understand that you can't exactly come naked to your alchemy exam, and partially because I can't just send a letter, or the guards will read it.

If you already have enough dresses or don't like this one, you can give it to your sister or sell it. I asked a servant if she thought it was ugly and she said no, but she was probably afraid I would behead her if she upset me, so I don't know how honest her answer was. But please know I have endeavored not to send you ugly clothes.

I probably won't be allowed out to see your final exam, but I know you will pass.

All my best,
Li Hong

PS: I have ordered 100,000 gold to be sent discreetly to your home address in Guangzhou, which I got from the census records. Apologies if this is presumptuous.

PPS: You asked me to pay for the stones you used, so I sent 1,000 gold. I'm not sure if this is enough? Let me know next time if not.

I sighed, holding the note over a candle until the flames devoured it.

"What kind of fool signs a treasonous note with both his real name and mine?" I said. "I don't know how he's stayed alive this long."

"At least it came with a present," Yufei said, holding up the dress. "If you're going to risk your life for him, you might as well get something nice out of it."

"Is it really so easy to win girls over?" Wenshu said, grimacing. "If I send a girl a pretty dress, will she forgive me for putting her life at risk?"

"You've literally sent girls buckets of fertilizer before," Yufei said. "You don't understand how girls, or gifts, work."

"Fertilizer is a very useful gift, unlike silk dresses."

"Well, I can't wear fertilizer to my final exam," I said, gesturing for Wenshu to turn around so I could take my dress off. It was the only clothing I had besides my nightgown, which I didn't particularly want to wear to my exam, so it seemed the prince would have his way.

The material felt cold on my skin, like a river running down my arms. The skirt tied high on my chest with gold ribbons, the sleeves hanging past my fingertips. I'd never in my life worn so much fabric—every time I turned, the skirt rustled, a thousand folds of silk whispering as they spun around me.

"Oh no. You like it," Yufei said. "You have expensive taste now."

"I don't like it," I said, rolling the sleeves up and looking away. "It's all I have to wear now, so I will wear it."

"What a pity," Yufei said, shooting me a knowing smile.

On the day of my final exam, I expected everything but fairness. I filled my pockets with three of every stone I had, bound knives under my clothes, and arrived at dawn. I wouldn't put it past the royal court to change the time and "forget" to inform me, so I needed to arrive there first.

*This is it*, I thought, my heartbeat traitorously loud as I approached the building. All the money we'd saved in Guangzhou for years, all the corpses I'd had to manhandle, all the nights of too-thin soup and secrets and shame could end today.

Yufei had tried to force cucumbers down my throat, but my stomach had felt so tight and small that I was sure I'd be sick if I had anything more than water.

For a moment, I allowed myself to imagine being a royal alchemist. Not an orphaned hùnxiě from the dirty south but a member of the imperial court. I thought of standing beside the Moon Alchemist with her sharp and perfect edges, her presence that demanded respect. I thought of Auntie and Uncle buying a new house and bragging to their neighbors that their daughter—not their niece—was a royal alchemist who sent them all the money they could ever want.

More than anything, I thought of Wenshu and Yufei. I'd barely even said goodbye to them this morning because they were both whispering over their scrolls, words and concepts that made no sense to me. Soon, they would trade in their hemp rags for purple silk robes and begin their new lives. I could either pass my test and stand beside them, or leave Chang'an alone.

For a terrible moment, I saw a future where Wenshu and Yufei walked to their offices together side by side and forgot about the sister they used to have, half a world away.

No. That would not be my life.

I had freed the prisoners under the nose of the Empress, I had brought back the dead from the river of death, and I would not let a coward like Zheng Sili stand beside the Moon Alchemist in my place. I would surpass my father's skills and leave this palace as a royal alchemist, just as I'd told the prince all those months ago. I would stay here with my family.

As the sun rose higher, more and more alchemists began to gather outside the gates. Some of them paused to stare at me, frowning like they didn't know who I was, and I remembered that I was wearing the silk dress from the prince, red as dawn. Did they see me as one of them, or as a child playing dress-up? It didn't matter. None of them mattered anymore.

Soon, the guards opened the gates, and all of us filed inside. I remembered the first day, when there had been enough of us to fill the courtyard. Now there was hardly more than a dozen.

A guard led us deep into the palace, past the courtyard where the second exam had taken place. Soon I could no longer hear the sounds of the streets at all, as if we'd crossed into another world entirely.

At last, we reached a small courtyard filled with rows of wooden tables. The guard directed me to a table full of glass jars containing every stone in existence, the exact same setup as the other tables. But even knowing that I was being treated equally, I couldn't relax. Surely they were going to put me at a disadvantage again. Because the alternative was that the test was so difficult that they didn't think I could pass.

Zheng Sili was one of the few remaining alchemists, at a table on the far end. I shot him a glare harsh enough to corrode metal, but he looked ill and didn't seem to notice. The official who had overseen the previous rounds was nowhere to be seen. I hoped he'd been fired.

The doors to the inner courtyard swung open, and the Empress herself emerged just as day was breaking over the horizon.

She wore a dress of pure gold silk, a train of it flowing behind her in a shimmering river. She was beautiful when I'd first seen her from a distance, but up close, she looked ethereal, like the sun itself had descended to earth and all of us were wildflowers hopelessly bending toward her light. She could more easily pass as the prince's sister than his mother, with the same knifelike sharpness to her features, the same round golden eyes. Guards and servants followed close behind her as she took her seat in a golden throne at the front of the yard. All of us dropped to the ground, bowing, and I was grateful for the chance to hide my reaction.

This was the woman who had destroyed the House of Li, who wanted the prince dead, who had tried to kill his little sisters. Rage burned inside me, and I bowed for a second longer than necessary, careful to iron out my expression to not betray my thoughts.

"As all royal alchemists report to me, it is only appropriate that I supervise the final exam," the Empress said, her voice echoing against the stone walls, pinning me in place. "However, this exam will be different from the previous ones."

The courtyard fell still, no one even daring to breathe as we waited for the Empress's next words.

"I am sure none of you know what to expect for today's test," the Empress continued. "This is intentional. The work we do here, and what we ask of you, is confidential. It will remain a secret of the House of Li, now and forever. That is why those of you who do not succeed today will not be leaving my palace."

My whole body went numb, like I was about to faint again, but my bones were locked tight in place, feet rooted to the ground. The runners-up couldn't leave? What were they meant to do in the palace? Become servants? I glanced at the other alchemists, their carefully controlled expressions, the fear bright in their eyes. No one was brave enough to ask for clarification.

"Now that you know this," the Empress said, "I will give you one last chance to leave. You may forfeit your chance and walk away freely to do whatever you want with your life. Aside from practicing alchemy, that is. This privilege is reserved for my alchemists alone. If you wish to leave now, no one will stop you."

I swallowed and gripped the edge of the table, thinking of how I hadn't even said a real goodbye to Wenshu and Yufei this morning. What would they do if I never came home?

*Would they even care?* a bitter voice whispered in my ear. I clenched my jaw and shoved the thought down. I needed to get home to them, but I couldn't come back empty-handed, stripped of my right to do alchemy.

I would return to them as a royal alchemist, or not at all.

The Empress waited for a long, breathless moment, but none of the other alchemists moved.

"All right," the Empress said. "Now that we're finished with formalities, we can begin. I have only one task for you today. If none of you can do it, then none of you will pass. No one has succeeded in the last four years."

I tasted sweat on my lips and tried to still my shaking hands. What kind of challenge was so impossible?

"Before you are the hundred most common stones used in alchemical transformations," the Empress said, gesturing to the tables. "If you desire any that aren't here, you may ask for them, and they will be provided to you."

*Any stone I could ask for?* Surely that would make this easy.

"Your task," the Empress said, her lips curling into a vicious smile, "is to create life."

At first, I thought I'd misheard her. But the deathly silence of the other alchemists, their gray expressions and petrified gazes, only confirmed it. The echo of her impossible request faded away, trees shifting above us as if unsettled by her words.

Life alchemy was strictly forbidden in all of China by the Empress herself. But apparently her own alchemists were exempt from her rules. That explained her secrecy.

But legality aside, this wasn't something even the wealthiest scholars could study. No one would dare publish writing on this kind of alchemy. If she'd given me a dead person, or even an animal, I'd be finished in moments, having done it a thousand times over. But we had nothing but stones to use as catalysts. How could we create life where none had ever existed? Was that even possible? Surely the cost would be too high.

The sudden silence in the courtyard told me the other alchemists were probably thinking the same thing. None of them so much as breathed, their eyes flickering across the stones as if the answer would reveal itself.

"Do not dare present me with a plant," the Empress said, rolling her eyes. "I want to see a living, breathing creature. Only the first one of you to succeed will pass."

I swallowed, glancing at the remaining alchemists. I'd always thought I was a good alchemist, but I knew I wasn't the best. I had clawed my way here through anger and luck and determination, but that couldn't possibly be enough to finish first.

"Do you have any questions?" the Empress said.

"Can we have any other materials besides stones, Your Highness?" one alchemist said.

"No," she said, a sharp frown creasing her face. "You are supposedly the greatest alchemists in this kingdom. Don't tell me that all the stones in the world are too limiting for you?"

The alchemist paled and shook his head, bowing in apology.

"Any other questions?" the Empress said, even though her tone made it clear they would not be welcome. At the resounding silence, the Empress crossed her arms and sat back. "You may begin."

Not a single alchemist moved, staring in stunned silence

at the stones before us. I had never had such an immense library of stones at my disposal, yet I had no idea what to do with any of them.

Where could I even begin? What sort of stone could create life? I closed my eyes and thought of my father's notes on all the minerals in the human body. I could hear the low, wordless rumble of his voice in my head. *Calcium, phosphorus, potassium, sodium, chloride...* But I doubted that simply putting all those things in a bowl and fusing them together would actually create life. There was no way the final exam could be so straightforward. Life wasn't just a bunch of rocks—it was qi. If it wasn't too far gone, qi could be called back, but how could it be created where none existed?

Some of the other alchemists had started assembling piles of stones with trembling hands. The one next to me had molded a bunch of iron into the shape of a small person and stared at it like it would tell him the answers.

"Quit copying me, hùnxiě," he said, glaring at me and shielding his stones from view.

I rolled my eyes. As if he was doing anything worth copying. But it wasn't like I had any better ideas.

I took a steadying breath. *Just think of a theory and test it*, I told myself. *Anything is better than gaping like a fish at your rocks while the other alchemists actually try things.*

The key to eternal youth was derived from gold, so surely gold had something to do with creating life. I grabbed a handful of gold nuggets and brought them to the center of the table. Maybe, if I could somehow create qi and meld it with the gold, I could create life. 氣, the character for qi, could also be read as *air* or *breath*, and the Empress had specified that she wanted a "breathing creature," so surely that was an essential part of it. Air came from the plants and oceans, so I chose a woodstone and waterstone along with a piece of gold and closed them into a fist.

It wasn't a good idea to do alchemy without a clear intention, but I needed to try *something* and see what happened.

The reaction was instantaneous—the stones burst into blue light, singeing my palm. I yelped and dropped them to the ground, where the grass flashed into flames. I quickly stomped them out, daring to glance back at the Empress, who was watching me coldly, lips pressed into a tight line.

"I've got it!" one of the alchemists said.

I whirled toward the sound, where a man in the front row was bouncing on his heels. He held some sort of catlike figure made of blue cobalt and placed it on a flat sheet of iron. The creature lifted a stiff paw and began to crawl forward, raising its tail. The other alchemists stifled gasps, peering around me to get a closer look.

The Empress leaned forward, squinting at the creation, and I cursed myself for not watching him more closely to see what he'd done. Surely he hadn't made life so easily and quickly? Fear clamped around my rib cage, choking my breath away. After all this time, had I already lost?

"Oh, please," Zheng Sili said, rolling his eyes. "That's not life, it's magnets. He's using lodestone."

He fished through one of his own jars and waved a grayed stone over the cobalt cat, which jumped toward the stone and stuck there as if nailed in place.

The Empress's eyes darkened. "Were you trying to deceive me?" she said, her voice like low thunder.

The alchemist shook his head frantically. "No, Your Highness, I was just experimenting, I thought magnets were allowed, I—"

"You have lost your chance," the Empress said evenly. "You

are disqualified. Guards?" She gestured to the alchemist cowering at the front. Without a word, a guard stepped forward, drew his sword, and plunged it into the alchemist's stomach.

The others gasped and stumbled back as the man crashed into the dirt, red spilling quickly from his stomach, soaking the ground beneath our feet. He cried out for help, but no one moved toward him, not with the armed guard still hovering nearby.

One alchemist backed up into another's table, stumbling as if heading toward the door.

The guard moved faster, leveling his sword with the alchemist's face.

"You already had an opportunity to forfeit," the Empress said, resting her chin on one hand. "You will complete the task now, one way or another."

More guards arrived, dragging the bleeding alchemist's body somewhere deeper into the palace, a trail of blood staining the dirt behind him. My hands trembled and sweat pooled under my palms as I slowly raised my gaze to the Empress's face.

*Those of you who do not succeed today will not be leaving my palace*, the Empress had said. This was why no one knew what the final round entailed. Either you won and served her, or you died to keep her secrets.

The other alchemists had already resumed their experiments with shaking hands, averting their eyes from the trail of blood. With a flash of light to my left, another alchemist's miniature human statue took a few faltering steps forward before bursting into a choking cloud of copper dust. The alchemist let out a panicked sob, sweeping the remains off the table.

I took a steadying breath, blocking out the scent of blood from my mind just like I did during my resurrections. I sank my fingers into the stones on the table, as if the right one would reveal itself to me by touch. *Creatures aren't made of stones*, I wanted to scream. *How can any stone create life?*

I looked down at my palms, the calluses and lines and deep blue veins. Too late, I realized I couldn't feel them at all anymore, that my vision was tunneling, as if I was staring at someone else's hands from the bottom of a well, a loud roaring in my ears. I should have expected this, should have tried harder to stomach those cucumbers Yufei gave me. My ridiculous fire imbalance always made me look weak at the worst possible times.

All at once, I crashed back into myself as if waking up from a dream. My fists clenched, hands shaking, sun burning on my back.

*It's imbalanced, but there is still fire in me*, I thought. *Every element is in me.*

Everyone was supposedly a mix of the five elements—wood that fuels fire, fire that forms earth, earth that holds metal, metal that carries water, water that feeds wood. We never noticed them until they were unbalanced, but they were always inside of us.

I dragged a pile of iron to my right, then picked up an earthstone. Suddenly, my hands couldn't move fast enough. I transformed three earthstones into identical disks, then did the same to three waterstones, metalstones, and woodstones, lining them up to make sure they were the same size. Everything had to be perfectly balanced. For the firestone, I made three disks of chicken-blood stone—if it was strong enough to resurrect people, maybe it could create new life as well. When I had three of each of the five types of stones, I arranged them all in a circle. Alchemy buzzed in my fingertips—a warm, tingling sensation, like my hands were falling asleep. I had never tried to combine so many stones in a transformation before, but if there was any hope of creating life, this was it.

The stones would form the body. Now all that was left was qi.

I caught a glimpse of another alchemist trying to use his own saliva like some disgusting form of qi transfer on his stone rabbit, and I prayed he gave up before experimenting with any other bodily fluids. Qi didn't simply leak out every time something left the body—it was much deeper inside of us than that. Spit wasn't the same as qi. Neither was breath, or even blood.

*Unless…*

I held out my hand again, tracing the blue rivers of veins under my skin. Blood itself wasn't the same as qi. But maybe it could be the path that led me to it.

I grabbed several pieces of iron and transformed them into a blade. Before I could second-guess myself, I dragged it across my palm. Blood rushed to the surface, dribbling over the stones. I clenched my fist, forcing more of it to splash onto the table. The Empress narrowed her eyes, leaning closer.

"Is blood alchemy the only kind you know?" Zheng Sili said. "Just because it worked for you once doesn't mean it's the answer to everything."

I ignored him, squeezing more blood out of my palm as he told the other alchemists how I'd never even gone to school, how I was the prince's pet, and a thousand other reasons I didn't deserve to be here. But his words didn't matter, because he wouldn't have been standing around talking if he knew how to win.

The trickle of blood had started to dry up, so I carved another one into my palm, deeper. It spilled faster this time, splashing across the front of my dress, soaking the stones in glistening red, the air reeking of iron.

I couldn't hear the stream of insults anymore, or feel the fiery glare of the Empress. The edges of my vision grew hazy, my breath coming faster, skin prickling with cold even as sweat beaded on my face. I fell onto my knees, gripping the edge of the table with my right hand, my left still bleeding over the stones.

"All you're doing is draining yourself dry, hùnxiě," Zheng Sili said, somewhere far away. "You can feed all the blood that you want to those stones, but it's not going to work."

For once, Zheng Sili was right. All the blood in the world wouldn't make this transformation happen.

But I wasn't feeding the stones my blood. I was feeding them my life.

Darkness eclipsed the sky in a single breath, Chang'an blasted away with nothing but night in its wake. I was kneeling at the bank of the river. Water crashed against the riverbed, twisting over jagged rocks and roots, ice-cold as it splashed onto my knees.

*You aren't supposed to be here.*

The words rose up from the dirt, from the whisper of rushing water, from the dark expanse beyond the trees. There were many things I wasn't supposed to do, but if I only did what was allowed, I wouldn't be kneeling before the Empress, a breath away from becoming a royal alchemist.

I cupped my palms and lowered them into the river, the coldness flaying my skin, and raised a handful of its dark waters.

The river disappeared and I was kneeling before my alchemy table once more, the sun searing overhead. I opened my hands and the liquid crashed over the stones, no longer freezing water but hot blood.

I felt the qi leave my body with a sudden rush, my vision grayed and mouth tasting like metal. This was what it felt like to touch death, to divert the river and force your life out of you.

Red light carved lines across the table between the stones, a pentagram scorching itself into the wood. The stones melted into the table in a swirl of marbled black, heat waves rippling the air around it. I snatched a couple moonstones from the table and managed to stop my hand from bleeding before backing away.

The black liquid bubbled over the edge of the table and spilled into the dirt, the red light searing brighter, casting the whole courtyard in a fiery glow. I raised a hand to shield my eyes as the transformation ripped all the colors from the sky, replacing everything with glaring crimson. The other alchemists retreated against the walls or hid behind their tables, but I couldn't lift myself from the dirt as the molten liquid ate holes in the wood.

*What have I done?* I thought, my fingers sinking into the soft ground. There was a reason you weren't supposed to experiment with life alchemy. Life was the greatest good, and that called for the greatest evil in return. I could flatten Chang'an with my carelessness.

With one final burst, like a shock of lightning, the light disappeared, the black liquid dripping like sludge onto the ground.

*That's it?* I thought, rising to my knees. *After all that, I've burned a table in half and created mud?*

I crawled forward and sank my hands into the swampy substance, searching for something, anything at all in the mess that now reeked of scorched meat and blood.

I was distantly aware of the other alchemists peeking out

from behind tables, guards making sure the Empress was un-harmed, but I couldn't tear my gaze from the wreckage be-fore me and the crushing feeling that I'd failed. I had no other ideas, and I definitely didn't have enough blood to try again.

The Empress let out a choked cry of anger, and I realized that sludge was dripping down her hair and face, the front of her dress stained black.

"She's finished!" the Empress said. "Guards?"

But then my hands brushed over something firm and sharp within the mud, making me jerk back in surprise. A guard yanked my arm, but I pulled away, scooping up the object and wiping away the sludge on my ruined dress. A white eye blinked up at me.

Two more guards grabbed me and I lost my footing, still clutching the object in my hands. It was moving, stirring in my palms.

"Wait!" I said, when the guards tried to drag me to my feet. "Wait, wait, I did it!"

The Empress held up a hand and the guards dropped me to the ground, the other alchemists hovering closer. I tucked the small, squirming creature against my chest and scrubbed it with my sleeves, sloughing off the black sludge. But my hands trembled too much, and the creature rolled off my lap onto the dirt, twitching as it spread its matted wings to steady itself. My throat clenched. What kind of abomination had I made from my experiment? *You cannot create good without cre-ating evil.* Life was the greatest good, so whatever this was must be pure evil. It shook itself, shrugging off more mud, revealing yellow fur.

"Is that a *duck*?" Zheng Sili said.

The creature toddled forward a few steps, then turned

around and looked at me, tilting its head to the side. It was a baby duck, hardly the size of my palm.

I let out a sharp, delirious laugh. The prince would never let me live this down.

I cupped my palms and the duck toddled back into my hands, resting there happily. My legs felt like paper, but I managed to stumble down the rest of the courtyard and kneel before the Empress, holding out my creation to her.

For what felt like a lifetime, the Empress watched the creature in my hands. I was dizzy, caked in my own blood and alchemical sludge, and before the Empress's glowing presence I felt like a monster who had crawled her way up from hell.

"I have heard much about you," the Empress said at last, her voice glass-sharp, like every word was supposed to be an insult. "You intrigue me, Fan Zilan. But being unique cannot make up for skill, education, or talent."

My heart sank. I lowered the duck, who nuzzled into my palm.

"I have a sense for greatness," the Empress said. "That is how I became the Empress. That is how I knew which alchemists to trust in my search for eternal life, and why I'm not dead like the Emperors before me. I sensed something in you from the moment I saw you in my city. But my advisers told me you were uneducated, that you were too brash and unrefined, that you would be a disappointment."

The Empress rose to her feet, and I couldn't bear to look at her anymore. As her shadow fell over me, I dropped into a bow that I wasn't sure I could get up from, each cruel word crushing me deeper into the ground. I clutched the duck to my chest and waited for my fate.

"It is clear that you are uneducated," she said, "and you

are indeed brash and unrefined. Yet, somehow, I am not disappointed."

My fingers tensed in the dirt, my whole body shuddering as I started to rise from my bow.

"I cannot say that I've ever seen an alchemist lay their life on the line as you have, or paint my courtyard red with their blood. That is why, as of tomorrow, the name Fan Zilan will no longer be allowed in my court."

I dared to lift my head, peering up at the Empress, backlit by the sun, like every part of her was made of gold.

"From now on, you will be known as the Scarlet Alchemist."

# CHAPTER EIGHTEEN

I left the courtyard in a daze, the duck stuffed into my pocket, feeling like I was stumbling through a dream. The floor tilted at sharp angles and spilled me against walls, my vision bursting with sun flashes that were almost definitely from the blood loss, but I pushed myself toward home with one goal in mind:

Paper.

The first thing I would do as a royal alchemist would be to tear out a sheet of scroll paper, slam it onto my desk, stab my brush into an inkstone, and write the words I'd dreamed of telling Auntie and Uncle for years.

*I did it.*

I pictured Auntie opening the letter and yelling for Uncle, shaking him awake. They'd tell all their friends about their daughter, the royal alchemist. And when I sent them enough money to move to a street that didn't bleed, all the neighbors would watch them pack their things onto a carriage while they bragged that their *daughter* bought them a new house, they didn't have to work anymore, didn't have to worry about anything. Anything they wanted, they could have it.

Wenshu's success had always been a given. Yufei always

managed to worm her way into whatever she wanted. I was supposed to be the purple weed destined for nothingness, and now I would stand beside the alchemists who had created eternity.

For the rest of my life, there would be no more cowering before blue-robed officials, pretending to be weaker than my brother. Never again would I hide my face and say I was someone's bride for safety. I could no longer be purchased, because I belonged to the House of Li. I stared down at my trembling hands, blood painted into the creases, and even with my body in this state, I felt as though I could rend marble apart, tear down handfuls of the sky, shove mountains out of my way. The name that my spineless father had cursed me with was gone, wiped away by the Empress herself. I had become a great alchemist without him.

I'd left the courtyard before I saw what became of the other alchemists, but I heard Zheng Sili shouting at the guards from the other side of the wall. I felt a twinge of guilt, but I knew for certain that none of them would have tried to save me if I'd lost. If they wanted to live, they could save themselves. I wouldn't waste my sympathy on the rich.

The ground seemed porridge soft, my ankles rolling as I tried to walk. I needed to go tell Wenshu and Yufei, if I could manage to make it home without falling flat on my face.

When I turned the same corner for the third time, I realized that I might be lost, or maybe too dizzy to find my way out of the labyrinth of the palace. I groaned, spinning around and heading back down the hallway again. In my pocket, the duck chirped and snapped at the fabric.

"I'm doing my best," I said, my words loose and slurred. "You think you can do better?"

The duck fell silent, then hopped to the floor and started waddling in the opposite direction.

"Where are you going?" I said, bending down to scoop it up. But the ground rushed up too fast and my forehead hit the tiles before my hands. I groaned and sat up as the duck scurried around a corner.

The duck seemed innocent enough, but I doubted that an alchemical animal was safe to set loose in a palace. There was no way I had created a creature of such pure good without even a touch of evil, and my position here was already precarious enough without being responsible for a dozen servants dead by duck attack. The only reason I hadn't gotten rid of it already was that Wenshu would probably be devastated if I deprived him of the chance to study it.

"You were literally just born—how are you so damn fast?" I said, following sludgy duck footprints deeper into the palace as a headache hammered behind my eyes, threatening to pop them out of my skull. I had the distinct sense that this wasn't a place where I was meant to wander—the paper doors rather than majestic wooden ones suggested these were residences and not offices. Perhaps this was where the members of the royal court lived.

The footprints disappeared between sliding paper doors left ajar at the end of the hallway, darkness spilling out from within. At least that meant the space was unoccupied, and I wouldn't be bursting into someone's room to collect my feral duck while they were in the middle of dinner.

I slammed the doors open, my gaze snapping to the duck sitting inside a shoe by the doorway.

"There you are, you little monster," I said, grabbing the shoe and shaking him out into my palm. "I've eaten duck before, you know. I'm not above doing it again."

But as I set the shoe down, the floor rippled beneath it, and I realized that dark liquid coated the ground. The sharp scent of blood knifed up my nose. I probably would have noticed it sooner if I wasn't drenched in my own blood and scorched alchemical sludge.

I peered into the room, but the shades were drawn, and dense shadows blanketed everything aside from the tiny circle of light in front of the door. I could make out the shapes of futons and low tables and scattered shoes, but not much else.

Then the darkness began to shift.

I grabbed hold of the door frame as the whole floor shivered, a river of blood spilling into the hallway. A creaking echoed through the dark, like dry branches splintering in winter, and a shuddering breath reached my ears. *Someone is in here*, I thought, even though I should have known because the blood rushing past my feet was sickeningly warm.

With trembling hands, I fished a few firestones from my bag and ignited them in my palm, stripping the darkness from the walls.

First, there was a woman's face, upside down.

Blood rushed from her mouth and nose into her eyes, hair tangled in the swampy darkness of the floor. White spikes jutted out of her at jagged angles, like the porcupines of the southern forests, her arms crooked and pale on the floor beside her. She shifted, writhing from her center, and a second face turned to me, rising from the base of her throat.

The man's eyes were two polished white spheres like faraway moons. His skin gleamed, my flames shivering in ribbons of light across his cheeks. The lower half of his face dripped like a melting candle, his lips lost in the dark mess of blood weeping down his jaw.

He grabbed the spikes on either side of the woman and used

them as leverage, raising himself up with a sharp *crack*, jostling the woman's limp frame as he emerged from within her.

I realized, with a dawning sense of horror, that the spikes were the woman's ribs wrenched apart, her chest opened like a book.

I stumbled back, tripping over the shoes in the doorway, and hurled my glowing firestones at the man's face. It should have scorched his skin, but the stones only bounced off his cheek with a sound like they'd struck hollow metal, clattering to the floor with a few errant sparks.

I clamped the duck in one hand as I scrambled to my feet. If I were going to fight a monster with indestructible skin, it sure as hell wasn't going to be right after losing half my blood.

A surge of pearls filled the monster's mouth, stretching his lips and pouring to the floor with the sound of heavy rain. I thought of the monsters lurking through the western wards— the beheaded pig, the blood-soaked pearls I'd found there, how my cousins *hadn't believed me.*

I took off running, careening around corners and slamming into banisters, trying not to crush the duck in my hand. My heartbeat sounded like a gong in my ears, my breath coming too fast but not reaching my lungs. I didn't know where I was running, but in the distance, I could still hear the clattering of pearls and lumbering footsteps.

I dared to glance over my shoulder and crashed straight into a body, sending us both to the ground.

My face slammed into the porcelain tiles. For a moment, shapes danced across my vision until the duck came into focus hopping around my face.

"*Zilan?*"

Hands gripped my arms and peeled me from the floor. I

looked up at the prince, his hair askew, lip split open. "What are you doing here?" he said. "Are you all right?"

"It's not safe," I said, gasping for breath, pocketing the duck with numb fingers. "We have to...have to get out of here."

The prince glanced around, but thankfully didn't ask any more questions before gently taking my arm and pulling me into a study, locking the door behind us.

I sank down to the ground and pressed my ear to the door, listening for the sound of clattering pearls. But as the minutes went by and my heartbeat began to slow, I heard nothing but the distant chirp of cicadas. I put my hands over my face and sagged against the door, letting out a shaky sigh.

A warm hand rested on my knee.

"What happened?" the prince asked quietly.

I closed my eyes. I couldn't bear his sincerity, his worry. "You have monsters eating people in your palace," I said.

His hand tensed on my knee. "Did they hurt you?"

My next breath caught in my throat, my heart rate picking up again. He didn't seem surprised at all. "You know about those things?" I said.

"I didn't know you were here," he said, even though that wasn't what I'd asked. "I would have told you not to wander the halls at this hour. I'm sorry, Zilan, I—"

"Is this normal to you?" I said, my voice rising. "Court ladies being dismembered in their rooms?"

The prince grimaced. "They don't often hurt other people, I swear," he said. "Usually they're only interested in me."

"They come after you?" I said. My gaze dropped to the healing scratches on the prince's collarbone, his robes tugged loose from our fall. Was this why he always looked like he'd been mauled by a cat?

But that wasn't even the worst of it. The prince was alive,

but because of these monsters, other people were dead. "You know that they're loose in other wards too?" I said.

He sat back, wrapping his arms around his knees. "Zilan," he said, "do you remember how I told you that my relatives across China have been turning up dead?"

I nodded stiffly.

"The official reports say they were all killed by wild animals," he said. "But, after the things I've seen in this court, you can imagine why I find that hard to believe."

"They were sent after your family?" I said, pressing my palms to my eyes. "That means the Empress is behind this, right?"

"I think at first, they were only meant to kill my family," he said, "but now they kill anyone she dislikes, and innocent people tend to get caught in the crossfire. Her experiments are not the most precise."

"What are they?" I said, shuddering at the thought of the creature's hardened skin.

Something flashed in the prince's eyes, and he looked away. "I'm not sure," he said, his voice wavering.

"You're a terrible liar."

"No, honestly, I'm not sure. All I know is that..." He shook his head. "I didn't... Zilan, you're so good at alchemy, and you worked so hard for this. I wanted to warn you, but I didn't want to take this away from you."

"What does me being good at alchemy have to do with this?"

The prince leveled his gaze with mine, taking a deep breath.

"Zilan, the royal alchemists create the monsters."

I shook my head slowly. The duck chirped in my pocket, struggling to break free. *They wanted to see if I could create life,* I realized, feeling like I was being dragged to the bottom of the ocean, chest crushed in.

"I won't," I whispered. I thought of the girl burning in the western ward, the smell of charred flesh that I still couldn't scrub from my mind.

"You won't have a choice," the prince said.

I rose to my feet and backed against the door. Making gold was bad enough, but creating monsters? This was what I'd dreamed about my whole life? The privilege of helping the rich live forever and crafting an infallible army for the Empress? My stomach clenched and my hand fumbled for the doorknob. I couldn't stay here.

"Wait."

The door wouldn't open. I turned around as the prince pressed his hand to the door to hold it shut, gold bracelets rattling on his wrist, caging me in. My gaze traced from his golden eyes down to his bleeding lip.

"Please, Zilan xiǎojiě," he whispered, his words ghosting across my face, "you look pale. Let me at least walk you home."

I swallowed, my mouth suddenly dry. He was so close that I could feel how our breathing was in sync. But this was the man who let monsters roam free in his kingdom. And maybe it wasn't his fault, but he still knew about it and did absolutely nothing.

"I don't need an escort," I said.

The prince sighed, his hand sliding down the door and falling to his side. "I'm sorry," he whispered.

"Don't apologize to *me*," I said. "Apologize to the family of the court lady who was ripped in two. Or the girl who was burned to death in a western ward because she was blamed for what your monsters are doing."

"Zilan, they're not *my* monsters."

But I couldn't stand his excuses anymore. I shoved the door open and stepped into the silent hallway.

"Zilan, please," the prince said, his warm hand reaching for my wrist.

I smacked his hand away. "Don't touch me!" I said.

But instead of the flustered apology I'd expected, the prince's face went white, eyes focusing behind me.

Before I could turn around, someone grabbed my shoulders and slammed me into the floor, my cheek smashing against the tiles. Then a thunderous voice above me said: *"You dare to touch the Crown Prince?"*

I tried to get up, but a foot on my back pinned me in place, my jaw biting into the stone. I turned my head to the side and caught a glimpse of one of the Empress's guards, three more appearing at the end of the hallway at the sound of shouting.

"Release her," the prince said, his voice even, as if he wasn't troubled at all. I knew he was probably feigning impartiality the same way Wenshu did, but it stung all the same. "I can handle her myself."

The guard lifted his foot and I hurried to sit up. "The punishment for touching the royal family is death," he said, his voice booming down the silent corridor.

"You are speaking out of place," the prince said sternly. "This is a private matter."

The guard scoffed. "The Empress has made it very clear that we answer to her, not you. If you don't like her rules, take it up with her. I will enforce her wishes."

The prince looked at me as if I would somehow have a solution, and I realized all at once that he truly had no power compared to the Empress. *That's it?* I thought. *I risked everything for this spoiled prince, and now I'll die for him?*

"It's not like she was attacking me!" the prince said, pulling at the guard's sleeves as two of them wrenched my arms behind me and hauled me onto my feet.

I considered throwing my head back and breaking their noses, but even more guards and court ladies were appearing around the corner or peering out of windows at the commotion. It wasn't as if I could kill them all to keep this a secret. I swallowed the lump forming in my throat, blinking away tears. I'd earned my place here, nearly died for it, and in less than an hour, it was already over.

Somehow, the prince was still rambling uselessly. "It was my fault for grabbing her in the first place," he said, "I think she tripped backward, so it was probably an accident—"

"The only people who can touch the Crown Prince are royal healers or concubines!" the guard said, his harsh tone finally silencing the prince. "She is clearly not a healer, and—"

*"She's my concubine!"* the prince said.

Everyone fell silent, turning to me. I didn't dare move, as if my stillness could hide my dress covered in sludge, blood, and sweat. The duck hopped out of my pocket and made a shrill, impatient sound.

"*She* is your concubine?" the guard said slowly.

I clenched my jaw and glared down at the tiles. I knew the prince was only trying to help, but did he have any idea what this would mean for me? I'd already been fighting accusations that the prince bought my place here, and now he wanted to prove all the other alchemists right? I briefly considered murdering every single witness before they could tell the Empress, but the prince kept talking, his face flushed red, words spilling out unstopped.

"What I mean is, she's *going to be* my concubine," he said. "You wouldn't have heard a formal announcement yet as we're still working out the logistics, but I promise it will be official very soon. Father has been telling me to choose a concubine for ages now. You remember three years ago when he had fifty women sent over for me to choose from and I didn't want any of them and he said it was an 'utterly emasculating spectacle,' or something to that effect? I've taken that failure to heart and, well, here's Fan Zilan!"

He gestured to me awkwardly and I closed my eyes, wishing the guards would slam me into the floor again so I would pass out rather than have to listen to this.

The guards exchanged glances, then promptly released me. I staggered forward, slipped on sludge, and fell to my knees.

"It would be in your best interest not to wander the halls at night with commoners," the guard said to the prince. "To avoid this sort of confusion in the future."

The prince clenched his jaw. "Is that another one of the Empress's rules, or is it just your opinion?"

The guard bowed stiffly. "I beg your pardon, Your Highness," he said, turning to leave.

When we were alone again in the hallway, the prince offered me his hand with a thin smile. I took it with more force than necessary, nearly dragging him to the ground as I stood up. He steadied himself quickly and pulled me closer, one hand on the small of my back, ignoring the hardening sludge beneath his fingers. I held my breath, my whole body tense at his closeness.

"There are court ladies watching through the windows, and the guards are still listening," he whispered. "Come to my room and we can talk."

I nodded and forced my muscles to relax, allowing him to lead me down the hallway. My questions could wait until my life wasn't on the line. He froze at the sound of chirping behind us and turned to see the small, dirty duck in the middle of the hall. I rolled my eyes and scooped it up. "I'll explain later," I said, jamming the bird into my pocket.

Lights still burned beyond the paper doors as we passed, shadows shifting behind them, so I knew some of the court ladies were lingering close by, listening. We entered a wing of the palace I'd never seen before, where jeweled murals covered the walls in cold jades and cut rubies and shaved pearls, sharp enough to draw blood.

Two guards stood in front of a set of double doors painted with gold cranes. They bowed as the prince approached and opened the doors for us.

We stepped into a room bigger than my entire house in Guangzhou, the walls glittering with jewels carefully glued into constellations across the wallpaper. Red silk shrouded a bed in the center of the room, and my skin burned as I remembered that I was his *concubine* now.

I jumped away as soon as the prince released me, backing against a dresser, rattling the scrolls on top of it.

"Zilan," the prince sighed, "I'm so sorry. The guards all report to my mother. I panicked. I didn't know how else to—"

"Let me be very clear," I said, gripping the dresser behind me. The prince closed his mouth and nodded. "I am not your concubine. At least, not when we're alone. And if that's not all right with you, then you might as well turn me over to your guards now."

The prince shook his head frantically. "I don't want you to be my concubine," he said.

It was the answer I'd wanted, but somehow it stung anyway. Of course he didn't want someone like me as a concubine. The royal concubines were chosen from the most beautiful girls in all of China. He'd said he'd had fifty to choose from, and yet not a single one had been good enough for him.

"I mean, you should live here as an alchemist," the prince said, his gaze softening. "That's what you want, isn't it?"

It's not like I had much of a choice anymore. I belonged to the House of Li now, and I could be a royal alchemist or leave in a coffin. Then a horrible thought rushed through me. "I can still be a royal alchemist, can't I?" I said. Had the prince just thrown away my new title?

He shrugged. "I don't see why not."

"I won't have to spend all day doing concubine things?"

"What is it you think concubines do?" he asked, frowning.

"I... I don't know," I said, looking down. "Whatever their master wants?"

The prince laughed. "Well, when my father had concubines, most of their days were spent sewing and gossiping with the eunuchs, but seeing as you're the first alchemist my mother has selected in years, I think she'll agree that you have better things to do. Though you would need to move into the inner palace and sleep in my room at times so that mother doesn't suspect anything."

My face burned, but the prince quickly waved his hands as if to scrub the thought from the air. "And I'll sleep on the floor, of course."

But I couldn't meet his eyes, and he kept talking as if to drown his last sentence with a deluge of words.

"You'll have access to the royal libraries as well, which might help you with your studies. And clothes and food will be provided for you, of course. You may need to attend some dinners with my mother to keep up appearances, but I'll make sure they understand you're an alchemist first and foremost, so they won't send you off to mend clothes or some other nonsense like my father's old concubines, and—"

"My siblings?" I asked at last, partially because I had never lived farther than a short walk away from them and partially because I wasn't sure if the prince would ever stop talking otherwise. "Can they come as well?"

The prince grimaced. "The families of concubines do not typically move with them to the palace," he said. "Maybe in time, I could bring them both here under a similar arrangement, though I don't want to draw too much attention to your family at the moment."

"A similar arrangement? Surely my brother can't be a concubine as well."

"Well, the term is not *concubine* for men, but he could certainly come here eventually. Unless... I don't suppose your brother is interested in being a eunuch?"

"Umm, I think he'll be fine waiting," I said.

"I want to help them," the prince said. "Please, believe me. I just need to be careful."

"I know," I said, dropping my gaze. The prince always meant well, even if he was a fool who didn't know when to stop talking.

He shifted from foot to foot, glancing over his shoulder at the door. "It might look suspicious if I sent you away right now," he said quietly.

I nodded, rubbing my eyes. After this hellish day, I wasn't sure that I could trudge all the way back to the western ward, which was probably closed by now anyway.

"I'll stay," I said. "Just for tonight."

The prince nodded, wringing his hands, gaze twitching around like his room was suddenly a foreign country. "You can have the bed, of course."

"Can we skip the part where I pretend to offer to sleep on the floor out of politeness?" I said, and when he chuckled softly, I waved for him to turn around while I shed the outer layer of my dress.

"I wouldn't make you sleep on the floor," he said with his back to me.

When I slipped onto the bed, I practically melted into it. "This is like Heaven," I said. "How do you ever get out of bed?"

The prince glanced over his shoulder, turning fully around when he saw I was already under the covers. "The constant fear that I'm going to be murdered in my sleep is pretty motivating."

"Well, if someone comes to kill you tonight, you're on your own," I said.

Something shifted in my discarded dress on the floor and I remembered the duck in my pocket. I leaned over and fished it out, setting it on top of the covers. The prince all but threw himself to the ground, reaching out a trembling finger to stroke its head.

"This is my alchemy duck," I said. "Freshly made."

"You *made* him?" the prince said, cupping his hands and letting the duck hop into them. "I shouldn't be surprised. Of course you can make ducks at will. Have you named him yet?"

I raised an eyebrow. "My brother will probably want to dissect him."

The prince tensed, holding the bird close to his chest. "Over my dead body." After a moment, he raised it to his face, mouth pinched in concentration. "He looks like his name is Durian," he said at last.

"Does he smell that bad?"

"Not the smell, the color," the prince said.

I shook my head. "You are objectively horrible at naming animals."

"Well, what would you call him?"

I shrugged. "Lunch."

"Fan Zilan, I will have you executed," he said, far too sincerely.

I yawned, turning over in bed. "That's not my name anymore," I said. "Now, I'm the Scarlet Alchemist."

The prince didn't respond at first, and I let my eyes fall closed. Sleep descended over me alarmingly fast, like it had been waiting for me to lie down so it could sink its talons into me and drag me to the bottom of a dark sea.

Warm hands brushed my hair back with reverence, a finger smoothing across my jaw, the shell of my ear. But I would never know if it was really the prince or the hands of sleep. And when someone whispered, *I knew you could do it*, I would never know if the words were real, or just what I'd wished for years that someone would say.

# CHAPTER NINETEEN

I threw open the door to my cousins' room and tripped straight over Wenshu, tumbling inside. He let out an indignant sound and knocked a pot of ink over his scroll, black bleeding across the floor.

"Sorry, sorry!" I said, soaking up the ink with my sleeve and quickly using alchemy to put it back in its pot as the bewildered guard appeared in the doorway behind me. Yufei, who was lying on her side in bed, raised an eyebrow and sat up.

"Zilan," Wenshu said warningly, frowning at his ruined scroll.

"Please don't murder me," I said. "Last night, I was—"

"We know, a messenger came to tell us where you were," Wenshu said. "Yufei almost stabbed him."

Yufei shrugged. "It was too late for visitors."

"Though he didn't tell us what you were doing," Wenshu said, crossing his arms. "Nothing dangerous again, I hope?"

"I passed!" I said, because if anything could distract him, it was this.

Wenshu's anger melted away instantly. He smiled, reaching out and ruffling my hair like when we were kids. "Of course you did," he said. "You're the best. You always were."

At his words, my throat closed up and my vision blurred with tears. I'd never thought I needed Wenshu's praise, so I wasn't prepared for the wave of relief it brought, like I could breathe for the first time since we'd dreamed of coming to Chang'an. I wasn't a failure who had to be sent home alone. I wasn't deadweight for my perfect cousins to drag around. They weren't going to leave me behind.

"Why are you crying?" Wenshu said, horrified. "Stop that!"

"Shut up, she's happy," Yufei said, crushing me in a hug so forceful that my ribs squeaked in protest.

"Be happy some other way!" Wenshu said, grabbing a rag and passing it to Yufei, who scrubbed at my face until I took the hint and blew my nose.

"What about you?" I said. "Which office will you work in?"

They looked at each other, then down at the floor. Their silence stretched longer until it became its own answer. I crushed the rag in my fist. "You didn't pass?" I whispered.

"It's not about passing or failing, Zilan. There are ranks," Wenshu said. "We're in the third tier. That means we'll train for another year, then they'll send us somewhere else."

*They have to leave Chang'an?* I shook my head, pressed up against the wall like I could back away from their words. I'd worked as hard as I did so we could stay together. I didn't want any of this if it meant saying goodbye.

"But you did so well on the second round," I said, my voice small.

"Yes, the written round, not the oral one," Wenshu said, expression pinched, unwilling to meet my eyes. "I swear they talked faster just to confuse us. And I think they try to force Southern candidates back to the South, since Northerners can't speak our dialect as well."

"For now, we can stay," Yufei said, reading the devastation on my face.

I opened my mouth to tell them to just stay with me at the palace before remembering that I hadn't exactly mentioned that part yet. I glanced at the guard behind me before switching to Guangzhou dialect to explain what had happened last night, watching as Wenshu's and Yufei's faces slowly darkened.

Maybe the palace monsters hadn't killed me, but Wenshu would.

"You're his *what*?" he said.

I winced, turning to Yufei for help, but she flopped back into bed like she couldn't stand to be conscious for this discussion.

"I'm also a royal alchemist," I said quietly. "Can we go back to talking about that part?"

Wenshu let out a strangled sound. "Is that why the guard is here?"

"I think it's a royal court thing."

Wenshu seethed, shaking his head. "Zilan, it's not a royal court thing, it's a concubine thing. He's making sure you don't get pregnant."

I whirled around to face the guard. "Is that true?" I said in his dialect. "You're not here to protect me from monsters but from men?"

The guard shrugged. "You can only have the Crown Prince's children."

"*He's my brother!*" I said, jerking a hand at Wenshu.

"I'm just following orders," the guard said.

I silently vowed to murder the prince when I returned to the palace.

"Zilan," Yufei said, sitting up again, "this is a terrible idea."

"Well, it wasn't my idea, and it's too late to take it back."

"You shouldn't have touched the prince in the first place!"

Wenshu said. "You shouldn't have snuck off with him at all! He's not supposed to even know who you are!"

"He risks nothing and you risk everything," Yufei said.

My gaze jumped between the two of them. Somehow, no matter what I did, I was the target of their anger. It was supposed to be the three of us against the rest of the world. Now we were all being sent off to separate places, and they were mad at me for something I couldn't control.

"I asked him to help you, you know," I said to her, raising my voice. "Maybe I shouldn't have."

Yufei barked out a laugh. "No offense, Zilan, but I'd rather gouge my eyes out than sleep with that rich fool."

"I'm not going to sleep with him!" I said, my face hot. "I already told you—"

"That's what you think *now*," Yufei said, "but men don't stop asking, and you don't know how to say no to him."

"That's not true! When he came to me in Guangzhou, I told him I wouldn't help him even for one hundred thousand gold!"

"Yes, and then you came to Chang'an and helped him anyway," Wenshu said.

I shook my head. "Look, there's nothing I can do about it now. I only came to pack."

Wenshu crossed his arms and turned to the window, but Yufei helped me gather my things into a small satchel the prince had provided. Even though I was mad at my cousins, it felt strange to stand in the doorway with a packed bag, leaving them. I had never really been apart from Wenshu and Yufei. Even when my parents were alive, we'd only lived down the street from them, and I'd slept in their room so often that it felt like my room too.

"When you're in the palace," Yufei said in Chang'an dialect, "try to pocket everything you can. Their wallpaper is probably pure gold. Just rip off a few corners in subtle places."

"She's joking," I said to the guard.

"I'm not joking," Yufei said. "Bring us back food."

"That, I can probably do," I said. Yufei hugged me while Wenshu watched with crossed arms.

When I got the sense that he wasn't going to say good-bye, I turned to go, but Yufei grabbed my arm and pushed me at Wenshu.

"Stop being angry. Zilan is leaving," she said, punching Wenshu in the shoulder.

"I'm not angry," he said, finally uncrossing his arms. "What's done is done. But know that I will be absolutely furious if you get yourself tangled up in any more of the prince's business and the Empress executes you. I swear, I will make one hundred míngqì of rabid wolves and cram them into your coffin so you get chewed to pieces in the afterlife."

I slung my bag over my shoulder, waving away the guard's offer to carry it for me and shooting Wenshu a smile. "As if the Empress would give you my corpse back."

"Fan Zilan, I will spit on your grave!"

I laughed and waved as I turned away, forcing myself to smile until they couldn't see my face. It was the same feeling as leaving Auntie and Uncle, the door swinging closed and all the air gone in a sudden punch to the chest. Even though I had never died like my cousins, I imaged that it felt a little bit like this.

"I have my things," I said to the guard, stomping down the pathway, forcing him to hurry after me. "Now what?"

"Now," he said, "I'll take you to meet the royal alchemists."

The guard led me through the maze of halls, pointing out a small room where I could drop my bag before heading deeper into the palace. We moved to the northern corner, where the walls grew so tall that shadows cooled the pathway, making me shiver. The dirt looked grayish in the dark, like we'd traveled to the surface of the moon. What kind of secrets were important enough to build such high walls around? Surely the whole palace knew that the alchemists dabbled in life magic.

Maybe it had something to do with the making of pearl monsters. I still hoped that what the prince had told me was wrong, that the royal alchemists weren't responsible. But regardless, it wasn't as if I could go to the Empress and say *Sorry, I don't want to be an alchemist anymore.* She'd probably make my organs into sausages just for wasting her time.

The guard stopped before a wooden door with leaves creeping through the cracks. "Is this an alchemy training ground or a prison?" I said.

"The Empress doesn't want alchemical activities interfering with the life of the court," the guard said, knocking twice on the door.

"Ah yes, what a pity if the alchemists who gave her eternal life get too noisy."

The guard cast me a stern look. "Remember that I report back to the Empress," he said.

I grimaced. I'd thought he only answered to the prince. "I don't suppose you could pretend you didn't hear that?"

Before he could respond, a slot opened in the door, where a pair of sharp black eyes glared at both of us before the panel slammed shut. The door creaked inward a few inches.

"Do you really need to follow me in here?" I whispered to the guard, shuffling in front of him so we weren't standing side by side like mismatched friends. I didn't want to look like a child in front of the other alchemists.

"I am to accompany you everywhere outside the inner

palace," the guard said. "You should be grateful you're even granted that much freedom."

Then the door swung open and a rush of light spilled out. I raised a hand to shield my eyes as I stepped into the training grounds.

The courtyard had sturdy stone walls that rose above the trees, cutting off the rest of the city so that everything beyond them was pure, uninterrupted sky. Rows of tiny houses lined the perimeter, framing a pond so clear that the entire sky was reflected back in it, like the ground was a portal to Heaven. Instead of the red dirt of the other courtyards, the ground here was silvery gray, like ashes.

About a dozen people mulled through the grounds, sitting on the dirt and eating fruit, reading scrolls, or napping in the shade. I heard muffled yelling inside one of the houses, and a cloud of purple smoke spun through one of the windows, followed by flashes of light and garbled screams. *Yes, these people are definitely alchemists*, I thought.

"I see you've made it, Scarlet."

I turned toward the Moon Alchemist as she approached from the center path. All the trees seemed to bend and bow in her direction, the sun behind her outlining her silhouette in white light. The wind nudged me a step closer and I realized, as she drew to a stop, that I had to look up at her. I'd never met a woman taller than me before, and I didn't understand how her height commanded respect and majesty while mine only made me feel like an overgrown flower that needed trimming. She drew to a stop a short distance away, gaze flickering to the guard and expression souring.

"I'm supervising her in here," she said. "You wait outside the door."

The guard straightened. "My orders are to—"

"Our alchemy practices are confidential. I don't make exceptions, and I outrank you."

She gestured for him to leave, and after a tense moment of silence, he pressed his lips together and bowed before heading toward the door.

"What an annoyance," the Moon Alchemist said. She turned back to me, her expression only slightly softer. "I don't think we've been formally introduced. I am the Moon Alchemist, head of the royal alchemists, and I will oversee your training."

*As if I don't know who you are*, I thought, bowing. She was impossible to look away from—like the moon itself, she seemed like the brightest point in a dark sky, majestic and eternal.

"I heard that you earned your name by pulling the moon down from the sky," I said before I could stop myself. "Can you really do that?"

The corner of her lips curled up in a smile. "I'm a healer known for using moonstone," she said. "That is where it comes from."

She hadn't answered my question, but I decided not to ask again. She didn't seem like the kind of person who would tolerate pestering.

"What was your real name again?" she asked, waving for me to follow her deeper into the compound.

"Fan Zilan," I said, bowing again as I walked. I felt like I shouldn't be allowed to look someone like her in the eye. Forget the Empress—*this* was someone I wanted to throw myself to the ground for. Could she really be responsible for all the pearl monsters?

The Moon Alchemist stopped, a frown creasing her forehead. "*Fan* Zilan?" she said, as if it was my surname and not my flowery given name that surprised her. As far as I knew, Fan was a common, unremarkable name.

"Yes," I said, feeling like a child scolded for giving the wrong answer.

She pursed her lips, gaze searing into me for a long moment, then turned and kept walking. "I heard you're from the south, Scarlet," she said, seamlessly switching dialects. She sounded like the people of southern Jiangnanxi, which bordered my home province, and while it wasn't the same as Guangzhou dialect, I'd spoken to enough people on trade routes to get the gist.

"I am," I said. "Are you—"

"Walk faster," she said.

I doubled my pace, tripping over a hole in the ground that oddly resembled a burn mark. "Where are you..." I trailed off, not sure how to finish the question. I'd hated when people in Guangzhou asked me where I was from, as if *here* couldn't be the right answer. But the Moon Alchemist seemed to transcend every map, maybe even time itself—she spoke both Southern and Northern dialects flawlessly, braided her hair like the nomads, had tan skin and harvest-moon eyes and a magnetic pull. I would have believed her if she claimed to be the daughter of the moon goddess herself.

"I grew up in southern Jiangnandong," she said, not even looking at me as she spoke, like she'd heard the question a thousand times. "My father was a teacher there, and my mother was from Persia."

My feet ground to a halt. Annoyance flickered in the Moon Alchemist's eyes as she stopped and looked over her shoulder, but I couldn't bring myself to move.

"You're a hùnxiě?" I said quietly.

She raised an eyebrow, waving for me to keep walking. "Was that not obvious?"

I could only shake my head. I had never met another hùnxiě before, and now, somehow, the most powerful alchemist in China was like me? It felt wrong that there was a single word that could describe both of us, when she felt like the sharp light of every star in the sky while I was just an overgrown weed scorched in the sun. Maybe if she taught me, I could be like her one day—commanding respect, not ridicule. She waved again and I hurried to catch up with her, neck craned to look up at her instead of the path in front of me.

"I'm not the only one," she said. "The River Alchemist is Bǎiyuè and Hàn Chinese. She helped invent the water clock, hence her name. And there are many of us who aren't Hàn. There's the Paper Alchemist, who's Uyghur. And that explosion inside the house earlier was the Comet Alchemist. She's from Tubo. You'll meet all of them soon."

Across the courtyard, a few alchemists waded through the pond, screaming with indignation when someone turned the water bright purple. Another swung from a tree branch onto an alchemist's shoulders, falling over laughing as the peach tree rained fruit over them. Some cast blue clouds of smoke across the courtyard and vanished into its mist, which smelled like burnt sugar. There were alchemists from lands I'd never dreamed of seeing in my lifetime. The alchemy grounds no longer felt like another part of the palace but a gateway to an entirely different world.

"I don't understand," I said. "I thought the court didn't want people like us. They kept trying to make me lose." I thought back to my first and second trials, the unfairness I'd been dealt at every turn, the messages from the capital that had mysteriously never reached Guangzhou.

The Moon Alchemist pursed her lips, looking past me as if considering her words. "The disadvantages at your trials were not meant to eliminate you," she said at last. "They were meant to push you to be better."

I tensed. "You knew?"

"Yes. Because they did the same thing to all of us," the Moon Alchemist said. "The Empress instructs the exam officials to put anyone who isn't a Hàn Chinese scholar at a disadvantage."

*"Why?"* I said, my mouth dry. "Aren't we at enough of a disadvantage already?"

The Moon Alchemist glanced over her shoulder, then back at me. We came to a stop in the shade of a small building with several locks on the door. "I will tell you what the Empress thinks," the Moon Alchemist said, her gaze restless, as if she sensed others listening. "She believes that alchemy favors the 'peculiar,' that hùnxiě and foreigners have a proclivity for it if they're challenged."

*There's a genetic component to alchemy,* Wenshu had said, and I hadn't realized until now how desperately I wanted him to be wrong. I had stayed up later than Wenshu and Yufei to study, had wanted to succeed more than them because they were already loved and valued and had nothing to prove. *That* was why I was an alchemist, not because of my father, who'd abandoned me. I would sooner die than owe my success to him.

"I can see why the Empress would come to that conclusion, given how many of us become powerful alchemists," the Moon Alchemist continued, "but she's only half-right. Alchemy is not about what's in your blood. It's about what's in your heart."

I nearly laughed out loud, but didn't want to offend the Moon Alchemist. Customers had called me heartless for years.

"And what is that?" I asked. What was in my heart but greed and stubbornness?

"Alchemy is not something you can master just by studying," the Moon Alchemist said. "Alchemists need to break themselves into pieces. They want to rebuild the world around them so desperately that they would give their blood, body, or soul. But people in power cannot fathom breaking a world that already bows to them. Alchemists are forged from pain."

I frowned, thinking of my second cousins, who worked the sugarcane fields. Surely they knew more pain than I did. "The world is cruel to many people," I said. "I'm hardly the unluckiest person in the empire. Shouldn't all the farmers be the best alchemists, if that's the case?"

"I'm sure many farmers would make great alchemists," the Moon Alchemist said, "but we'll never know, because the Empress lets them starve. They live and die in the fields, too busy surviving to study alchemy. The fact is, Zilan, this world was made for a certain kind of person, and it's not you, or me, or anyone who was not handed greatness at birth."

I lowered my eyes to the dirt. "I don't like the idea that I'm only here because of things I can't control," I said. It somehow felt worse than if I'd won because of being rich and well educated. Like the prince handing me stale bread out of pity, except my prize was a dream that I thought I'd earned for myself. "I'm a good alchemist because I'm unlucky?"

"You misunderstand," the Moon Alchemist said. "You are not an alchemist because you are a hùnxiě, or a southerner, or a poor merchant girl. You are an alchemist because you traveled across the world to stand before the Empress while some men didn't even leave their own wards. Maybe those born into greatness could do the same as you, but they'll never have to, so most of them will never try."

Then she straightened and turned back toward the houses. "Now, Scarlet, you've stalled for long enough. It's time to begin your training." She fished out a ring of keys from her pocket and slid one into the first lock with a heavy *thunk*. "You are a good alchemist," she said, "but I intend to make you a great one."

# CHAPTER TWENTY

At night, the palace breathed.

Jagged shadows rolled across the paper windows, formless specters whispering over the lattice. Far away, just soft enough that I couldn't be sure if it was a dream, the sound of marbles clattering like hail echoed down the hallway.

My room in the inner palace had four locks. I'd checked them again and again before curling up in my bed, which I'd pushed to the center of the room, not convinced that the lattice was strong enough to keep anything out. I drifted halfway into dreams, jolting awake at every sudden sound. I dreamed that I was lying on the riverbank, my hand dipped into the warm waters, watching the current pull steadily onward, the ground growing moist and spongy under me, the river lapping up over the edge, filling my mouth.

From everywhere and nowhere all at once came the words of the imprisoned alchemist: *Stay away from the royal family. They don't want your alchemy. They want your soul.*

I opened my eyes, shaking myself out of the dream. I grabbed a few firestones and lit a candle to scorch away the shadows and resigned myself to lying awake the rest of the night. The duck looked up from its box beside my bed, chirping faintly.

I still didn't know what the imprisoned alchemist meant, despite uncovering so many of the royal family's secrets. The Moon Alchemist hadn't mentioned any soul-sucking component to my training. All she'd done was lock me in a library room with a pile of scrolls taller than me and told me to read. My role as a concubine seemed to be the more soulless job of the two.

When I'd first come back to my room after training with the Moon Alchemist, I'd found a maid who looked at me like I was a piece of rotten fruit while she laid silk dresses across my bed and stuffed my sleeping garments into a bag.

"These hemp clothes are garbage," she said. "If you try to wear anything but silk, I will tear it off you no matter where you are or who's watching." She then gave me a "tour" of the concubines' quarters by pointing to a common area and a garden, then alluding to several other rooms that she didn't even bother showing me.

"So I'm just a concubine now?" I'd said. "I don't need to be initiated or something? I just move in and put on a new dress?"

I didn't want any sort of concubine ceremony or whatever strange affairs the royal family practiced, but it was oddly anticlimactic to just dump my bag onto a bed and suddenly begin a whole new life. I felt a bit like the prince had just smuggled me into the palace.

The maid squinted at me, gaze raking all the way down to my reed shoes. "You're a concubine, not a wife," she said slowly, like she didn't think I could understand her dialect. "Your status is just barely higher than mine."

"Oh," I said, not sure how else to respond with the maid

burning holes into me with her eyes. "So no one but the prince expects much of me?"

"You are expected not to embarrass the royal family, and to have the prince's children," she said. "Do you think you can manage that?"

"Umm, definitely the first one," I said, my face suddenly hot.

The maid raised an eyebrow. "You've sold your body for a place in the palace and you can't even talk about it? You're going to be eaten alive here."

*Perhaps literally*, I thought.

The maid kept walking into a courtyard and I shuffled behind her, not sure if she actually wanted me to follow. "Because you're an alchemist," she said, "the prince has ordered the Moon Alchemist to supervise you from sunrise to sunset. From sunset to sunrise, you are a concubine, and need to be available in your room in case the prince calls on you."

"Great," I said, with all the enthusiasm of a wet pair of socks. If the prince expected me to wait around for him, he would be sorely surprised.

"Don't leave the inner palace without a guard and don't bring any men here unless you want them executed," the maid said. "Now stop following me. I have work to do."

I ground to a stop, feeling a bit foolish standing by myself in the middle of a courtyard far more beautiful than me, unsure where to go.

The maid stopped just before she reached the end of the bridge.

"Oh, and one last thing," she said. "There are four locks on your door, and they're not for decoration. I suggest you use them all."

The training ground was deserted in the evening, nothing but white mist and hushed winds whispering over the walls.

But I didn't trust quiet in a place like this. Night was when the palace opened its eyes.

I rolled a piece of amethyst between my fingers, then tossed it into the middle of the courtyard, where it burst with a small flare of light and hiss of pale pink smoke.

There was no responding attack, no sharp intake of breath, no answer at all in the shattered stillness. I took a deep breath and ran out into the clearing.

With a white flash, the dewy ground beneath me turned into a sheet of ice. My next step slid out from under me, sending me spilling forward onto my palms. I rolled onto my back just as a figure descended on me, and I kicked them in the chest before they could pin me down.

"Ow, what the hell, Scarlet?" they said, coughing.

I reached for the tree behind me with my ringed hand, ready to reshape it to trap them under its heavy branches.

But the tree reached for me first, squeezing me around the rib cage and forcing my hands apart with its smaller branches. It yanked me off the ground, holding me high up above the courtyard, where all I could do was kick my legs at the air.

"You didn't say this was two against one!" I said, sagging against the branches.

The Paper Alchemist appeared from behind the tree, adjusting the embroidered cap on her head. "You're supposed to be practicing alchemy, not breaking ribs," she said.

"It's a reflex," I said, while the River Alchemist rose to her feet, coughing.

"It's okay, I have plenty left," she said.

The Paper Alchemist had startled me awake in the reading room by shaking my whole table. The first thing I saw after opening my eyes was the bright green of her irises. She wore a red dress with flowered embroidery so detailed that it looked like the fabric held a thousand worlds inside it. Her gloves had small pieces of alchemical stones stitched into them, making her hands twinkle. The River Alchemist popped up behind her in the reading room's doorway, grinning and waving a tattooed hand. It had been their idea to smuggle me away to practice sparring. I was hesitant after how terribly my last sparring session had gone, but I was too curious about the other royal alchemists' powers to say no.

*It will be an easy warm-up*, the Paper Alchemist had said, showing me a piece of purple silk fastened to a stick. *Just grab the flag before one of us can catch you.*

It turned out that trained royal alchemists could catch me in about thirty seconds.

"Your problem is that you fight like a viper," the Paper Alchemist said, leaning against the tree. From up here, I could see the top of her cap, embroidered with interlocking gold flowers. I kicked my foot to at least get the satisfaction of knocking it off, but she ducked without even looking. "You lash out hissing, unthinking," she said.

"Vipers are deadly," I said, falling limp against the branches. "Can you let me down now?"

"Vipers are deadly, but *you're* not," the Paper Alchemist said. "You should be fighting like a fox."

"Have you even seen a fox before?" I said. "They're lazy. They just steal eggs when birds aren't looking."

"Exactly!" the River Alchemist said. "Minimal effort, no confrontation, all the eggs they could want." She nodded to the icy ground. "I had you down before I even touched you."

"I...guess you're right," I said.

"Sorry, I didn't catch that?" the Paper Alchemist said, cupping a hand around her ear and grinning.

"I said let me down or I'll tell the Moon Alchemist you kidnapped me."

"It's okay, Scarlet," the River Alchemist said, patting my foot. "We'll teach you to win while barely lifting a finger."

I kicked out again, only because it was easier than acknowledging that they were actually going to help me, and what that meant. I'd never had real teachers before, unless I counted Wenshu, and his teaching style was basically yelling at me to rewrite characters. No one had ever cared whether I succeeded. No one had ever thought I was worth their time. As the Paper and River Alchemists took off my shoes and pretended to throw them over the wall if I tried kicking again, I wondered just how much I would be able to learn if I wasn't fighting against the entire world.

And more importantly, how could these people be the ones making the monsters that were running around the city?

"Why is my alchemist in a tree?"

The alchemists below me froze, dropping my shoes. The Moon Alchemist appeared from behind another tree, arms crossed.

"*Your* alchemist?" I said.

"She climbed it," the Paper Alchemist said, shrugging. "Nothing to do with us at all."

"She was sleeping in the library anyway!" the River Alchemist added as I aimed a kick at her head.

The Moon Alchemist sighed, then reached up and grabbed a low-hanging branch. The tree instantly dropped me to the ground, the sheet of ice crackling underneath me.

"Well, this has been fun, Scarlet, but we have important business to return to," the Paper Alchemist said, rapidly backing away, the River Alchemist close behind her. The Moon Alchemist rolled her eyes as they departed, then glared down at me.

"I wasn't actually sleeping," I said, before she could scold me. "I just closed my eyes for a moment."

"It doesn't matter," the Moon Alchemist said, her voice flat. "You're done for today."

I tried to stand up but slipped on the ice and found myself kneeling at the Moon Alchemist's feet. "I'm sorry, I can go back to studying now. I just—"

"You're not in trouble," the Moon Alchemist said, gazing somewhere over the wall, her expression gray. "The prince has sent for you."

I crossed my arms. "Well, it's not sunset yet, so he can wait."

The Moon Alchemist shook her head. "He's sent for you now so that you have time to get ready. The Empress wants you to attend her dinner tonight."

"Oh," I said, sinking back to my knees. I wasn't particularly eager to make small talk with a scheming Empress, but I hadn't eaten meat in ages and couldn't help imagining what a royal dinner would entail. An entire pig? A whole deer? Maybe even a bear? But the Moon Alchemist looked like she'd just invited me to a funeral.

"Is this bad news?" I said.

She pressed her lips together. "Personally, I prefer not to dine with the Empress."

*That's easy for you to say, since you've lived in a palace for a century*, I thought. I preferred not to do a lot of things as well, but most of life's unpleasantries didn't come with a feast.

"It's what the Empress wants, so don't overthink it. You don't have a choice," the Moon Alchemist said, turning to the faint ghost of the moon overhead, just starting to brighten before nightfall. "Just do as she says, and everything will be fine."

"I'm sorry," the prince said. I glared at his reflection in the mirror while a servant brushed my hair and stabbed jeweled combs into it. She'd already manhandled me into a gold dress, choked me with a jade necklace, and slapped powder on my face. Now she was determined to skewer hairpins straight through my skull into my brain. Apparently my red dress wasn't formal enough for this occasion, despite it being by far the nicest clothing I'd ever owned. That gave me high expectations for the food, if nothing else.

"Mother insisted on inviting you," he said, cradling my alchemy duck. "I tried to talk her out of it, but she is—" his gaze drifted to the servant, who was undoubtedly listening "—not easily swayed."

"Why is everyone so solemn about dinner?" I said. Then a horrible thought crossed my mind. "I won't have to eat gold, will I?"

"*Have to?*" the prince said, frowning. "You don't want to?"

"I don't want to look seventeen forever," I said. My body was still wiry like a grasshopper. I hoped that in a few more years I would start growing out instead of up.

"But you're..." The prince hesitated, clamping his mouth shut as he blushed.

"I'm *what*?" I said, narrowing my eyes.

He shook his head. "I'm just surprised you want to change," he said to the floor. "It doesn't matter, the Empress wouldn't give you gold. You're not part of the royal family."

"Small mercies," I said. If I *were* part of the family, I would probably be dead already. "How long have you been eating gold, anyway?"

The prince thought for a moment, stroking the duck's head with one finger. "About a year," he said. "Unlike my sisters, I had a 'political purpose,' so I needed to age. A crown prince isn't very useful as a helpless child."

"So you're not a sleazy old man in a young man's body,"

I said as the servant pierced my hair with one final pin and began cleaning up her supplies.

"*What?* Is that what you thought?" the prince said, squeezing the duck so hard that it squeaked and pecked his hand.

I shrugged. "I thought you seemed too naive to be an old man, but I didn't know if life gold stunted your brain growth as well."

"I don't even eat that much of it!" the prince said, his face pink. "Only once or twice a week! I'm still aging, just slowly."

"That hardly seems worth the expense," I said, raising an eyebrow.

"Fan Zilan, *you* try eating rocks instead of real food for every meal."

"Okay, fair enough," I said, turning back to the mirror and regarding my reflection with distrust. The servant had painted the center of my lips bright red, so my mouth looked the size and color of a cherry. Between my eyebrows, she'd drawn a red plum blossom. I looked like someone who'd grown up learning to sing and read poetry and make small talk with important men, not someone who spent her summers elbow-deep in mud and sweating beside a kiln. I knew I was supposed to feel prettier this way, that this was the face of someone of great importance, but it felt just like when I pretended to let Wenshu punish me, or be the Emperor's foreign tribute bride. Not all lies required words, and this one was painted all over my face.

"We should go," the prince said, setting the duck back in the box with seemingly great reluctance. "I'll bring back food for you," he whispered to it.

Then he offered me his hand. "To keep up appearances," he said. "We're supposed to be young and in love."

I grimaced. "I don't think 'love' is the purpose of a concubine."

"Well, no. But after turning down the last fifty girls, I

think indifference to the one concubine I've chosen might make mother suspicious."

"Are those the only two options?" I asked. "Love or indifference?"

He sighed. "I know I am not as smart as you, Zilan xiǎojiě, but if there's one thing I've succeeded at so far, it's delaying my own death in this court. I would like to live at least one more day." He held his hand out closer to me. It was clean and uncalloused, the hands of someone who only ever held paint brushes and chopsticks and gold coins.

I slipped my hand into his. "At least one more day," I said quietly, letting him pull me out into the hall.

The members of the court stared and whispered as we passed through the courtyard. I wished I could melt into the dirt and bury myself alive rather than feel so many eyes on me at once. The prince held my hand tighter, drawing me closer as if that would shield me from their words.

"It's not because of you," the prince whispered as we crossed over a bridge. "They're just surprised I have a concubine after the...fuss of last time."

"Yes, they're wondering why you turned down the fifty prettiest girls in the kingdom and then chose a hùnxiě," I said, glancing down at my rippling reflection in the lake, stretched long like a morning shadow. Surely the Empress would see right through this charade.

"Those girls..." The prince shook his head. "It's not as simple as how pretty they were. There were other factors to consider."

"If you're truly that picky about your concubines, I don't know how your mother will believe this," I said, tearing my gaze from my reflection.

"It's not about what *I* want," the prince said. "Most of those girls were either plucked from poor districts with the promise of food or pressured by their fathers to earn them a higher position in court. They weren't choosing me—they were choosing this life."

"Can you blame them?" I said, frowning. "Why do you think I'm here? Why do you think anyone wants to be part of this court?" *That's what happens when you hoard all the kingdom's riches in the capital*, I wanted to say, but there were too many people who might be listening.

"I just wanted to be chosen," the prince said quietly. "But those girls didn't have a choice, not really. I don't want to be the cause of someone's suffering just because my father has purchased me the right. I want to be chosen freely, or not at all."

"That's very..." I trailed off, because none of the words I could think of felt right. *Foolish? Naive? Oddly endearing?*

"I know," he said, grimacing. "Whatever you're thinking, my father has said worse. At least he should be happy now, because of you. As for mother..." He squeezed my hand tighter. "Just stay close to me."

The prince turned toward a hallway on the left, but the guards stationed in the doorway didn't move.

The prince sighed. "The Empress has requested our presence at—"

"She wants you to use the western entrance," one of the guards said.

The prince gripped my hand tighter. "That's not necessary," he said. "We can just meet her—"

"Empress's orders," the guard said.

The prince let out a tense breath between his teeth, then trudged to the left. We drew closer to the central palace, where the guards bowed and opened the doors, letting us into a hallway tiled with rubies and sapphires and diamonds that cast my reflection back at me in a thousand prisms across the walls. I felt like I was walking through a cave of a dragon's hoarded treasures. The doors shut behind us, sealing out the setting sun, the gems sparkling quietly in the candlelight like sharp whispers. We turned down another hallway, the lights growing dimmer, the walls paneled in dark wood.

"I'm sorry about this," the prince whispered, leading me around another corner.

Bones hung from the ceiling by threads of silk, swaying from the quiet breeze spilling through the lattice. The bones formed the shapes of animals, a whole menagerie suspended in the air like strange constellations. I discerned the short snout and claws of what was probably a bear, the needlelike ribs of a fish, the dangling long arms of an ape. Pelts decorated the walls, their jagged edges and outstretched paws making them look like exotic moths.

"Mother conducted experiments on many animals," the prince said, averting his gaze. "She didn't want to waste the bodies when they died."

"What kind of experiments?" I asked, my gaze tracing hairline cracks in a panda's skull, oozing with dried glue.

"I've never asked," the prince said. "I don't think I would like the answer."

He tugged my hand as if to pull me into the next room, but something caught my eye. I let go of him and ducked under the curled spine of a snake, moving deeper into the crypt.

"Zilan?" the prince said. "You shouldn't go back there."

But I ignored him, sliding around the hollow gaze of a goat's skull and the sharp bones of a bird swaying overhead, drawing to a stop in front of a pale, leathery pelt with scorched edges. Fine hair grew in patches, the surface creased like old scroll paper. Toward the top edge, a mess of black thread held the pelt together, one long line of stitches like a slanted smile.

"This is not an animal," I said quietly.

The prince lingered near the door, half a room away from me. "No," he said, the word so quiet, hardly more than a thought. A breeze whistled through the lattice, rattling the bones overhead, the whole room shivering.

"Who is this?" I said, my words rising over the sound of wind.

"Their name doesn't matter anymore," said a woman's voice.

At the other end of the room, the Empress stood in an arched doorway, light spilling inside. In the dim light, she looked less like a person than an idea of a person, her skin not even creasing when she offered me a sharp smile.

"I'm not particular about my subjects," she said. "When an opportunity presents itself, I seize it. Do you like my exhibit, Scarlet?"

My mouth felt too dry to speak. I glanced back at the pelt behind me. "You buried someone without their skin?" I said. "You're not afraid of angry ghosts?"

"I don't believe in ghosts," the Empress said. "I believe in gold." Then she turned and stepped through the doorway, swallowed by the light. The prince shot me a weak smile and reached for my hand again. This time, I huddled closer to him as we crossed over the threshold.

A cavernous dining hall opened up before us, arched ceilings so high that light couldn't reach them, like an empty night sky yawned overhead. The Empress sat at the center of a long table, its silk tablecloth spilling onto the floor like a waterfall of gold crashing into the pearly tiles. The table was set for many people, but the hall was empty except for the three of us and a few servants. Smaller tables around the room had the same place settings, with gold incense burners in the center. The smoke rose in spirals overhead, the ceiling churning with misty ghosts and the scent of jasmine. By the far left wall, seven red-crowned cranes with chains around their necks pecked at rice from golden troughs.

The prince let go of my hand, leaving me adrift. The light reflected off the tablecloth burned sharply in my eyes, the cranes' pecking the only sound in the sea of white mist, this world at the bottom of a well.

"Zilan," the prince whispered. I shook myself from the daze, kneeling on the floor in a deep bow. When I stood up, the prince took my hand once more.

"Darling," the Empress said to the prince, "Come sit." She waved us over, palm facing up, like she was calling a dog.

The prince led me to the far end of the table, five seats from the Empress, where two servants pulled out our chairs.

"I'm so glad you're joining us, Scarlet," the Empress said.

I bowed as much as I could at the table, coming face-to-face with my dinner plate. "It's an honor, Your Highness."

"It certainly is," the Empress said.

Servants began filling the cups at all of the tables, even those at the empty place settings, the green tea's steam deepening the blurry mist around us.

"Will others be joining us?" I whispered to the prince.

"No," the Empress said, as if I'd spoken to her. She rapped a sharp nail against the table. As if summoned, a servant emerged from the fog, refilling her cup. "We don't have room for anyone else."

My gaze drifted to the empty place settings, then back to the prince, who seemed to be searching for the right words. "The other seats were for my brothers and sisters," he said at last.

The table seemed to stretch longer, the absence heavier now that I knew the seats were for the dead. The table was littered with fine porcelain plates and teacups and bone chopsticks, like a ceramic graveyard. I imagined the table once filled with children talking amongst themselves, laughing and sharing food. I hadn't known the prince had so many siblings—only the ones in line for the throne were important enough for commoners to talk about. But now I realized that the prince would have sat here every day and watched as one by one his brothers and sisters never returned to their chairs, the table growing quieter, the absence yawning wider, until finally, there was no one but him left.

He gestured to the empty tables behind us. "The others are for my ancestors."

I shifted in my seat, conscious of the Empress's gaze on me. In Guangzhou, we set out plates for our ancestors during festivals, but certainly not every day. "Your ancestors must be pleased that you honor them so faithfully," I said at last, because that felt like a safe observation.

The Empress laughed, the sound bright as lightning in the silence of the hall, echoing up to the blurred ceilings. *"Honor,"* she said. "You're adorable, Scarlet. I like to remember those that came before me, that's true. But we do not honor the weak in this palace."

She took another long sip of tea, her red lips leaving a bloody smear across the gold rim of her cup. "The secret to eternal life was right in front of them," the Empress said. "But they were too lazy, too stupid, too afraid to find it. Their failures remind me why I deserve this kingdom. So no, Scarlet, we do not *honor* the dead here. We laugh at them."

The incense seemed even thicker than before, the scent of it coating my throat, creating a blurry haze around the Empress, only pierced by her golden eyes.

"Now," the Empress said. "Let's eat."

# CHAPTER TWENTY-ONE

The doors creaked open and servants carrying golden trays streamed into the hall, cramming the tables full of lidded dishes.

"Eat quickly and then we can go," the prince whispered, squeezing my hand.

"Hong, where did you say she was from?" the Empress said. It took me a moment to recognize the prince's name.

"Guangzhou, mother," he said.

"Ah." The Empress nodded, taking another sip of tea. The pure gold rim sparkled against her red lips. "That explains the accent."

I hid a frown against my teacup, drinking even though I felt that I could drain an entire lake and my mouth would still be bone dry. I hadn't thought my accent was that noticeable. People in Chang'an understood me well enough.

"My guard said he heard you speaking Guǎngdōng huà," the Empress said, swirling her tea around. "I don't know if anyone has informed you, but we only speak the language of scholars here."

"Yes, Your Highness," I said, worrying too late if my sour mood was leaking through to my words. I wondered if the

Empress actually thought lesser of my dialect, or if she just didn't want me keeping secrets. A small part of me prayed that the prince would protest, but he stayed still and silent.

The servants placed bowls of rice on the table, but the Empress and prince ignored them.

"My son tells me you're a hùnxiě," the Empress said, tilting her head to the side.

I gripped the edges of my chair, not trusting myself to meet her eyes without saying something that would get me beheaded. Couldn't we talk about how I was unschooled again? How I was a dirty southerner who had sold my body to her son?

"Yes, Your Highness," I managed to say.

"Where are your parents from?"

I swallowed. "My mother was from Guangzhou, and my father was from Scotia."

"What an intriguing mix," the Empress said. "I've met some hùnxiě with Slavic fathers, but Scotia is very far away. I think that's a better mix, personally. Scotians have such fair skin. Don't you think so, Hong?"

"Yes, Zilan is very beautiful, mother," he said evenly.

I blushed. I doubted that was what the Empress had been implying, but hopefully his comment would redirect her from talking about me like a recipe for soup. *He doesn't mean it*, I reminded myself. *He has to pretend because he chose you as a concubine.*

"Hùnxiě girls usually are," the Empress said. "Either they're pretty or they look like warthogs. There's no in between."

*I'm definitely the latter*, I thought, staring down at the forbidden rice.

Warm fingers touched my face, and I nearly jumped out of my skin before I realized it was the prince, angling my face toward him and smiling. He tucked a loose strand of hair behind my ear, the gesture so simple yet so delicate, like I was the kind of girl that needed to be gently cared for, not someone who shoved pearls down people's throats. My face burned, and I hoped all the white powder was enough to hide it. The prince pulled back and promptly dumped the rice from his bowl into mine.

"I don't need this," he said, before I could protest.

I eyed the rice, remembering the prince talking about all the poison in his food. "Don't you have taste testers?" I whispered.

"Yes, they sampled everything an hour ago," the prince said, setting his hand on my leg. "They're all alive and well, though the food is a bit colder than it would be otherwise."

The servants swooped in and cleared all the bowls but mine, and I caught a glimpse of the Empress watching us from across the table. I looked away, trying to focus instead on the absurdity of serving decorative dinner courses. I hoped they at least let the servants eat the rice.

Next, bowls of soup were brought out and promptly ignored.

"I'm curious, was your father very tall?" the Empress said, her gold eyes searing from behind the cloud of steam rising from the food. "You're almost as tall as Hong."

"I don't know," I said, staring at my reflection in the soup. "I don't remember much of him."

"He left you?" the Empress said, raising an eyebrow. When I didn't answer right away, the Empress shook her head. "You can't rely on foreigners. Though I'm curious, as I've never had the opportunity to meet a Scotian. I hear they have eyes the color of amethyst?"

"I don't—"

"Of course you don't know," the Empress said, sighing. "You're uneducated. I bet you never even left Guangzhou until now, you poor thing. No matter, I can figure things out for myself."

She gestured to a servant, who pulled a length of string from his pocket. The servant held the string to my shoulder with one hand, then took my wrist and laid it flat across my arm, all the way to my fingertips. I sat still and limp, too confused to protest.

"One quarter chǐ," the servant said, dropping my arm.

"Mother, is this necessary during dinner?" the prince said.

The Empress waved her hands like the prince's words were flies to swat away. Another servant appeared, hefting a scroll under one arm and unrolling it before the Empress with a bow. The Empress squinted, gaze dancing across the lines of text.

"That's above average," she said, turning to me. "You're like a crane, Scarlet. You could practically fly away."

"You measure all the concubines?" I said, forgetting that I wasn't supposed to speak unless the Empress asked me a question first. But she only smirked as the servant wound the string around my head.

"Of course not," she said. "Just the hùnxiě."

A hollowness opened up in my stomach. I thought of the bones in her menagerie, the pelts, the discarded remnants of her animal experiments. I barely heard the servant call out my next measurement before he wrapped the string around my waist.

"Mother," the prince said, slamming his palm against the table, soup sloshing over the rim. "That's *enough*."

The Empress raised an eyebrow. "Your defiance was cute when you were a child, Hong. Now, it's unwise."

He moved to stand up, but I grabbed his hand, yanking him back down. He was sweet to be angry, but for me, this wasn't worth dying over. I couldn't remember the last time

I'd felt fresh outrage at something like this, rather than stale and bitter acceptance.

I laced my fingers with the prince's, anchoring him to his seat.

"It's fine," I whispered. "One more day, remember?"

He let out a breath, unclenching his jaw, and leaned his forehead against mine. The closeness made me tense, but I didn't dare pull away with the Empress watching.

"I'm sorry," he whispered. "I wish I could—"

"This is the least of our problems," I said.

He nodded, pressing a hand to my cheek, then leaned back. The Empress watched us with narrowed eyes, then whispered something to her servant, who made another note on the scroll before rolling it up once more.

Servants leaned between me and the prince, setting down sparkling trays, and I realized that the time for decorative food was over. The real dinner was about to begin.

Servers placed trays overflowing with gold nuggets and pearl garnish in front of every seat but mine. I couldn't help leaning closer to the prince's plate, for I had never seen life gold up close before. It had a ghostly glow around it and strangely perfect symmetry to each piece, like it was a dream of gold rather than actual gold.

I drew back as the servants set a steaming bowl of stew in front of me. I hadn't eaten enough meat in my life to know for certain what kind it was, but it smelled of scallions and citrus. Another servant set a plate of sausages in front of me, and yet another set down a bowl of soup that smelled of salted pork with bok choy bobbing on the surface. There were so many dishes that a servant had to shuffle them around to make room for more. How could anyone eat this much food in a single meal?

The Empress raised a handful of gold to her mouth and

bit down with a sickening crunch, like all of her teeth were shattering. But rather than pain, her eyes rolled back in ecstasy. She surged forward into her palm, her tongue lashing out to lick the stray pieces from between her fingers, beneath her honed nails. Her hands glimmered from gold residue as she snatched another fistful from the table, cramming it into her mouth.

I turned to the prince, but his palms and chin were stained with gold as well, the residue splashing down the table and pooling around his feet. He seemed to have forgotten I was there, his irises suddenly pure, blazing gold.

It felt like the room around me was melting, hot sweat pooling under my clothes as the sound of crunching scraped my eardrums. I didn't feel hungry anymore, but I couldn't just stare at the Empress and I knew better than to ignore free food. I raised a spoonful up to my lips with a shaking hand.

The moment it touched my mouth, spices sizzled across my tongue and warmth spread through me, like I'd taken a bite of sunlight. Before I could help it, I'd shoveled down another spoonful. I couldn't eat fast enough, and soon the bowl was empty, half of it spilled down my neck. Before I could even pause to mourn how quickly it had gone, a servant took my bowl and replaced it with a full one.

"Do you like it, Scarlet?" the Empress said, sucking gold from her finger.

Something about her tone made me hesitate, my spoon hovering over the second bowl. Her words had an odd edge to them that I couldn't quite decipher. My stomach felt tight, my lips scorched.

"We have all sorts of exotic foods here," she said, popping another gold nugget in her mouth. "Foods you've probably never dreamed of trying."

I had the sudden urge to vomit across the table. The spoon fell from my lips and I grabbed my teacup, draining it in a single gulp. The haze of smoke had swallowed the ground beneath my ankles, like nothing existed in the whole world except for the three of us and the table piled with gold.

The Empress wiped her lips, then leaned closer. "Did you come to Chang'an alone, Scarlet?" she asked, her voice low, all pretense of politeness stripped from her tone. This wasn't a question, but an order.

The words spilled from my lips all at once, like the Empress had jammed her hand down my throat and yanked them out.

"I came with my brother and sister," I said. "They're still in a western ward."

The Empress hummed, drumming her fingers on the table. "Why did you really come here?" she said.

"To make money," I replied, my tongue heavy in my mouth. It was hard to shape words, but they surged forward anyway.

"Is that your god, Scarlet?"

I shook my head, incense stinging my eyes, clouding my vision. "What?"

"Everyone worships something, whether they know it or not," the Empress said. "The old gods are dying. I'm asking which new one you'll choose."

My throat clenched, the pain like being sick on an empty stomach, trying to force words up even though I couldn't figure out what I wanted to say.

Something crashed against the door, straining against the wood with a gnarled scream—another one of the palace monsters? But the Empress didn't even flinch, licking gold from the crevices of her hand as a sound like jagged claws raked across the door. The whole room rattled from the force, teacups trembling, my reflection shivering in my soup. Something hot and wet pooled under my feet, though I couldn't see it through the mist of incense. My heartbeat thundered in my ears, nausea choking my throat. I closed my eyes and gripped the edge of the table, feeling like I was going to faint face-first into my food.

"Zilan?"

A hand rested on my leg, making me jolt. The prince had slid his chair closer to mine. His face and hands had been wiped clean of gold, but his skin still sparkled with its remnants.

"I want to leave," I said. I really shouldn't have been making demands to the prince in front of the Empress, but he nodded anyway.

"I'm finished," he said to the guards.

"Already?" the Empress said, frowning.

"I ate earlier today, since your invitation came late," the prince said, pulling out my chair before a servant could. He took my hand and all but yanked me to my feet, as if he didn't want to give his mother the chance to object.

"Scarlet," the Empress said.

The prince seemed inclined to keep dragging me out of the room, but I looked over my shoulder.

"I know it's all a bit...overwhelming at first. I was not born into this court either. I understand."

My iron grip on the prince's hand loosened.

"But you don't need to worry," she said, picking up another gold nugget and holding it up to the light. "You won't be here for long."

The prince pulled me away through another set of doors that the servants held open for us. I greedily inhaled a breath of clean air as the incense floated away, stumbling over to a banister and holding tight.

He took one of my arms, fingers sliding down to the base of my wrist, feeling my racing pulse.

"I'm sorry," he said. "Mother sometimes asks for too many herbs in the soup."

*"Herbs?"* I said, cuffing drool from my mouth. "Are you joking? She drugged me!"

The prince shook his head quickly, releasing my wrist. "It's a mild sedative," he said. "She's done it to me before. Let's get you some more water and you'll be fine."

*"Fine,"* I echoed, staying rooted even when he tugged at my sleeve. Did he truly not see how horrific that meal had been? I could suffer through being treated like a pet by the Empress, but when I looked at the prince's face, all I could see was the lingering stain of gold on his lips.

"You've known all your life that the Empress was like this," I said. "You watched her kill your entire family. But you only came to Guangzhou for my help when you realized your own life was in danger. No one else mattered enough."

"I won't let her hurt you," the prince said. He reached for my face, but I slapped his hand away.

"I'm not talking about myself!" I said. "Why did you ask me to resurrect you in the first place? Did you want to come back and stop her, or just play dead while she destroyed the rest of China?"

He looked away, jaw tense as he stared out across the garden. Both of us knew the answer.

"What am I supposed to do?" he said at last. "You really think I can stop my mother?"

"Have you ever even *tried*?" I said.

He flinched, still refusing to meet my gaze. "I never asked to be who I am," he said. "I can't—"

"*Stop talking about what you 'can't' do!*" I said, shoving him back against the banister. I was too loud for such a quiet night, but I didn't care. "You are the Crown Prince of China! Don't you dare tell me that you're powerless."

I turned to leave, but he grabbed my wrist. "Zilan, please," he said. "You can hate me if you want, but please don't run off alone. The monsters—"

"As if *you* could ever protect me from any monster!" I said, twisting my wrist out of his grip. "You can't even protect yourself."

I took a step back, waiting to see if he would argue. *Tell me that you would try to save me*, I thought. But he only dropped his shoulders and stared at his feet—the same way he looked away from everything that mattered. Like always, he would let me leave, knowing exactly what he could say to make me stay.

My eyes watered. I took another step back, only starting to realize how badly I'd wished I was wrong, how much I didn't want him to be like the other rich men who only cared for themselves. But I should have known from the first day we met, when he'd tried to buy my dreams from me. He would never fight for me because the rich never fought. They turned and ran away.

# CHAPTER TWENTY-TWO

The prince wasn't foolish enough to call for me the next few nights, so I tried my best to forget he existed. During the day, the Moon Alchemist kept me busy doing almost everything but alchemy. Studying for the imperial exam seemed easy compared to the mountain of scrolls she stacked in front of me every day and the questions she'd ask me afterward to make sure I'd understood.

"What element is spessartine?" she said.

I didn't lift my forehead from my scroll. "Fire," I said.

"No."

"Isn't it orange?"

"Yes, but it's a desert stone, so it's Earth."

I peeled my forehead from the desk. "But diamonds are desert stones, and they're considered metal."

"Desert diamonds are Earth stones. Mountain diamonds are metal."

"But aren't mountains part of the earth?"

The Moon Alchemist shot me a cold look. "Arguing about it doesn't change what it is."

I sighed, flopping back onto the table. I'd spent the whole

morning going back and forth between scrolls on stone types and scrolls on the history of alchemy. Most of them traced the source of alchemy back to Penglai Island, a place in my father's notes that I'd thought was only a myth. But I didn't see how any of that was supposed to help me make gold. "I need a break. I can't fit any more stones into my brain."

"You're distracted," the Moon Alchemist said.

I shook my head. "It's just that all of this is theoretical. I like actually *doing* alchemy."

"The kind of alchemy you'll be doing is dangerous," the Moon Alchemist said. "Handling these stones needs to be as easy as breathing to you."

I doubted making gold would be the most dangerous thing I'd done. If only the Moon Alchemist knew about my cousins, the walking corpses, courtesy of my sloppy childhood resurrection. I hadn't gone to see them in a few days, too caught up in my training.

"Do you have any scrolls on alchemical resurrection?" I asked.

The Moon Alchemist froze. Her sharp gaze slid over to me. "That is forbidden," she said, each word clipped. "You know that."

"Yes," I said, "but is reading about it also forbidden?"

The Moon Alchemist watched me for an uncomfortably long moment, as if searching for something in my face. "We will cover that—and everything else—in time. But only under my supervision. It's very dangerous."

"But why?" I said.

Something in my voice must have sounded too desperate, because the Moon Alchemist's eyes narrowed.

"Zilan," the Moon Alchemist said stiffly, "I heard that your parents passed."

I opened my mouth to tell her this wasn't about them, but hesitated. Maybe it was better if she thought I was just a sad orphan instead of running an illegal resurrection business. I sank lower in my seat, dropping my gaze to my lap.

"My mother passed," I said, keeping my voice quiet, weak. "My father left. I just wish my mother could have seen me being a royal alchemist. I wish she could have been proud of me."

The words were true, but somehow I felt the Moon Alchemist would sense the lie behind them. I didn't dare look up, certain she would see straight through me.

At last, she sighed. "Zilan," she said, "if you were to resurrect your mother, she would not be human anymore."

I felt like a rock had lodged in my throat. I pictured Yufei braiding my hair, Wenshu making tea. How could they not be human? They were more human than the gold-guzzling court scholars.

"When you die, all of your qi goes back into the universe," the Moon Alchemist said. "You can't simply call it back to an empty husk. Your mother would need another source of qi."

My stomach clenched. My cousins didn't have enough qi? Was I supposed to be finding more of it for them? I cleared my throat, trying to keep my tone even. "So if I brought her back, I would have to give her—"

"You can't *give* someone qi," the Moon Alchemist said slowly. "They take it."

I clasped my hands together to still their trembling. "From where?"

The Moon Alchemist crossed her arms, her eyes burning amber.

"From you," she said.

My heart felt like it stopped in my chest, my whole body suddenly marble stiff and deathly cold. "From me?" I whispered. "You mean—"

"From whoever they love," the Moon Alchemist said. "The dead are like a parched riverbed, sucking up anything they can find. They can siphon off the qi from their loved ones, one drop at a time, until they grow sick and die."

I shook my head, wishing I could take the question back, return to the life when I'd innocently wondered what the true cost of resurrections was. If the Moon Alchemist was right—if the cost of one life was everyone they loved—then I had never really brought back the dead through some alchemical miracle, I'd just traded one life for countless others and doomed the revived to a life of grief and loneliness. I'd ended more lives than I'd restored.

My thoughts snapped to my aunt and uncle in bed, inexplicably growing sicker and sicker. Yet, as soon as we'd left, they'd claimed they felt better. I'd thought they were lying for our sakes, but what if Wenshu and Yufei had slowly been killing them?

If I told my cousins the Moon Alchemist's theory, they would never want to go home again. They could never see their parents because of what I'd done.

I'd tried so hard to fit seamlessly into their lives, never give them a reason to question my presence, to regret me. But now our family was fractured in half because I'd played around with alchemy as a desperate child. Would they all hate me if they knew? I prayed the Moon Alchemist was wrong, if only so I would never have to tell them.

And what about *me*?

If my cousins had been stealing qi from their parents, surely they'd been taking mine as well. Perhaps I'd lasted longer because I was younger, but did that mean I was going to drop dead at any moment?

"How long?" I said, unable to hide the shaking in my voice. "How long does it take to...to take all of someone's qi?"

"It's not an exact science, but about four years," the Moon Alchemist said. "The closer you are to the dead, the faster it happens."

The trembling in my hands stilled. I gripped handfuls of my dress, pinching my legs beneath the fabric, the distant pain the only thing keeping me tethered.

That didn't make any sense. It had been about three and a half years since I'd resurrected my cousins. Surely if three quarters of my qi was gone, I would have noticed by now. I wouldn't have been able to do alchemy, wouldn't even be able to stand up, unless...

...unless they didn't love me.

The thought cut off my breath, washed all the heat from my body. I couldn't hear anything at all but my heartbeat, so mockingly loud.

I thought of Wenshu and Yufei walking side by side to take their tests, whispering to each other, trading secrets about me in the dark. Even in death, they were together, bonded in a way I could never understand. Maybe they thought they loved me because they'd grown used to my presence, but alchemy had a way of unveiling truths that even alchemists didn't know.

"Are you sure?" I whispered, hot tears burning at the corner of my eyes.

"Why are you crying?" the Moon Alchemist said, the words a sharp accusation.

I shook my head, swallowing down my tears. "How do you know?" I said. "If it's so forbidden, how can you be certain of the cost? Have you even resurrected anyone?"

The Moon Alchemist's eyes darkened. She stood up slowly,

and as her shadow eclipsed the section of the floor where I sat hugging my knees, for once I felt incredibly small.

"I wanted to make this easy for you," she said, "but if you're so certain that you're ready, wipe your face and come with me."

I rubbed my eyes on my sleeve. "Where—"

But the Moon Alchemist had already turned away, storming out the door. I hurried after her, nearly tripping over the low table. She didn't even check to make sure I was following, striding swiftly across the courtyard. I walked a few paces behind her as she charged out of the alchemy ward, across the central palace, where the walls grew shorter and pathways narrower. The walls had a different cast in daylight, but as we drew closer, it slowly dawned on me that I'd been here before.

The guards to the dungeons bowed and unlocked the doors for us without question. Once more, I headed into the cool underbelly of the palace. The Moon Alchemist grabbed a candle and strode unwaveringly into the darkness, down the spiral staircase, deeper and deeper until we'd long passed where the princesses had been kept. The farther we went, the more the air smelled of death. Not exactly rot quite yet, but the sour scent of decay creeping in. My breath rose in shuddering clouds and I hugged my arms around myself, annoyed at the thin, decorative silk of my dress.

At last, the staircase came to a stop on dirt ground, so cold and parched that it cracked beneath our feet. A curved doorway led into darkness thick as a wall of painted black.

The Moon Alchemist handed me the candle, then pointed ahead.

"Go on," she said.

I looked between her and the doorway. "Why—"

"You wanted to know," she said. "Go find the answers you wanted."

I swallowed. The Moon Alchemist might be terse, but she wasn't wrong—I had asked for this. Besides, this was my job now. I needed to stop acting like the prince, who turned away from the palace's ugliness.

I stepped into the shadows, the weak light of the candle illuminating little more than my own feet and the cracked ground in front of me. Maybe it was my nerves, but the air here seemed harder to breathe, so moist with decay.

My circle of light swallowed a pale hand lying in the dirt, palm facing down. The skin had started to peel back from purple nails, revealing red muscles underneath. I drew closer, fishing out a firestone and brightening my candle so I could see better.

A thousand faces stared back at me.

Bodies stacked from floor to ceiling, stiff arms and legs jutting out, jaws slack in silent screams, eyes shrunken into pools of jelly dripping out of their sockets, bloody foam oozing from nostrils, flaps of skin hanging off limbs and shuddering like limp flags.

My heel crunched down on something as I backed up. I whirled around, jumping when I realized I'd stepped on another hand, stumbling into a mountain of bodies on the opposite wall. I tripped over another arm, jostling the corpse at the bottom of the stack, the whole pile trembling at the disturbance. Each of them had thin strings tied around their wrists or ankles with names written on scraps of paper.

How had all of these bodies ended up here? Corpses were supposed to be buried in coffins crammed full of míngqì, not stacked in a frozen dungeon.

"Who are they?" I said, turning to the Moon Alchemist, who stood in the doorway with her arms crossed. "Why are we hoarding corpses under the palace?"

"I don't know who they were. They have names, but it hardly matters now," the Moon Alchemist said. "And we don't *hoard* them, Zilan, they're here for a reason. Wipe the shock from your face and start asking the right questions. You are a royal alchemist, so speak like one."

I took a deep breath of stale corpse air and tried to organize my thoughts. "Who brought them here, and how?"

"The Empress's night guards," the Moon Alchemist said. "At the end of every week, they go to the poor districts. They'll buy blood for fifty gold, and fresh corpses for one hundred."

*One hundred?* That's a week's worth of food in this city. But I supposed many couldn't afford a burial anyway. "Why does the Empress need either of those things?" I said.

"It's not the blood she wants, but the qi. If you take enough blood to bring someone near death, you can access it. It's the key ingredient in life gold."

So she was after the same thing I'd used in my final alchemy trial. It made sense that qi was needed for life gold, but something that valuable seemed worth more than fifty gold pieces. One bowl of rice at the palace probably cost more.

"The bodies are used to make soldiers," the Moon Alchemist went on. "I'm sure you've seen them in the palace by now. The Empress isn't one for subtlety."

"Soldiers?" I whispered.

The Moon Alchemist walked past me, waving for me to follow her deeper into the darkness. We approached a hall full of bamboo cells, where people were chained to the floor, rats scurrying around them. We stopped in front of a man who lay so still that at first I thought he was a corpse, but he flinched away from the light and curled into himself like a dying spider. He had a name carved into his cheek, the wound still raw, like someone had sliced it haphazardly with a blunt knife.

"He's been resurrected, but I think you already knew that," the Moon Alchemist said.

I ripped my gaze from the soul tag, face red. "I—"

"I don't care what you've done in the past, but these are the only people we are allowed to resurrect now," she said. Then she drew a handful of pearls from her pocket. "The Empress is expecting this one to be done today."

"What do you mean, 'done'?"

She held the pearls up to the dim light. "Life pearls," she said. "The kind that the Empress eats." Then, with one hand, she reached through the bars and opened the man's slack jaw.

"Eat," she said, popping the pearls in his mouth.

Maybe a more conscious man would have refused, but this one was half dead from starvation, and everyone knew that pearls were sustenance for the rich. He chewed through them with a horrible shattering sound.

Slowly, the man sat up. He shuttered like a rickety old house in a typhoon, and with a thousand tiny cracks, glossy pearl began to envelop every inch of him in a second skin. The colors in his irises vanished, his eyes replaced by two smooth pearls, his white teeth sharpening. His jaw hung slack, tiny pearls spilling past his lips, clattering to the floor.

I backed up against the other wall. These monsters had tried to kill me and my cousins, yet the Moon Alchemist didn't seem afraid. In fact, the pearl monster wasn't doing anything at all. He was just staring forward, drooling pearls.

"Eating alchemical gemstones may provide eternal youth to the rich," the Moon Alchemist said, "but this is what happens when you perform too much alchemy on one body. You get eternal life, but not the kind you wanted."

I crept closer, waving a hand in front of the man's face. But his eyes didn't even track the movement.

"I've seen people like this before, but they were dangerous," I said. "Why isn't he doing anything?"

Instead of answering, the Moon Alchemist snatched a rat from the floor. It writhed and angled to bite her, but she pulled out a knife and slashed a shallow line across its spine, then tossed it into the darkness of the cell. She turned to the pearl man, cranked his jaw open, and held her bloody blade over his tongue, tapping a few times until the drops fell into his mouth.

The man's jaw clapped shut, nearly splitting his lip on the Moon Alchemist's knife.

His head cranked around to face the rat, tiny pearls rushing from his slack lips. He lunged back into his cell, rattling his chains as he crushed the creature in his bare hands. It squeaked and twisted, but he held it by the tail and sunk his teeth into its torso.

"They only hunt what they're told to, unless you try to stop them," the Moon Alchemist said. "They are lethal, but of no danger to their creators."

"Why did you do that?" I asked, wincing as the pearl man crunched down on the rat's skull.

"Why did *I*?" the Moon Alchemist said. "Because if I send the Empress a pearl monster that doesn't perform properly, she'll throw me in the cell next."

"Do you know what these monsters have been doing?" I said. *Devouring the House of Li? Getting girls burned alive in western wards?*

"We don't know where most of the blood we feed them is from," the Moon Alchemist said. "We're still running a lot of experiments, and at times, there is collateral damage."

I remembered the slaughtered librarian, the bloodied pearls in my satchel he was supposed to protect. Maybe Wenshu was right and the pearls were lost in a robbery gone wrong, their owner one of the unfortunate victims of the Empress's experiments. The monster had probably killed him first, then still smelled his blood and come after the pearls next. The librarian had only gotten in the way.

"We bring them back here eventually," the Moon Alchemist said, "and destroy them when they've served their purpose."

"Destroy them?"

She pointed to the man's cheek. "We remove the soul tags."

The man continued to tear the rat apart, its tendons snapping wetly, bones crunching, blood dribbling into the dirt. I'd always maintained that it wasn't my problem what happened to the bodies I resurrected, as long as I got paid. But did the families who sold these bodies know that this was what would become of the people they loved?

"I don't know if I can——"

"If you refuse to help, then you'll be chained up here as well," the Moon Alchemist said. "You will starve to death and the rats will eat you, then the other alchemists will be forced to resurrect you. If you're lucky, you'll be made into a pearl monster, kill someone who nobody else liked, and be put out of your misery quickly. Do you want to know how I know that, Zilan?"

I swallowed. "We're never allowed to quit?" I said quietly.

The Moon Alchemist let out an incredulous laugh. "You think the Empress would let anyone else hire the best alchemists in the country? Once you're an imperial alchemist, you serve the Empress until you die, and after that as well."

I felt like the walls were drawing closer on all sides. The man was sucking on rat bones, loudly licking his fingers.

"Do you understand now, Zilan?" the Moon Alchemist said. "You spilled your blood at your last trial, so the Empress almost certainly has it. Even if you fled, her monsters would find you anywhere."

I shook my head, leaning against the wall, afraid I would fall over. This was the dream I'd so desperately wanted? I'd needed money so badly that I'd signed myself up for something without really knowing what it meant, and now there was no way out.

A warm hand fell on my shoulder. The Moon Alchemist stood in front of me, her eyes the only brightness in the dungeon.

"You're overthinking this," she said. "Do you want to be inside the cage, or outside?"

"Outside," I whispered, even though outside only felt like a bigger cage.

"Then you've got your wish," the Moon Alchemist said. "We'll start resurrections tomorrow."

I walked back to the western ward, two steps behind my guard, feet dragging and nails stained red, paper-wrapped pork from the palace kitchens in baskets in each hand. Despite the smell, I was too nauseous to eat. My skin somehow reeked of rot, even though I'd barely touched any of the dead. I felt their soupy eyes on me even when we'd left the dungeons and the sunlight had bleached away the darkness, as if everything below was a hazy nightmare. But night would come again, and I didn't want to be alone.

The Moon Alchemist's words still haunted me.

*They can siphon off the qi from their loved ones, one drop at a time, until they grow sick and die.*

I had no reason to doubt the Moon Alchemist anymore, but even if she knew alchemy better than anyone, she didn't know my cousins. I'd bring them food, and we'd chat and poke fun at Wenshu, and their smiles would wash away any doubts. *I* had resurrected them, I knew them better than the Moon Alchemist ever could.

But when I opened their door, they were halfway through dismembering a man in Yufei's bed.

*"Shut the damn door!"* Wenshu said, mopping up blood with a bedsheet while Yufei startled to a stop, holding a severed hand. A man with a pearly sheen to his skin—or what was left of him—was sprawled face-down over Yufei's sheets, which were now hopelessly stained red, seeing as she'd chopped off both of his hands. The baskets of pork fell to the floor.

I whirled around to the guard, who'd gone pale. "Wait outside, or I'll stab you," I said, slamming the door shut.

"What happened?" I said. "Did it hurt you?"

"He came in through the window," Yufei said, nodding to the shattered lattice before plunging a knife back into his arm. "Tried to bite me, so I snapped his neck."

"And, as you can imagine, getting caught dragging a grown man's body out in the middle of the night isn't the most flattering look for southern travelers trying to not get burned at the stake," Wenshu said, wiping sweat from his forehead. "We're trying to get rid of him discreetly."

"Then why did you start with the hands?" I said, rushing forward and shoving Wenshu aside. "And stop cleaning while he's still bleeding!"

"Because our knives aren't sharp and our resident corpse-handler was *busy being a concubine!*" Wenshu said, casting his rags to the floor.

"I wasn't being a concubine, I was being an alchemist," I said, stepping closer and frowning at the pearly coating on his skin. If what the Moon Alchemist said was true, then someone had sent this monster after my cousins.

"How big of a bag do you have to stuff him in?" I asked.

"Here," Yufei said, holding up a burlap sack the size of a pillowcase.

I fished some firestones out of my satchel and leaned over the man. My hands hovered over the nape of his neck, where a name was etched into his skin and outlined in ink, cracked down the middle where Yufei had snapped his neck. I prayed Wenshu hadn't—

"And yes, we've seen the fucking soul tag," Wenshu said, "so as soon as we get away with this murder, we'll be discussing what the hell you're doing in the palace."

I raised an eyebrow. "You're giving a lot of orders for someone who has no hope of hiding this body without me."

Wenshu clenched his bloodstained fists. His face and clothes were spattered with red. "You won't have to worry about the monsters anymore if you keep wasting time being a brat. I'll kill you myself."

For once, I didn't think he was exaggerating.

I turned to the corpse and broke it down into pieces with firestone, soaking the bed with blood and passing Yufei feet and kneecaps and squishy organs while Wenshu yelled that she needed to put the biggest pieces in the bag first or else it wouldn't all fit. Somehow, she managed to cram everything in, save for a few toes poking out the opening. I decided to take mercy on Wenshu and use some stones to strip the blood from the bedding. Then at last, we stood in a clean and silent room, a bag of body parts on the floor between us.

"I think you need to stay at a different inn," I said.

"You *think*?" Wenshu said, his face red. He grabbed the bag from the floor and stormed across the room, throwing the door open to where the flustered guard stood waiting. "Get rid of this," Wenshu said, shoving it into his arms, then slammed the door before the guard could answer. He turned to me, his eyes murderous.

"I know a soul tag when I see one," Wenshu said. "Do you want to explain to me why alchemists are making monsters that want to eat us?"

"I don't know why they came for you," I said. It could be that the Empress knew I'd set the princesses free and was trying to punish me, or maybe the monsters knew the taste of my blood and had come after my family because they smelled similar.

"So what did you do?" Wenshu said, glaring. "Because it's a bit strange to me that once you moved into the palace, monsters start bursting through our windows."

"I thought the point of us coming here was so we could work for the Empress!" I said. "Just because I passed my test and you didn't, suddenly it's too dangerous?"

Wenshu's face pinched. "There are a lot more scholars than alchemists, Zilan," he said, not exactly unkindly, but there was something just barely sharp about his words, like I'd pricked my finger on a thorn. "The competition is different, and we don't have a crown prince looking out for us."

Heat rushed to my face. "You think he had anything to do with—"

"He just means that the prince is dangerous," Yufei said. "If rich people know your name, you're going to make enemies no matter what you do."

"*I had to stay alive!*" I said. "I don't know what you want me to do! Roll over and die? Even if I wanted to, I can't leave now!" My life wasn't mine anymore, and the more I learned about alchemy, the deeper I fell into the sticky secrets of the palace. And what did I get in exchange?

Money.

I'd sold my soul for gold, the only god I believed in. The Empress was right.

I thought of Auntie and Uncle and couldn't bring myself to truly regret it, but I had a sinking feeling that the palace would gut me like a pig and turn my bones to wind chimes and still want more and more, and I could do nothing at all but keep bleeding.

"I can ask the prince to find you a safer place to stay," I said quietly, because that seemed to be the only thing I could offer them.

"No," Wenshu said. "Don't tell the prince anything. We'll find our own place under different names and write to you when we get there. Leave the royal family out of it."

I jumped at the sound of knocking, but the guard's timid voice followed soon after. "I, um, did what you asked," he said.

"Go," Wenshu said.

"Are you—"

"We can handle it," Wenshu said.

"We'll let you know as soon as we figure out where to go," Yufei said.

I didn't want to return to the palace, but it seemed that both of them were pushing me out. "I brought you food," I said, gesturing to the parcel on the floor. But I hesitated in the doorway, remembering the monster the Moon Alchemist had showed me, the sounds of rat flesh being torn apart.

"Whatever you do, don't eat any jewels," I said. "The Moon Alchemist said—"

"Jewels?" Wenshu said incredulously. "If we have any extra jewels, the last thing we'll do is eat them. Be serious, Zilan."

I clenched my jaw, wondering how my warning them had somehow turned into me being scolded again. Could I do nothing right in their eyes?

"Never mind," I said stiffly, sliding the door open then slamming it shut behind me.

The guard followed me back to the palace, where I curled up in my bed and told myself that tonight didn't mean anything, that the Moon Alchemist was wrong. I fell asleep repeating my own lies until they seeped into my dreams. *The Moon Alchemist is wrong, and everything is fine*, I thought, even as the words dissolved like waterlogged paper that floated down a bloodred stream. Then the waters dried up and there was only the red dirt road, and the five empty doorways, their emptiness screaming for me.

But the name they called was not mine.

I drew closer and the shadows prickled across my fingertips, devouring my skin, gnawing holes in my bones until I was a nothingness as loud as the empty arches. When I woke in the morning and turned toward the brightness of the sun shattering through the lattice of my windows, I couldn't remember who the darkness had called for.

# CHAPTER TWENTY-THREE

The Moon Alchemist was keeping a secret.

She didn't even watch as I jammed a pearl into the mouth of today's corpse, didn't comment when I pulled my hand out too slowly and nearly lost my fingers, and only cast a cursory glance at the freshly born pearl monster ripping a rat to shreds.

"Good enough," she said, standing and waving for me to follow her out of the dungeons.

She observed as I made a batch of gold and then she disappeared, leaving me alone to stir the qi out of a cauldron of hot peasant blood, the smell so sharp that I didn't even realize when my own nose started bleeding. Instead of thinking about the bodies it came from, I thought about the pay I'd received at the end of last week, an amount so eye-watering that I'd immediately sent half of it to Auntie and Uncle, certain that everyone would smell the money on me and rob me the second I stepped outside.

The Moon Alchemist burst into the room an hour later, looking like someone had spit in her tea.

"You're not using enough iron," she said, barely glancing at my pitiful pile of finished life gold. "You need to draw up more of it from the blood, or the gold doesn't hold together. It's not supposed to crumble to pieces once you touch it."

"Is anyone really that picky about their nuggets of eternal youth?" I said, ladling another glob of blood onto my tray.

"Do you think I'm teaching you this for my own entertainment?" the Moon Alchemist asked, slamming her fist onto the table and rattling all the gold nuggets. "Don't waste my time with more pointless questions."

My hand froze before setting the ladle down. *"More?"* I said. I'd hardly asked her anything today.

The Moon Alchemist sighed and leaned back in her chair, glaring up at the ceiling. "You need to deal with the prince," she said at last.

I dropped the ladle in surprise, trying to snatch it again, but the handle sank to the bottom of the cauldron. "I... What?"

"He comes here every day asking about you," she said.

"He *does?*"

The Moon Alchemist crossed her arms. "He's constantly inquiring as to how you're doing, how your training is going, if you need anything. I tell him to talk to you himself, but he refuses. I'm not even supposed to tell you this, but if you want to report me for treason, go ahead. I don't care anymore."

I gripped the edges of my chair, mortified. I wanted to apologize on his behalf, but it wasn't like he was my pet that I could scold for bad behavior. He wasn't *mine.*

"He's an annoyance and a distraction," the Moon Alchemist said, "but I can't tell him that because he's the Crown Prince, so go deal with your problems yourself. Quickly."

That was how I found myself trudging to the prince's room in the middle of the afternoon. I figured I might as well use the opportunity to ask him if he could subtly find someone to guard my cousins, despite Wenshu's wishes. Every time I closed my eyes, I remembered the pearl man in the dungeons sucking rat bones clean. That could be my cousins next. Even if they hated me for it, I needed to try to help.

I'd asked the Moon Alchemist about the monster who came for Wenshu and Yufei, but she'd only scowled and said, *I already told you, we don't know whose blood we're using. It's possible that someone got your cousins' blood, or diluted some of yours, but there's no way to know and we can't stop making the Empress's creatures. Get your family some swords and sturdier windows. This is what you signed up for, Scarlet.* In hindsight, her impatience might have had something to do with the prince's visits.

But the prince was not in his room when I came for him. I so rarely sought him out on my own that I felt strangely foolish just standing in his dim bedchamber, so vast without him.

But something else was there.

In the delicate silence of the palace, slow breaths came from inside the closet. Something was waiting for the prince to return.

I hadn't spoken, so maybe they thought I was him and were preparing to jump out. I thought of the way the Empress looked at him across the dinner table, and a dark ember of rage began to glow within me. I pictured myself returning to his room at night to find him slashed to pieces, his blood spattered across the silk sheets.

As quietly as possible, I drew three pieces of iron from my satchel and transformed them into a blade. As I drew closer to the closet, the sounds silenced.

I curled my fingers around the lip of the door and shoved it open.

Two girls screamed, cowering against the back wall.

It was the Princesses Yiyang and Gao'an.

The girls who were supposedly safe in an eastern convent, though apparently not anymore. The older one peeked through her fingers at me, then gasped and shook her sister.

"It's Fan Zilan," she said. "Hong's girlfriend."

I felt my face twitch. "I'm not—" I shook my head. Now wasn't the time. "What are you two doing here?"

"The convent burned down," the older one said, hugging one of the prince's robes to her cheek. "Monsters came and killed all the nuns and knocked over a candle. We ran here through the tunnels. We didn't know where else to go."

I sighed, squatting down in front of them. So much for the safe sanctuary until the prince could figure out a better plan.

"Are you hurt?"

They shook their heads.

"Is this really where the prince put you?" I said, leaning against the doorframe. "Surely there are better hiding places."

"We couldn't find him," said the younger one. "We didn't want to be seen, so we came here."

I sighed, rising to my feet. So much for quickly dealing with the prince before returning to alchemy training. "I'll find him for you," I said. Surely the palace had some sort of fortified safe room he could put them in, at least temporarily.

"Don't leave!" the older one said, grabbing my wrist. "What if the monsters find us?"

I paused to think, then handed the girl my dagger. "This is just in case," I said. "I'm going to seal the doors shut, okay? I won't be long."

Their eyes watered, but they nodded and scooted back into the shadows of the closet. I felt like a monster shutting the door on them and locking them in the dark, but I didn't want to drag them out into the hallway without a better plan. After using up all the iron in my bag, I didn't have many strong stones left, so I jammed the locks with granite, testing the handles to make sure they wouldn't move, then took off running.

The hallways were near deserted as the servants prepared for lunch, but I managed to grab a maid, who told me the prince was in a meeting with foreign diplomats on the other side of the palace. I flew past bewildered servants carrying trays of food and guards who had probably never seen a woman run in their lives. I tripped and skinned my knees in the dirt, then gathered up my skirts and ran faster. The prince had said that the monsters had tracked members of the House of Li across the country—it wouldn't take them long to follow the scent of the princesses' blood from the convent.

I reached the meeting hall panting and covered in dirt, the guards so bewildered that at first they didn't even try to stop me from entering. A hand grabbed me just before I could reach the door.

"The prince is occupied," he said.

I was too out of breath to argue, so I twisted my arm out of his grip and stormed in before he could stop me.

A room full of bearded old men in blue silk spun around, all of their golden eyes focused on me. The prince sat at the opposite end, brush hovering over an unfurled scroll. He locked eyes with me, the brush slipping from his fingers, splashing ink across the page.

"Zilan?" he said. His gaze twitched to the men around him. "You can't be here right now," he said, the same even voice he used to talk to crowds and guards and everyone beneath him. I knew it was only because of the diplomats, but I wanted to wring his neck all the same.

"Your Highness," I said, bowing. "Forgive me for interrupting, but you're needed immediately."

The prince only gaped at me like I'd dragged a dead body

into his meeting. "Zilan, *you can't be here*," he said again, a desperate edge to his words.

"Isn't that your concubine?" one of the diplomats said.

The prince pressed his lips into a tight line. When he didn't answer, the diplomat to his left let out a stiff laugh. "How progressive of you, Your Highness," he said, "letting your concubine interrupt your meetings."

"It's urgent," I said, but the prince only winced at my words.

"She's not even guarded," the man to his right said, his tone light but his words sharp. "How will you know if her children are yours?"

The other men laughed, because the comment would be treasonous if not a joke, but the prince only stared at the slowly bleeding ink across his scroll.

*I'm making him lose face in front of important diplomats*, I realized, wishing I could just tell the prince about his sisters. But there were too many people here—surely word would get back to the Empress. I could tell him that a convent had burned down, but in the eyes of foreign diplomats, that alone wouldn't be a good enough reason for him to leave. What could I say that would make these men listen? What did they even care about enough to stop a meeting for?

*Themselves*, I thought. But I couldn't just threaten them directly. My gaze drifted across their gold embroidered robes, the gold flecks in their teeth, their pearl necklaces and jade earrings. Those who ate life gold didn't need to fear aging, but they all feared the other ways their expensive lives could end.

"My guard fell ill when I was in the outer courtyard," I said, bowing again. "I didn't want to be unguarded, so I came to you first."

"Your guard?" the prince echoed. He knew that I was supposed to be with the Moon Alchemist right now, that I had no guard when I was with her. His expression shifted, a cold mask wiping away his distress, like he was too aware he was being watched. He picked up his brush with stiff fingers.

I nodded. "Yes, the one from the east, just outside of Chang'an."

"Near the convent?" he said quietly.

I could have melted into the table from relief. "Yes, that one," I said, even though we both knew no such guard existed.

The prince hardly seemed to breathe, casting a quick glance at the diplomat on his left before meeting my gaze. Getting the prince to understand was one thing, but excusing him from an important meeting without losing face was another.

Luckily, I knew how to scare rich men.

"He had red spots all over his face and arms, like beans," I said. "His mouth was full of sores. He said he felt like his head was full of dragonflies, then he vomited blood."

The diplomat to the left of the prince let out a strangled sound, while others dropped their brushes, hands stiff, faces stripped of color. *Disease* was a dirty word among the rich, one of the only things they feared. I'd seen the way smallpox ravaged Guangzhou, ripping through the city with no regard for who was poor or wealthy.

"Perhaps we should reconvene another time," one of the other men said, his voice remarkably steady despite how quickly he bowed, already rising to his feet.

"Yes, we should let you attend to your duties and resume when it's more convenient for you," said another, throwing himself down in a bow before following the other man.

"I… Yes, I suppose that's for the best," the prince said, watching palely as the rest of the men bowed and hurried for the door. I caught a glimpse of one of them sprinting once he made it outside. I turned to the prince, ready to reassure him that the plague was a lie, but he slammed the door shut and grabbed my hand.

"What's wrong with my sisters?"

The door to the prince's room was, mercifully, still sealed when we arrived. I unjammed the jade with the touch of my hand and burst inside, where the closet was still shut.

I should have known from the smell alone that something was wrong. But I told myself it couldn't be true and slammed a stone against the door, shattering the granite binding and throwing the doors open.

The back wall of the closet gaped outward, as if torn open from behind. The doors to the prince's room hadn't mattered at all, because whatever had come through here hadn't needed a door.

The princesses lay in a pool of syrupy blood, their throats slashed open, windpipes gaping like second mouths, necks snapped at severe angles, papery white faces and glassy eyes with tiny burst veins like bloody fireworks.

The prince fell to his knees with a shattering cry, scooping them up, blood sloshing over his silk robes. My mind felt like it was full of buzzing insects. Only moments ago, they'd been fine. I'd been so sure they were safe.

"Zilan," the prince moaned, his hands trembling where he gripped his sister's stiff arms. "Can you fix them?"

I swallowed, thinking of what the Moon Alchemist had told me. That those I brought back weren't truly human. I still didn't know if she was right, but could I really inflict that on these little girls?

"Zilan," the prince said, a bloody hand twisting in my sleeve. *"Please."*

"Yes," I said, before I could think about it more. Maybe it

was selfish, but I couldn't just leave these girls dead. I couldn't do nothing while the prince cried over their corpses.

But there was another problem. I hadn't resurrected anyone without my cousins in years. Wenshu hadn't written to me yet, so I had no idea where they were staying. Would they even come if I asked?

"I need your help," I said, picking up my abandoned blade from the ground. It was clean—the girls hadn't even had a chance to fight back.

"*My* help?" the prince said.

I nodded. "Put her down," I said, passing him the other knife. Normally, for these resurrections, Yufei was Heaven, I was Earth, and Wenshu was Man. But we were one person short, and the prince looked too shaken to be the stable pillar that I needed. Three legs had to be sturdy to hold up a cauldron. I would have to hold it up myself.

I sliced my palm with the blade and painted 天 on my left arm, 地 on my right, and 人 on my cheek with my fingers.

"Hold her down," I said, fishing three bloodstones out of my satchel, all of them slick with my blood.

The prince nodded, looking ill as I placed the stones over the girl's heart meridian and closed my eyes.

The first girl was easy enough, so simple in fact that I was sure I'd done something wrong. Just as I'd walked with her through the tunnels under the palace, I led her easily down the river, her trusting hand in mine until we resurfaced and I carved her name into her inner elbow, telling the prince that she'd need a tattoo before the scar healed.

She woke up clutching her mended throat, coughing as the prince cradled her close. I wiped the sweat from my brow and moved to the next girl, my breathing coming fast and hot, the air a dizzy swirl of iron and salt around me in the tiny closet.

This time, the transformation began to fall apart.

I felt it in my bones, the arm marked with 天 pulling away from the arm marked with 地, my cheek burning, an ache blooming in my face like all my teeth were being yanked out. I stood on the riverbank, but the ground swirled and swayed, knocking me into the thin stream, where I choked on murky water.

*You cannot create good without also creating evil,* my mind said again and again and again until it was the only thought that existed. I'd done unstable transformations before, where I'd tried to sew together pieces of fabric with only two moonstones, or been too exhausted to concentrate properly on the practice pig I was trying to resurrect, and it was always as if the alchemical cauldron in my mind had toppled over and spilled across the floor. The world had turned soft like the earth after a typhoon, wet dirt that slid around and sucked you into it, fallen trees and drowned rats and overturned soil where the sky was supposed to be.

I saw myself walking in flashes down the riverbank, falling to my hands and knees on the rooted basin. There was the girl, curled up in a ball on the ground, and the dam, still dribbling water. I fell against it, my head bashing against stones, and then the waters were breathing me in. Blood filled my lungs and stones pummeled me, but I couldn't find the girl. My hands reached out in every direction, scraping at frigid red water. My lungs screamed for air and my eyes threatened to close and the roots on the riverbed scratched at me and tugged at my clothes. I crashed into a bed of stone, and the world turned black.

"Zilan!"

The prince was shaking my shoulders, the darkness of the closet sloshing around me. I was slumped across the little girl's body, my face covered in her blood. Underneath me, she was warm, her breaths slowly rising her chest.

I pushed myself up dizzily, but I could already tell I hadn't done it right.

Her body wasn't shaking the way suddenly uprooted souls were supposed to. Instead, she breathed shallowly, as if asleep. I reached for the knife to carve her soul tag into her skin, just in case, but my hands trembled too much, and I knew it was useless. I had restored her qi, but I hadn't brought her soul back with me. She was hollow inside.

"I'm sorry," I said, the words blurring together, "I'm sorry, it's the best I can do right now. Her soul—"

"It's okay," the prince said, cupping my cheek. "It's okay. She's alive, Zilan."

"She's empty," I said.

"Maybe she'll wake up later," the prince said, tucking the other girl against him. "We need to…need to… What should we do?"

I rubbed my eyes, which felt coated in sand.

"Get the Moon Alchemist," I said. "Tell her what happened." She would probably be furious with me for resurrecting the girls—even more furious that I'd failed with one—but she would handle it.

The prince nodded quickly and cast aside the outer layer of his bloodstained robe, pulling on something clean before charging out into the hallway.

I must have fallen asleep leaning against the closet, because I woke to the sound of the door sliding open, the Moon Alchemist and the prince carrying two stuffed hemp bags. Strangely, it reminded me of old man Gou back in Guangzhou, dragging a corpse into the míngqì store. How much things had changed since then.

"You're a fool," she said to me, dropping a bag. "You could have died, and I'm tempted to kill you myself. Do you even care what you've done to these girls?"

I couldn't quite bring myself to apologize, too tired to even form words. The Moon Alchemist went on grumbling about how foolish children were forcing her to risk her life as she dumped out the bodies of two young girls from the sacks while the older princess huddled in the prince's arms.

Once she'd finished berating me, the Moon Alchemist worked in silence. She laid the bodies out in the closet, switched their clothes with the princesses' dresses, then used a firestone to shatter their faces inward like crushed melons until they weren't recognizable.

"Give me five minutes, then report their deaths," she said, wiping her brow with the back of her arm. "Once it's confirmed, I'll be allowed to dispose of the monsters."

She narrowed her eyes at the older girl, then picked up the younger from my arms, which finally fell limp at my sides. "I'll have the River Alchemist take them to a western convent through the tunnels, but destroying the monsters that can track them has to be my priority."

"What about Gao'an?" the prince said, looking to the girl unconscious in the Moon Alchemist's grasp.

"They have healers at the monastery," the Moon Alchemist said. Then she offered me a hand and all but yanked me to my feet before I could even accept it. The world spun, but she shoved me against a wall to hold me steady. "In five minutes, call the servants," she said. "That's all you have to do."

"Call the servants," I repeated, nodding even though it made the world slide back and forth.

The Moon Alchemist took the older girl's hand, but she reached out for the prince.

"You'll be safe this time," he said, patting her hair. "I'll come for you soon."

She cried as the Moon Alchemist tucked the younger sister against her chest and left, the door closing quietly behind her.

Then it was only me and the prince, standing before a pool of blood, by the stiff corpses of the girls who were not his sisters, but maybe they had been someone else's.

I rested my head against the wall, not sure how I was even going to stay awake for all the commotion that was sure to follow. "You need to change back to your other robes," I said quietly, because I had no idea what else to say. "Ten men saw what you were wearing. The change will be suspicious."

"Zilan."

I looked up. The prince stood stiffly before the closet, hair hanging over his face, hands clenched into fists.

"You were right," he whispered.

"I'm right about many things," I said, thumping my head back against the doorway. "What is it this time?"

"I should not have waited this long," he said. "I can't sit around and hope my father recovers enough to handle this for me."

"Okay," I said slowly. "What do you want to do?"

The prince turned to me, his eyes fierce, blistering gold.

"The Empress must die."

# CHAPTER TWENTY-FOUR

"You're out of your mind," Yufei said, taking another bite of lamb leg.

I sat on the floor of Wenshu and Yufei's new quarters, a basket of food spread out before us, my guard just outside the door as we spoke in Guangzhou dialect. Though I still needed a guard for the sake of the prince's image, he'd instructed them not to follow me into every room. The prince had also stationed plainclothes guards in the western ward on my behalf and ordered them to watch over my cousins at night.

I had asked the chefs for a more elaborate meal than usual in order to break the news to my cousins that we were going to kill the Empress. Part of me had hoped they would help, but as Wenshu sat with his arms crossed, food untouched, I thought that might have been too optimistic.

"Gēgē?" I said, tearing a piece of bread to bits as I waited for his response.

He let out a long sigh, closing his eyes. "Please tell me you're joking," he said at last.

Yufei slowed her chewing, glancing uneasily at Wenshu.

"I've told you what the Empress does," I said. "Don't you think she deserves to die?"

"It doesn't matter what *I* think about the Empress," Wenshu said, his eyebrow twitching. "I'm a third-tier scholar from Guangzhou."

"Of course it matters!" I said. "You're the one who's always said the mandate of Heaven is a lie, that the royal family should get their authority from the people."

"There's a difference between a moral objection and *planning an assassination*," Wenshu said, covering his face with his hands and taking a steadying breath. "Why are you even telling us this? It's not like you listen to anything I say anymore. You're going to do it anyway."

The bread had crumbled to bits in my hands, falling through my fingers. "I thought you might help us," I said quietly. "You're smart, Gēgē. Maybe with your help, we could—"

"I'm smart enough to not want anything to do with this," Wenshu said.

I turned to Yufei, but she stuffed her mouth with rice and gave a noncommittal shrug that could have meant anything.

"Someone at the palace is already after our heads," Wenshu said. "What do you think they'll do to us if you're caught?"

"They're going to come after us regardless," I said. "They won't stop until the Empress is dead."

"The Empress will never die!" Wenshu said, rising to his feet. "Do you think she wiped out the entire House of Li and locked up the Emperor through sheer idiocy? You think *you* of all people can stop her?"

"What's that supposed to mean?" I said.

"You're seventeen," Wenshu said, clenching his fists. "You're a girl, not an army general."

"I'm a royal alchemist."

"Yes, because she *let you become one!*" Wenshu said. "How do you not understand that? She controls everything!"

"She doesn't control me," I said. "The prince and I—"

Wenshu let out a strangled sound, hands twitching like he wanted to grab something and wring the life out of it. "Don't get me started on the prince," he said. "This is all his fault."

"What?" I said, clenching my teeth.

"Soup is getting cold," Yufei said, ladling some into both of our bowls. "Eat now, talk later."

Wenshu shook his head. "You'd follow him anywhere because he's the first man who's ever liked you," he said. "It's not even real, but you're throwing away your life for him."

I slammed my fist onto the table. Soup sloshed over the rims of bowls, rice jumping up in white sparks, cups overturning and gushing hot tea across my knees, but I didn't care.

"I'd follow him anywhere because unlike you, *he treats me like a royal alchemist!*" I said. "He believes in me! He looks at me and sees someone great, not an annoying little sister too foolish to make her own decisions."

"You're not making your own decisions!" Wenshu said. "You're doing whatever the prince wants!"

"I'm doing what *I* want!" I said. "You're just mad because it's not what *you* want!"

"*I want to live!*" Wenshu said, hurling a bowl against the wall. It shattered in a burst of soup, pooling at his feet. "I've already met death once, Zilan. I'm not doing it again. If you want to die so badly, then go do it alone."

I turned to Yufei, who flinched away from my glare. "Jiějiě, say something!" I cried.

She took a long moment to finish chewing, gaze darting around the dishes on the table like she didn't want to look at either of us. Yufei was good at calming Wenshu down, or at least distracting him. She would convince him—

"Zilan," she said, and the heaviness in her tone made my stomach drop. "You're good at alchemy. That can make you money, even if it's not in Chang'an. I can only be a scholar or a wife, and I don't want to be a wife. I don't want to die, or lose what we have right now."

I shook my head, wishing I could dissolve into the wallpaper. "Why are you both so sure I'm going to fail?"

"Why is that something you're even willing to risk?" Wenshu said.

*"Why?"* I echoed, the question so absurd, so unexpected, that it took my breath away.

Because when I closed my eyes, I saw corpses stacked in wet dungeons and their crying families with one hundred gold in their palms instead of a proper funeral. I thought of the girl in the pink dress burning, the leathery smell of her charred flesh, her screams that could rend the world in half. I saw the old man begging me for fabric in the streets, and my dead cousins in the fields, and little princesses shredded like cuts of meat, and the empty chairs where all the prince's brothers and sisters used to sit. And above it all, like the re-sounding light of daybreak, was the Empress, lips painted with gold, laughing at the dead. If she was the ruler Heaven had chosen, then I would gladly burn through every layer of hell.

"Someone has to," I said, but the words came out too weak, my eyes burning with tears because I knew Wenshu hadn't seen what I'd seen, that he couldn't understand.

"And that someone has to be you?" he said.

I nodded, a single tear racing down my face. I wiped it away, but Wenshu had already seen it. He sighed, crossing his arms.

"Fine," he said.

I looked up. "Fine?"

"Do what you have to do," he said. "But stop coming here."

I froze, my heart stopping at his words. "What?"

"Stop visiting us," he said. "Tell your secret guards—yes, I've noticed them—to stop watching us. Stop talking about us. And stop calling yourself a Fan."

"I *am* a Fan," I said, but I didn't sound certain anymore. All the blood in my body was pooling in my feet.

Wenshu shook his head. "That's the name our mother gave you when she thought you wanted to be part of our family."

I didn't realize I was backing away until my spine pressed against the wall and there was nowhere for me to go.

"Gēgē—"

"Stop calling me that," Wenshu said.

"*Gēgē,*" Yufei said, frowning. But she didn't argue with him. Didn't defend me. "He just means it's safer for us if we're not associated—"

"I know what he meant," I said. He meant that "sister" had never been something that I was, but a name he'd let me borrow. A familiar feeling began to fester in my stomach, and after a moment I remembered the last time I'd felt this way— the day they'd died, leaving me alone in the world.

They would be dead without me, and yet they were casting me aside. It was clear that they couldn't love me. If I had ever needed any proof that the Moon Alchemist was right, this was it. They had cut me off like a dead petal off a flower.

I clenched my fists and turned to the doorway so they couldn't see me cry.

"When you died, I should have let them bury you," I said. "I wish I'd let you both rot."

Before I could take it back, I grabbed my coat and ran into the night, slamming the door behind me.

Of course, there was the matter of how we were going to kill the Empress.

Physically attacking her seemed impossible with four burly

guards constantly at her side, not to mention that it would be hard to hide our identities if we failed. Poisoning would be difficult because she ate nothing but gold and drank nothing but tea, both of which were sampled by a servant before she touched them. The prince only recalled one poisoning attempt during her reign, after which every servant and their families had been executed.

I pored over alchemy texts for some sort of poison that would work on one person but not another, but past scholars had unfortunately been smart enough not to write such treasonous things down and store them in the imperial library. Surely, if alchemy could resurrect people, then it was advanced enough to produce a poison that was inert until activated—something to kill the Empress without hurting the taste tester. The prince reluctantly gave me a box of mice that would have otherwise been snake food and said I could experiment on them, but I didn't even know where to begin.

After three days of research that turned up nothing at all, the Paper Alchemist and the River Alchemist found me sitting under a tree in the training grounds, glaring into my mouse box. Durian the duck sat sleeping by my side. He peeped so incessantly whenever I tried to leave him alone in the room that I'd had no choice but to bring him along.

"What did those rats do to offend you so much?" the River Alchemist said.

"They're mice," said the Paper Alchemist, peering into the box. "Is this one of Moon's new training techniques?"

I shook my head. "I'm studying anatomy to better understand blood alchemy," I said, my prepared excuse in case the Moon Alchemist found me.

"Studying mouse anatomy?" the Paper Alchemist said. "I heard you've already been doing blood alchemy on humans."

I glared harder at the mice, as if my bad excuse was their fault.

I couldn't exactly tell the other alchemists I was trying to poison the Empress. "I'm working on a…personal project," I said.

"*Personal* as in something Moon doesn't want you to do?" the River Alchemist said, raising an eyebrow.

"No!" I said. "I mean, she hasn't objected. Mostly because I haven't asked her."

"Sounds dangerous. I'm in," the River Alchemist said, sitting down.

"Explain, Scarlet," the Paper Alchemist said, sitting next to the River Alchemist and crossing her arms.

I hadn't wanted anyone else involved, but somehow I'd ended up with two alchemists staring at me expectantly. Saying *It's such a big secret that I can't tell you either* felt more dangerous than saying nothing at all.

I pressed my lips together, taking a moment to select my words with exquisite care. "I want to transform some mice but not all of them," I said slowly. The other alchemists stared at me blankly, waiting for more. "Can some creatures be made impervious to alchemy?"

"All bodies are different, so they respond differently to alchemy, but no one is completely impervious," the Paper Alchemist said, frowning.

"Okay, but…" I bit my lip, gathering my thoughts. "What if all the mice were exposed to the same substance. Is there a way I could use alchemy to change how some of them react to it?"

"It depends on the substance," the River Alchemist said. "Are you talking about something environmental, or something they consume?"

"Something they consume."

"Like fruit and seeds?"

"Like…arsenic."

The alchemists across from me went quiet, their expressions suddenly too careful, too reserved.

"You mean, hypothetically?" the Paper Alchemist said, her posture rigid. "Because you know that we don't experiment with arsenic here. You're asking because it's a thought exercise and not something you would actually do, right, Scarlet?" Her words had an odd edge to them, a sharp sort of desperation.

"Yes," I said quickly. "Of course."

"Because you know that talking about this sort of thing in front of people you don't trust is dangerous, don't you?" said the River Alchemist, her eyes wide. "*We* can talk about it, because we know that you have no way to actually get your hands on arsenic, anyway."

They knew no such thing, but I nodded anyway.

"Then, hypothetically, what are you actually asking us?" the Paper Alchemist said.

I swallowed, looking between their fearful expressions. In the tense silence of the empty courtyard, it seemed as if the whole world was waiting for my next words.

"If I were to feed arsenic to two mice, but I only want one of them to die, how could I do that?" I asked quietly.

For a long moment, the alchemists only stared at me. The longer they took to answer, the more I started to realize how much of a mistake this was. It was all fun and games when we were fooling around in trees, but that didn't mean I could trust them with my life.

"You can't," the River Alchemist said at last.

I dropped my gaze to the box of scurrying mice, too afraid that the alchemists would be able to read my disappointment, would know exactly what I was doing from my eyes alone.

"You would need to feed them something other than poison," the Paper Alchemist said.

I looked up. "What else besides poison would kill them?"

The Paper Alchemist shrugged, but I knew from the tightness in her face that there were words she didn't want to say. "I thought you said the Moon Alchemist had you studying until your eyes bled. I'm surprised you haven't found anything useful."

I clutched my mouse box tighter to my chest, frowning. The Moon Alchemist had me studying stones, not practical alchemy. I was certain I hadn't come across a stone capable of killing some people but not others.

At the other end of the courtyard, the doors swung open and several alchemists burst inside, one of them on fire, the others laughing while he ran to extinguish his hair in the pond.

The Paper Alchemist sighed, then rose to her feet. "Sorry we can't be more helpful," she said. "This has been a fun thought experiment, but you should probably get back to whatever Moon wants you to do."

"Thanks," I said, dropping my gaze to my mice. I was certain they knew more than they were letting on but were too worried about getting in trouble to help me. I couldn't say I blamed them, but it stung to feel so close to the answer yet so far.

The Paper Alchemist strode away, but the River Alchemist lingered a moment longer after rising to her feet, her shadow cast over me, her silhouette backlit by the sun.

"I heard about your final trial," she said, pointing down at Durian, who was still sleeping beside me. "May I?"

I sighed, scooped up the duck, and held it out to the River Alchemist, who tucked it against her chest and stroked its head. "I'm impressed," she said. "It's not easy for an untrained alchemist to make something like this."

"It's just a duck," I said.

The River Alchemist shrugged, moving to give Durian back but hesitating before our hands touched. She leaned forward, the curtain of her hair swinging down, shielding us from the sun. In the darkness, the flecks of amber in her eyes gleamed brighter.

"I don't mean that the duck is impressive," she whispered. "I mean, what you did to make it."

I blinked, my hands frozen in the air, reaching out. "I hardly knew what I was doing."

"Yes, I know," she said. "You need to be careful when combining different stone types. You never know what sort of danger you could create."

Then she passed me the duck and stood up sharply, sunlight spilling between us, and ran after the Paper Alchemist without another word.

Durian shuffled and settled down in my palms. I remembered the burst of light and alchemical sludge that he'd been born from, the uncontrollable reaction that could have ripped a hole in the universe if I'd been just a little less lucky.

All because I'd combined stone types.

I stuffed Durian into my pocket and snatched my mouse box off the ground, jostling all the mice inside, and took off toward my room.

I hadn't found a single stone that could do what I wanted because none existed.

But multiple stones could.

As long as I could make sure the Empress used a different taste tester for each of her meals, I could put traces of a different stone in each one. The taste testers would be unharmed. But the Empress, once she swallowed both types of stones...

I pictured the burst of light, the hole seared in the table, black sludge and fire and raw, searing power.

I smiled.

The Empress was as good as dead.

★ ★ ★

The prince did not share my enthusiasm when I presented him with a box of dead mice.

"I would have believed you," he said as he slammed the lid back on and opened a window. "I didn't need to see exploded mouse guts. Those poor things."

"You were going to feed them to your pet snake anyway," I said, rolling my eyes. "You think that would have been painless?"

I'd spent the afternoon breaking my stones into smaller and smaller pieces and feeding them to the mice until I'd found a combination that worked. In the destruction cycle of the elements, earth soaks up water, water controls fire, fire melts metal, metal cuts wood, and wood breaks earth. I'd focused on the last combination, grinding woodstones and earthstones into fine powder, then activating them with a simple fire transformation that kept the alchemy in them simmering. It turned out that citrine and jade, once they met in the stomach, made the mice bleed from the mouth and fall over dead. Other combinations had caused more…explosive results, but this one was the most consistent.

I thought, fleetingly, how much Wenshu and Yufei would have appreciated my discovery. But I couldn't think about them right now. I had an Empress to kill.

"Are you sure this is enough?" the prince said, examining the small bag of activated citrine I'd passed him. "Shouldn't we use more, just to be safe?"

I crossed my arms. "If the Empress receives a cup of rocks instead of tea, she's going to notice."

The prince nodded, setting the bag down, his gaze lingering somewhere past me.

"You're not having second thoughts, are you?" I said. The prince was oddly sentimental about animals, so it wasn't out of the question that he'd be squeamish about murdering his own mother, even if she'd killed his little sisters.

He shook his head, looking down at the mouse box. "I was just thinking... None of my taste testers have died this week," he said quietly. "No monsters have come to my door. I've stayed up, waiting for them, but there wasn't a single sound."

"Isn't that good?"

The prince sat down on the bed and gripped the sheets. "Zilan, ever since our dinner with my mother, no one has tried to kill me. I've been dodging assassination attempts for months, but all of a sudden, it's like she's given up. I know I shouldn't question a good thing, but it only makes me feel like something worse is coming. If my mother doesn't want me dead, it means she needs something else from me."

"It doesn't matter what her plans are," I said. "She won't have time to execute them. She'll be dead by morning." Still, the prince's words unnerved me. It was hard to accept that my arrival in the palace and the sudden ceasefire were a coincidence. Was I part of the Empress's plan as well?

The prince hung his head, so I sat beside him and shoved his shoulder. "Stop worrying," I said. "If you're too anxious, you're going to make mistakes."

"I am quite literally always anxious," he said, "so that might be a problem."

"I've practiced more than enough!" I said, jerking a finger toward the mouse box. "Don't you trust me?"

"I trust no one else but you," the prince said. "Was that not obvious from the moment I found you in Guangzhou and asked you to break the law for me?"

"You didn't even know me then," I said. "That just means you were a fool for trusting a stranger."

The prince seemed to think this over, studying my face for

a long, quiet moment. "I might be a fool for plenty of other reasons," he said at last, "but trusting you will never be one of them."

I turned away rather than acknowledge the sentiment. His words unlaced me, softened me like a flower that unfurled in the sunlight. "That's easy to say in hindsight," I finally said, feigning indifference. "I could have just mugged you and run away the day we met."

The prince laughed. "It would be an honor to be robbed by you, Fan Zilan."

"It's not too late for that," I said, jokingly tugging at one of his rings.

But the prince simply slipped the ring off and set it in my palm. "You don't need to steal from me," he said. "I'll give you anything."

I shoved the ring back at him. "You can't just say things like that," I said. How could he sit there and promise me the world so effortlessly? "Normal people don't say things like that."

"Are we normal people?" the prince asked, raising an eyebrow. "*You* certainly aren't."

He smiled, slipping the ring back on. "Then I can say whatever I want."

The Empress's afternoon tea came just after high noon every day, delivered by one of the kitchen servants. The prince said the consequences for delivering lukewarm tea were severe, so the servant always walked quickly.

*Is there some sort of alchemy that could make her fall?* the prince had asked during our planning.

*Yes*, I'd said. *It's called "soap and water."*

So we'd crushed up soap beans that definitely did not make

me think of Wenshu and spilled water in the hallway outside of the kitchen.

A girl about my age backed out of the kitchen with a tray, hair wet from steam, gaze focused on the rattling teacups in front of her. Part of me felt bad for involving her in our plan at all. But no one in the palace was safe if the Empress went on with her monstrous experiments, so in a way, I was helping her.

"Excuse me!" the prince said, stepping out into her path far too soon, and I had no choice but to follow.

"Your Highness!" the girl said, the words a surprised shout. She bowed awkwardly while holding the tray out so her hair wouldn't fall over the Empress's cups.

"Stand up, it's fine," the prince said, walking toward her too quickly. *You're going to slip on the soap before she does*, I thought, grabbing his hand and forcing him to slow down. He didn't act surprised at all, simply squeezing my hand and pulling me along with him, thankfully slower this time.

"Scarlet xiǎojiě," the girl said when she saw me, bowing again.

"No, no, don't bow to me," I said, mortified that even the kitchen servants already knew my name, and worried that she'd fall face-first into the tea tray before we could reach her.

The girl looked perplexed, but the prince only kept drawing closer, flashed his I-am-the-Crown-Prince-of-China smile, and let forth a torrent of nervous babbling.

"Zilan and I were just taking a walk, discussing different kinds of tea leaves, which I know is a suspiciously boring topic of conversation but I assure you I am a thoroughly boring person—Zilan will tell you—and I wanted her to try all the different kinds we have, so we headed for the kitchen rather than call for someone because we were already so close and you know how impatient royalty can be! So could you—"

The girl was saved from more of the prince's word vomit

when she finally, mercifully, reached the puddle on the floor and slipped backward with a startled yelp.

The prince grabbed her arm to steady her. The teacups rattled, but the prince took the tray in his other hand and smoothly passed it to me. "Zilan, it's spilled a bit," he said. "Clean it up, would you?"

He turned back to the servant girl, standing closer than he should have. He grasped her arm with sickening gentleness, examining her hand.

"Are you all right?" the prince said, while I slid out a packet of citrine from my sleeve and dumped it into the teapot, then slammed the lid back on quickly. But all my subtlety was utterly unnecessary, because the servant was wholly transfixed by the prince.

"You didn't get burned, did you?" he said.

"No," the girl said, the word a stunned whisper. "I mean, no, Your Highness, I'm fine. Please forgive me."

"There's nothing to forgive," he said, smiling.

"Here's your tray," I said, probably too loudly, shoving it at her. "I cleaned up the spill."

The prince immediately released the servant and took a step back. The girl bowed to me, fumbling for the tray, her face bright red. She looked at me like she thought I would eat her alive.

"I'm sorry, Your Highness, but what is it that you wanted?" she whispered.

"Nothing," I said, grabbing the prince's arm. "You shouldn't keep the Empress waiting."

The girl's eyes went wide at the reminder, and she bowed once more before hurrying off. The moment she turned the corner, I slapped the prince's shoulder.

"I said distract her, not seduce her!"

"I only spoke to her!" he said, holding his hands up. "Are my words that seductive?"

I smacked him again, harder. "You can't just touch servants!"

"I was helping her!"

I raised my hand again, but this time, I halted when the prince started laughing.

*"Why are you laughing?"* I said, clenching my fist.

He shook his head, trying and failing to hide his smile behind his sleeve. "It's just that, the last time you hit me, you became my concubine," he said. "Are you sure you want to do it again? Who knows what will happen this time."

I turned away so he wouldn't see my burning face. "This time, there's no one to stop me from beating you to death," I said, grabbing his sleeve and dragging him back down the hall.

We waited in the prince's room because I felt sick with nerves and feared the prince would simply blurt out our plan to the first member of court he ran into. All afternoon, I was certain that someone would burst inside to tell us that someone had tried to poison the Empress and that every servant was going to be executed as penance. But as the hours passed and both the prince and I pretended to read our scrolls, the halls stayed still and quiet.

I passed the packet of jade back and forth in my hands. It was almost time for the Empress's evening tea, the dose that mattered. The servants would have changed shifts, so a different girl would be serving the Empress and it wouldn't be hard to pull the same trick twice. Just to be certain, the prince had sent the first servant girl home early.

It was my day off from training, and normally I would have spent it with my cousins. I felt like a guest overstaying my welcome in the prince's room as the shadows grew lon-ger, the day stretching quietly on. The prince seemed equally uneasy but had given up the pretense of reading, instead fo-cusing on overfeeding Durian.

"He's already grown so much," he said, holding the duck up to show me, as if it didn't follow me around all day long. It used to be half the size of my palm, but now it sat com-fortably in the prince's larger hand.

"You feed him too much," I said. "He's going to explode from bread crumbs like all your other pets."

"Do you think he's old enough to meet them?" the prince said, clutching Durian to his chest. "Do you think they'd like him?"

"They'd probably attack him."

The prince grimaced, petting Durian and setting him down on the bed. "We'll wait until you're bigger," he whispered.

As the hour drew nearer, we decided to take a walk around the palace and loop back around to the kitchens, neither of us wanting to stay in his chamber any longer.

The prince took my hand the moment we left his room. I didn't think it was a necessary pretense—most of the court also took tea around this time, or was relaxing in their quar-ters before their evening meal—but I didn't pull away, even as we strode through the empty courtyard.

The prince came to a stop before a shallow pond, turn-ing his face up to the setting sun, the gold flecks in his skin sparkling.

"I've been thinking about what I want to do when I'm the Emperor," he said quietly, in Guangzhou dialect.

I tensed, nearly yanking my hand away out of surprise, but the prince held tight.

"Is it that bad?" he said, turning toward me, mouth sliding into a frown. "I hired a tutor to help me."

It wasn't bad at all, but I was too stunned to answer him. I swallowed, my mouth suddenly dry. "Your mother told me I wasn't allowed to speak that dialect," I said, in Chang'an dialect.

"I know," the prince said, grimacing. "I hated that she did that. Which is why I wanted to learn. I think your dialect is beautiful."

I cast my gaze down to the lake, my hand too warm in the prince's palm. I hadn't expected the prince to remember his mother's offhand comment.

"I'm still learning," he said, his grip on my hand loosening. "I know it's not very good yet but—"

"No, it's good," I said in my dialect, holding his hand tighter, not letting him pull away. "Tell me what you'll do when you're the Emperor."

He smiled, taking my other hand, pulling me a breath closer. "Well, the monster problem seems to be the most pressing."

"Agreed."

"But once that's sorted out, I think we need to scale back on gold production. The inflation is getting out of hand."

"And you need to pay more for infrastructure in the south."

"Yes, that too," he said. "We can bring the rest of your family here if you want, but I hope economic conditions in the south will improve so that they'll have a choice. I hope everything will be better. No, actually, I don't *hope*. I *know*. I'll make sure it happens."

I had never seen the prince's eyes like this before—they always contained whispers of gold, but they'd never before appeared so bright and endless, sharper than the sun's rays reflecting off the pond beside us, exquisitely painful to look at. He leaned forward and I couldn't breathe at all, positive he could hear my heartbeat crashing against my ribs. I'd never felt so unbalanced in a way that had nothing at all to do with alchemy—it was like when I'd first set off for Chang'an and saw a whole new world unfold across the horizon in front of me.

*This is pretend*, I reminded myself, loosening my grip on his hand. *When he becomes the Emperor, he'll need a wife from a noble family. He can't marry the hùnxiě daughter of a mìngqí merchant. Will you really stay here as his concubine when he marries someone else?*

I turned toward the pond. "It's about time," I said, the words stiff in Chang'an dialect.

He nodded. "Right," he said quietly, slipping back into his own dialect. "Zilan, I—"

"Let's go," I said, looking away before I could see his face, before I could forget who I was born as, who I would die as.

# CHAPTER TWENTY-FIVE

The afternoon sun fell lower in the sky, and no one emerged from the kitchens.

"Maybe they're running late?" the prince said, peering down the hallway before I yanked him back by the sleeve.

"Stop looking so suspicious," I whispered.

"Or maybe *we're* too late?" the prince said, eyes wide. "What if she took her tea early?"

I tried to keep my expression neutral, but the prince's panic was contagious.

"Maybe we should check," I said. "You go toward your mother's quarters while I check the kitchens."

I took out my packet of jade and grabbed the prince's hand, pouring half of it into his palm. "Just in case."

He nodded, then took off running very unsubtly down the hall. I sighed but turned toward the kitchens, which were oddly silent for a time when they were supposedly preparing dinner. I slid a hand into my satchel just in case and shoved the door open with my shoulder.

The kitchen had shattered into a thousand pieces. Every dish and cup laid broken on the floor, a sharp carpet of porcelain crunching under my feet. The shelves had been ripped from the walls, lying in splinters on the counters, the tables cleaved in half, pots and pans warped on the floor. Blood trickled slowly toward the drain at the center of the room.

At the far end of the kitchen, a starburst of blood painted the wall, dripping down to a pile of corpses beneath it, spines snapped at odd angles, still clutching kitchen knives and iron pans that hadn't helped them at all. No human could have done this.

I grimaced and kicked a pot out of the way so the blood rushed faster toward the drain, then tightened my satchel and approached the servants.

I lifted one of the cook's wrists, the limb still pliant, skin bloodless but not yet cold. He hadn't been dead long, so whatever monster had razed through here couldn't be far. I jammed the cook's eyes closed with my thumb but couldn't quite bring myself to climb the pile of corpses to do the same for the rest. Had the Empress noticed something wrong with her tea and sent her monsters after the kitchen staff? Guilt closed off my throat, the wide eyes of the corpses pinning me in place.

I shook my head. The prince had said that the last time someone tried to poison her, the executions had been a public spectacle to deter future attempts. Besides, none of these bodies even had bite marks. I knew too well that the monsters always went for the throat and drained bodies dry before tearing them apart to lick out the juices. These people looked more like they'd been snapped in half when they got in the way. Judging by the weapons in their hands, they'd definitely tried to confront the monster.

*They only hunt what they're told to, unless you try to stop them,* the Moon Alchemist had said. If these people had just cowered or run away, they'd still be alive.

But if the monster had only passed through the kitchens, who was it hunting?

My thoughts flashed to the prince, who I'd just left alone in the halls with nothing but half a packet of jade.

I spun around, slipping and crashing onto all fours, porcelain shards knifing into my hands and knees. I pulled myself up on a counter and took off running toward the Empress's quarters.

I sprinted across the courtyard, then shoved through the heavy doors to the inner palace, ignoring the sloped decorative bridge in the garden and charging straight through the shallow water to the other side. A sudden *bang* in the nearest building vibrated under my feet, rippling the water. I charged toward it, following the sound of splintering wood and tearing wallpaper.

The door to one of the inner libraries had collapsed inward, the archway gaping open to the chaos inside. Every shelf had toppled over, covering the floor in wood and paper carnage. It reminded me of the windstorms that raged through the wooden houses of Guangzhou, like a great beast had chewed them up and spit them out. The air smelled of blood.

"Li Hong!" I called, shoving a shelf out of my way so I could see farther into the room.

"Zilan!" a voice called.

I pulled apart the barrier of broken wood and stepped fully into the room.

At first, I thought I was looking at a man made of pure sunlight, only a silhouette of thorny sparkles and violent brightness. Then it stepped forward, out of the light streaming through the painted window at the far end of the library.

Unlike the smooth, river-softened surface of the pearl monsters, this monster's skin had knife-sharp facets the color of sapphire, each one reflecting a dark image of the room, like a thousand portals into a world of night. Its eyes were an endless blue, the whispers of light in the translucent gemstone like bright tears. Through the rough silhouette, I could barely make out the shape of a man within, the soul tag burned into the back of his neck. I had never seen a sapphire monster before, but I knew from my tedious studies that sapphire was much, much harder than pearl.

The prince had crammed himself into a corner of the library, wielding a jagged piece of wood, the front of his robes painted in blood that I hoped wasn't his. Our eyes met and he smiled with relief before the monster took a thundering step closer.

I could never cross the chaos of overturned bookshelves to reach him in time. Instead, I fished three firestones from my satchel and slammed my palms onto the floor.

The broken shelves covering the room exploded upward in a flurry of wood chips and clattered down over the monster like heavy rain. With his path now cleared, the prince hurried out of the corner and toward me.

But the monster was faster.

It swiped a jeweled claw in the prince's path, barely missing his face as its fingers sank into the floor. The prince swung at it with his piece of broken shelf, which instantly burst in his hands.

"You're not going to break sapphire with wood!" I said, scanning the room for a solution while the monster tried to dislodge its arm from the floor.

"Well, sorry, but *my choice of weapons at the moment is a bit limited!*" the prince said, dodging a swipe of the monster's other hand.

I grabbed a wooden plank and one of the metal backs of

the overturned chairs, burning up the ring on my left hand to transform them into a mallet and handle. While the monster was preoccupied with its claw, I managed to heft the hammer and strike at its leg. It hit with a hollow *clink*, knocking the mallet out of my hands and sending it spinning across the floor. The monster turned and swung at me, the *whoosh* of its claws tearing through the air far too close to my face.

Clearly, I wasn't going to stop this monster by breaking it.

As the monster struggled, the light reflected off the soul tag burned into its neck. The Moon Alchemist had said that removing the soul tags was how she killed the monsters after they served their purpose. So maybe I didn't need to completely disarm the monster. Maybe I could just crack its soul tag until it was unreadable.

I plunged my hand into my satchel and felt around, realizing I only had two firestones left. I'd put off restocking in favor of planning the Empress's demise, not really expecting to fight for my life tonight.

Without stones of destruction, I would have to break off the soul tag some other way. But I knew for a fact none of the stones on my fingers or in my satchel were strong enough to crack sapphire.

The prince tried once more to run from the corner, but the monster swung out its free arm and tore off the prince's sleeve, rattling the bracelets on his wrist. One was gold with smaller jewels I couldn't make out, one was smooth jade, and the other was a blue-green gemstone.

"Give me your bracelets!" I said.

*"How is that going to help?"* the prince said, crushing himself back against the wall.

"Just throw them!" I said.

The prince let out a frustrated sound but pulled off his

bracelets with shaking hands and tossed them over the monster's head. They hit the ground and spun off in three different directions, but I quickly snatched them from the floor and held them to the light.

I tossed aside the jade one immediately. Jade was softer than sapphire and would shatter just like wood. I held the blue gemstone up to the light, praying it was some sort of blue diamond. But the bracelet had red and yellow hues, so it was probably topaz, which wasn't hard enough.

"Zilan?" the prince said uneasily as one of the monster's claws began to unlatch.

I ignored him, dropping the blue bracelet and examining the gold one. The gold itself was useless—surely the crown prince wore jewelry made of pure gold, which was butter-soft. But the tiny decorative gemstones in the pattern were clear. I jammed my nail under the base of the stones and popped them out one by one, until I had a handful of tiny glittering shards. I closed them in my fist and used up my iron rings as catalysts to meld them together into a single diamond the size of a fingernail, sharp like a dagger on one end with a flat surface on the other. It wasn't very big, but it was the hardest gemstone in the world.

"Distract it!" I shouted.

The prince's eyes went wide. "*Distract it?* With what, exactly? My death?"

"Something else, if you can manage," I said, clambering up a pile of broken wood.

The prince sputtered and tossed another plank at the monster, shielding his face when it bounced straight back at him.

I reached the top of the wood pile, as high as I could hope to get. For once, I was grateful that I was tall. I needed to be in order to reach the towering monster's soul tag.

The monster yanked its claw once more and, in a spray of splintered wood, freed its arm from the floor.

"*Zilan!*" the prince said, shrinking into the corner.

Then, at the worst moment possible, my vision swirled.

I saw flashes of crooked roots and black water in the parched river of my soul, then scorched red earth, a dirt road unfurling, the five gates of darkness rising up before me like a tidal wave. My own face reflected back at me a thousand times in the prisms of sapphire, eyes hollow, my ears burning with the name that the darkness screamed. I felt myself falling and reached out into the nothingness.

The sharpness of sapphire beneath my fingers shocked me back into awareness, its jagged edges biting into my palm. I'd wanted to jump onto the monster's shoulders, but I'd only managed to grab onto its back while falling.

The monster twisted around, reaching for me, but its limbs were too stiff to touch its back. I locked my legs around its waist and hoisted myself up, and only then, as a jolt of coldness rushed through me, did I realize the diamond was gone.

I must have dropped it when I got dizzy, and there was no chance of finding it in the chaos of the library floor.

The monster arched backward and its fingers caught my dress, tearing a line across my leg. I winced and jammed a hand into my satchel, already knowing that there was nothing else strong enough, but I had to try *something*. I couldn't just hang on like a rag doll and wait for the monster to squish me against a wall.

My fingers pinched a stone I didn't recognize at first, before I remembered it wasn't a stone at all. It was a soap bean left over from this morning.

My gaze snapped to the soul tag scorched into the back of the monster's spine in dusty streaks of black. Whoever had made the monster must have realized that sapphire was too hard to carve a soul tag into, settling for burning the name into the surface instead. Maybe I couldn't damage the soul tag, but I could clean it away.

I crushed the soap bean between my fingers, spit on the soul tag—*that's what you get for ruining my plans*—and scrubbed the soap into the characters.

The name smeared at once with a long streak of black under my thumb, and the monster froze.

Cracks shot across every inch of the monster's skin, like tangled vines. I lost my grip and crashed to the floor as chunks of sapphire molted off the monster, falling in twinkling shards of sharp blue rain.

A pale human crawled out of the steaming stones, then fell limp and still on the floor among its sparkling fragments. I crawled closer to him, both to make sure he was really dead and then to close his eyes and mouth.

The prince crossed the room, his shoes crunching over the shards, and before I could speak, he knelt on the floor and wrapped his arms around me. He smelled like blood and fire, and I didn't know what to do with my hands. In the stillness, I felt his heart beating fast against my cheek.

"I don't think the evening tea ever made it there," I said. "It's not over, if that's why you're hugging me."

He sighed, but rather than letting me go, his arms only pulled tighter.

"I don't think we should split up again," he said.

I laughed sharply into his shoulder. "Yes, you'd be dead without me."

"I thought you were already dead," the prince said, finally releasing me. "I saw the monster walk by covered in blood. I was sure that meant it had already found you."

"You really think that I'm more likely to die first?" I said. "If you believed it was after me, you should have just left it alone. They only attack if you get in the way of their target."

"You would ask me to walk away from the thing that killed you?" the prince said, eyes narrowing.

"You mean you attacked it first?" I said. "Do you have a death wish? Why would you—"

A drop of blood trickled down his collarbone, into my line of vision. I pulled back.

"You're hurt," I said. My hands hovered around his throat, where three parallel claw marks ran from the center of his throat down to his collarbone, shredding through the neckline of his robes.

"It's not deep," he said, gently moving my hand away.

*Only a little bit deeper and we wouldn't be sitting here talking about it*, I thought, my stomach tight. "I can fix it," I said, my voice wobbly. "Let's go back. It's not safe out here anyway."

"Zilan, it's fine. I—"

"Shut up," I said. I tugged him to his feet and dragged him back through the halls to his room. I locked the door, even though I didn't know anymore whether something as feeble as a lock could really keep out monsters.

I pushed the prince until he sat down on his bed and kneeled in front of him, my hands tracing over the wounds to get a sense of how deep they were. I peeled back a torn layer of his robe, and it was only then that I realized I didn't have any moonstone on me, that I had no way of actually healing him and he would have been better off with a palace nurse. He swallowed, and I felt the motion under my fingertips, my gaze drifting up to his eyes. They were burning amber, like the gold flecks had melted away into glowing pools.

My fingers slid down to his bare chest. He shivered, a warm

hand tucking my hair behind my ear. I leaned into his touch, my hand rising to his face, mirroring his gesture, my fingers staining his skin with blood.

My mind spun with a thousand reasons this was a bad idea. I thought of my cousins telling me how dangerous it was to be close to the prince, how he'd tried to buy me like a cow back in Guangzhou, and most of all, how this could never last once he became Emperor.

But I wasn't like the members of the royal court, who ate gold to try to keep the world the same for all of eternity. Nothing would last forever, including me. I didn't need something to be eternal for it to matter.

I leaned forward, but the prince's hand on my cheek held me a breath away.

"Zilan," he whispered, "you don't have to."

"I know," I said, frowning.

He shook his head. "Do you? I would still protect you, even if you didn't want me."

"You think I don't know how to refuse you?" I said, shoving his wrist away. "I've done nothing but say no to you since the day we met."

"I'm serious," he said. "This can be pretend, if you want it to be. You could still stay here. I would keep you safe no matter what."

I took his face in my hands. "Li Hong," I said, "I'm done pretending."

Then I leaned forward and kissed him.

He held me close, hands ghosting over me with reverence. He was everywhere all at once, his heartbeat singing through my bones, his left hand on the small of my back with exquisite gentleness, his right hand laced with mine, clasped tight in a wordless promise. He pulled me onto his bed and whispered my name, one I'd never before thought was beautiful, unraveling me beneath him like a secret.

He slipped my dress from my shoulders, his bright eyes turning to me for permission before I nodded and helped him slide me out of the bloodied layers of silk. But rather than undressing himself, he pressed a kiss to my palm and ran his hand down my bare arm, mapping my skin. I shivered as his fingers whispered across my collarbone, across the racing pulse at my throat.

"What are you doing?" I said.

"Remembering," he said, kissing the inside of my elbow. "You don't eat gold, so every moment, you change just a little bit. You will never look exactly like this again. I want to remember this moment forever."

My whole body glowed at his words and I turned away, unable to look at him, sure he could feel my quickening heartbeat.

"There is no forever," I said. "Not in the future we want."

The prince hummed, fingers tracing my other arm, all the way down to my fingertips, where he laced our hands together once more.

"Then let me remember it as long as I can," he said.

So I let his warm hands remember me, whispering across my stomach and hips, shivering across the knobs of my spine, his lips gentle at the back of my neck. I felt myself sinking into his touch, like a warm river rising over my head, ready to carry me far away. He brushed my hair aside and ran a finger across a spot between my shoulder blades.

"I thought your surname was Fan," he said.

"It is," I said, the words murmured and distant, my whole body boneless beneath him.

"Then who is Su Zilan?"

All the warmth drained from my body. I curled away from his touch, sitting up, my skin suddenly cold and tight. I hadn't heard that name in a long time.

My mother and Auntie So were sisters, and since my father didn't have a surname they could write in Chinese, they'd given me my mother's name. I'd been born as So Zilan. In the dialect of Chang'an, my name would be read as Su Zilan. But the prince wouldn't know that unless he saw my name written down, and I hadn't written that name anywhere since Auntie and Uncle had adopted me.

"Where did you read that?" I said, turning around.

The prince pulled back slightly, as if sensing the danger of his question. "I didn't mean to offend you," he said.

"I'm not offended, I just don't understand. Where did you see that name?"

"Your scar," he said quietly.

I was already on my feet, my fingers fumbling to light a candle by the mirror.

"What scar?" I said, the wick finally igniting, singeing my fingers.

The prince rose from bed and tried to drape a sheet over me, but I swatted his hand away, scanning my body in the mirror.

"I didn't mean to upset you," he said.

I shook my head. *"What scar?"*

He pointed to my back, between my shoulder blades. I pulled my hair over my shoulder and tried to twist to see it in the mirror, but the light was too dim.

"Here," he said, picking up the candle for me and nudging my shoulder forward until I could barely see the center of my spine in the mirror. There, in small, jagged lines, the skin was raised and white, a ghost of a scar.

蘇
紫
蘭

Su Zilan.

"I'm sorry," the prince said, "I didn't mean to make you uncomfortable. I was only curious."

But I could only stare at the mark—my real name—branded onto my skin. For so many years, I'd tried to be one of the Fans, but, as always, alchemy unveiled the truth. I pressed a hand to my throat, feeling like the golden walls were crushing closer, like the world was a cold, dark box, no air left for me to breathe.

"It's very small," the prince said, shifting from foot to foot. "I probably wouldn't have noticed it if I hadn't felt it. If it bothers you that much, I can see if there are any healers who can remove scars..."

*It's not a scar,* I wanted to scream, staring at my horrified reflection.

*It's a soul tag.*

# CHAPTER TWENTY-SIX

I ran across the palace grounds, my untied hair lashing my face as the wind tore through it. I didn't know where I was going, but I couldn't be around the prince right now. What would he think if he knew I was just a hollow shell living on stolen time, no different than any of the corpses chained in the dungeon? He thought I was beautiful, but he didn't know that I was rotting inside.

I'd dragged so many people back from the shores of death without ever really thinking about what that meant. Was I even a person anymore? Or was I like one of my old hemp dolls, just a soulless piece of fabric stuffed full of rags? I pressed a hand to my racing heart—I could feel all the blood rushing through me, nausea twisting in my stomach, cold sweat running down my face. How could I not be alive?

And more importantly, how could I have died without knowing it?

The name on my spine said *Su Zilan*, so it must have happened before my father left, before I was a Fan. Maybe I didn't remember because I was so young at the time. But I had still grown up down the street from my cousins, who were older than me and surely would have remembered me dying. And who could have resurrected me? My father's notes had theorized about how one might revive the dead, but he hadn't written about attempting it.

I came to a stop in the middle of an empty courtyard, my legs shaking. I'd jammed on my dress and hadn't bothered to grab a jacket before fleeing, and somewhere along the way I'd lost one of my shoes, my toes sinking into mud.

I had no idea where to go.

I wanted to talk to my cousins, the only people who would understand, but would they even open the door for me after what I'd said? Who else could I possibly talk to? Who else even knew the first thing about resurrection?

I turned my gaze toward the southern quarters, the high walls that marked the alchemy compound.

I started running before I could stop myself, shivering as I waited for the bewildered guard to let me in, wanting to tear my own skin off just to feel something other than this nauseous panic. Finally, I sprinted past the gates to the last house on the right, pounding my fists on the door until I heard grumbling and footsteps from the other side.

The door slid open sharply. The Moon Alchemist stood in the shadowed darkness, her hair in a tangled crown around her face, her grip tight on the doorframe.

"*Fan Zilan*—"

"I think I'm dead," I said.

She blinked, the anger gone from her face in an instant, then let out a heavy sigh. She turned, waving for me to follow her inside. I hurried in before she could change her mind, locking the door behind me.

"I think—"

"Shh!" she said, rubbing her eye with one hand and throwing a couple cushions onto the floor around a small table. "Tea first."

I wanted to scream at how slowly the Moon Alchemist began to boil water and measure out tea leaves. The moment she sat down with a steaming cup, the words poured from my mouth.

"I found a soul tag on my back," I said. "I'd never seen it before."

The Moon Alchemist hummed in acknowledgment, taking a sip of tea. "Did you tell anyone?" she said.

I stilled. Her calmness unnerved me. Was she going to turn me in to the Empress?

"Just the prince," I said. "He saw it, but I don't think he understood. I left before explaining."

"Good," the Moon Alchemist said, setting her cup down loudly on the table. "Make your excuses to him later. He's well-educated but not particularly perceptive. He'll believe you if you lie."

I reached for my teacup, wanting to hold on to something, but my hands shook so much that the hot water spilled onto the table, scalding me. I pulled away out of reflex but hardly even felt it. The Moon Alchemist was so eerily calm that it only heightened my panic. Did she understand what I was telling her?

"Do you not believe me?" I said. "I know what a soul tag looks like. I resurrected people long before I came here."

"That was obvious from the start," the Moon Alchemist said, frowning at me through the haze of steam rising from her cup. "You have no memory of dying?"

I shook my head. "It must have happened when I was very young, because the soul tag doesn't say Fan Zilan. It says—"

"Su Zilan."

I froze. All the blood rushed from my face. Across from me, the Moon Alchemist took another sip of tea.

"How did you know that?" I whispered, my bones screaming for me to *get up and don't stop running*.

She set down her cup, pushed it to the side, and crossed her arms. "Because," she said, "I'm the one who brought you back."

I shook my head slowly, unable to form words. I wanted to flip the table over and storm out into the night, but my limbs felt like granite. Why was the Moon Alchemist suddenly lying to me? I'd never even left Guangzhou until this year, so how could she have met me?

"When you came to Chang'an as an alchemist, I wasn't sure if it was really you, at first," she said. "Zilan is not a common name for your class, and a hùnxiě named Zilan is even less common. But you said your surname was Fan, and I knew that was not the name I wrote on a child's spine so many years ago. That is not a day I will ever forget."

"I met you for the first time this year," I said.

The Moon Alchemist shook her head. "It's unusual that you don't remember, but then again, your resurrection was also unusual. If I hadn't known your father, I don't think I would have tried to bring you back at all. Recalling your soul was a very long and difficult process. Maybe that's why you don't remember."

*"What are you talking about?"* I said, slamming my fists into the table.

The Moon Alchemist looked at me with something resembling pity. It was the softest expression I'd ever seen on her face.

"Ten years ago, I met a Scotian alchemist here in Chang'an," she said. "He'd brought his wife and daughter from Guangzhou. They intended to move here so he could study alchemy."

I wanted to tell her that I'd never been to Chang'an before this year, but the words died on my lips. That strange day when the world went dark, the memory I knew was real but could never place, the certainty that I'd seen the gates of Chang'an before, the dizzy feeling of remembering something I wasn't supposed to.

"I didn't need his help," the Moon Alchemist said, "but he had some interesting ideas, so I let him work with me. Then, one day, the Empress's horse brigade ran over his daughter in the market."

I shook my head, remembering the feeling of my body snapping apart, my name being called across an empty expanse. The way that our horses we rode to Chang'an had terrified me in a way Yufei and Wenshu couldn't understand.

"I'd never heard a mother scream so loudly," she said. "The thought of resurrecting you didn't cross my mind at first— you hardly had a face left, and alchemists aren't supposed to go around resurrecting all their friends. I would have been killed if anyone found out, and why would I take that risk for a family I hardly knew?"

She leaned back, glaring into her empty teacup. "But, in the whole market, no one tried to help. Even when your mother begged for a healer, no one would look at you. They kept selling their beans and porridge and just walked around you, like you didn't even exist. This was just after the Yangzhou massacre. No one wanted foreigners—or their children—in our markets."

*But I'm not a foreigner,* I thought, although I knew what the Moon Alchemist meant.

"No one wants people like us to exist," she said, her grip

so tense around her cup that I thought it might shatter. "So I decided to spit in all their faces and bring you back. I led your parents here through the tunnels and warned them that if I resurrected you, you would drain their qi, and they would be dead within four years if they stayed with you. But they didn't care. They told me to bring you back, no matter what."

"Stop," I said, gripping the edge of the table. Maybe she thought it was kind to tell me how much my parents had loved me, that once I had been wanted more than life itself. But I didn't want to hear it. Their love didn't matter now, because it was gone. It was easier to pretend I had always been a Fan, to say I was too young to remember my real parents, to hate my father for leaving us. I couldn't be Fan Zilan while mourning the life that Su Zilan might have had. I couldn't think about whether my aunt or uncle would have done the same, would have given up their lives for mine. I was too afraid of the answer.

"I did the best I could with what was left of your face and hands, and somehow, I brought you back," the Moon Alchemist said. "Your soul was very hard to find, and even when I retethered it, you didn't wake for several days. But once you did, I told your parents that they could never tell anyone what happened, or else the Empress would chain you up as one of her monsters, and I would be killed as well. Your parents decided to spend their last four years with your mother's family in Guangzhou, and I thought I'd never see you again."

*This is why my cousins never said anything about it*, I thought. They didn't see me die, had probably been too young to remember me disappearing for a few weeks, and my parents had never spoken of it.

"Your father returned to Chang'an four years later, looking for a cure for your mother," the Moon Alchemist said. "He was half-dead already, and I told him the same thing—that the only way to live was to stay away from you. He was angry with me, so I sent him off with some gold and never saw him again. My guess is that he died somewhere in the city. He wouldn't have made it far."

I stared at my hands in my lap, the long, spidery fingers that Auntie So said were so unlike my mother's, the alchemy rings on each hand, the dream I'd chased just to spite the man I thought had left me. But maybe he'd wanted to come back and had died in a drainage ditch in Chang'an, ending up in the dungeons like the other bodies, hollowed out and forged into a monster by another alchemist. I'd thought my mother was delusional for saying he'd return, but he'd *tried*. He hadn't wanted to leave us, but to save us.

My fists closed tight, alchemy rings biting into my palms. My father had been with me this whole time, the warm and wordless voice ringing in my ears whenever I studied alchemy, and even if I'd long forgotten his language, his presence had pushed me forward until I became a royal alchemist. He'd given everything for me, and in the end, I'd become exactly like him—standing beside the Moon Alchemist, trying to fight death.

"I didn't mean for them to never tell *you*," the Moon Alchemist said. "That was dangerous. One piece of gold past your lips and you would have turned into a monster like the ones crawling around the palace. You truly never noticed?"

"How could I?" I said, staring at my hands and imagining them cracking apart into a thousand pieces, being sewn back together by the Moon Alchemist.

"Because all of your qi is stolen," she said. "Every four

years, the people closest to you must have died after you drained them. Is that not the case?"

My head throbbed, but I closed my eyes and tried to organize my thoughts. The Moon Alchemist said I'd died ten years ago, when I was seven. My mother died and my father disappeared when I was eleven, four years later. Three and a half years later, Wenshu and Yufei died. Now, two years later, Auntie So and Uncle Fan were sick, though miraculously recovered the moment my cousins and I left for Chang'an.

*We were killing them*, I realized. Not just Wenshu and Yufei, but all three of us.

I'd been so certain that my cousins hadn't loved me because they weren't killing me. But I had no qi for them to steal. I was as hollow inside as them, siphoning qi off Auntie and Uncle. I slumped my shoulders, letting my hair hide my face, finally feeling as dead as I truly was inside. I'd been so cruel to my cousins because I'd believed in a lie.

"You need to be careful," the Moon Alchemist said, taking my silence for an answer. "One body cannot withstand too much alchemy. I have never been able to resurrect someone twice. This life is your last, Zilan. Do you understand?"

I nodded slowly. "What am I supposed to do now?" I said.

"Do?" The Moon Alchemist frowned. "You continue what you've been doing."

"How can you make it sound so simple?" I said. "I'm dead."

"You are not dead," she said. "You died. There's a difference."

"How is there a difference?"

She grabbed my wrist and yanked me forward. My pulse hammered in her hand, mockingly alive.

"The difference is that I gave you a second chance, and people like us don't get second chances every day. Stop thinking about how and why and just figure out how not to waste what I've given you, what I risked everything for."

I shook my head. "I'm no different from those monsters in the palace who rip apart little girls. How can I possibly just keep living normally?"

"I'll tell you how," the Moon Alchemist said. "You never let anyone see your soul tag. You never let a piece of gold or a jewel past your lips. And you never get close to anyone you aren't willing to destroy."

I tried to sleep for a few hours after that, but I dreamed of my flesh falling off in stiff chunks at any moment, my muscles rotting away, my bones crumbling. My whole body felt stolen and wrong, like I was wearing gloves and silks instead of my own skin, and part of me wanted to tear myself apart until I was left with nothing but my soul, the only thing that was real.

The Moon Alchemist said nothing had to change, but that was easy for her to say. She wasn't risking her last life by betraying the Empress. I'd never thought much about dying until now, because ever since I'd learned to resurrect people, death had seemed like a temporary state, an inconvenience. But now I felt death watching me from the dark and empty oceans of the moon, whispering to me in the wind that rustled the silver grass beyond my windows, deepening the shadows across my bed and curling around me when I tried to sleep.

*Death remembers me*, Wenshu had said. And now I remembered death as well, the day of darkness, the feeling of becoming nothing and everything all at once. Was that what permanent death would feel like? Nothingness that stretched on for eternity?

I sat up in bed, feeling sick. *I want Wenshu and Yufei*, I thought, even though I doubted they wanted me anymore.

But I felt so much like an untethered boat drifting from shore, and only they would understand.

I cast my blankets to the floor and put on my shoes, then slipped out into the night. The guards at the gate would never let me past them without an escort, especially at this hour, so I carved a new door in the wall with some iron and slipped through, hurrying into the street.

I hardly felt my feet as I ran. No part of my body seemed like it belonged to me anymore. I wasn't even supposed to exist.

When I finally reached their ward, my lungs burned and sweat coated my face, but just the thought of running into their arms made me feel like all of this would somehow be fine. Wenshu would be angry, but he would tell me how to fix things. Yufei would pat my hair and stuff food in my face, and we would figure out what to do.

Their door was already open when I arrived.

"Gēgē?" I called, trying to peer through the darkness. "Jiějiě?"

My voice echoed back in the stillness. I grabbed a candle and sparked three firestones in my hand, casting weak light across the room.

The beds were overturned, scrolls unfurled across the floor with muddy footprints blurring the text. Wenshu's jar of soap beans had shattered, coating the floor in sparkling shards and the aching smell of too much soap. They must have been in a hurry to leave if Wenshu hadn't tried to clean up.

I stepped into the room and stumbled over one of Yufei's shoes, still muddy. In fact, both of her and Wenshu's shoes were scattered near the doorway, their coats still hung up on hooks. I knew for a fact that they only owned one pair of shoes and one coat each, and they hadn't bothered to take them before leaving? My mouth went dry.

"Gēgē? Jiějiě?" I said again, rushing forward, shoes crunching over broken glass. Maybe they were out back somewhere. Maybe Yufei had just made a mess, and Wenshu had stormed off into a backyard I didn't know about, because they wouldn't leave willingly without their shoes or coats, so that meant—

A note was staked into the far wall, neatly folded, the blade coated in pristine gold. The paper bore the imperial seal, a crane stamped in red ink around the characters for *eternity*.

I yanked the blade out and cast it aside to unfold the note with hands I could hardly even feel.

There were only three words on the paper.

*Nice try, Scarlet.*

# CHAPTER TWENTY-SEVEN

The sun rose over the alchemy courtyard, where I lay on my back in the dirt, birds circling overhead, probably debating if I was dead. My feet ached from running around the city all night and my palms had blistered from the alchemy of breaking into so many buildings. After returning to the palace, I'd stormed through the dungeons, but my cousins were nowhere to be found. Wherever they'd been taken, it was a place I had never been before.

The Empress must have noticed something in her tea. Maybe the taster had said something about the texture, or the strange encounter with us in the hall. Maybe the River Alchemist or the Paper Alchemist had reported me for asking about arsenic. Only now did I realize how many open ends we'd left, how it had been a foolish and doomed plan from the start. Now my cousins were probably chained up in some moldy cell like the rest of the corpses the Empress bought. And if what the Moon Alchemist said was true, I couldn't bring them back this time if the Empress killed them.

I curled onto my side, cheek scraping into sharp grass and

roots. *My cousins will die for a second time because of me,* I thought, my tears darkening the dirt.

The only thing I didn't understand was why I was still walking around freely. The Empress definitely had my blood. She could have easily made a monster to eat me. Surely it could have found me and ripped my throat open by now.

I felt like the prince, worrying over the fact that I was safe, and what that meant. The Empress was clearly keeping both of us alive for a reason, and I had a sinking feeling that it wasn't mercy.

The Moon Alchemist hadn't been in her quarters when I'd come back after scouring the city, or at least she hadn't answered the door, perhaps sick of handling all of my problems. I knew it wasn't her job to unravel the mess I'd made for myself, but I had no one else to turn to.

The doors to the courtyard creaked open and I sat up straight, backing against the tree trunk. A man entered first, and for a paralyzing moment I thought it was the prince. The last thing I wanted was to answer his questions about my abrupt disappearance. My head started swimming. I couldn't handle my cousins maybe being double-dead and me being single-dead and my first kiss all at once. I had to prioritize, and finding my cousins was the biggest problem right now.

But I didn't need to worry, because it wasn't the prince. It was the Empress and her guards.

*This is it,* I thought. *She was waiting to execute me on her perfect schedule. She'll reveal me as a traitor in front of all the other alchemists and have me carried away in chains, then she'll behead my cousins in front of me.*

I must have looked like an animal, drenched with sweat, rising on shaking legs, palms scraping against the bark as I hauled myself to my feet, watching the Empress draw closer. Was it even worth trying to fight her guards off? Surely they'd just threaten my cousins the moment I resisted. I fumbled for my satchel anyway, my hands shuddering against the stones.

The Empress met my eyes as she approached, a sharp smile cutting across her perfect face.

"Scarlet," she said, nodding at me as if she hadn't noticed the fact that I hadn't bowed, that I was glaring at her.

Then she cut through the rest of the courtyard, her guards brushing past me before the entire party exited through the southern door.

I felt like I'd been doused in cold water. *That's it?* I thought, sinking to my knees. Either the Empress truly had nothing to do with my cousins' disappearance—which I doubted—or she had something bigger planned for me. Something more terrible than humiliating me in front of the other alchemists. She wanted to watch me squirm like a pinned insect.

A hand closed around my wrist.

I nearly jumped out of my skin, yanking away so violently that both me and my assailant spilled onto the ground.

"Fan Zilan!" the Moon Alchemist said, shoving me so she could rise to her feet and brush off her skirts. "You're late."

"Late?" I echoed as she hauled me to my feet, moving toward the gate. "Where were you last night?"

"Working," she said, yanking my wrist harder. "We have more to do today."

I pulled away and drew to a stop. "You have to help me. My cousins—"

"We can't talk about that now," the Moon Alchemist said under her breath. "Now *come with me.*"

"This can't wait!" I said. I wasn't being particularly polite, but I hadn't slept all night and my brain felt like porridge leaking out of my ears. She was the only person who could help me, the only one in this palace I thought I could trust with all of my secrets. Who else could I go to when all of us talked in circles, terrified of what the Empress might hear?

I glanced around the courtyard, which was empty aside from a groundskeeper trimming flowers.

"Have you ever thought," I whispered, slipping into Guangzhou dialect, "about what all the alchemists could do to stop the Empress if we worked together?"

The slap echoed across the courtyard. I hardly realized I'd been struck until the ground rose to meet me, my face stinging and jaw aching.

The Moon Alchemist stepped over me, her shadow eclipsing the sun, her expression grave.

"You are a fool," she said, this time in Chang'an dialect. "*Never* ask me that again."

"Are you really that scared of her?" I said, trying to push myself up, but the Moon Alchemist shoved me back into the dirt.

"You are too young to understand anything," she said. "Your words are more dangerous than you know."

"I understand that she has my family!" I said, rising onto my elbows. "I understand that I have to save them, and that the Empress wouldn't stand a chance if all the alchemists—"

"*I have already explained this to you!*" the Moon Alchemist said. "The whole court says that you're unschooled and ignorant, and right now you're proving them right. The things you want are nothing more than foolish childhood dreams. We obey because we don't have a choice."

I ground my fingers into the dirt, my hands trembling.

*No.*

That wasn't a good enough answer.

The Moon Alchemist had a choice, and she had chosen her own life over the lives of others. Part of me could hardly blame her for that.

But then I thought of the piles of corpses in the dungeons, all the people who didn't get to choose whether they lived or died.

I rose to my feet, cuffing bloody spit from my lip. "That's all that anyone ever says around here—*I can't do it, it's not that simple, you wouldn't understand.* But I understand perfectly. You know that there's a price for change, and the people who have the most power never want to pay it. They always want someone else to pay it for them."

The Moon Alchemist kicked me hard in the stomach, stealing my next words from my mouth. I gasped, curling into myself in the dirt. Was she trying to scold me or kill me? I reached out for her ankle, but she stepped down hard on my hand, then knelt in front of me.

"You think that just because you were the best alchemist in some backwater village, you know better than the alchemists who have been here for centuries?" she said. "Once she has you, and your blood, the only way to live is to serve her."

She kicked me again and I rolled over onto my face.

*"You're a coward!"* I said into the ground. I didn't care how much she beat me. Let her kill me again and waste all her hard work. I didn't care. "You think you're the greatest alchemist in the empire, but you're spineless just like the rest of the royal court."

I braced myself for another strike, but it never came. When I dared to look up, the Moon Alchemist was staring down at me with a perfectly even expression, like she didn't know me at all.

"We're done for today," she said, turning around. "Get out of my sight."

I shuffled back to my room, trying not to draw too much attention to myself even though I couldn't help wrapping a hand around my stomach. I tasted blood running from my nose and wiped it away with my sleeve.

"Zilan!" the prince called from somewhere behind me.

I hesitated, wishing the Moon Alchemist had just killed me when she'd had the chance.

The prince had frozen halfway across a courtyard, his flock of wide-eyed servants all turning toward me in confusion. I thought about last night, how gentle his hands had been, even when they traced over my soul tag. I felt like he could see straight through me, right down to the bone.

He was already crossing the courtyard, servants toddling behind him like startled ducklings.

"Your Highness, your meeting—"

"Not now," he said, waving a hand behind him, not tearing his gaze from me. He looked at me with the same gray expression that people had always worn when they first heard my mother died, like I was too-thin ceramic that would break apart. He reached for my hand when he came closer, frowning at the dirt ground into my knuckles.

"What happened to you?" he said, examining my face. "Who did this?"

"Training exercise," I said, looking away. "You don't need to execute anyone, I promise."

He frowned, but nodded and released me.

"Are you all right?" he said, his voice lower, and I knew he wasn't talking about my bloody nose.

I had an overwhelming urge to wrap my arms around him and cry, to have him lie to me and say everything would be fine, that all his money and power could fix everything for me.

"We need to talk when you're free," I said instead, my words soulless as I glanced pointedly at his servants.

"We can talk right now," he said, spinning toward them. "Everyone go away."

"Your Highness," one of them said, grimacing, "your meeting—"

"Not right now," I said to the prince. "I need to…" Change into non-bloody clothes? Try to sleep? Cry? Even if he figured out where my cousins were, I was going to be useless when it came to rescuing them if I still felt this shaky and nauseous and ready to burst into a thousand shards. My last attempt at overtired alchemy had left his little sister in a coma.

"Whatever you want, Zilan," the prince said, thumb tracing under my eyes, like he knew I hadn't slept but didn't want to say it out loud.

I thought about the Moon Alchemist telling me not to explain what I really was to the prince. His eyes were so bright and earnest that it felt cruel to lie to him.

"I'm sorry. About last night," I said at last. "I… I just panicked." That much was true, at least.

He took my hand and pressed a kiss to it. I tensed up, casting a nervous glance to his servants just behind him, but he didn't seem bothered.

"There's nothing to be sorry for," he said. He raised his sleeve, wiping the blood from my nose. "I know your training is important, but I wish they wouldn't damage your pretty face," he said with a soft smile.

I tried to smile in return, but it probably looked more like a grimace. I imagined a horse stomping on my face as a child.

"I'll see you tonight?" he asked.

I nodded. "You should go before your servants start to cry," I said, gesturing to the man who had begun nervously pacing.

"I think they'll live," he said, squeezing my hand. I turned away, knowing he wouldn't leave unless I did first. I could hardly feel my feet carrying me away, my stomach such a nauseous mess of worry that I wanted to throw up until every part of me was empty. Everything with the prince was so spectacularly poorly timed. It was too hard to appreciate him when I was busy imagining my cousins being strung up and tortured in dungeons while my mentor shrugged and said *It's my duty.*

Could my father have convinced the Moon Alchemist to help, as he'd convinced her to resurrect me? I closed my eyes and tried to imagine the warm cadence of his voice, but it felt quiet and far away. I'd thought myself so much better than him for rising to the royal court, but what did I have to show for it? My words were powerless, my wishes just childish dreams.

I locked the door to my quarters and fell into my bed, then drifted into a weary half sleep, my heart still racing too fast to let me truly rest. I resurfaced just as the sun had set—as winter drew closer, the days were becoming thinner, the sunlight paler. I'd already missed dinner with the other alchemists but couldn't bring myself to care.

I hoped they were at least feeding my cousins, wherever they were.

I sat up at the sound of my door rattling. I'd thought the prince would wait for me to find him, but maybe he'd grown too worried.

"Wait a moment," I called as I rubbed my eyes and smoothed down my hair a bit.

But before I could even stand up, the lock clicked.

I froze. The prince didn't have a key to my room, did he? And he never would have unlocked it to let himself in. I reached for my satchel of stones as the door slammed open.

Two figures in red opera masks rushed into my room and grabbed my arms. I tried to scream, but one of them shoved a cloth into my mouth. They yanked my arms behind me and bound my wrists, then the world went dark as one of them wound a black piece of fabric over my eyes.

*The Empress is ready for me*, I thought, trying to drag my heels, to kick at them and trap them in the doorway, but something warm flashed near my knees, and my legs turned limp like wet noodles. *Alchemy?* I thought. Of course, the other spineless alchemists would help the Empress kidnap me. If they didn't mind draining the blood of peasants to feed the rich, why would they care about hauling me off to my death?

My feet dragged across pebbles and dirt, my shoulders aching where their hands clamped down. I tried to work the cloth out of my mouth with my tongue, but someone shoved it back in even harder.

At least I would probably see my cousins now. More than anything, I worried what state I'd find them in. They had no inherent value to the Empress other than forcing my hand, so she wouldn't have a problem hurting them.

A heavy door swung open, then another, then another, footsteps echoing against stone. Just how deep into the palace were they taking me?

Finally, they shoved me into a chair, and I heard the sound of a lock clicking. I would have risen to my feet if I could feel my legs at all, but I could do nothing but sit and wait to meet my fate.

Someone yanked the fabric out of my mouth, then ripped away the blindfold.

I squinted in the dim light. The other alchemists stood around what looked like an old classroom, their expressions grave. The Moon Alchemist was closest to me, a blindfold in her hand, the River and Paper Alchemists beside her.

But the Empress was nowhere in sight. And this didn't

exactly look like a place where she would deign to visit. It smelled damp and moldy. There weren't any windows, so we were likely underground.

I turned to the Moon Alchemist, but before I could speak, she slapped me hard.

"Haven't you done enough of that today?" I shouted, tugging at the rope around my wrists. "You made your point this afternoon."

But the Moon Alchemist only looked angrier at my words.

"You're a fool," she said. "You wanted to talk about rebellion in the middle of the courtyard in broad daylight? The Empress has ears everywhere. You would have gotten us both executed."

"There was no one around, and I was speaking in a southern dialect!" I said. "Where else was I supposed to…"

I trailed off, my gaze sliding over the other alchemists. There were no royal guards, nothing that indicated the Empress had anything to do with this. "Why have you brought me here?" I said.

"Because," the Moon Alchemist said, crossing her arms, "we've been planning to stop the Empress for years, and it sounds like you want to help."

I swallowed, scanning the stony faces of the other alchemists. They looked like they'd rather eat me alive than have me help them. Besides, they were far more experienced and skilled than me. What could I possibly offer them?

"You talk so much about people in power doing what's right," the Moon Alchemist said. "Did you mean any of it?"

"Yes, but…how can I help you?" I asked.

"We can't tell you anything specific until you vow to stand with us," the Paper Alchemist said, holding out a bowl and a small knife. "All of us have blood samples stored here," she said. "If you turn on us, we'll feed it to all the monsters in the dungeons."

I hesitated, and one of the alchemists at the back scoffed. "She's just a child," he said. "I told you she was gutless."

"Sorry if I think it over before giving alchemists my blood," I said, glaring at him. I wasn't one to make blank promises, but truly, what did I have to lose? The Empress had already taken my cousins.

"I'll do it," I said. "Whatever you need, I'll help."

The River Alchemist untied me, and I offered my hands to the Paper Alchemist, who pricked my finger and collected the blood in a shallow bowl. She passed it to another alchemist, who put it in a vial and started writing my name across the label.

I saw them starting to write *Fan* and my stomach clenched, remembering the look on Wenshu's face when he'd told me I wasn't a Fan anymore. I'd thought him so cruel at the time, but all of his fears had come true. He and Yufei had been taken because of me. I'd spent so much time worrying that they didn't think of me as a true sibling, but I was the one who hadn't listened to them, hadn't trusted them. I thought of Auntie and Uncle chastising me when they found out what I'd done to their real children.

"My surname is Su," I said quietly.

"You said your name was Fan Zilan," the Paper Alchemist said, frowning.

"I lied," I said, looking down. "Since we're being truthful now. The Moon Alchemist knows."

The Moon Alchemist peered at me strangely but nodded to the other alchemist, who sighed and scratched out my name.

"Which Su?" she said impatiently.

"Su as in Jiangsu province," I said.

"Su as in fùsū," the Moon Alchemist said, staring at me. "*To come back to life.* How appropriate for an errant resurrection alchemist." Then she turned and drew a small chest from the shelf behind her, unlocking it. The inside glimmered like pure snow, and in the dim light it took me a moment to realize the chest was packed full of diamonds.

"We don't make quite enough money to buy many of these," she said, "so we've been saving up for a few years. There's enough here to make small blades that can cut through any jewel. If we can destroy every monster's soul tag, they'll be gone in a matter of minutes."

"How many monsters are there?" I asked.

"Right now, fifty-four," the Paper Alchemist said.

I glanced around the room. "But we're outnumbered," I said. "Nearly four times."

"We are not the only alchemists in the palace, Zilan," the Moon Alchemist said.

I was about to ask who, but my mind drifted back to the dungeons, the hand around my coat, the gaunt face of the man who'd warned me. "You want to release the prisoners," I said.

The Moon Alchemist nodded. "We'll have more than enough on our side."

"That's why you needed me?" I said. "For greater numbers?"

"No." The Moon Alchemist drew closer. "We need you because no one else has access to the Empress like you do."

A lump lodged in my throat. "I have to kill her?"

One of the other alchemists barked out a laugh. "As if we'd entrust something that important to a child," he said. "We need you to get us her blood."

"Why do you—"

"The Empress has over a hundred guards, and more that she can call if needed," the Moon Alchemist said. "If we can feed the Empress's blood to a dozen or so monsters, they'll fight off any guard trying to protect her. Even if they don't make it to her, they'll reduce the number of obstacles in our way."

"Besides," the Paper Alchemist said, grinning wickedly, "it feels appropriate for the Empress to be ripped limb from limb by her own pet projects."

"She means that it's safer for us if we're not fighting off five guards each," the Moon Alchemist said, glaring at the Paper Alchemist. "This is more efficient than getting the blood of every single guard. We don't have enough monsters for that, anyway."

"And you need me to get her blood for you," I said. "I can find a way." I thought of the Empress sitting across from me at dinner, passing me in the halls, so close that I could reach out and touch her.

"Then there's the matter of what happens after," the Moon Alchemist said.

*After?* I hadn't thought much beyond the Empress keeling over dead, and rescuing my cousins.

"We're not going to depose the Empress just to hand China over to someone who will continue the same policies. The Emperor has been kept ill for over a century. There's probably not much of him left, if he can even be saved. The prince would have to rule as regent at first, if not permanently."

*That's what I'd been counting on*, I thought. But I didn't think now was the best time to mention that I'd already tried to kill the Empress without them.

"We've been watching him for years," the Moon Alchemist said. "He's soft. He let his sisters out of jail, and cries reading about death and war. He's openly defied his mother more than once. We think he could be agreeable to our counsel, or if that fails, afraid of our power."

I shook my head. "It won't come to that," I said. "He hates his mother and her policies."

"No offense, Scarlet, but you're not the most unbiased source," the Paper Alchemist said. "The House of Li has been decimated, so our options are quite limited. He can be agreeable to us, or he can rule with a knife to his back. It's his choice."

"He'll help us," I said. "I'm sure of it."

The Paper Alchemist nodded. "I hope, for all of our sakes, that you're right."

"When are you planning on doing this?" I said. When no one answered, I tried to stand up, swaying because my legs were still numb. "Please, we need to do it as soon as possible. She's taken my cousins."

"It depends on how fast you can get us her blood," the River Alchemist said.

I nodded quickly. "Okay. I'll get it for you as soon as I can."

"Zilan."

I turned. The Moon Alchemist pressed a vial into my palm, closing my fingers around it, her hands warm. "I know you want to save your family," she said, "but please be careful. If the Empress finds out that her alchemists are against her, this will be over before it's even begun. She won't give us a second chance to strike."

"I can do this," I said, a promise to myself. This time, there would be no mistakes.

# CHAPTER TWENTY-EIGHT

I opened my eyes to the gold-embossed ceiling of the prince's room, a swirl of painted cranes and diamond whirlwinds sparkling across my vision. I blinked a few times before I realized the prince was shaking me.

I was on the floor, legs twisted under me, Durian peeping in my ears. I vaguely remembered bursting into the prince's room and telling him about my cousins and the plan to get the Empress's blood, then the world went black halfway through a sentence.

"Zilan?" the prince said, somewhere above me. "You need a healer," he said, standing as if to fetch one.

I shook my head, sitting up. "I'm fine," I said, but the prince was already speaking to his guard in the hallway. What would his healer find if he examined me? Would something about my pulse give away the fact that I was dead? He hadn't noticed anything when fixing my tooth, but surely this would be a more thorough investigation.

"Wait!" I said.

The prince turned around. "Zilan, you need—"

"Can you get the Moon Alchemist?" I said.

The prince frowned.

"She's a healer," I went on before he could argue. "I'm more comfortable with her than with your male physicians."

The prince's expression softened. "Of course," he said. "If that was the problem, you should have just told me earlier." He turned to the guard. "Go bring the Moon Alchemist here, please."

He sat down on the bed with me and waited, his hand on my knee so gentle that I felt guilty for deceiving him. The Moon Alchemist arrived soon after, her hair down, a bag of stones clutched in her hands.

"What happened?" she said to me, ignoring the prince.

"Zilan has been fainting," the prince said.

*It's not that simple*, I thought, but didn't want to contradict him. The Moon Alchemist studied my expression for a moment, then turned to the prince.

"You can wait outside, Your Highness," she said. "This may be a…women's matter."

The prince looked disappointed but stood and shuffled to the door.

The Moon Alchemist crossed the room and pushed my legs to the side, sitting on the bed in front of me.

"What's going on?" she said.

"I don't know," I said, staring at my hands in my lap. "I didn't faint."

The Moon Alchemist sighed. "I know you don't want help, but—"

"It's not that," I said. "I think there's a problem, but I don't think I actually fainted."

The Moon Alchemist frowned. "Explain."

I tugged my sleeves, picking at the loose thread. "Sometimes, I feel like a piece of driftwood carried out to sea," I whispered. "I see myself from far away, or I see places that I've never been. I don't feel ill, I just feel like I've gone somewhere else. Is it because of..." I trailed off, wary of the prince waiting outside the door. "...what we talked about before?"

The Moon Alchemist's expression pinched down further. "Come here," she said, waving me closer. She pressed one thumb to the space between my eyebrows and the other to the shell of my left ear, then closed her eyes. I listened to her breathing and tried to remain still. After a few moments, she drew back.

"Your soul is loose," she said.

I stiffened. "What does that mean?"

"Soul tags are supposed to tether your soul to your body like a sheep on a short lead, so it can't go anywhere. Your lead is too long, and the sheep is wandering out into the fields to eat flowers before it deigns to come home."

Coldness burned through my chest. My soul could just drift away? What if it drifted too far and never came back?

"How can that happen?" I said, trying to keep the tremor out of my voice.

The Moon Alchemist gestured for me to turn around and started unbuttoning my dress, pulling it down until it revealed the scar on my spine. "You grew so tall that your scar stretched and faded. I'll trace over it again."

"And that will fix it?"

"I don't know," she said, pulling a sharp needle from her bag, which she held over a candle until the tip started to glow. "The revived dead don't normally last as long as you."

Any other questions I might have asked left my mind as soon as she pressed the needle to my skin and started carving the name into my spine. I waited for the moment my soul would snap back to me, when my vision would clear and my body would stop feeling like a pile of soggy rags, but the Moon Alchemist set down her needles and I felt exactly the same. She wrapped my back in a thin layer of gauze and buttoned my dress again before calling to the prince.

"Her elements are unbalanced," she said when he returned, tightening the drawstring on her bag and standing up. "I corrected it with needles."

The prince thanked her for an embarrassingly long time before she managed to escape, then sat on the bed, plucking Durian from his box and petting him anxiously.

"I can get you out of your alchemy training if you need time to rest," he said.

"I don't need rest, especially not from alchemy," I said, frowning.

The prince sighed, resting his hand on top of mine. "Ever since I met you, I've done nothing but ask more and more of you," he said.

"You know I don't do anything I don't want to," I said.

His gaze dropped to our hands. "Oh?" he said, smiling. "So you want me to hold your hand right now?"

Before I could answer, the prince yelped and wrenched back, standing and flapping his left arm like a crooked bird.

"What are you doing?" I said. "I didn't even answer yet."

"Durian bit me!" the prince said, outraged.

I rolled my eyes. "Hold still," I said as I grabbed his sleeve, then reached inside until my fingers closed around the baby duck. He came out clinging to a golden thread in his beak, more of it unraveling as I set him on the bed.

"No way you're still hungry after all he feeds you," I said to Durian, pulling the thread away.

"I thought he liked me," the prince said, sitting heavily on the bed and crossing his arms.

"Be grateful that at least one person in here likes you. Two is pushing your luck."

"So you admit you like me?" he said, raising an eyebrow.

He leaned toward me, but I moved to the left and transformed his sleeve with my iron ring, tying him to the bedpost. "Don't kiss me while I'm thinking about how to kill your mother," I said.

He tugged his sleeve and slumped against the post. "That's not fair," he said. "I didn't know you could transform fabric."

"It's not the fabric. It's the gold," I said, tugging at a loose strand on his other sleeve. It unraveled easily, a long, thin strand of gold pooling in my palm that Durian tried to bite once more. I reached to pull it away from him, but my hands froze.

"Zilan?" the prince said.

I grabbed his arm and yanked the thread even farther out of his sleeve.

"There are easier ways to undress me," he said. "If you—"

"Wait," I said, backing up halfway across the room until a thin line of gold was suspended between us, only visible when the light hit it exactly right.

"Zilan, what—"

I clenched my fist around the thread, crushing it against my iron ring.

The prince's sleeve around the bedpost unknotted itself, bursting into frayed gold threads. He stared at his sleeve like it was the most marvelous thing he'd ever seen, then looked up at me with a wide grin.

"You can use the thread as a conduit," he said.

"And you can hide it," I said. "She expects *me* to do alchemy, but not you."

"Me?" the prince said, his smile fading. He looked down

at his frayed sleeve. "I'm not exactly in the habit of touching her," he said. "I can certainly get closer to her than you, but probably not close enough."

I rolled the thread between my fingers, sitting down on the bed. The prince was right—the Empress was far from foolish, and anything even slightly unusual would alert her that we were up to something.

The light shifted as clouds passed overhead, the room blooming with sunlight, everything shimmering—the gold-woven curtains, gold-embossed tables, gold flowers in the wallpaper. I'd heard that past dynasties had revolved around worshipping gods, but this one only worshipped gold. Everything in this damn palace down to the washcloths had some sort of gold ornamentation. I remembered the foiled gold of the Empress's makeup, the gold in her eyes, the gold rim of her teacup that she slammed onto the gold-embroidered tablecloth.

I grabbed the prince's hand so sharply that he jumped, squeezing Durian.

"Hong," I said, "I think it's time we had dinner with your mother again."

The Empress was not in the royal dining hall that evening.

The servants outside the door bowed and led us farther down the hallway, explaining that the dining hall was being cleaned. I doubted the Empress would ever let something like that interfere with her dinner plans, but we had no choice but to follow, the prince's hand clutching mine, his rings cold against my sweaty palm.

He wore gold rings on each finger, a gold thread tied from one hand to the other, connecting them under his clothes. If I held his left hand, I could do alchemy through his right.

At least, as much as one could do with a soft metalstone like gold—simple transformations that could change shape, but not much else.

Our plan was to use alchemy to make the Empress bleed without even touching her. Alchemy would flow from me, through the gold thread to the prince's ring, across the gold-embroidered tablecloth, into the Empress's golden teacup, where I could sharpen the rim as if the cup had cracked while being washed. The crack would be subtle enough that it looked like an accident, but just sharp enough to cut her lip when she drank. A servant who had been bribed—or possibly threatened—by the Moon Alchemist would whisk the cup away and present the Empress with a fresh one. The Paper Alchemist and River Alchemist were already waiting by the kitchens to snatch the dishes from the servants before they could be washed. And if all went to plan, the Empress wouldn't think much of a few drops of blood on the dish, since she'd have no way of knowing that I had caused it.

We followed the servant out to a courtyard beneath a canopy of willow trees, their broad shade softening all of the garden's colors. The Empress sat at a long table, where a servant held an umbrella over her and the creature chained beside her...

I stopped short, yanking the prince to a halt.

The Empress sat beside a golden beast with a wild crown of wispy hair around its face, its mouth curved down in a frown. Its chest made a rumbling sound, like the ground before an earthquake. It rose to its feet at the sight of us, bearing massive yellowed fangs.

"Mother," the prince said, his voice wavering, "I think—"

"I wanted to eat in the garden today," the Empress said,

petting the creature's head. "I don't think your concubine has had the chance to see one of our gifts from the West."

The prince sighed and took a small step forward, but I stayed rooted in place. Was this some sort of alchemical creation like the pearl monsters?

"It's a lion," the prince whispered. "They're dangerous, but this one is chained and obeys mother."

I didn't know if that was supposed to make me feel better. But I supposed the pearl monsters were dangerous as well, and they'd yet to kill me. I tightened my grip on the prince's hand as we crossed the courtyard, the lion's yellow eyes tracking us.

"Don't be afraid, Scarlet," the Empress said as we sat down. "He only bites when I ask him to."

I tried my best to ignore the rumbling beast as the servants started pouring tea. It wasn't until I reached for my teacup that I realized what was wrong.

There was no tablecloth.

I'd counted on the gold embroidery in the fabric to conduct alchemy, but this table was bare. I took a long sip of tea to hide my panicked expression and prayed the prince wouldn't react too strongly when he noticed.

"How is your family, Scarlet?" the Empress asked.

I stiffened, nearly choking on my tea. I took a long moment to swallow before I felt controlled enough to meet the Empress's gaze.

"My parents are dead, Your Highness," I said, because that seemed safer than talking about my cousins.

"Yes, but you came here with family, didn't you?" she said. "Are they well?"

She raised a napkin to wipe her lips, and my response died in my throat.

I recognized the embroidery immediately. Auntie So had

always hemmed the edges of Yufei's dresses with the same blue thread, the same tight stitches that had become looser over the years as her hands had grown stiff.

The Empress had made rags out of Yufei's clothes.

"Zilan has been busy with her duties at the palace," the prince answered for me when I took too long to speak. "She hasn't had much time to visit her family lately."

I swallowed, my throat dry already despite draining my teacup. The Empress was clearly trying to unsettle me, but I shoved her mockery out of my mind and honed in on what I knew—alchemy.

I needed a clean line of metal from me to her. The bare wooden table wouldn't do, but once the table filled with dishes, perhaps I could use them somehow. It was risky to do alchemy on materials without knowing what they were, but everything about this plan was already risky. Maybe it was safer to just choke down dinner and try again another day. But then the Empress wiped her mouth again with Yufei's dress and I clenched my fists under the table.

"I've requested a special dish for you, Scarlet," the Empress said. "I hear they eat this where you're from."

Then the servants began filling the table with gold plates, soups and rice and vegetables. At the center of it all was a large bird, skin glazed red and crispy. I recognized the dish, but it was surprisingly large—usually leaner birds were used to make it crispier. I didn't think I'd ever seen a bird this large, except...

Another servant placed a tray in front of the prince. Five duck heads, brown and crisp, sitting on a bed of lettuce.

The prince went very still, gaze shifting from the duck heads to the larger bird in the center of the table. "Mother," he said, his words oddly delicate, "is this duck—"

The doors to the courtyard swung open, and a servant came in holding another fat duck by its neck. It flapped and made a choked honking sound. The prince leaped to his feet, but the Empress shot him a searing look.

"Don't be a child, Hong. Animals need to eat too," she said as the lion rose onto its front paws.

The servant stopped a careful distance away and tossed the duck at the lion, who snatched it out of the air, teeth clamping around one of its wings. The duck let out a scraped wheezing noise, its free wing beating frantically, but the lion crunched down on its bones and dragged it to the ground, then pinned it with its claws as it ripped the wing clean off.

The prince sank down to his seat, gripping the edge of the table and closing his eyes. The Empress petted her lion as it ate, the duck growing quieter, its dying sounds drowned out by the wet crunching and low rumbling of the beast.

"Are you going to cry?" the Empress said. "You, the Crown Prince, crying over a dead duck?"

"No," the prince said, the quietest word I'd ever heard him say. He stared at his lap, refusing to meet her gaze. I clutched my gold chopsticks so hard that the soft metal warped in my hand, bending into a shallow curve. I slammed them on the table, ignored the flustered servants rushing to replace them, and tried to hide my treasonous anger by shoving a spoonful of rice into my mouth. It wasn't enough for the Empress to destroy everyone in her path, but she had to make them suffer as well.

I forced down more rice and tried to focus on the arrangement of dishes, nudging my bowl closer to another plate. The dishes were packed together tightly enough that their gold rims almost formed a clear path to the Empress's cup. The prince's soup bowl was just slightly too far to the left, breaking the bridge, but I couldn't exactly reach across the table and move it for him without calling attention to myself. I looked at the prince and wished he could read my thoughts, but he was sulking into his soup.

I took my soup bowl with both hands and poured it into my mouth. I didn't know if it was rude to eat this way in the palace, but the Empress thought I'd grown up in the gutter anyway. I drained it dry, choking down noodles, then grabbed the prince's hand and gestured for his soup bowl.

Without comment, he picked up his bowl and poured the contents into mine, then moved to set it back in place. I grabbed his free hand and gave it a sharp squeeze. He turned to look at me, eyes wide as if snapping out of his daze. He would only have a moment to figure out what I wanted before the silence grew too long, his hesitation too obvious, making the Empress suspicious. She was already watching us across the table.

I glanced pointedly at the plates before turning back to my soup, still wringing the life out of the prince's hand in the hopes he got my point. I heard the sound of him setting the bowl down but didn't look up right away to see where he'd placed it, in case the Empress could sense my thoughts.

Then the prince squeezed my hand back.

*He understands*, I thought, a strange warmth filling me that had nothing to do with the bucket of soup I'd just inhaled. In all my life, I'd always felt that even my cousins never had a clue what I was thinking, at least not beyond surcharging customers and scowling at men—nothing that wasn't obvious on the surface. No one had ever tried to look deeper. But here was someone who knew me the way that sailors knew the stars, charting each constellation with reverence, looking for my light when lost at sea. Maybe he didn't know my whole life story, but he knew where I was headed and would throw everything away to voyage there with me, something my family had never done.

The Empress reached for her teacup.

At the same time, the prince reached for his rice, ring clinking against the side of the bowl.

I gripped the prince's hand even harder, not sure that it would help at all with the transformation, but unwilling to let go. Alchemy rushed from my hand into his. I could sense it flashing across the thread under his clothes, rushing from his ring into the bowl, across the plate of bok choy and dumplings and bowls of rice and gold-painted chopsticks, charging like invisible lightning toward the Empress's golden teacup. It skimmed up and down the golden leaves painted across her soup bowl and—

The bowl burst, spraying all of us with a hot mist of soup.

The Empress flinched back, teacup in one hand, whirling around to glare accusingly at the servants.

"What kind of porcelain is this?" she said.

My hand went limp in the prince's palm. Our timing had been off. The Empress had moved her cup too soon, and the alchemy had cracked the wrong dish. One glance at the prince's golden ring on his right hand told me the transformation had already burned it away, and I could feel the thread in his palm that was now slack. He could no longer be a conduit for me.

The servants were all bowing and apologizing, hurrying to clear the table. I sank into my seat, thinking about my cousins rotting away in a cellar while I sat here and failed at alchemy. The prince threaded his fingers with mine, even though it was pointless now, his pulse hammering through his palm.

The lion let out a low rumble from where it lay beneath

the table, and I suspected the warm liquid pooling under my shoes was duck blood.

After the servants had finished cleaning up the mess, they brought out trays of gold for the Empress and the prince, leaving me to stare at the roasted duck that I couldn't bear to eat.

"This is dinner, not a funeral, Hong," the Empress said, popping a gold nugget into her mouth. "Try not to look so glum. This is why no one wants you at events. You couldn't put on a face if your life depended on it."

"I'm sorry, Mother," the prince said, staring at his plate.

"That's all you ever say," she said, licking gold juices from one of her long, thin fingers. "It's laughable that you think you can be the Emperor one day."

The prince looked up sharply. "I don't—"

"We'd be better off crowning the corpses of your brothers and sisters," the Empress said, sorting through her gold with one hand. "You think the fact that you live while they're dead makes you some sort of victor? All it means is that you've been saved for last because no one sees you as a threat. You're as inconsequential as a fly buzzing around meat on a summer day. Not even worth the effort to kill. Just an annoyance."

The prince slammed his fists into the table.

The dishes rattled against each other, his pile of gold spilling over the lip of his plate onto the ground. His face was red, jaw clenched as he rose to his feet.

"I am the Crown Prince of Dai, the last living son of the Emperor, and you *will not speak to me like this*," he said. "You forget that you're only the Empress consort. My father lets you play your games while he's ill, but China does not belong to you. It belongs to him and me."

For a long moment, the Empress said nothing at all. She stared at the prince like he'd spoken another language, pinching a single piece of gold between her fingers until it crumbled to bits. I grabbed the prince's sleeve, but he refused to sit down, glaring back at his mother. I'd wanted him to stand up to her, but not now, when we already had a plan to end her.

At last, her expression spread into a vicious smile, and she popped another piece of gold into her mouth. "Careful, Hong," she said. "You'll live much longer as a fly."

He opened his mouth to reply, but I yanked hard on his arm. His gaze snapped to me, and his expression softened.

*Don't ruin everything now,* I thought, praying he could read it in my eyes. *She'll get what she deserves soon enough.*

"Yes, obey your concubine, Hong," the Empress said. "That's what your father did and look what happened to him."

"Zilan is not like you," the prince said.

"You don't think so?" the Empress said, raising an eyebrow. Her sharp gaze turned to me, and I felt like a million arrows on taut bowstrings were aimed at my face.

Then, to my horror, she spoke her next words in perfect Guangzhou dialect.

"I think we're quite alike, actually."

*The Empress has understood everything I've said,* I realized. My words weren't safe just because they weren't in the dialect of Chang'an. How foolish I had been.

"I also wanted a lot of things I couldn't have when I was your age," she said, "but the difference is that I got them, and you never will. So let me be clear about a few things, Scarlet. Whatever power you think you have is an illusion. Whatever your dreams are, they belong to me. And wherever you run, I am already there waiting for you."

Then she leaned back in her chair, stroked her lion, and picked up a fistful of gold.

"Now, if you don't mind, I'd like to eat my dinner."

The two of us stared at the Empress in silence as she ate with the kind of unbothered ease of someone who had absolutely no fear of losing. For the first time, I wondered if it was impossible to beat the Empress. Maybe it would be better to go back to the Moon Alchemist with my tail between my legs and say we needed a different plan, one that didn't depend on me outsmarting her.

The prince took my hand under the table again, his touch gentle. He knew as well as I did that we wouldn't get the Empress's blood, at least not today. Another day for my cousins to suffer in a dungeon. Another day for the monsters to carve open court ladies, for little girls to burn in the western wards.

When my hand stayed limp, the prince laced his fingers between mine, thumb rubbing across the back of my hand. His pulse beat in my palm, the rush of blood saying everything he couldn't in front of the Empress.

As his heartbeat stayed furiously fast even as the minutes wore on, I remembered what one of the scholars had said when I'd first come to Chang'an.

*You are the keepers of gold, which runs through the veins of the family that Heaven has chosen for us.*

I knew the blood of the Lis wasn't literally gold, but if you ate enough life gold to stop aging, some of it must end up in your bloodstream.

Maybe we didn't need a golden thread after all. Maybe the prince himself could be the conduit.

I hesitated. There was always the possibility that I'd accidentally tear all his veins open or explode his heart. I thought of the soup bowl I'd shattered instead of gently reshaping a teacup.

But I was a royal alchemist. If I couldn't perform alchemy correctly when it mattered the most, then what good was I?

I did a quiet transformation under the table, sharpening the ring on my right hand into a small point, mentally apologized to the prince, then jammed the spike into his leg.

He flinched, leg twitching, but must have trusted me enough not to make a sound as my alchemy wound its way through his body, through the rushing rivers of his veins, around the delicate organs in his abdomen, the pulsing muscle of his heart, up to his mouth until finally—

Blood gushed from his nose, splashing across the table and spreading fast. He let out a choked sound and clapped a hand over his nose while servants fluttered around him, offering him rags.

The Empress rolled her eyes. "Hong, honestly, you're not making a very good case for yourself. You have the constitution of a sickly peasant girl."

She popped another piece of gold into her mouth and didn't notice the alchemy that rushed across the surface of the table, carried by the metals in the prince's blood. It soaked into the bottom of her golden plate, wound up through her pile of gold, all of the energy tunneling into the next piece that she reached for.

*It is easier to destroy than to create.* One of alchemy's central tenets. Creating the life gold that filled the Empress's plate was a complicated alchemical endeavor, the secret of the royal alchemists. But breaking it down into its constituent parts was simple, lazy alchemy.

Gold, qi, blood, iron.

Before the Empress picked up her next piece, the gold sloughed off of it like dead skin, the qi and blood trickled down the rest of her plate, leaving only a hardened sphere of iron.

She popped it into her mouth and bit down, expecting the usual crisp shell of gold that gave way to a buttery interior.

The resounding *crack* of her next bite silenced the frantic servants. I caught a quick glimpse of blood on her lips before she clapped a hand over her mouth and shot to her feet. The servants abandoned the prince, leaving me to hold a rag to his nose as they flocked around the Empress. Her eyes watered, one hand frozen over her mouth, the other gripping the edge of the table like it was the only thing anchoring her to the earth.

*I did something that surprised the Empress*, I realized, warmth swelling in my chest. The look in her eyes as her perfectly plotted dinner began to slip away was glorious. She might have made me a royal alchemist, but just like every judge and scholar I'd encountered on my journey, she was still under-estimating me. I was not her science experiment anymore. I was the end of her story, the girl who would stand over her when she died, prying her kingdom from her withered hands.

The Empress stood up sharply and turned away, one hand still over her mouth. "We're finished here," she said, then hurried out of the garden.

"So are we," I said to the prince. A healer was about to be called to fix the Empress's cracked tooth, and someone needed to intercept him.

Just after sundown, I pounded my fist on the Moon Alchemist's door.

She answered within moments, and before she could speak, I shoved a handful of bloodied rags into her hands.

The Empress might have been difficult to outsmart, but her healer wasn't. I'd taken a servant's uniform and offered to throw the rags away for him, and he'd handed them over without question. I'd even managed to get the Empress's ex-tracted tooth.

"How soon can we do it?" I asked.

The Moon Alchemist looked down at the blood-soaked rags as if she didn't understand them.

"Zilan, did you really—"

*"How soon?"* I said. "I need to find my cousins."

I waited a few torturous moments as the Moon Alchemist took in the bloodied rags, her hands slowly clenching around them as if to make sure they were real. When she finally looked at me, all the gold in her eyes burned, like a comet rushing overhead in one brilliant flash.

"I'll gather the others," she said. "We'll strike tomorrow."

# CHAPTER TWENTY-NINE

I remembered being eight years old when old man Leoi had caught me and my cousins climbing on his roof. Yufei and I had run away, but Wenshu hadn't been able to climb down on his own, and old man Leoi had dragged him home, face covered in snot and tears and nervous vomit.

Auntie So had apologized to old man Leoi, then shut the door and spun around, not to Wenshu, but to me and Yufei.

*You don't leave your brother behind*, she'd said. *Come back together, or not at all.*

*But Mama, he's so slow*, Yufei said, crossing her arms and pouting. Yufei's stubbornness was usually enough to exasperate Auntie So and make her move on to an easier problem, but this time her eyes went dark and she shook a soup ladle at us.

*We have nothing without each other, you understand? Our house, our shop—all of it can burn down tomorrow. Fans don't leave each other behind.*

Now, as I stared into the candle the Moon Alchemist had given me—marked with red notches that would tell me the hour as the candle burned down—I couldn't help but wonder what Auntie So would say about me now. I was kneeling in the bedroom of the Crown Prince, wearing a gold-embroidered dress, while Wenshu and Yufei were probably choking on mold spores, shivering in some lightless dungeon.

*Fans don't leave each other behind.*

But I'd left them, because I wasn't a Fan and I never really had been. We'd come to Chang'an to save our parents, but when it mattered the most, I'd only managed to save myself.

When the candle melted down to the last line, the other alchemists would feed the Empress's blood to this week's crop of monsters and release the imprisoned alchemists. The Moon Alchemist had tasked me and the Comet Alchemist with finding the Emperor and keeping both him and the prince safe while the monsters ravaged the palace around them. *They're the last of the House of Li,* she'd said. *One of them needs to live, or there will be another war for power.*

The prince came into the room as the candle was reaching its last notch, his expression nauseous. He locked the door and lingered in front of it for a breath too long.

"What is it?" I said. "Has something happened?"

He avoided my gaze and came to sit on the bed beside me. "Durian has been pulling at your dress," he said, tugging at a loose gold thread on my sleeve. "What if it snags on something when you're running?"

I reached over him and grabbed a spool of thread from the drawer, the same one we'd used to try to trick the Empress.

"Somehow, I don't think that will be my undoing," I said, as I threaded a needle and wound it through the loose thread to knot it back into the fabric. "Do you want to talk about what's actually bothering you?"

"There's nothing bothering me," he said, far too quickly. "I just worry that if you pull at the wrong thread, the dress will fall apart, and we don't want you undressed. I mean, not in public at least. Maybe we need to get Durian something else to chew on? I think—"

"Hey," I said, threatening to poke his leg with my needle, "what's going on?"

The prince met my gaze, then sighed and dug into his pocket, took my hand, and slapped a cold piece of metal into my palm.

"What is this?" I said after a moment, holding it in my palm like a dead thing.

"A ring," he said.

I turned it over in my hand, feeling its cool, smooth edges. My alchemy rings were rough and sharp, made with haste. They were never polished or beautiful like this. "Thank you, but I use iron rings for alchemy. Gold is a weaker metal, so it's less practical."

"I know," he said, shifting from foot to foot. "This isn't for alchemy."

"Then what is it for?"

"Well," the prince said, "I figured there would be too much excitement afterward to really talk about this for a while, what with, you know, all the corpses we're probably going to have to clean up tonight, and there's probably a lot of paperwork that goes along with a change in power, so this seemed like a good time—"

"Li Hong," I said, frowning, "why are you giving me this?" It didn't take an imperial scholar's mind to sense that the prince was hiding something, but I didn't understand what was making him so nervous.

He scratched the back of his neck, looking anywhere but at me. "I just think that, when I'm Emperor, the court may look down on us if my wife only wears iron jewelry. Not that it matters to *me*, but it gives the impression that I don't treasure you, and—"

"Your wife?" I whispered, the ring suddenly a thousand pounds in my hand.

The prince nodded quickly, his face pink. "If you prefer bracelets, or necklaces, that can be arranged, but I thought a ring might work better with your alchemy, even if it's not as good as iron."

I slammed the ring down on the bed like it was made of fire, startling Durian awake. "You can't marry me," I said.

"Oh," the prince said, his shoulders drooping, all the light sapped out of him. "Well, I intended to ask you rather than tell you, but words get away from me sometimes when I'm around you."

I shook my head, inching away from the ring. "Hong, I'm not from a noble family. I don't think you're even allowed to marry me." Anyone at all could be a concubine without the court making a fuss—even a peasant girl, as long as she was pretty. But the wife of an emperor needed to be someone of importance.

"My father would probably take issue with it," he said, shrugging, "but I will be Emperor one day, and no one will question me then."

"Have you lost your mind?" I said. "I can't be the Empress."

The prince frowned, scooping Durian up and cradling him. "I don't understand," he said. "Do you not want to be the Empress, or my wife?"

I shook my head again, my mind feeling like hot soup leaking out of my ears at the absurd question. I had never imagined either title for myself. When I'd pictured the rest of my life, I'd always seen myself as a royal alchemist until the end, and what came after was a story entirely unwritten, because what could matter more? I'd never even considered that I could be a part of someone else's dream.

The prince sighed. "If you don't want to be the Empress, that's fine. I just won't have an Empress."

*"You can't just not have an Empress!"* I said, gripping my hair. "Your mother has killed all of your relatives in the line of succession. It's dangerous not to have an heir!"

"What am I supposed to do, then? Marry some random noblewoman?"

*"Yes!"*

His expression dropped even further. "I don't want to marry anyone else," he said, hugging Durian to his chest.

"You don't *want*—" I scoffed, unable to repeat his ridiculous sentence, clapping a hand over my eyes. "You'll already be changing so much of what your people are used to," I said, "and you think it's worth making them even angrier because of me?"

"Yes," he said, taking my hand and pulling it away from my face.

"They would hate me."

"It wouldn't matter."

"Think about this. Abolishing gold will cost you the rich. Marrying me could cost you the poor as well."

"Zilan," he said, taking my other hand, "I don't care if it costs me the world."

Heat bloomed in my face. I turned away, but he only squeezed my hands harder, and while I knew the rich were skilled at spinning beautiful lies to get what they wanted, somehow the prince's words rang true. I wanted to believe in him the way some people believed in gods or gold, their promises all that you could cling to when drowning.

"I won't eat gold to live with you forever," I said quietly. *Not unless you want me turn into one of those rabid beasts,* I thought.

He shook his head. "There won't be any more life gold to eat. We'll live short, normal lives together."

"Normal?" I said, laughing. "Nothing with you could ever be normal."

"Are you referring to the current assassination plot, or just me as a person?"

I shrugged. "A bit of both."

"I am offended," he said, making a show of crossing his arms and turning away. "I may forgive you if you kiss me, though."

I glanced at the candle, burning down toward the last notch. "How about we make sure your mother is dead first?"

The prince groaned, closing his eyes, and fell back onto the bed. "How does my mother ruin everything even when she's not here?"

I rose to my feet, tugging the prince's hands. "Come on," I said. "I'd like to live at least one more day, and that requires you to get up."

The prince cracked an eye open. "One more day?" he said, as I hauled him to his feet. "I think I can manage that."

"Promise me," I said, because his words felt more real than any religion, as bright and true as the summer constellations.

His expression sobered. He picked up the ring and placed it in my palms, then closed my hands around it. His grip was bone-crushing, like he also knew the secret weight of his words.

"One more day," he said.

When the candle burned to the last notch, we were already gone.

We needed to be well on our way to the Emperor's quarters when chaos broke loose in the dungeons, because the first thing the guards would do when they caught wind of trouble would be to secure the Empress and Emperor. By the time the guards came looking for him, we wanted to be deep in the tunnels on our way to a monastery, where we could shelter the Emperor until the fighting ended. The Moon Alchemist promised to send alchemists to protect him when they had any to spare.

The Comet Alchemist was supposed to meet us outside the Emperor's quarters, but when we arrived, the only people in the hallway were the guards.

"Have we messed up the timing?" the prince whispered.

"How could we mess up burning a candle?" I said, unease simmering in my stomach. How could our plan already have gone wrong? We waited another minute in the shadows, but we couldn't linger forever and risk being caught up in the carnage that was sure to follow.

"We'll find the Comet Alchemist later," I said. "Let's just get the Emperor."

Unsurprisingly, the guards outside the emperor's room weren't thrilled with our demands.

"The Empress says you're not allowed in," one of them said, while the other didn't even acknowledge us.

"And what does my father have to say about it?" the prince said. "Because you answer to him, not my mother."

"Look, I'd like to keep my head attached to my shoulders," the guard said. "The Emperor can't help me with that at the moment."

The prince sighed and held up a satchel of gold. "Is five hundred enough? Just a quick visit. No one has to know."

The guard frowned. "My head is worth a hell of a lot more than five hundred gold."

"One thousand."

The guard's eye twitched, lips pressed tight as if considering it. But I knew the look in his eyes. You couldn't buy people's fear away. I glanced out the window at the sinking sun and elbowed the prince.

"We don't have time for this," I said. "You tried playing nice."

"It was worth a shot," the prince said, sighing. Then he wound back and smashed the satchel of gold into the guard's face. I grabbed some silver from my bag and pressed it to the other guard's thigh, making his legs go numb—a trick that the Paper Alchemist had recently taught me as an apology for my unwarranted kidnapping. Both guards collapsed to the ground and one crawled away. He wouldn't get far, and we would be long gone before he caused us any problems.

I pressed a firestone to the door and snapped the lock, and the prince rushed inside.

We stumbled into a dark room, full of cobwebs and settled shadows, no light but the pale murmurs of gold embroidery on the silk curtains. The room felt carved out like a gourd, the patterns of dust telling the stories of everything that used to be but no longer was. The prince tore back the canopy around the bed, but the sheets were flat, the bed empty.

"He's not even here?" the prince said. The curtains trembled in his hands for a moment, then he let out a furious sound and ripped them down, blasting clouds of dust into the air.

"We should go," I said, placing my hand on his shoulder. First the Comet Alchemist, and now the Emperor was missing. Something had gone wrong, I was sure of it.

"Without my father?" the prince said. "Who knows what the Empress has done to him. I can't go without him."

I wanted to tell him that the Emperor was as good as dead, that he hardly mattered anymore, that Hong's survival was the only thing that mattered now.

But then I thought of anyone telling me to leave Uncle Fan or Auntie So behind.

"Okay," I said, gripping the bedpost, trying to figure out our next step. "Okay, so where could the Emperor be?"

"The palace is massive," the prince said, shoulders drooping. "We're not going to just stumble across him."

He was probably right. Where would the Empress hide him? I thought of her staring at me across the table, sipping her tea, smiling as if she knew all my secrets. She knew damn well what I was up to, yet she was so confident that she'd shared a meal with me.

"I think wherever the Empress is, your father can't be far," I said. "She keeps her enemies close."

The prince trembled for a moment, then turned and stormed past me. He drew to a stop in front of the fireplace and picked up a long fire poker from the metal stand. I saw a flash of Wenshu stabbing the magistrate in the inn—what felt like ages ago. The prince whirled around, gripping the poker in both hands, his eyes dark.

"Let's find Mother," he said.

As we ran, the palace began to crumble. The wallpaper had been torn off in the wake of the pearl monsters, windows shattered in, floor tiles crushed into soft powder. Like a lizard sloughing off its grayed skin, the palace trembled out of its gold shell, revealing the pale stone foundations underneath.

Members of the court were screaming and sprinting down the halls, slipping on bloody tiles. Bodies of prisoners bobbed in the courtyard ponds with ducks floating around them in scarlet waters. Some guards led the court ladies across the rickety bridge toward the northern gate, while others fought back the prisoners. I could tell them apart from the other alchemists by the deathly cast of their skin, the scent of mildew that clung to their clothes, the way they fought like they had seen things worse than death.

The alchemist who had grabbed my sleeve in the dungeons

caught my gaze as he forced a guard facedown into the pond, pinning him in place with a knee to his back. In daylight, he looked like a beast wrenched up from the pits of hell, drenched in blood that I doubted belonged to him. He tossed the guard aside and shifted toward me, but another guard tackled him into the pond and he vanished in the black waters.

Pearl monsters tore across the courtyard, their skin a spectacular flash of white in the afternoon sun, leaving stars in my eyes as they raced past.

"They must be going after the Empress," I said, tugging the prince's sleeve. He didn't move at first, staring at the ruins of his palace, but I yanked his arm harder until he stumbled after me.

We rushed around a corner, my feet slowing at the sight of the Comet Alchemist with a spear through her neck, insides splashed across the hallway. She'd been wrenched in half from just below her rib cage, her jaw gaping open in a silent scream, the floor so thick with blood that it formed a glazed red mirror in front of us.

The prince stumbled to the wall and vomited behind me, but I couldn't turn away from my own scarlet reflection on the floor.

The guards couldn't have done this. No human could have. The Empress must have managed to find some monsters and fed them the blood of the alchemists.

"We have to go," I said, my voice shaking as I reached for the prince, tugging at his sleeve with hands I could hardly feel. "Something isn't right."

But before I could pull him up, someone grabbed me by the collar and slammed me against a pillar. My head smashed against the stone and my vision swirled into a hazy cloud of gold. I reached for my stones but the hands around my shoulders shoved me back again and my hands fell limp beside me.

*"Where the hell did you get that blood?"* she said.

It took me a moment to realize it was the voice of the Paper Alchemist. A cut on her hairline had gushed across her face, painting her tan skin with a mask of blood. The prince was trying to wrench her off me, but she pushed him away with one hand.

"What are you talking about?" I said, my tongue heavy in my mouth.

"The blood that you gave the Moon Alchemist!" she said, her knuckles white where she gripped the front of my dress. "That wasn't the Empress's blood, Scarlet. It was *ours.*"

I shook my head. "No, no, that's not possible," I said, my voice trembling. "I gave her the Empress's blood."

"Then why did the monsters turn on us the second they tasted it?" the Paper Alchemist said, her eyes wild and bloodshot.

"I saw the healer leave the Empress's room," I said. "The rags had her tooth in it!"

"Did you actually *see* the healer use the rags on her?"

I felt like she'd dropped me from a rooftop, like I was falling faster and faster toward an earth that would swallow me whole. Humiliated tears burned at my eyes, and that was the only answer the Paper Alchemist needed. She let out a furious cry and shoved me hard against the wall, releasing me. "Scarlet, half the other alchemists are dead!"

"I'm sorry!" I said, folding into myself, gripping my hair and wishing I could disappear. "I'm sorry, I'll bring them back, I—"

*"There's nothing left of them!"* the Paper Alchemist yelled, jerking a hand at the remains of the Comet Alchemist. "The monsters are tearing them apart!"

A window across the courtyard burst open. A pearl monster crashed into the pond, sending waves of red water across the dirt. Its eyes locked on us, and in half a breath, it tore through the pond, vaulting the gate, skidding through blood puddles toward us.

The Paper Alchemist cursed and reached for her stones, but I pushed her behind me. I threw a handful of firestones at the monster, singeing its face, but it only stumbled back a moment before surging forward.

"Scarlet, get out of the way!" the Paper Alchemist said, grabbing my arm, but I elbowed her and she slipped in the pool of blood.

"Go find the Empress!" I said. Maybe the Paper Alchemist would know a way to salvage the mess I'd made, to make sure all the others hadn't died in vain.

*This is your last life*, the Moon Alchemist had said. My last chance. So many people had died for me, for a life that never should have been mine. The Paper Alchemist wouldn't be one of them.

The prince threw his fire poker at the monster, but it bounced off its surface with a hollow *clang*, skittering across the hall. I transformed a small iron blade, even though I knew it wasn't sharp or hard enough. I'd never thought I was the kind of person who would sacrifice myself, but in the end, it wasn't even a choice. It was easier to meet death than to watch someone else die for me.

The monster rushed toward me, its teeth bared, and I stepped forward to meet it.

# CHAPTER THIRTY

Blood hit the floor like a warm rain. Heat bloomed in my side and ran down my leg, my whole right side numb. The crunch of bones sounded so much like the Empress eating gold that for one brief flash I saw her across from me at dinner, her blazing eyes pinning me in place, gold juice running down the thin line of her neck, pooling in her collarbone.

The prince called for me from somewhere far away, then his hands were closing around my arm and pulling me to the side. I stumbled, barely processing that my legs were still there, that my lungs hadn't been torn open.

The pearl monster had sunken its teeth into the Paper Alchemist's neck, ripping through her like a starving animal, raking apart the tendons of her throat, gnawing through her collarbone. Her head tipped back, staring up to the ceiling, choked breaths gurgling and gasping. *The blood on me isn't mine.*

I grabbed the monster's arm and tried to yank him away from her, but my fingers slipped off the blood-slick pearl, and the monster didn't budge, like he couldn't even feel me. It hunched farther over the Paper Alchemist, her throat screaming open wider, hands twitching, eyes darting around the room. *That was supposed to be me*, I thought, my stomach clenching with nausea. Why was the monster ignoring me?

"Zilan!" the prince said, pulling me away. "It's too late for her."

My hands shook as the Paper Alchemist fell still. I couldn't resurrect a body broken up into so many parts. That had been her last and only life.

*The Empress outsmarted me*, I realized, my whole body suddenly numb.

I pictured her in her bedroom, pouring the alchemists' blood over her rags and sending them out with the physician, grinning and drinking tea from her gold-rimmed cup while knowing I'd just sentenced all the other alchemists to death.

I fell to my knees, hands sinking into the growing pool of hot blood, and let out a scream that barely sounded human, the red mirrored surface trembling at the sound. Once, I had dreamed of being a royal alchemist, and that dream had devoured everyone around me, had razed a palace to ruins, drowned the halls with blood. Once, I'd thought I could save everyone if I was only brave enough, and now everyone was dead.

All because of the Empress.

I rose to my feet, a dangerous quiet inside me.

"Zilan?" the prince said.

I wiped the Paper Alchemist's blood from my face, walked past the pearl monster still devouring what was left of my friend, and made my way deeper into the palace.

It wasn't hard to find the Empress—all of her guards were gathered in the garden just outside the throne room, fighting off the remaining alchemists.

I could have cried at the sight of the Moon Alchemist and River Alchemist still alive, wrestling guards to the ground.

Their shoes crunched over shattered white shards and cracked limbs, as if the pearl monsters had crashed to pieces at their feet. The Moon Alchemist pressed a stone I couldn't see to a guard's face and blood burst from his ears and eyes, brain matter oozing out of his nose as he collapsed to the ground. She whirled around at the sound of our footsteps, expression softening when she met my gaze.

"Zilan!" she said, rushing to meet us. "Are you all right?"

*She doesn't hate me*, I realized, stumbling toward her. I couldn't help wrapping my arms around her, crushing my face into her chest and sobbing. *"I'm sorry,"* I said. "I didn't know, I didn't mean to—"

The Moon Alchemist held me back at arm's length, bending down to my height. "Zilan, it's not your fault," she said. "The Empress tricked all of us." Then she looked at the prince and let out a tense sigh. "You're supposed to be securing the Emperor."

"We can't find him," I said, wiping my face.

"Then forget about him," she said. She jerked a finger at the prince. "Get him out of here. If he dies, we have no one to put on the throne. The rest of us will handle the Empress."

I nodded quickly, taking a steadying breath. The Moon Alchemist wiped the tears from my face with her sleeve. "Leave," she said. "It's not safe for you here."

Then she strode back to the guards.

The prince took my hand and gently tugged. "There's a tunnel entrance around the corner," he said. "If we—"

But he didn't finish the thought, because a pearl monster burst through a window and tackled the Moon Alchemist into the pond.

My hand tensed, crushing the prince's fingers. The Moon Alchemist was capable, but how could I leave her to clean up my mess? I thought of the Paper Alchemist twitching beneath the pearl monster. So many had died because of my mistake. I turned to the prince. "I—"

"Go," he said, squeezing my hand, his eyes gentle, understanding. "Help her."

I gripped his sleeve, shaking my head. "I can't just send you off alone. This is all for nothing if we lose you."

"The tunnels are gated, remember?" he said. "They're the safest place here. I'll cut across the grounds and look for my father."

I knew he was right, yet I couldn't let go. He took my face in his hands and pressed a searing kiss to my lips, and for a moment, I wasn't standing in the bloody ruins of a kingdom I'd destroyed. There was no world but him and his soft smile and the dream I'd once believed in. He pulled away and my hands fell to my sides. I felt the same way as when I left Auntie and Uncle in Guangzhou—that this was the last time I would see them, and neither of us wanted to say it out loud.

"Give mother my regards," he said, backing up. Then he turned and ran for the tunnels.

I took a deep breath, then ran for the Moon Alchemist, who was knee-deep in bloody water, fighting off a monster as it latched onto her forearm and tried to wrench it from her body. I jumped onto the monster's back, locking my arms around its neck and forcing it away from her. It reared backward, trying to jolt me off, but I dug my knife into its spine and hacked away its soul tag.

It shattered apart, dropping me heavily onto the courtyard stairs. I rolled to my feet as the Moon Alchemist yanked me up by the collar.

"I told you to leave," she said. "The prince—"

"I'm not going to let you die," I said.

She scoffed. "Adults are supposed to die for children, not the other way around."

"I don't want anyone to die," I said, the threat of tears closing up my throat. "Not because of me."

The Moon Alchemist opened her mouth to answer, but another pearl monster thundered across the courtyard. She spun around and hurled firestones at it before it could take a bite out of the River Alchemist. The monster burst into blue flames, illuminating the whole courtyard until it rushed into the bloody pond. The Moon Alchemist pulled out three stones, hurled them into the water where the monster flailed, then stomped her foot into the ground, sending quakes across the yard.

The pond dropped down as if the earth had cracked open. The pit was suddenly too deep for the monster to claw its way out of. I realized, for the first time, that I had only ever seen a fraction of the Moon Alchemist's true power.

But it wasn't enough.

Two more monsters leaped through nearby windows. One of them sank its teeth into the River Alchemist's throat, silencing her scream as it bit down with a sharp *snap*.

The Moon Alchemist spun around before I'd even realized the danger, and the next thing I knew, a pearl monster had plowed past me and tackled her. I stepped back for balance, but there was no ground beneath me, and I toppled into the pit.

My hands closed around a root on the wall of the pit and my fall halted abruptly, yanking at my shoulders. My feet dangled just above the trapped pearl monster, who hissed and swiped for my shoes. I remembered, with a sickening wave of nostalgia, how the Paper Alchemist and River Alchemist had pulled my shoes off when I'd dangled in the courtyard like this, and now both of them were dead.

I staked my knife into the wall and tried to use it for leverage, but it slid through the mud like cream. The branch I clung to creaked ominously and I clamped the hilt of my knife between my teeth so I'd have a free hand to fish through my satchel. With my hands so muddy, it was hard to tell the stones apart by touch alone, and I couldn't see them from this angle.

"Zilan!"

The Moon Alchemist appeared at the edge of the pit, holding out a hand. I reached for her, my wet fingers sliding through hers.

"Give me your other hand," she said, nodding to the one wrapped around the branch.

I hesitated, sinking my nails into her skin, not sure if she could truly hold my weight.

"Zilan, I'll catch you," she said. "Hurry."

Before I could second-guess myself, I let go of the branch and grabbed her wrists with both hands. For a moment, I sunk in the wrong direction, my weight yanking her down. Then her grip tightened and she hauled me up over the edge onto solid ground.

The pearl monster laid in shards around her. I could only bear to look at what was left of the River Alchemist for a moment before biting my lip and turning away.

"We have to find the Empress," I said. "We have to finish this."

But the Moon Alchemist wasn't standing.

She clutched her abdomen, panting, her face pale and beaded with sweat.

I took a step closer. "Are you—"

Blood gushed from her lips and she collapsed onto her side. I fell to my knees and rolled her onto her back. Vomiting blood meant organ damage. Maybe a skilled healer could have helped her, but I only knew how to help dead people.

"Don't worry," I said, my hands shaking as I pulled matted strands of hair from her face. "Don't worry, it's only internal damage, your body is still intact. I'll bring you back, I promise. I just need to deal with the Empress first."

She shook her head, more blood spilling past her lips.

"I can do it," I said. "I promise, I'll finish this and come back for you."

"No," she said, coughing. Her skin had gone papery white, her breaths fast. "Don't bring me back."

I stiffened. "What are you talking about?" I said. "Of course I'm going to bring you back."

She gripped my wrist. "Why?" she said. "So that I can watch everyone I love suffer and die? Only to bring them back so they can watch *their* families die?"

"Isn't that better than death?" I said. "Isn't anything better than death?"

"To *you*," she said, coughing. "This isn't how it's meant to be, Zilan. People are supposed to die. I don't want to be the cause of people's suffering anymore."

"You don't cause suffering," I said, even though I knew what she meant. All the alchemists had built this kingdom that hinged on blood and death and pain. Even if we thought we didn't have a choice. "You helped me."

"I'm glad," she said, smiling softly. "But you don't need my help anymore."

"Stop it," I said, my voice wavering. "Are you saying you regret bringing me back? That I'm such an abomination that I'd be better off dead?"

She shook her head, but couldn't seem to turn it again, staring off to the side. "Raising the dead is evil, Zilan," she said. "But you can't create evil without also creating good.

You are the good thing—the best thing—to come out of all the evil things I've done."

"Don't," I said, tasting tears that I couldn't feel on my face. "Stop talking like that. You can't—"

"Promise me you're not going to bring me back, Zilan."

"I—"

"Put my body in the pit."

"I can't do that. I—"

"Zilan," she said, gripping my hand, her eyes bright, "if you don't get rid of my body, someone will use it."

I thought of the corpses stacked up in the dungeons, the paper name tags, their glassy eyes once we dragged them back to the land of the living.

"Please don't let them use me," she said, her voice small, tears streaking down her face. "I don't want to be used for evil anymore."

"Okay," I said, so softly that I didn't even know if she could hear it. "I promise."

Then her grip went slack, and she wasn't the Moon Alchemist anymore.

I rolled her body into the pit, my breath catching as she tipped over the side and the sounds of tearing flesh echoed up into the air.

I rose to my feet, my muddy knife clutched in one hand, my whole body shaking as I crossed the courtyard, past the empty eyes of the dead, the growing puddles of blood, the crushed fingers and split rib cages and organs. I trudged up the stairs, pressed a muddy hand to the door, and pushed into the throne room.

The Empress was sitting on her throne, a glass of wine in one hand and a servant trembling at her feet. In the fireplace behind her, a wall of flames blazed. The rancid scent in the room nearly brought me to my knees, so thick and sticky at the back of my throat. My footsteps crunched over broken pearls as I stumbled closer.

"Ah, Scarlet," the Empress said, taking a sip of wine as if I wasn't wielding a weapon at her, trailing dirt and blood. "I was wondering when you'd arrive."

I pointed my knife at her. "All your guards are dead," I said.

She shrugged, swirling the liquid around her glass. "I have more in the western ward on the way."

"They won't get here in time," I said.

She watched me for a long moment, the flickering light of the fire gleaming off the string of pearls around her neck. "Pour Zilan some wine," she said to her servant, who leaped to his feet instantly. "Zilan, drink with me."

The servant approached me with a gold chalice, but I swiped it off the tray and it clattered to the floor. "Do you not hear me, *Empress*? Your reign is over. You can't hurt the Emperor anymore. He'll wake up and see—"

"Scarlet," the Empress said, "really, you disappoint me." She set down her glass. "There is no Emperor."

I tensed. "Of course there's an emperor. People have seen him—"

"He's been dead for months," she said, waving her hand like this was inconsequential. "Arsenic dosing is not a perfect science. I admit, his death wasn't part of my original plan. But it turns out it's surprisingly easy to dispose of a body in this palace."

"You hid his death?" I said. I'd thought the Empress wanted nothing more than the Emperor to die so she could claim her place as Empress dowager instead of Empress consort. Then understanding dawned on me. "He died before changing the line of succession," I said.

The sour look on the Empress's face told me that I was right. That must have been why the attacks on the prince started so recently—the Empress had been trying to get rid of him before anyone found out the Emperor was dead.

"That means that you're not really the Empress," I said. "The country belongs to Hong now."

"Hong will be dead within the hour," she said. "Then the people will learn of the tragic passing of their beloved prince and emperor, in that order."

"What have you done with him?" I said, tightening my grip on the blade even as my hands trembled harder. I thought of the look on his face as he'd kissed me goodbye in the garden, eyes bright with hope not yet extinguished. This wasn't supposed to be the end, not yet.

"I've been thinking of posthumous names for Hong," she said, as if she hadn't heard me. "We can call him Emperor Xiaojing, even though he was never really Emperor, but I think the people would find it endearing. It would show how much I loved him."

*"Where is he?"* I said, raising my knife. "And where are my cousins?"

"Your cousins?" the Empress said. She hummed as if thinking. "Apologies, but their names have slipped my mind."

Then she waved over her servant, who brought her a gold tray with a lid. She lifted the lid and tossed it aside with a clatter, then picked up what looked like two stained strips of parchment ripped from a weathered book.

"Ah, yes," the Empress said, squinting at the strips. "Fan Wenshu and Fan Yufei, right? How lucky that I saved these."

"What are those?" I said, stepping closer, my whole body thrumming with so much adrenaline that my knees felt like wet paper. "What are you reading?"

"Just a little souvenir," she said, extending the strips to me in her palm. I took them with shaking hands.

For a moment, I didn't understand what I was looking at. The paper was stained deep brown, with black ink scratched haphazardly into the surface. A ringing began in my ears when I realized this was my own handwriting. The soul tags I'd carved into their backs all those years ago.

This wasn't paper, but skin.

I threw the soul tags to the floor, dizzy with nausea. I imagined my cousin's souls floating away, lost in the river, no way to return.

"Where are they?" I said, my voice low. The Moon Alchemist had said I couldn't resurrect people twice, but maybe I could find a way. I would try, no matter what it cost me, no matter what evil it brought into the world. I just needed their bodies.

The Empress took a long sip of wine, then pointed a thin finger at the roaring fire behind her, piled high with ashes and blackened bones. The foul smell in the room was of flesh, like the fires in the western wards.

I sank to my knees, choking on the rancid air, clutching my throat. I didn't remember much of death, but I was sure that this was what dying felt like, your whole body a scream that didn't make a sound.

There was only one person I had left.

The doors to the throne room slammed open, and a guard dragged the prince in, throwing him to the floor.

"Hong," the Empress said, smiling, "finally, you've joined us."

# CHAPTER THIRTY-ONE

"Zilan!" the prince said, rising to his feet. "I'm sorry, I couldn't find him, I—"

"Hong, shut up," the Empress said. She rose from her throne, her gold robes trailing behind her, then drew a knife from her sleeve and pressed it to the prince's throat.

"*Wait!*" I said, reaching for my stones. My hand froze as the Empress shot me a warning glare, wrenching the prince closer to her, a thin bead of blood trickling down his throat. Only hours ago, I'd thought I was going to overthrow the Empress. Now I had no one and nothing left but Hong.

"Get in the cage, Scarlet," the Empress said.

I looked over my shoulder at a metal enclosure behind me, just like my first exam. At my hesitation, the Empress only pressed the knife harder into the prince's throat, drawing more blood. I didn't know if the Empress was familiar with the rules of resurrection—if she were to tear his body to shreds, he would be gone forever, and I couldn't bear to lose him too. So I clenched my fists, bent down, and crawled into the cage, which the guard instantly slammed shut and locked.

"Give the guard your stones," the Empress said.

I bit back a sound of frustration and passed my satchel through.

"There," the Empress said, smiling. "Now we can have a pleasant conversation."

"Pleasant?" I said, gripping the bars.

"Yes," the Empress said. "You see, Scarlet, I think we can help each other."

I thought of my cousins' bones burning in the fireplace and spit on the floor. "As if I would ever help you."

"Oh, but I've already helped *you*, Scarlet," the Empress said, tracing the prince's jaw with the tip of her knife. "Both you and Hong, actually. As you may have noticed, neither of you is dead yet. Do you think that's a coincidence?"

I thought of the monster that had shoved me aside and devoured the Paper Alchemist in my place. None of them had even glanced at me, let alone tried to kill me.

"The two of you are only alive because I needed a backup plan," she said.

My grip tightened on the metal. "What do you mean?" I said.

"This morning, there were fifteen alchemists in the entire world who knew how to make life gold, but it turns out that all of them are traitors. You know what I do to traitors, Scarlet. But I had to save at least one of you to make me more life gold, and you were always my favorite."

"Why me?" I said, my throat closing. Why would she want to keep me around rather than someone like the Moon Alchemist, who knew so much more?

The Empress shrugged. "You have a certain sharpness about you that reminds me of myself when I was younger. And you flaunted your weakness right under my nose. I didn't even have to leave the palace to find him." She looked pointedly at the prince, and I began to understand why it was so important to have both of us alive. As long as she threatened one of us, the other had no choice but to obey.

"I thought your siblings were the better leverage, at first," she said, "but do you know what they told me? That you wished they were dead."

I shook my head, hands trembling against the bars. "That's not what I meant."

"It's inconsequential," the Empress said. "They were disposed of. You might have cared for them, Scarlet, but there's a difference between someone you care for and someone you would do anything for. I needed the latter, and luckily, I've found him."

I let myself fall forward, my face crushed against the cold metal of the cage. Did my cousins really think I wouldn't have saved them? Had they died believing that?

"Here's what's going to happen," the Empress said. "You two can wait in the dungeons while I select a new crop of alchemists. Scarlet, you will teach them what you know, and when they can make gold to my satisfaction, I'll let both of you go. Officially, you'll be dead, but you can run off somewhere else."

"I don't believe you," I said through clenched teeth. The moment I taught another alchemist to make gold, the Empress had no reason to keep me alive.

"It doesn't really matter if you do," the Empress said, her blade scoring another line across the prince's throat, "because you won't let him die."

Tears burned down my face. The fire blazed behind them, the floor coated in blood, and I realized at last that I had lost. My family was dead, and it had all been for nothing. I would be the Empress's slave until she grew tired of me.

The prince moved suddenly, and at first I thought he was foolish enough to try to wrestle the knife away from the Empress, but instead he pressed the blade harder into his throat, splitting skin.

The Empress flinched backward, but kept her grip firm on the knife. "Hong—"

"Do it," he said.

Her eyes narrowed. "Do you think I won't?" she said.

"I know you will," he said, his voice unwavering.

"Li Hong, stop it," I said, slamming a fist against the cage. "None of this matters if you're dead! There's no one left but you to put on the throne."

He shook his head slowly. "Yiyang and Gao'an are alive."

The Empress frowned. "They're not," she said, though she no longer sounded certain. Had she really not known? It seemed that out of all of us, the Moon Alchemist was the only one half good at keeping a secret from the Empress.

"They may be disgraced, but they're still the Emperor's children," the prince said, his gaze burning gold. "You know where they are, Zilan. Bring them back here."

"No," I said, shaking my head furiously, wishing I could wrench the bars apart. "I won't."

The prince smiled sadly, his eyes wet as he clutched the Empress's hand around the blade. "You heard her, Zilan. I'm just a weakness. Without me, you can stop her."

"*I can't!*" I said. "I'm in a cage and I don't have my stones! There's no one left to help me!"

"Stop talking about what you can't do," he said, a cruel echo of the words I'd once spoken to him. "You can, Zilan. If anyone can, it's you."

"*I hate you!*" I said, thrashing against the bars, the sound quaking across the floor. "You can't just die and leave me here to fix everything!"

"Zilan, *please*," he said, tears falling freely down his face. "In my whole life, I've never done anything meaningful. Please, just once, let me do something that matters."

*"No!"* I said. "You think that dying for me absolves you of anything? Everyone dies. It doesn't make you a hero. It just makes you another body in the ground."

"Better me than you," he said, smiling even as a line of blood trickled from the sharp edge of the blade.

"You don't get it," I said. "I'm already dead, Hong." I hadn't meant to tell him this way, but the words rushed out like a well spilling over from too much rain. Anything to change his mind, even if he never looked at me the same way again.

"Zilan, I know," he said quietly. "I saw your scar, remember?"

"You understood what that meant?" I said, my hands slipping from the bars. "You never asked about it."

"It doesn't matter, Zilan," he said, his eyes as warm as ever. "None of it matters. You're still you."

*He's actually going to do it*, I thought, wishing I could rend the bars apart, tear the whole world in half. So many people had died for me, for a life that I'd ruined and wasted, and I couldn't let the prince do the same. But the Empress held a knife to his throat, he had no weapons to defend himself, and I was caged across the room. I still had my rings, but those were only good for small transformations with things I could touch.

I patted my sleeves and pockets for something, anything I could use to break free. But no stones fell out. Just a tiny spool of gold thread that I'd used to fix my dress that afternoon.

I froze, clutching it in my fist to be sure the Empress wouldn't see it. Maybe the prince didn't have any weapons on him. But I could be a weapon for him.

I pinched the loose end of the thread and twisted it around my finger.

"Li Hong," I said, "you promised me one more day."

"I'm sorry," he said, his voice breaking. "I tried."

I pulled the thread slack under my sleeve.

*"Try harder,"* I said, reaching through the bars and hurling the spool across the room.

It arced over the room like a comet, a tail of golden thread marking its path. The Empress's gaze followed it, eyes narrowed as she tried to discern what I'd thrown.

The prince would know. He would understand it sooner than the Empress, and if he was smart, he would use that half second to his advantage.

*This is all the time I can give you*, I thought, pressed against the bars, clutching the other end of the thread, praying he would understand.

He didn't even hesitate.

As the Empress arched her neck toward the spool, the prince wrenched her wrist down, forcing the knife from his throat. Her gaze snapped back to him, and she raked the blade across his chest, drawing a line of blood through his clothes, but he had already broken away from her, reaching out, hand closing around the spool.

I never should have doubted him—the prince knew me the way the moon knows its shadowed face. He knew all of my secrets even if I never said them out loud.

He turned back to the Empress and pressed the spool to the bare skin of her sternum.

Gold was a soft metal. Not ideal for stabbing someone, especially not through bone.

But if I could break her skin, I would have access to her bloodstream, filled with the gold and iron that I could warp into any shape. I could force all the blood to pool in her feet, knocking her unconscious. I could sharpen the iron into tiny spikes that tore her veins open, making her bleed out inside herself. I could rip her organs apart, I could drill spikes into her brain, I could destroy the indestructible empress, and the empire would finally belong to Hong.

The Empress raised her blade, aiming for the prince's throat. This time, I was faster.

Alchemy shot like lightning across the golden thread, singeing the palm of my hand raw. The tangled threads congealed into a thin point that bit into the Empress's sternum, splitting her skin and sending a curtain of blood spilling down her chest, soaking her gold dress. Her necklace burst, pearls clattering to the ground as my alchemy raced into her veins, rushing toward her heart.

She struck wide at Hong but missed, and in my moment of relief, I realized too late that she hadn't been aiming for him at all.

The thread snapped, spool clattering to the floor. The transformation cut off like a wall had slammed down between me and the rushing river of the Empress's veins. Hong took a surprised step back, then the Empress readjusted her grip on her knife, and in one fluid sweep, slit his throat.

"*Hong!*" I said, grabbing the bars. The cage lurched with my weight, threatening to spill me onto my face.

The prince remained on his feet for a moment, like a swaying stalk of silver grass, hand clamped around his neck. Then blood rushed past his fingers, weeping down the steps before the throne, racing through the grooves between the tiles. He tried to speak, but the words came out wet and distorted. He coughed, sinking to his knees, and I realized that in a few minutes, I was going to lose everyone who mattered to me.

The prince fell to his elbows, blood dribbling past his purple lips, veins a stark blue against the papery shade of his skin.

I thought that I knew death well. I had waded into its thorny waters and plucked souls from its jagged teeth. I'd been chewed to pieces by death and spit back out on the streets of Chang'an. I knew the stages of decay the way scholars knew the words of philosophers. Death was not supposed to scare me.

But as the prince wilted into the ocean of his own blood, already a quiet echo of himself, I realized that no one could really know death. The hundreds of bodies I'd handled could never have prepared me for the look in the prince's eyes when he died, the moment he went from seeing only me to seeing nothing at all, the moment he went from someone I loved to nothing more than a corpse.

*I've never done anything that mattered*, he'd said.

*You mattered to* me, I thought.

My arms shook as the Empress drew closer, her heavy footsteps like a death knell as she crossed the room, then kneeled in front of my cage. She swiped a finger across the blood on her chest, grimacing. It pooled down the front of her golden dress, dribbling onto the floor.

"There was no need for that, silly girl," she said. "You're only delaying the inevitable."

I surged closer, swiping a hand through the bars, but the Empress only leaned back a breath, just past my fingertips.

"His organs are intact," she said. "I didn't even touch his pretty face. I'll let you resurrect him while he's still warm. You just have to work with me, Scarlet."

I bit my lip, my head hanging low. Surely the Empress

would chain me in the dungeon for the rest of my life, force me to spend my days making gold for her.

But the prince could live.

I didn't know now how we could defeat her, but with both of us alive, maybe we could try. As long as we lived, we had choices, we had a chance. I looked over her shoulder at the prince spilled across the stairs and thought of him memorizing every part of me, squeezing my hand and knowing my heart even when I didn't know it myself.

But if I refused, and no one made gold for the Empress, then she would eventually die. I could end her reign if it meant losing everyone that I loved.

Tears splashed onto the floor of the cage. Hadn't I given enough?

*You know that there's a price for change, and the people who have the most power never want to pay it,* I'd said to the Moon Alchemist. Surely no one in the history of the empire had ever held as much leverage over the Empress as I did in this moment. But even now, I didn't want to pay the price either. I wanted to be a child who looked to her elders and teachers and government to hold the world together. I wanted to run home to Auntie and Uncle and cry because none of this was supposed to be my job. I'd never asked for this.

But someone had to pay.

*You cannot create good without also creating evil.* That was the most important rule of alchemy—that behind everything beautiful was a hungry shadow. I had thought everyone else cowards for not being willing to make sacrifices, but in truth I hadn't known the depths of what I was asking.

It didn't matter if it was me, or the prince, or the children burning in pyres, or old man Gou. There was always a reason to say *It's not my fault. Why should I have to pay?* But if no one paid, this would never end.

*Say the words, Zilan*, I thought. *Look the Empress in the eyes and say,* Let the prince die. I will never help you.

That was all I had to do, and the Empress's reign would end. The insatiable rich would wither and die.

I pressed my forehead to the bars, slumping boneless against them, letting out a croaked sound of despair. I saw my reflection in the dark puddle of the Empress's blood, the dirty pearls, the singed remnants of golden thread.

"Don't cry, my perfect little alchemist," the Empress said. "Just say the word, and you can leave the cage."

My hand slipped down, splashing in the shockingly warm liquid. I lifted it back up, watching the Empress's blood run down my wrist. I almost laughed at the irony—this was what I was supposed to give the other alchemists, and I had plenty of it now, far too late.

"Say the word, Scarlet."

*Say it, Zilan.*

My whole body shook, my fingers rolling over broken pearls.

"Hurry, while he's still warm."

*Tell her, Zilan.*

I whispered my answer, the words like jagged chunks of ice.

"Speak up, Scarlet," the Empress said.

I cleared my throat. "I will never help you," I said, my voice raw and cracked. "I would rather die."

The Empress's expression hardened. "Then I suppose you won't mind if I burn Hong like I did your family?"

"No," I said, my fist closing around the pearls. "That's not what I said."

"Well, you—"

The Empress froze as I held up a handful of bloody pearls in my palm.

"What are you doing?" she said, her eyes wide.

I tilted my head back and let the blood drip from my hand and pool under my tongue, my mouth filling with shattered pearls. I rolled one between my teeth, and bit down.

# CHAPTER THIRTY-TWO

The pearl scraped down my throat, my abdomen clenching as my body tried to reject it.

I folded into myself, my stomach seizing up, my insides full of sharp teeth. An infinity opened up within me, a screaming emptiness in the center of my chest, demanding more blood, more darkness, anything to feed the night.

My skin grew tight and stiff, sealing me in a shell of pearl, burying me in ice. My vision fractured, all my breath stolen and choked out, moisture sapped from my mouth. I was the impenetrable walls of Chang'an. I was the endless gray of the northern sky. I was the darkest shadows in the dungeons, the gods that no one wanted to pray to, the end of days that the rich thought would never come for them.

And deep in my core, something new blossomed—a hunger so voracious that I could see nothing else but the Empress and the blood pulsing in her throat, the veins in her neck as bright as molten steel. Pearls spilled from my mouth, clattering to the floor. I grabbed the metal bars of my cage and wrenched them to the side, then stepped through.

A door burst open somewhere far away and guards started

shouting, but they were too late. I could hardly even feel their touch through the shell of my skin. I grabbed one by the throat and pinched until his neck splintered like kindling. Others poked at me like swarming flies, so I jammed my fingers into their eyes and shattered their ribs with a swipe of my hand and pulled their arms from their sockets. It was as easy as breathing, their bodies dough-soft, their dying silence a breath of Heaven. When they lay in pieces around me, I turned back to the Empress, her rushing blood just beneath her thin skin the only color in the dark landscape.

She ran for the back door, but tripped up the stairs and grasped at the feet of her throne. She had just reached the armrests when I sank my teeth into her throat.

I ripped through coarse tendons, my mouth filling with sweet blood. I felt like I'd been dying of thirst my entire life until this moment. The need yawned wider as my teeth forced more blood from her flesh, broken gasps croaked from her lips, body twitching, bones rattling. More guards tried to pull me away, scratched at me with their useless knives, but the blood dribbled down my neck and I didn't care, I didn't care at all. Nothing mattered but the syrupy sweetness spreading warmth through my frostbitten bones.

Until something sharp slipped between the knobs in my spine.

Lightning lanced up my back, the crackling spreading through me, and all at once, my jaw unlatched, my whole body going numb. My hands shook, the blood tangy and nauseating in my mouth. The hard shell of pearl flaked away from my skin, leaving me pale and soft and trembling. The spot between my shoulder blades burned, and I didn't understand what had happened until one of the guards threw something on the ground, and I saw my own name staring back at me in the flickering cast of the fire.

*They cut out my soul tag.*

I clenched my teeth and dug my knuckles into the ground, but I felt like a kite holding on to earth by the thinnest string. I was just an untethered soul clinging to stolen bones, my whole body corpse-cold. I collapsed onto my side, teeth biting into the stairs, my own hot blood mixing with the Empress's.

I rolled my gaze up to her, where she lay slumped in her throne, her silk robes painted with blood, a pale hand clutching the wound at her throat. She wouldn't live long, not without an alchemist to stop the bleeding, and there were none left. By the time they found one from outside the palace, it would be too late.

Then I couldn't breathe at all, and as much as I didn't want to die at the Empress's feet, death didn't wait for anyone. My chest ached for air that wouldn't come, and my limbs felt as heavy as mountains. My fingers twitched, the discarded soul tag lying a few feet away.

Maybe everything was ending, but at least I'd brought the Empress down with me.

My vision flashed with images of the dark river, flickering between the throne room and the in-between plane, but wouldn't settle on either one long enough for me to sink into it. I caught glimpses of Wenshu and Yufei sitting on the riverbank, the prince smiling in the sunlight of the courtyard, the Moon Alchemist offering me her hand, my mother braiding my hair, the hazy face of my father and his low voice. *Zilan,* he said, and this time I understood the words that came next, his language no longer forgotten, a prayer and a memory all at once. *Get up, Zilan,* he said. *Please.*

The floor jolted with heavy footsteps, dragging me back to the throne room, and blue robes fell into my line of vision.

"Your Highness, we've found one," a guard was saying.

I managed to look toward the sound and saw Zheng Sili, a sword at his throat. My vision was hazy, but he seemed ragged and unshaven, robes caked with dirt, face stark white. I thought the Empress had killed him, but perhaps he'd been thrown in the dungeons?

"Save her," a man said, and at first, in my dizziness, I thought he meant me, but then Zheng Sili was rising to his feet, drawing closer to the Empress.

"I need moonstone," he said shakily.

*No.*

I tried to push myself up, but it was like trying to topple a mountain with my bare hands. After everything I'd given, Zheng Sili was going to save the Empress, and everyone would have died for nothing at all.

My vision blurred, the world graying at the edges. I couldn't see anything but the blood on the stairs and the soul tag at my feet.

蘇
紫
蘭

So Zilan.

Just a useless merchant girl from the dirty south who could have lived if she'd been smart enough to stay there, if she hadn't mistaken herself for someone great. I stared at the name I'd always hated, unable to look anywhere else, the characters mockingly sharp even as the rest of my vision had gone hazy. Everything began and ended with my ridiculous flowery name and the surname that wasn't even mine.

I choked on a breath. I didn't know I'd been breathing at all, but the thought slammed into me so hard that it forced the last bit of air from my lungs.

*That's not my name.*

I had been born as So Zilan, but that was a name with no hopes attached, a pretty flower who was meant to die in winter. The name painted on the list of victors at every round of the royal exams was Fan Zilan. The name the other alchemists had laughed at, that the Empress had banned after giving me my title, that my brother and sister yelled when they were angry with me—it was Fan Zilan. For so long, I'd thought that using the name Fan was a privilege that could be revoked at any moment if I wasn't a good daughter or sister, if I shamed my family, if I failed. But even now, in the darkest moment of my life, alchemy unveiled the truth.

The Moon Alchemist had said my soul was "loose" but hadn't known why, hadn't been able to fix it just by carving the same characters deeper into my skin. For years, I'd caught glimpses of my death, been wrenched between the two planes as I grew out of the soul tag meant to bind me to my body, as So Zilan became further and further from who I was.

*Get up, Zilan*, my father's voice said again.

I wheezed out a thin breath and threw an arm in front of me. It felt like I was dragging a thousand iron bricks, but I hauled myself across the floor until my numb fingers closed around the Empress's knife. None of the guards noticed me, all focused on the Empress as Zheng Sili worked on her.

My vision flickered, but I held tight to the hilt and pressed the blade to my arm, carving a new soul tag into my skin.

範
紫
蘭

All at once, my sight cleared, my body shocked awake with burning blood beneath my palms and the sharp scent of iron knifing up my nose and the sting of torn skin on the back of my neck. I gasped, feeling like I'd been clinging onto the edge of the earth my whole life and had only now found solid footing.

The guards finally noticed me, one of them catching my gaze and backing up, slapping the other on the arm.

"I thought you cut out her soul tag?" he said.

"I did!" he responded, jabbing a finger at the discarded skin on the floor.

"That's not mine," I said, my voice oddly steady. Zheng Sili hesitated where he bent over the Empress, looking over his shoulder.

"Then who the hell are you?" the guard said.

I rose to my feet, steadying the blade in my hand, no longer trembling.

"Fan Zilan," I said, and stabbed him in the chest.

The other guards didn't even try to fight. They grabbed their fallen friend and scurried like rats out of the throne room. I whirled around to face Zheng Sili, who knelt pale and frozen before the Empress.

"Did you save her?" I asked, gaze sliding to the Empress, whose throat was now whole and unharmed, though she lay unmoving.

He shook his head quickly. He looked pale and dirty, trembling like a newborn calf. I wondered what the guards had done to him, but it wasn't my problem.

"I didn't finish," he said. "She's dead."

I raised my blade and he flinched away, but I only cut the drawstrings on his satchel, spilling gemstones across the stairs. I grabbed a handful of chicken-blood stone as he fled the throne room.

On the stairs, I saw my cousins' soul tags in my childhood handwriting, marked with bloody footprints.

Wenshu had thought I wouldn't go back for him and Yufei, but he was wrong.

*Fans don't leave each other behind.*

I rolled the Empress onto her stomach and tore her dress, exposing the skin along her spine. Yufei's body was gone, but her soul might still be at the river. The Moon Alchemist had said that two resurrections would never be successful, but I doubted she'd ever tried to attach a soul to a different body.

I held my breath, three bloodstones crushed into my palm, and closed my eyes.

The river rushed around me in a stormy torrent, sticks scraping against my bare legs, shredding through my silk dress. I didn't know if this would work, but I called Yufei's name out across the expanse, the rain swallowing my words.

I stumbled over roots, the river knocking me to my hands and knees, filling my mouth with murky water. I trudged across it as the expanse opened up like an endless ocean, deeper and deeper. When I could no longer walk, I swam even as my arms went numb, the current dragging me toward an unseen endpoint. I erased all other thoughts from my mind but my sister's name until I washed up on a sandy shore beneath an overcast sky. I couldn't lift my head, but I heard footsteps crunching across the sand, then coming to a halt in front of me.

"Took you long enough," Yufei said.

★ ★ ★

My sister gasped awake and ran her hands across her blood-ied chest, over the sealed wound on her neck.

"This isn't me," she whispered, startling at the sound of the Empress's voice. "Zilan, what did you do?"

I couldn't find the words to answer, could barely raise my-self from my hands and knees, still feeling like I was under-water.

"Are you okay?" Yufei said, dragging me upright and then leaning me against the side of the throne.

I nodded, wiping my forehead with the back of my arm, even though I felt half-dead again. My gaze fell to the prince, still lying in a pool of his blood, and I forced myself to crawl down the stairs.

"Jiějiě, are there any guards left?" I said, taking the prince's hand.

She rose to her feet, tripping over her skirts, and peeked out the front door. "No," she said.

"Are there any bodies that aren't ripped to pieces?"

She paused, then turned back to me, shaking her head. "Can't you use that one for Wenshu Ge?" she asked.

"This is the prince," I said, my mouth numb.

"But it's the only body we have," she said. Then her eyes widened and she crossed the room quickly. "Zilan, you're going to bring Wenshu Ge back, aren't you?"

I said nothing, my hand tightening around the prince's.

*"Aren't you?"* Yufei said, her eyes wet. "You put me in an-other body, so you can do the same for Wenshu Ge, right?"

I twisted my fists harder into the prince's clothes. I thought of the prince finding me in Guangzhou, of telling me I was special, of looking at me like I was every constellation. I thought of Wenshu stabbing the magistrate for me, of always feeding me his portion when food was scarce, of carrying me on his shoulders when we were kids.

I couldn't bring back both Wenshu and the prince into one body.

"Zilan," Yufei said, grabbing my sleeve.

"Shut up!" I said. "Shut up, I need to think."

"To *think*?" Yufei said.

But I couldn't listen to her anymore, so I slammed three bloodstones into the prince's chest and closed my eyes.

I combed through the river for what felt like years. Somewhere above me, I sensed Yufei hovering, but I had to ignore her. After ages of darkness and sour water, I opened my eyes and carved a name into the white skin of his forearm. At last the prince gasped, back arching. He rolled over and coughed blood onto the floor.

Yufei lingered behind me as I cupped his face in my hands.

"Zilan?" he whispered.

I smiled, even though I tasted tears.

"Welcome back, Gēgē."

# CHAPTER THIRTY-THREE

The following week, Empress Wu halted the production of life gold.

While the palace servants were busy fishing bodies from the ponds, the new guards took shifts keeping the nobles from tearing the walls down. Magistrates from the nearby provinces joined the uproar by nightfall, and surely those from the south would come once word reached them. Almost all of them scattered when the Empress took her favorite pet lion on a stroll a bit too close to the front gates—if there was one thing that the rich hated more than aging, it was risking their lives.

The royal court was in quiet hysterics, no one wanting to offend the Empress and end up with their head in a bucket, but her advisers had red-rimmed eyes and bald spots where they'd tugged their thin hair out.

"Your Highness," one of them said, pacing back and forth while the Empress ate her third bowl of soup, "your people are...unsettled."

"You mean *the rich* are unsettled," she said, waving her spoon at the man, as if she could cast a spell and make him disappear. "I bet the farmers and merchants couldn't care less. I need more soup."

A servant hurried away to fulfill the order while the adviser clenched his jaw so hard that he almost definitely shattered some of his gold teeth. I sat at the far end of the table beside the prince, gnawing on a cucumber.

"There will be uprisings," the adviser said.

The prince scoffed. "The rich are afraid to even leave their homes in case they scratch their perfect skin," he said. "For all we pay the royal guards, are you saying they can't handle them?"

"Well, no," the adviser said, "but the morale of the people—"

"Which people?" the prince said, his glare silencing the adviser.

"Oh, that reminds me," the Empress said, wiping her mouth on her sleeve. "Morale in the south is low. Tomorrow, I'm lowering the imperial tax back down to five percent and sending rice to all families in the southern provinces until harvest season."

The adviser dropped his scroll, barely even reacting when it hit his foot with a heavy *thunk*.

"Your Highness," he said, voice trembling, "the cost—"

"Demolish one of the guesthouses or rhino farms and sell it for parts or something," the Empress said, turning to the servant carrying her new bowl of soup. "I have no more alchemists to pay and cellars full of gold. Rip off some of this gold wallpaper if you have to. It's hideous."

"Your Highness, it's not that simple," the adviser said, closing his eyes. "I'm not sure what's caused your sudden… *benevolence*, and I can appreciate your sympathy for our country's poor. Truly, you are a kind and gracious ruler. But this childlike idealism simply won't work. There are important people you need to please if you want to stay in power. You will have to make compromises."

"Compromises?" I said, crossing my arms. All eyes turned to me, except for the Empress, who continued eating. "Compromises like drinking the blood of peasants to make more life gold?"

"Cutting off production entirely is jarring," the adviser said. "Perhaps a slower process—"

"So, only drinking a little bit of peasant blood?" I said.

The adviser frowned, turning to the prince. "I'm sorry, why is your concubine part of this meeting?"

"She's not my *concubine*," Wenshu said, making a sour face. "She's the head alchemist."

"The *only* alchemist," Yufei added through a mouthful of rice. "She's more valuable to me than you, who can be replaced easily."

The adviser shook his head. "You must be willing to compromise—"

"We can compromise on tonight's dinner menu," I said. "We can compromise on the color of silk used for the Empress's dresses. We don't compromise on scamming the poor out of their corpses."

"What Zilan said," Yufei said, waving her spoon in my direction. "Just pretend I said it."

*The things you want are nothing more than foolish childhood dreams*, the Moon Alchemist had once told me. I hoped, more than anything, that she was wrong. I hoped that growing old didn't mean growing complacent with other people's suffering, like the adviser Yufei had dismissed, who I could hear letting out an anguished scream in the hallway.

The good news was that Yufei adored pretending to be the Empress. She'd learned too quickly that she could quite literally have any food in the world prepared for her within an hour. She spent her mornings solving the city's problems with alarming but efficient bluntness, her afternoons floating in one of the palace's many pools, and her evenings arranging for Auntie and Uncle to move in.

Wenshu handled the more practical matters. He'd arranged a funeral with a fake corpse for the Emperor, since we had no idea where the body had gone, as well as a funeral for the alchemists. He'd hired new servants and guards and had the palace interior repaired and the exterior fortified so the rich couldn't burn it down. He drafted all the legislation that Yufei enacted.

And I did…nothing.

I thought I'd earned that right after all I'd done to overthrow the Empress in the first place. The truth was that I'd thought once the Empress was gone, everything would magically repair itself. I would marry Hong, I would keep studying with the Moon Alchemist and playing in the courtyard with the Paper Alchemist and River Alchemist. That future still felt so vivid, so foolish. I often sat in the empty alchemy training grounds and tried to remember all the laughter and games that had once filled it, but now the rustling of leaves and wind humming off the clay walls was the loudest sound in the world.

I spent most of my time in my room, feeding Durian berries and watching him grow bigger.

At the start of a new week about a month after the Empress's death, the door to my room slammed open.

Durian made a venomous hissing sound at the intruder, but he was still small enough for me to put him back in his box when I saw Wenshu in the doorway carrying an armful of scrolls.

"You've been avoiding me," he said.

I stared out the window and didn't bother denying it.

I'd worried at first that it would be awkward seeing Wenshu in the body of someone I'd wanted to marry, but that wasn't the problem—Fan Wenshu was nothing at all like Li Hong, and I could see it in everything from his facial expressions to the way he tied back his hair to his choice of swear words.

But that didn't mean I liked seeing his corpse walking around, speaking words he would never say. It felt like desecration, somehow.

"For what it's worth, I'm not thrilled by this arrangement either," Wenshu said.

"Should I have just let you die?" I said.

He set the scrolls down on the floor, avoiding my gaze. "Probably," he said quietly. "I mean, I would have understood if you had."

"You would be dead if I had."

"Zilan," he said, shoulders drooping, "when you were at the palace, I hardly slept. I worried about you constantly."

The words were so oddly gentle that he almost sounded like the prince. I sat back, hugging my knees.

"All I wanted was to keep you safe," he said, "but you kept running off with the prince. You would do whatever he asked and didn't care what I had to say anymore."

"I don't want to talk about him," I said, glaring. "Not with you, of all people."

He shook his head. "I'm just explaining," he said, looking pained. "I was so afraid that one day you weren't going to come back to us, either because the prince got you killed, or because you didn't need us anymore."

I frowned, my hands falling to my sides. "What?"

"That was why I said those things to you," he said. "Because I thought you didn't want us anyway. I'm sorry, Zilan."

"That's what you thought?" I said, grabbing a handful of Durian's berries and hurling them at Wenshu's head. "You're supposed to be the smart sibling!"

"I know," he said, wincing. "It wasn't my finest moment. That's why I've brought you these." He gestured to the pile of scrolls.

"Homework?" I said.

He shot me a glare before unfurling one, but instead of columns of text like I expected, it was a map, the world blooming in strokes of blue and black ink across the page. He pointed to the cove around the Bohai Sea.

"Do you remember when we were in the library and you asked me about Penglai Island?" he said.

"You said it wasn't real."

"No, I said it was spoken of in myths, but that doesn't mean it's not real. Frankly, after all the monstrously impossible things you've done, I'm not sure I believe alchemy has limits anymore. Penglai Island is the island of the Eight Immortals, where it's said they have an elixir of immortality."

"We already had one of those, and Yufei just banned it," I said.

"Zilan, *listen*," Wenshu scolded, unrolling another scroll, this time with words. The writing was in a strange language, and it took me a moment to recognize it.

"How did you get my father's notes?" I said, shouldering Wenshu aside to get a closer look. These weren't the ones he'd left in Guangzhou, that was for sure. I'd read those a thousand times over.

"The Moon Alchemist had some in her study," Wenshu said quietly. "I was just looking. I didn't throw anything away."

I ran my hands over the ink, the swooping brushstrokes. I'd thought my father's story was over, but here I was discovering more of him. "Have you translated any of this?" I asked.

"Kind of," Wenshu said. "He seemed to be working together with the Moon Alchemist, so the topics of their notes overlap, which makes it easier to translate. It looks like they thought the elixir can break the most fundamental rule of alchemy."

*You cannot create good without also creating evil.* Without that rule, you could create infinite goodness without paying a price. "Alchemy with no limits?" I whispered.

"Well, it's an elixir of *immortality*," Wenshu said, "so it probably has to do with life."

I swallowed, my mind spinning with a thousand possibilities of what I could do with that kind of power. I closed my eyes, cutting off that train of thought. "What are you saying?" I asked. It was all well and good to fantasize about dreams, but saying them out loud made them real.

He crossed his arms. "I'm saying I want to get my body back, and you can return your ugly boyfriend's soul to this one."

I couldn't help but tackle Wenshu into a hug, ignoring when he complained that we were squishing scrolls and squirmed around like a mealworm.

We all knew that Yufei had to stay in Chang'an for now. Uprooting the country's way of life and then fleeing would completely destabilize her authority.

When I told Yufei we might be able to get her body back, she averted her gaze, tearing apart a piece of bread distractedly.

"Don't you want your old body?" I said.

Her hands slowed. "I never wished to be anyone but myself," she said, "but as the Empress, I can do so much more than Fan Yufei."

"You're still you," I said. "Fan Yufei abolished life gold, not the Empress."

Yufei popped a piece of bread into her mouth and turned back to the window. "You're sure we can really hand the kingdom over to your boyfriend once he returns? He can handle it?"

"I know he can," I said. "Besides, I can't leave him out there."

"You mean you can't leave Wenshu Ge in his body," Yufei said, smirking.

I groaned, collapsing onto the bed. "Don't forget that you're technically his mother now, which is arguably even weirder."

"That just means I can boss him around," she said.

"When have you ever *not* bossed him around?"

By the end of the week, Wenshu had gotten us two horses and enough rations to make it to the next province. I eyed my horse nervously as Wenshu tightened its saddlebags. He noticed my hesitation and rolled his eyes.

"Get over it," he said.

*He's definitely not Li Hong anymore*, I thought.

"A horse has literally killed me before," I said. "You could be more understanding."

"You defeated death twice," he said. "You can ride a horse."

And that was how I ended up on horseback for the second trip of my second life. We rode through the streets, past the five arches that had once been my first memory, past the gates of the city that had once been my greatest dream.

The first time we came here, we were only allowed to walk on foot within the city walls because horses were for the rich. Now the faces of the poor merchants and barefoot children and foreign traders turned as we rode past, squinting up at us through the sharp sunlight, not knowing that we were just children in costumes, muddy míngqì merchants wrapped in gold and silk.

Some nobles in blue robes glared and spit as we rode past. Soon, the wrinkles in their faces would deepen, their skin would grow loose around their bones, their teeth would fall out, and they would die like they deserved, like all of us deserved someday. Their lives locked away eating gold and throwing parties in their mansions weren't worth the blood they'd cost.

The Moon Alchemist probably would have liked me to learn that resurrection is evil, that we can't question the ways of the universe. But, as always, I was a disappointment.

The evil wasn't in the alchemy, but in the world that let children in rice fields die of thirst in the summer, that made people desperate enough to sell off their family's corpses for money, that let some people eat handfuls of gold while others starved. *Alchemists need to break themselves into pieces, to want to rebuild the world around them so desperately that they would give their blood, or body, or soul*, the Moon Alchemist had said. She had wanted to rebuild the world in her own way, but I wanted to crack it wide open, raze the fields, and start again.

What I didn't tell Wenshu was that I would bring them all back.

Not just Hong and our family, but all the alchemists, all of Hong's murdered siblings, the princess whose soul I'd left trapped in the void. Fans don't leave anyone behind.

The river of my soul was filled with the blood of my mistakes, the bones of everyone who had saved me. I could feel it inside me, roaring so loudly with the cries of wandering souls. In my sleep, I waded deeper and deeper until I was swimming into open waters and woke up with the taste of blood in my mouth.

*We don't know for a fact that any of this is possible,* Wenshu had told me over and over again, ever the pragmatist. I sensed that this trip was more for me than any true objections he had about being in the prince's body, which was much taller than Wenshu's. *If we get to the coast and there are no leads, we need to turn back and help Yufei. I'm not going to become a vagabond looking for a mythical elixir for the rest of my life.*

But I believed in the elixir in a way that Wenshu never could. He'd been dragged through his fair share of miracles, but I was always the one who sought them out. Besides, my father had believed in it, and he had a good track record for discovering the impossible.

Durian quacked inside my satchel, poking his head out to peer across the streets. He was growing alarmingly fast, and soon he would need an enclosure of some sort. But for now, it was best to keep my potentially evil alchemy duck within arm's reach rather than inflict him on a palace without alchemists.

Leaving Chang'an was a new start that felt somehow more significant than dying and being reborn, because this was my choice. As the sun sank and the sky cracked open to bright red across the horizon, we rode toward the bleeding sunset of our new kingdom, no longer trying to escape death but charging straight toward it, calling its name.

★ ★ ★ ★ ★

# HISTORICAL NOTE

*Alchemy*

There were indeed alchemists in the Tang Dynasty, but unlike Zilan, they didn't spar in muddy courtyards or set each other on fire. Originating around the fourth century BCE, Chinese alchemy had the singular goal of creating an elixir of eternal life.[1] The type of alchemy popular during the Tang Dynasty was called wàidān (外丹), meaning "external alchemy," and was a means of making medicines with different chemicals and devices. Tang Dynasty alchemists experimented with minerals such as arsenic, mercury, and lead in the hopes of attaining immortality. Five Chinese emperors died from ingesting their concoctions.[2]

---

1   Robert P. Multhauf and Robert Andrew Gilbert, "Alchemy," in *Encyclopedia Britannica*, accessed January 22, 2023, https://www.britannica.com/topic/alchemy.

2   Yan Liu, "Dying to Live," in *Healing with Poisons: Potent Medicines in Medieval China* (Seattle, WA: University of Washington Press, 2021), 148, https://www.jstor.org/stable/j.ctv1wmz491.12.

## Civil Service Examinations

There is a common theme in contemporary Chinese-inspired fantasy novels of federal examinations that lift a lower-class character out of poverty. This concept is rooted in ancient Chinese history: meritocratic examinations known as kējǔ (科舉) began in China as early as the seventh century CE.[3] These civil service examinations tested knowledge of Confucian classics and were a path to obtaining government positions.[4] In theory, these exams allowed for social mobility, though some government positions could be inherited.[5] Alchemy was not one of the disciplines tested in the real exams.

## Merchants

In the Tang Dynasty, merchant and artisan families like Zilan's were considered leeches who profited off the manual labor of peasants and were the least respected nonpeasant class. In the real world, a merchant like Zilan would not have been allowed to take the civil service examinations, even if she were a boy. The exorbitant tax rate that the market commandant charges the Fans is historically accurate, reflecting the disdain the government held for the merchant class.[6] When the Fans arrive at the inn in Qingyuan, Zilan laments that the punishment for kidnapping merchant-class alchemists like her is less severe

3    Rui Magone, "The Examination System," *Oxford Bibliographies* (Oxford University Press, 2014), https://www.oxfordbibliographies.com/display/document/obo-9780199920082/obo-9780199920082-0078.xml.

4    Charles Benn, *China's Golden Age: Everyday Life in the Tang Dynasty* (New York, NY: Oxford University Press, 2002), 255–256.

5    Benn, *China's Golden Age*, 24.

6    Benn, *China's Golden Age*, 36.

than for kidnapping alchemists of a scholar class—this class-based punishment scheme is accurate to the punishments described in the *Tang Code*, a penal code implemented during the Tang Dynasty.[7]

*The Royal Family*

The empress in *The Scarlet Alchemist* is a reimagining of Wu Zetian, China's first and last female emperor. Wu Zetian entered the royal court as the concubine of Emperor Taizong, and after his death, became a concubine for his son, Emperor Gaozong[8] (the Emperor referenced in *The Scarlet Alchemist*). When Gaozong fell ill, Wu Zetian controlled the government in his place.[9]

Though sources describing Wu Zetian are varied, highly biased, and often contradictory,[10] some historians suspect that she killed her own infant daughter in order to frame Gaozong's then wife, Empress Wang, for her daughter's death. Wang was consequently demoted and Wu Zetian became the Empress.[11] After Gaozong's death, Wu Zetian decimated anyone in China with even a distant claim to the throne, declaring herself emperor (not empress) and beginning the Zhou Dynasty in 690 CE.[12]

7   Wallace Johnson, "Status and Liability for Punishment in the T'ang Code," *Chicago-Kent Law Review* 71, no. 1 (October 1995): 224, https://scholarship.kentlaw.iit.edu/cklawreview/vol71/iss1/8.

8   Charles Patrick FitzGerald, "Wuhou," in *Encyclopedia Britannica*, last modified January 1, 2023, https://www.britannica.com/biography/Wuhou.

9   Jason Porath, "Wu Zetian," in *Rejected Princesses: Tales of History's Boldest Heroines, Hellions & Heretics* (New York, NY: William Morrow, 2016), 323.

10   Porath, *Rejected Princesses*, 323.

11   Lily Xiao Hong Lee and Sue Wiles, eds., *Biographical Dictionary of Chinese Women: Tang through Ming: 618–1644* (Armonk, NY: M.E. Sharpe, 2014), 464.

12   Porath, *Rejected Princesses*, 325.

Please note that Empress Wu in *The Scarlet Alchemist* is ruling as empress consort rather than emperor because Gaozong is both (allegedly) alive and refuses to give the empress full power. For this reason, I refer to this book as an alternate Tang Dynasty, rather than Zhou Dynasty, book. Similarly, the date that this book takes place (775 CE) does not align with the real Wu Zetian's reign—the first part of the Tang Dynasty (before Wu Zetian's brief interregnum) has been extended in this world thanks to the discovery of life gold.

The crown prince in *The Scarlet Alchemist* is inspired by Li Hong, the son of Wu Zetian and Emperor Gaozong. Shortly after angering Wu Zetian by requesting that his half sisters (the children of the emperor's former concubine Xiao) be allowed to leave the royal court, he suddenly died of poisoning.[13] Some historians speculate that Wu Zetian was responsible for his death.[14] As far as we know, no alchemist ever resurrected him.

13  Barbara Bennett Peterson, ed., *Notable Women of China: Shang Dynasty to the Early Twentieth Century* (Armonk, NY: M.E. Sharpe, 2000), 195.

14  Porath, *Rejected Princesses*, 323.

# ACKNOWLEDGMENTS

Thank you to my agent, Mary, who is always the first to champion my wild ideas and make my dreams come true. What feels like ages ago, I pitched this idea to Mary as an adult fantasy trilogy about an alchemist girl summoned by the Empress herself. I had very few concrete thoughts about it at the time, other than a burning obsession with The Poppy War series and vague aspirations of writing something equally as vast and magical. Mary mentioned offhandedly that if I wanted this to be a YA series, perhaps the Empress's son could be the one to summon Zilan. I loved that idea, and it ignited an excitement for this book that never dimmed even as I got down into the weeds of revision.

Thank you to Claire, for all your excitement about this story before it was even fully formed. Your faith in me made this the most fun writing experience I've ever had, knowing my unwritten story already had so much love and support.

Thank you to the Inkyard Press team for all the ways you've supported me and my books these past few years. I was lucky enough to experience so many amazing book events in 2022, which I owe to the endlessly supportive team at Inkyard.

Thank you as well to my UK publishing team at Hodderscape, for making another one of my greatest dreams come true!

Enormous thanks to my friend Kin, for naming basically all of my characters. Thank you for patiently answering my ridiculous questions and supporting my efforts to write this book so far beyond my expertise. It can be an isolating experience as an Asian diaspora writer to want so badly to explore your heritage, knowing that you will never be "authentic enough" for some people, so I am extremely lucky to have friends like Kin who help me explore the parts of my culture that have been lost without passing judgment or gatekeeping.

Thank you to Van Hoang and Yume Kitasei, agent sisters and publishing support buddies forever. May our stories only grow weirder and more popular. Thank you as well to all of my agent siblings in Mary's Squad!

Thank you to Rebecca Kim Wells, my mentor, writing buddy, and dear friend.

Thanks to Jialu, for being my friend and writing buddy, and also the best thing to come out of the hellscape that is Twitter.

Thank you as well to all of my friends outside of publishing who celebrated with me as this journey unfolded and cheered for my successes even when they didn't know what they meant. Thank you for coming to my book launch events, taking pictures of my books in the wild, and proudly telling your friends that you know an author. Thank you for sneaking into my signing lines, letting me stay with you while traveling for book events, taking me around your cities for book research, and listening to me ramble about my creepy book ideas.

Thank you to my extended family for reading my books just because you love me, even though I know that they gross you out.

And of course, thank you to my parents for supporting all of my dreams, for relentlessly promoting my book to all your friends, and for believing in me.